WWW.SIRENPUBLISHING.COM
EROTIC ROMANCE

SEX RATING: SCORCHING

This book is for sale to adults ONLY as defined by the laws of the country in which you made your purchase. Please store your files wisely where they cannot be accessed by under-aged readers.

SIREN SEX RATING

SENSUAL: Sensual romance with love scenes comparative to most romance novels published today

STEAMY: Heavy sexual tension; graphic details; may contain coarse language

SIZZLING: Erotic, graphic sex; explicit sexual language; may offend delicate readers

SCORCHING: Erotica; contains many sexual encounters; may contain unconventional sex; will offend delicate readers

SEXTREME: Excessiveness; many instances of unconventional sex; may be hardcore

The Polyamorous Princess

Erotic Sci-Fi
Ménage à Trois (F/M/M, M/M)

A passionate, spoiled princess. A brilliant intelligence officer. A tough marine.

Princess Allison, the coddled daughter of the Emperor of Mankind, is irreparably disturbed by the vicious war with the cat-like Arupians. Her social life is in shambles. Her friends are all on duty. Allie spends her days teaching old American history at the University or else hiding out in the royal Safe Room.

Then two fascinating men enter her life.

Second Lieutenant Damon Hyde is a swaggering and respected marine. Most people think he's fearless—except for Allie, who falls for his vulnerability.

Lieutenant JG Harrison Douglas is brilliant. Most people think he's also crazy—except for Allie, who is drawn to his eccentricity.

Brought together by fate, Allie falls in love, torn between the two men who love her and fight to win her. As new and disparate emotions blossom, Allie, Damon, and Harry are pulled into a passionate, polyamorous relationship. The three are forced to come to terms with their love for one another as they rely on their wits and skills, not only for their own survival, but also for all mankind on His Majesty's Star Ship Boone.

REVIEWS for Melodee Aaron's
The Polyamorous Princess

5 Angels: "The Polyamorous Princess is an intriguing book, and one that kept me interested. Although it is primarily an erotic novel, the reader will also discover a good grounding in science fiction allowing the action to take place in a believable spaceship in the middle of an epic war. This isn't a book that can be dipped into. The action slowly builds up but in doing so, allows the reader to completely understand all characters involved and to appreciate all the emotions that they go through.

Melodee Aaron has managed to produce a book that is very educational as well as highly entertaining. The romance scenes whether f/m, m/m or m/m/f have all been delicately and tastefully done although because of the nature of the book some readers may find the scenes uncomfortable. I thought this book was excellent and I would recommend to anyone who is looking for an erotic book with a difference or for anyone who is looking for an erotic science fiction novel. I will definitely be looking out for more of Ms. Aaron's work." —**Heidi,** *Fallen Angel Reviews*

4.5 Blue Ribbons: "*The Polyamorous Princess* takes a different look at the ménage relationship. I especially enjoyed the realistic portrayal of the men in the story trying to come to grips with Allie's feelings for the other as well as the preening and posturing that goes along with trying to make the other man go away. Once they accept that they could be a family, the rest was gravy. Each character was remarkably diverse and I liked how Ms. Aaron portrayed their differences. For a completely unique take on a ménage, or rather, polyamorous relationship, *The Polyamorous Princess* won't disappoint." —**Natasha Smith,** *Romance Junkies*

4.5 Kisses: "*The Polyamorous Princess* is a fascinating tale set in a bold world. Polyamorous relations are nothing new to the world created by Melodee Aaron. Allison's father is married to four women who are all in love with each other. There are no sexual taboos in Allison's world. Allison is a loving woman caught between two men. She loves them both and is torn apart at having to choose one. Damon and Harry are both yummy in their determination to win Allison. Damon is heroic when he leaves on his mission. I will admit to crying a bit when he was reported as dead. Melodee Aaron did an outstanding job bringing her characters to life. The story focuses on the relationship between the three characters, but the war with the Arupian Empire is very much a presence in *The Polyamorous Princess*. The book's plot has a wonderful flow and the story is a pleasure to read." —**Tara Renee,** *Two Lips Reviews*

4.5 Stars/Orgasmic: "If you are looking for a futuristic novel that focuses on relationships and exceptional sex, *The Polyamorous Princess* is a one stop shop for it all. The setting of His Majesty's Starship Boone, previously introduced in Ms Aaron's Ike Payne Adventure series, sets the tone for a joyful love affair with Allison and Damon, and then the introduction of Harry into the mix. Although this lengthy novel has a great deal of plot, the bond between Allison and her men sets this novel into motion. What I found particularly interesting is that this isn't just a story about Allison and the two men she falls in love with, but this is also a story about how deeply in love Damon and Harry are with her. I found every aspect of their connection believable and highly provocative. Harry is intelligent, almost to a fault, and extremely bold, with a sense of entitlement for Allison's love. Damon is more romantic and is the quintessential marine, strong with a powerful personality. To top it all off, Allison is a bit of a princess, in some ways very self-assured but in others, a bit spoiled. I loved even these negative aspects of her personality. Sexually, Allison knocks the socks off in a carnal explosion. There were several unusual sex scenes, including some surprisingly fiery settings that left me quaking for more. As a warning, there are scenes in which Damon and Harry express love for one another, but this only supports their friendly pursuit of Allison. Overall, with touches of imaginative futuristic ideas, *The Polyamorous Princess* left me feeling satisfied, in all the right ways." —**Francesca Hayne,** *Just Erotic Romance Reviews*

ABOUT THE AUTHOR

Born in the Ozark Mountains, Melodee Aaron comes from a long line of storytellers. Storytelling is a tradition in the Ozarks and one of Melodee's earliest memories is sitting on the front porch of her great-grandma's house listening to her tell stories.

Being an avid reader of anything, including both romantic and erotic, Melodee was popular with the guys at Southeast Missouri State University. For some reason, guys like a girl who reads Penthouse Forum. Add to that a passion for actually trying the things she read about. Anyway, after sixteen semesters and no degree, Melodee moved on to the real world.

Melodee decided to try telling stories on paper and has had success with a number of short stories, including flash works of fewer than 1,000 words.

Mel writes erotic and adult fiction, with a science fiction spin as well as incorporating a bit of crime, military, and political drama.

www.melodeeaaron.com

THE POLYAMOROUS PRINCESS

Melodee Aaron

EROTIC ROMANCE

Siren Publishing, Inc.
www.SirenPublishing.com

A SIREN PUBLISHING BOOK
First Printing, 2007
Copyright © 2007 by Siren Publishing, Inc.

IMPRINT: Erotic Romance

ISBN-10: 1-933563-69-9
ISBN-13: 978-1-933563-69-5

DESERT HEAT
Copyright © 2007 by Melodee Aaron

All cover art and logo copyright © 2007 by Siren Publishing, Inc.

ALL RIGHTS RESERVED: This literary work may not be reproduced or transmitted in any form or by any means, including electronic or photographic reproduction, in whole or in part, without express written permission.

All characters and events in this book are fictitious. Any resemblance to actual persons living or dead is strictly coincidental.

Printed in the U.S.A.

PUBLISHER
Siren Publishing, Inc.
www.SirenPublishing.com

The Polyamorous Princess

By Melodee Aaron
Copyright © 2007

Chapter 1

The Princess

Allison Jenkins threw the stylus against the screen of the data terminal. "Fuck!" Playing Vegas solitaire, she had lost just a little shy of a million credits. Today.

Allie reached to smack the screen of the cheating game, and the battle stations alarm began to wail its now familiar song. At war with the Arupian Empire, the Empire of Mankind sent His Majesty's Star Ship *Warren E. Boone* to the thick of the fighting. Normally, Allison's father, Jim, or as most people knew him, Emperor James the First, By Grace of God, Emperor to Mankind, wouldn't be near a battle zone with his flagship.

Allison remembered her father's words when he told her and the rest of the family that they would be going into harm's way. "Too many people, human and Arupian, have died already. I have to go so we can settle this."

That idea hadn't worked too well so far. In the nine months that *Boone* had been here, the war had actually gotten worse. At least that was what Allison heard. Other than the fact that it got in her way, she couldn't care less about the war. With most of her friends in either the Fleet or Marines, none of them were around because the war kept them busy these days. Instead of being with her friends having fun, Allison sat here playing cards with a computer that cheated.

"Fuck!" Allison stood to go to the Safe Room reserved for the royal family. This would be the twelfth trip there today. She slowly sat back down and picked up the stylus from the floor.

She started another game of solitaire, double or nothing.

* * * *

Admiral Q glanced around the bridge and saw the duty stations all manned by the primary staff. "Tactical, range to target?"

"Five million kilometers, Sir."

"Helm, bring us to heading zero seven five mark one niner two, hyperspace layer three, please."

"Heading zero seven five mark one niner two, HS layer three, aye."

Boone banked and moved ahead, turning toward the attacking Arupian battle cruiser. "Weapons, arm all systems and lock on target, please."

The Weapons Officer worked her control panel. "All weapons tracking and locked, Sir."

"Thank you." As a simulated human, people three thousand years ago would have called Q a cyborg at best or a robot at worst. His body was a synthetic biological system. His brain was a positronic system, nearly identical to the twelve positronic brains that were the central nervous system of *Boone*. The similarities weren't accidental. Empress Tanya, one of Jim's four wives, had designed both. She often said that she had practiced on Q for the work she did with *Boone*. Far from being emotionless, like cyborgs and robots, Q had the full range of human emotional and biological reactions. He and the other twenty-one simulated humans on *Boone* were fully functional. "Range to target, please."

"Two point four million kilometers."

"Communications, please open a channel to the Arupian battle cruiser and direct them to come to all stop, lower their shields, take their weapons offline, and prepare to be boarded for surrender."

"Aye, aye, Sir." The Communications Officer worked his console for several minutes. "No response on any channel, Admiral."

"Thank you. Please continue to hail the Arupians. Let me know immediately if there is any reply."

"Yes, Sir."

"Weapons, you are authorized to return fire to any target."

"Understand authorized to return fire, aye."

Q watched the screens showing *Boone* and the Arupian ship closing. "Weapons, full power to forward shields. Harbison Field to maximum power."

"Full power to forward shields and Harbison Field to maximum, aye." The Weapons Officer checked her displays. "Range to target one point six million kilometers. Fifteen seconds to weapons range."

Q nodded. "Thank you. Any response from the Arupians?"

"Negative."

"Thank you." Q watched the seconds tick by. The searing green light of Arupian laser fire stabbed out at *Boone*. The Harbison Field absorbed the energy, radiating it away safely to space.

He watched as the Weapons Officer carried out her orders, and the pure white beam of the disruptors lashed across space to touch the Arupian ship. A volley of four galvanic torpedoes followed, racing at the enemy with their deadly load of concentrated energy. The Weapons Officer's timing was perfect. The torpedoes reached the ship just as the defensive shield failed and the full energy of the four killer weapons, each more than the entire nuclear arsenals of old Earth, unleashed on the unprotected hull. Q's positronic brain made the instant association between the explosion of the Arupian ship and the energy pulse radiated by a black hole at the event horizon when it sucked in something of planetary mass. "Science, please scan for life signs. Helm, prepare for recovery operations for any survivors."

The Science Officer studied his instruments. "Negative life signs down to fifty centimeter resolution, Sir."

Q nodded. "Thank you. Please secure *Boone* from battle stations. Well done."

* * * *

Lieutenant JG Harrison Douglas sat in his cubicle in the Fleet Intelligence Office staring at the latest intercepted Arupian communication. They'd changed their encryption again, and he tried to see a pattern the ship's brains might have missed. His head hurt.

"Harry, you really should get a haircut before someone decides to skin you and me both." Harry's immediate superior, Lieutenant Devon Henson, leaned against the cubicle entrance.

"Yeah, I guess I should." Harry ran his hand over his long black hair, nearly to his shoulders now. "But if I don't, what are they going to do? Kick me out of the war?"

Henson laughed with him for a minute. "We should be so lucky. Any plans for this evening?"

"Not really. Assuming we all don't get killed before then, I may go to the Café and see what there is to see."

"Yeah, right."

"Are you and Mary still seeing each other?"

"Sort of, I guess. It's not going to work out, but we each fill a need for the other."

Harry laughed. "With filling being the operative word?"

"No comment. When are you going to find a nice girl to settle down with, Harry?"

"I have to wait for you to do that first."

"What? Am I your older sister, and I have to get married first?"

"Yeah. That way, I'll never have to get married."

"Everybody's a comedian." Devon looked at the screen. "Any luck with that new code?"

"Not really. Looks like at least four layers of redundancy, so this one may be tough." Harry smiled. "Maybe they'll change again before we crack this one, and we won't need to bother with it."

"Harry, if Admiral Q kills me, I'm taking you with me."

* * * *

The tiny robotic nanites in their bodies that repaired damage, fought illness, and in general kept them healthy made the Emperor and his family, and a number of others in the Empire, immortal. Allison thought she understood that after living for so long things could get a little regimented, and that explained the fixed seating at the dinner table.

Jim sipped his wine, staring at Allison. "Little one, I heard you didn't make it to the Safe Room this afternoon."

Ship's security must be his personal spies. "Um, no, Daddy, I didn't."

"Care to tell me why?"

"It's silly. Nothing ever happens. We spend all our time running back and forth."

Jim sighed and looked at Janelle, Allison's biological mother. "Do you want to try this time?"

"Sure." Janelle laughed a little. "What your dad is trying to say is that we're just trying to make sure you're safe."

"Mom, if *Boone* gets blown out of space, what difference does it make where I am?"

"That's the point, Allie!" Jim ran his hand through his hair. "The Safe Room will survive. It has oxygen, water, food, and everything else needed to survive for a month, waiting for rescue."

"Rescue by whom? If they can destroy *Boone*, what other ship can stand up to them?"

Jim tossed off his wine, and the steward came to refill his glass. "No, I need something stronger. Get me a scotch." He turned to Allie. "I don't like it when you're being logical any more than when your mothers are."

Paige spoke into the strained silence. "Allie, we know you're bored."

"I am that, Mom." She looked around the table at her four mothers and her father. "Daddy, you've got all the Empire stuff to do." She looked at Janelle. "And you have things to do in engineering with the drives and all. Paige, you can go to communications and make sure everything is working right." She turned to Tanya. "You've got the ship's brains to keep you busy, and Marilyn, if nothing else, you can go to the zoo and play with your animals." She looked around the table. "I don't have anything to do. I'm a historian, for crying out loud! Writing the history of this war comes down to saying how many ships blew up today!"

Tanya and Admiral Claire Reeves, the oldest of the princesses, were considered to be the most intelligent people in the galaxy. While Claire, probably because of her training as a medical doctor, was very personable and appeared comfortable with her intelligence, Tanya looked a bit self-conscious. She made people uncomfortable to be around her, mostly because she seemed to know what they were going to say days before they did. Because of the tiny problem deep in her brain's switchboard, Tanya also fought a stutter for her entire 2,800-year lifetime. "You're r-right, Allie. Your f-friends are all b-busy, we're all b-busy, Miranda isn't here, and you have t-t-to entertain yourself. M-maybe you should make some new f-friends who aren't m-military personnel so you can spend some t-t-time with them."

"Yeah, all my friends are either Marines or Fleet and doing double watches. Maybe you're right, Mom."

"I think she is." Marilyn wouldn't look at Jim. Allie knew that meant she was about to say something he wasn't going to like. "I know you haven't spent much time with Roland recently, either."

Allie had been going out with Roland for about a year, but he was Fleet, and in the nine months since *Boone's* arrival in the war zone, they'd had dinner less than a dozen times. "No, I haven't, but we decided to see other people."

"I'm sorry." Marilyn smiled a little. She still wouldn't look at Jim. "That means you could find a new guy, a civilian, to go out with!"

"Baby, if you're going where I think you are with this conversation, can I leave first?" Jim wasn't smiling.

"You don't need to leave. I'm just saying that she should go out and, um, have fun."

Paige tried not to spew wine from her nose. "Marilyn!"

"Well, I'm sorry, but Allie is twenty-seven, and she's a beautiful young woman. She needs to spend some time with young men. Doing, um, things."

"I'm leaving now." Jim stood and kissed the top of Allie's head. "Little one, please try to get to the Safe Room next time." He left the dining room.

"Mom! You're going to cause Daddy to have a stroke!"

"She might, but he'll get over it." Janelle reached across the table and took Allie's hand. "Marilyn's right, though. Go out and have some fun."

"What about the security guards tailing me all the time?"

"Why don't you talk to Ike?" Paige thought for a moment. "She's reasonable. Maybe she can help you with that. I know being a princess can cramp the social life a little."

"More than a little, Mom." Allie smiled slowly. "I'll do that and see what happens."

* * * *

"Please, Ike? Can't you do something?" Allie reached the point of begging.

"Are you crazy? Between the terrorists and the nutcases, you're too good of a target. And we may have Arupian agents aboard, too." Ike Payne was the Marine Master Sergeant in charge of security on *Boone*, and that included providing bodyguards for the royal family. "No, absolutely not. I am not pulling the guards off you." She sighed. "I really do understand what you're saying, though."

Allie had mastered a really good pout long ago, and she knew when to use it. "Please?"

"Jesus, Allie!" Ike thought for a moment. "OK, tell you what. Instead of one uniformed guard, I'll put two plainclothes people with you." Ike stared at the ceiling for a moment. "I must be out of my fucking mind." She sighed again. "They'll tail you and keep you in sight at all times, but they won't be as noticeable that way. That's all I can do. You can take it or leave it."

"Thank you, Ike! You're the best!" Allie hugged Ike.

"Shit! Stop that! Now, get the fuck out of here before I change my mind!"

* * * *

The Imperial Café was an interesting place. When Allie's grandpa built *Boone* eight hundred years ago, he wanted a nightclub on the ship. Stu Dayton was almost 4,300 years old, older than the Empire itself, and a bit of a sentimentalist. He called the Café a Classic Rock bar, and the food and music all came from when he was a young man in the last half of the twentieth century AD. Most people had never heard of the music.

As Allie walked to the club, she noticed the bodyguards following at a reasonable distance but never losing sight of her. While Allie was

Janelle's biological daughter, she had learned to dress from her sister Charlotte and from her mother Marilyn, both tall, gorgeous blondes with the most amazing sapphire blue eyes. Her mom and sister both also dressed very sexy and could grab the attention of any man within a parsec. Allie walked into the club. It was only about a third full. Too many military people worked twelve or more hours a day since the war started.

She went to the bar and ordered a drink as she surveyed the crowd.

* * * *

Damon Hyde was a Marine and damn proud of the fact. His family had all been Marines for seven generations, and he was happy to carry on the tradition. As a Second Lieutenant, he commanded an assault team and had the respect and devotion of a crack group of professionals. Other than boarding a few Arupian ships, Damon and his team hadn't seen much action and no combat in this war, but that was sure to change. It didn't matter how high-tech warfare became, it always came down to a Marine with a gun.

Damon shared a few drinks and a lot of laughs with his sergeant and corporals at The Imperial Café. At only thirty-one, Damon had gotten hooked on the music played at the nightclub. One of the few people on *Boone* who knew anything about the songs, he had a certain pride about the fact. There was no music less than four thousand years old, and most was far older. He recognized the song playing now as *Light My Fire* by The Doors.

Sergeant Williams asked Damon when they might have a chance to do more than baby-sit a few prisoners. "I don't know, Gabe. That's up to..." Damon's mouth remained open as his voice faded away. The most beautiful woman he'd ever seen had walked into the Café and gone to the bar.

Between the advances in medical care and transplant technology, human life spans approached four hundred years, and people in their three hundreds looked like they were forty. The woman might be any age between twenty and three hundred. It didn't matter. She was tall and slender, her shape full of soft, feminine curves. Her waist-length hair was a soft honey blonde, looking like the smooth, creamy head on the glass of Irish cream ale in front of him. She wore a very tight and short white skirt and a matching top tied around her chest, her flat stomach exposed. Her eyes were nothing less than amazing. Even in the semidarkness of the club, he could see them, like emeralds, throwing green fire around the room as she sipped her drink and watched the crowd.

Damon didn't know her and didn't recall ever seeing her before. He would have remembered her.

Gabe nudged him. "Are you OK?"

Corporal Emily Harden laughed. "He's been struck blind, deaf, and dumb!"

"No, but I have to meet that woman." Damon tossed off the rest of his beer. "With any luck, I won't be back."

* * * *

Allie leaned casually on the bar sipping her vodka on the rocks. Most of the people in the Café were civilians and the few military there were Marines. She saw a man stand up from a table and walk her way. He wore the casual uniform of a Marine officer and was good looking. A big, well-built man, his head well above the others, he had the typical short hair of a Marine. In the darkness, Allie couldn't tell his eye or hair color clearly until he stood in front of her.

"Hi, I'm Damon."

She took the offered hand. She managed not to jump at the electrical tingle that raced up her arm and through her body. "I'm Allie." His eyes were a pale blue and the short hair was blond.

His warm hand gently squeezed hers. "Allie, good to meet you." He laughed easily. "This is about the oldest line in the book, but it's all I can come up with. May I buy you a drink?"

"On one condition. You tell me why that's the best line you can come up with."

He flagged the bartender for more drinks. "That's a deal, but the answer will sound like another line. Since you walked in the room, I haven't been able to think straight."

"You're right, it does sound like another line, but I'll take the drink anyway."

"Thanks, Allie." The drinks came, and Damon swiped his credit card. "Would you like to find a table and sit down?"

"Sure." She led the way to a table on the far side of the dance floor. Damon held her chair as she sat down. She didn't think he'd seen the guards as they kept a discreet distance but always in sight.

"So, Allie, tell me your life story."

She laughed. "We really don't have time for that, I'm afraid." She watched him and thought he looked like the guy who should be on the Marine recruiting posters all over the Empire. His face was all angles and sharp, with a look of firm authority and devotion to duty and honor about him. When he walked, he held his back straight, his shoulders square, and his steps measured and even. Allie laughed to herself. Despite the tired, old pickup lines, she found herself incredibly attracted to him.

"I don't know. I've got plenty of time."

"So, why don't you tell me *your* life story?"

"I can do that. I'm Damon Hyde. I guess you can see I'm a Second Lieutenant. I'm thirty-one. I've been on *Boone* for four years now. I was born on New Moscow and stationed there since I enlisted at seventeen. My mom is Betty, and my dad is Ralph, and I'm the middle of three kids. I've never been married, and I have no children. I like watching and playing baseball, working out, and my favorite color is green. My favorite food is Italian, and I like beer." He pulled a pen and piece of paper from his shirt pocket and wrote quickly. "Here's my service number, my intercom number, birthday, and shoe size if you need any of them."

Allie laughed. "Well, you have a short life story." She looked at the slip of paper he'd given her. "I'll hang on to this."

"Other than a few details that would bore us both to tears, that's it." He smiled at her. "See, it doesn't take long."

"I guess not."

"Don't take this wrong, but your eyes are fascinating."

She'd been watching him. Like her mother, Allie had large breasts, but she hadn't seen Damon look at them more than briefly. He spent most of the time focusing on her eyes. She found it remarkably sensitive and attractive. "Is there a wrong way to take that?"

The Polyamorous Princess 11

"I don't know." His face went to a funny, soft expression. "I've never seen eyes that color before."

"Thank you." He had no idea who she was. She considered telling him, but she didn't want to scare him off.

"Don't thank me for being pretty, Allie. God made you pretty, not me."

She smiled at him. "You're smooth, I'll give you that."

He looked down for a moment. When he looked back into her eyes, Allie saw a slight blush touching his face. "I'm really not trying to be smooth. I'm just trying to talk and not babble like an idiot."

"That wasn't very fair of me. I'm sorry."

"That's all right. I guess you get a lot of lines from smooth talkers."

"I've had my share."

A song Allie didn't know came on, and she wondered what it was. Her question must have shown because Damon smiled. "This song is called *Diary*. A band called Bread is the artist."

"How do you know that?"

He shrugged. "I just like the music that they play here. I sometimes wonder what Mr. Dayton had on his mind when he set the Café up this way."

"You should ask him."

"Yeah, like that's going to happen!"

"You never know, Damon."

He smiled for a moment. "Would you like to dance?"

"Yes, I would." He held her chair and then her hand as they went to the dance floor.

After a moment's hesitation, he slipped his arms around her waist. She put her arms around his neck, and they moved to the slow music. "You're a much better dancer than I am."

Allie's breath was short, but she hoped she managed to hide the fact. "Maybe, but the last I heard, they didn't teach dancing in Marine training." The electric tingles faded to be replaced by major shocks as their bodies touched.

"No, they don't. What do you do to pay the rent, Allie? You don't act like you're military."

"No, I'm not. Technically, I'm a historian, but I do a little teaching at the high school, college, and even a little to the recruits and midshipmen." It was true, but she decided to leave out the princess part. She was afraid to look, but she knew the tingles had her nipples hard, and she hoped they weren't poking his hard chest.

The song ended, and they made their way back to the table. "A historian. That sounds interesting, but I'm just a grunt."

She laughed. "The history of the Marines goes back a long time and is pretty interesting. They were established in 1775 AD, almost five thousand years ago, and are the oldest continuously operating branch of the military."

"There must be a lot of things other than military history to talk about with the prettiest woman I've ever seen."

"Smooth."

"Maybe. You owe me your life history, Allie."

She thought for a moment. "Tell you what, let's go for a walk, and I'll tell you all about it."

"That's a deal."

* * * *

Another great thing Stu had built into *Boone* was the Observation Deck. More than ninety square kilometers, the OD looked like Old Earth from before the global war that nearly exterminated humanity. A dome covered the OD and could change from clear, to look out into space, to a number of effects to simulate the sky of Earth. It was after 2300 when Allie and Damon reached the OD. Studded with stars in the patterns seen from Earth, a bright full moon hanging among them, the dome was set to night-sky mode.

As they walked in the moonlight, passing from the glow of one streetlamp to another, she wondered about the guards. She hadn't seen them, but she knew they were there. Allie and Damon walked close together but not touching. She wanted to touch him but she was afraid to, fearing the tingles of his touch would push her over the edge.

"Let's sit down here. I'll tell you my life history instead of the Marine's history." They sat on the park bench quietly for a while, just watching the darkness, a gentle breeze blowing the crisp smell of trees and grass on the air.

"Well, where to begin. I'm Allison Jenkins." Most people had no idea of the Emperor's last name. "I'm twenty-seven and, like you, I've never been married. I have no kids, although I have several nieces and nephews that are almost like my kids." As one of 141 children of the Emperor, Allie didn't tell Damon she had over five hundred nieces and nephews. "You already know I'm a historian, and my favorite color is purple."

He smiled at her. "Don't I get your intercom number?"

"Not yet."

"I can accept that. Any brothers or sisters?"

"Obviously. I have nieces and nephews." She managed to dodge that question.

"Oh, yeah. I told you I'm not thinking clearly."

"Still?"

"Yeah."

Allie could see his eyes study her face in the half-light of the streetlamps. "What's wrong?"

He smiled a bit sheepishly. "I've been on missions into hostile fire. I've gone down as the first wave of assaults when we lost seventy percent of our teams. I've been in firefights and been shot three times, once seriously enough that I almost died. I've been way too close to explosions. I was even in a landing craft that was shot down once." He looked into her eyes, and his smile slipped from his face. "Why do you scare me, Allie?"

"I don't know. I don't mean to scare you." Ever since she was a little girl, she could remember her father telling her mothers that they scared him. She knew he wasn't scared of anything other than they.

"I know you don't mean to. It's nothing you're doing." He sighed, his broad shoulders slumping a little. "I'm not sure myself. Maybe it's because I want to impress you and I feel like I can't do that while I'm acting like a babbling idiot."

Allie watched him for a moment. His eyes were soft. She could see an almost boyish innocence there, and the fear he spoke of was clear on his face. The breeze wafted his scent to her nose, the crisp, clean scent of a man who worked hard for what he believed and wasn't afraid to sweat to do his job. She couldn't help herself. She leaned slowly towards him.

Hesitantly, they moved together, and their lips touched. His strong arms slid around her, pulling her close to him. His tongue moved slowly into her mouth, like he tested the waters. Her tongue, of its own volition, pressed against his in a tango of warm, moist passion. Their faces pressed tightly together, their lips slipping against each other.

The skin of his face was smooth, like he shaved only a short time ago. She didn't feel surprised that a Marine would shave more than once a day. His hands left warm tracks on her back as they moved over her body, and she trembled at the heat.

As her lips moved over his mouth, she tasted the unique flavor that his cologne, perspiration, and saliva made. His sweat brought a sharp salty tang to her mouth. Damon's cologne held distinct hints of pheromones, but not overpowering. The flavor and scent that filled her senses only added to the natural attraction she felt. His saliva and breath came sweet to her nose and tongue. She longed for more and pulled him tighter to her.

In the quiet of the Observation Deck night, the gentle smacking of his lips against her face played a chorus with the sounds of the crickets in the grass around them. She thought she heard a few low moans coming from him, but they might have been her own.

Somewhere in the distance, a moonflower released its sweet aroma to the wind, and it floated to her nose, adding to the remarkable blend that already drove her senses to near overload. The grass, recently mown, offered a fresh, clean backdrop to the other smells running through her system.

Damon moved his head slowly, his lips rolling over hers. As his tongue moved slowly and deliberately in her mouth, he flicked it against her teeth. When the tip fluttered over her gums, she trembled.

Her mind fogged from the passions his kiss awakened in her, and she found herself melting in his arms. Something about the way he touched her senses made her want him.

She ran her hands over his head and neck. Her pulse pounded in her head, her face flushing hotly, like lava flowing across her skin. Unlike her younger sister, Allie wasn't a virgin. She had her fair share of experience with men.

Through the fog of the passionate kiss, she realized that his hands

The Polyamorous Princess 15

behaved themselves, never moving toward her breasts. She found it pleasing, though she knew she wanted Damon to touch her.

Many minutes later, their lips slowly parted. Allie's eyes opened slowly, and she smiled at him. "I think I should give you my intercom number now."

"I'd really like that."

Allie considered, but only a moment. "Damon, there's something I need to tell you, though."

"What's that?"

"I, um, haven't been fully open with you. I haven't lied to you, but there are a few things I didn't tell you." She searched for words but couldn't find any, so she decided the direct approach would be best. "I am a historian, and I do teach history sometimes, but mostly I don't do much of anything, as you put it, to pay the rent."

Damon frowned. "I don't understand."

"Promise me you won't run."

"What?"

"I really am Allie Jenkins. Princess Allison Jenkins."

His eyes blinked rapidly, and his mouth worked like a trout left flopping on the riverbank. "Your father is..."

"Yeah, he's the Emperor."

He stood up suddenly and danced back and forth a little. She stood and grabbed his hands. "Damon, it's OK."

"No, it's not OK! You're a princess!"

"Yeah, but I'm also a woman. I'm really just Allie."

"I've been making out with the Princess?"

She laughed a little despite herself. "Well, it wasn't exactly making out, but it was a good start."

"This isn't funny!"

"Actually, it is. At least a little." Allie put her arms around his neck, her face very close to his as she looked up into his eyes. Her heart began to pound faster in her chest again, and her breathing raced to a pant. "Do I need to call my bodyguards out of the woods to make you kiss me again?"

"Sergeant Payne will shit."

"No, she won't."

"Your father will have her toss me out of an airlock, then."

"No, he won't."

"Something bad is going to happen."

"Shut up and kiss me."

A small smile played across his face as he put his arms around her waist. The thrill of his touch hadn't faded, and she smiled in anticipation as their lips pressed together again.

* * * *

It was 0145 when Allie and Damon reached the door to her suite, deep in officer's country with Marines in body armor at every intersection. She saw him glance down the corridor. "Yeah, that's my folks' suite down there." Six guards, all with heavy weapons, stood watch, and the shimmer of a force field was visible.

"I'm twenty meters from the Emperor's suite with his daughter."

"Yeah, that pretty well sums it up." The door swished open to Allie's command. "I really don't normally do this, but would you like to come inside?"

His eyes flicked from her face to look into the room behind her. "If you were anyone else, I'd love to come inside. Actually, I'd love to come inside anyway." His mouth worked soundlessly again for a moment, then he looked back to her eyes. "I'm not making any sense at all, am I?"

"No, not much." She reached to his face and ran her fingers softly around the firm line of his jaw. Allie knew she wanted him. "Was that a yes or a no?"

"Both." He swallowed several times. "I want to come in, but I'm afraid to."

"You don't need to be afraid of my family."

"I'm not afraid of your dad. I'm afraid of you."

"Me? Why?" His mouth moved again. Allie laughed a little. Watching his lips move, she wanted to kiss him again, to feel his lips on hers. "Tell you what. Let's go inside and sit down. Just talking, OK?" She smiled gently. "I promise not to bite." She let her best seductive smile ripple across her face. "Unless you want me to."

Damon nodded. "OK, just to talk." He followed her in.

"Have a seat." She indicated the sofa. "Would you like a drink?"

"Just water, I think." He sat down at attention.

She brought his water. "Just relax." He leaned back a little. "Now, what's this about being afraid of me?"

He made a couple of false starts. "Allie, I'm not sure how I feel about you."

"What does that mean?"

As Allie watched, she saw the Marine in Damon come out. His shoulders squared, and he seemed to become, somehow, tougher than he was already. His eyes became resolute and, maybe, just a little cold and hard. She imagined him preparing to rush, single-handed, against overwhelming odds, knowing he would die, but duty and honor required the sacrifice, and he was ready to do what was needed. As if his body wasn't attractive enough, she saw things in Damon that emotionally attracted her. He had many of the character traits she knew her father possessed. The combination pushed her desires higher.

"Allie, I know we've only known each other a few hours, but it's easy to see you're special. I've never known anyone like you."

She had to fight not to laugh at him. "I know that whatever it is that you're trying to say is hard for you. You look like you're ready to charge up San Juan Hill. The fact is that I really have no idea what you're talking about."

"Where's San Juan Hill? Oh, never mind." He took a deep breath. "I really like you, and I really want to get to know you a lot better." He seemed to sag a little.

"Is that all? I like you, too. If I didn't, you wouldn't be here now. In fact, you'd have been shot down at the bar." She took his hand in hers, feeling the tingles returning. Allie wanted him, but the shyness and fear he showed her made her want to hold him, to protect him, more than her passions wanted to make love to him. "Don't be afraid of me, Damon. I'd like to get to know you better, too." She smiled at him. "If I didn't like you, I sure as hell wouldn't have kissed you the way I did."

"Really?"

"Yeah, really."

He seemed to relax, at least a little. "Well, could I take you to dinner tomorrow?" He glanced at the clock. "I mean tonight."

"I'd like that, yes."

He sighed. "Good, I'll pick you up at 1800, then." He moved to stand, but Allie grabbed his arm.

"Where are you going?"

"I should leave."

"Oh, no! You just relaxed a little bit." She laughed a little. "We're just talking, remember?"

"Yeah, just talking."

Allie and Damon sat together on the sofa, just talking, until 0600.

Chapter 2

Turns

Harry started staring at the Arupian code when he walked in his cubicle this morning. Now at 1220, he still stared at it, no better off than he was more than four hours ago. He leaned back in his chair and rubbed his eyes. The encrypted data had a pattern, but he could only see tiny parts of it, enough to tease him and play games with his mind.

Harry knew he had to solve this puzzle. Devon Henson was a nice guy, but he'd be getting pressure from Commander Dalton. Dalton wasn't bad, as line officers went, but he'd be getting flack from as high up the ladder as Admiral Q. Even the Admiral was OK, but Harry would bet credits to donuts that the Emperor himself yanked on the Admiral's chain. Harry had only been in Fleet for twelve years, but he'd learned fast that shit flows downhill. He also learned that a Lieutenant Junior Garrison was at the bottom of the hill.

He stood and stretched, reaching over his head for the ceiling. What made the pressure worse was that everyone seemed to think Harry was some kind of genius. He could solve puzzles and see patterns better than most people, but he didn't consider himself a genius. The impression the officers had that Harry might be a genius let him be just a little different. His hair was one example. Straight, shiny, and pitch black, his hair almost touched his shoulders and was far longer than regulation, longer than any other Fleet member on *Boone*. His black, closely trimmed beard was another. The regulation book strictly forbade long hair and beards. Harry got by with both because the brass thought he was smart. They also thought him just a little strange. They tended to leave him alone.

Devon poked his head into Harry's cubicle. "Haven't you gone for lunch yet?"

"No, I was just thinking about that." He studied his CO for a moment. "I need to get out of here and think for a while."

"Bad timing. We need that code."

"I know, and I'll get it for you, but I need to be away from this office for a while."

Henson sighed. "Harry...Oh, damn it! Listen, it's going to be both of our butts, but do what you need to do. Any idea of a timeline?"

"Not really, but I know you need to tell Dalton something." He paused for a moment and deliberately kept a blank look on his face. "I'll have it cracked by 0900."

"Are you sure?"

"No, but that will give us time to walk out an airlock before they come after us with torches and pitchforks."

Devon blinked at him. "Shit. Get out of here."

* * * *

Allie wrapped up her lecture on ancient American history to the students at the Imperial University campus on *Boone*. It had been a rough four hours, trying to keep students interested in things that happened nearly five thousand years ago on a planet most of them had never seen. Most didn't care about Richard Nixon and wouldn't remember a word she'd said by the time they finished lunch. She really couldn't blame them. Just what was the impact of Richard Nixon going to be for them?

She decided to go to the bistro on the OD for lunch. As she walked the tree-lined paths, she kept thinking about Damon. She'd been ready to bed him last night, but the boyish way he'd acted, the shyness he'd shown, had made it clear to Allie that the man was actually afraid of her. She'd been around a lot of men who were afraid of her father, but that wasn't the case with Damon. He was afraid of *her*.

She'd asked her moms about it over breakfast. Marilyn had giggled a little. "He's afraid you'll hurt him. He's giving you the power to crush him, emotionally, and he's afraid, down inside, that you'll do that. His heart knows you won't, but his head is in the way."

The bistro was busy today, and tables were scarce. She found a table and ordered. As she waited for her lunch, a young fleet officer approached her. "Excuse me, miss, but things seem to be a little crowded today. I was wondering if you'd mind a little company for lunch."

She looked at him for a moment. He was nothing if not forward. She liked that. "Sure, have a seat."

"Thanks." He extended his hand to her. "I'm Harry Douglas."

"Good to meet you, Harry. I'm Allie." His grip was firm in her hand.

He sat down and smiled slyly. "Should I call you Allie or Princess Allison?"

Allie watched him for a moment. He wore the uniform of a Fleet Lieutenant JG, but his black hair was way too long, and he had a beard. His brown eyes sparkled at her as if he had some secret he wasn't telling. A chill ran through her as she looked into his lively, sparkling eyes. "I guess I can't convince you I'm not the Princess."

"Not a chance." He gave his order to the server. "I am curious why the Princess is slumming it here with the commoners."

She had to laugh at his easy banter. "We do that, you know." Allie decided that if he could be brazen, so could she. "I'm curious how a fleet officer can have hair that long and a beard."

"Fair question. My CO thinks I'm crazy and a genius."

"Are you either or both?"

He waved his hand. "I suspect I'm smarter than some, and I know I'm crazier than some."

"So they just leave you alone then?"

"That's right." He smiled at her, his eyes flicking to her breasts and back to her eyes quickly. "I like them being just a little afraid of me."

Like the rest of the royal family, Allie had a neural implant that allowed her to communicate with the ship's computers directly, as well as with anyone else with an implant. She called up the personnel file on Harry and reviewed it in her head. "Well, long-haired Harry, what is it you do for my father?"

"That's an interesting way to describe my position. I solve puzzles, and I see you're trying to solve one right now." He grinned a little. "Your implant link will tell you that I work in Intelligence as a cryptography specialist. Your facial expression gave you away."

"Well, I guess a girl can't have any secrets around you." There was something about his easy conversation and his confidence that Allie found attractive. When he smiled, his whole face smiled, not just his lips. His eyes twinkled, and she still had the feeling that Harry had some secret he wasn't sharing. The air of mystery was intoxicating.

"Oh, a few." Their lunches came. He glanced at her salad. "Rabbit food."

He had some huge slab of fried meat with fried potatoes. "Maybe, but it won't kill me nearly as fast as that will." She pointed her fork at his plate.

"Oh, that doesn't matter, Allie. We'll probably all die in the war long before diet can kill us."

"You're just a bundle of joy, aren't you?" Her scan of his file said that he was a genius, but a little strange sometimes. Having grown up around Tanya and her sister, Claire, Allie understood that the two often went hand-in-hand.

"Maybe." He wolfed down his meal. "I'm nothing if not entertaining."

She laughed and almost choked on her salad. "I'll certainly grant you that." He was more than entertaining. He was fascinating. She pointed at his plate again. "What is that?"

"This, my Princess, is a hamburger steak, so rare that the chef only showed it a picture of a match." He cut off a small piece and held it out to her on his fork. "Here, try it."

Allie stared for a moment. She rarely ate red meat, but his open and forward manner made her take the morsel he offered. "Hey, that's pretty good."

"You bet it is." He finished the rest in two more bites. "You never told me what you're doing here, so I guess you're not going to. Want to go for a walk after lunch?"

She felt like she'd missed something. "What?"

"I'm going for a walk down around the lake. I thought you might like to come along." He frowned. "I guess I should have asked if you're engaged or something."

"Um, well, no. I'm not engaged or anything like that."

He glanced toward the door of the restaurant. "Your two sidekicks would be welcome. I'm just looking for someone to have a little intelligent conversation with."

"Harry, are you always this direct?"

"Direct? I don't know. I spend all day looking for hidden meanings, and I see no point in hiding the meaning of what I say."

Allie smiled slowly. "All right. You've got a date."

"Oh, no! I'm not looking for a date! Just a little company for a walk around the lake."

"OK, then. Just a walk and intelligent conversation."

* * * *

As they walked around the lake, Allie was fascinated watching Harry. His conversation would swing from one topic to another without warning. He would run at birds and squirrels, causing them to scamper for cover. "Harry, why aren't you on duty?"

"Oh, I am on duty. I have a puzzle I'm trying to solve, and I needed to think."

"So, you're thinking?"

"Yep." He stopped suddenly. "I just realized that I should have told you something."

"What's that?"

"You're very pretty, Allie." He brushed his hair out of his eyes. "I know you hear that a lot from men. All men tell women that for several reasons. Seriously, though, you're very pretty, and I'm not saying that to get in your pants."

She stumbled a bit and he caught her arm. She wasn't used to a man being even close to as open and direct as he was being. The thought flitted through her mind that this could be an elaborate line, but even if it was, Allie had to give him credit. It was a very good line. "Thank you, I think."

"You're welcome." He watched the ducks on the lake. She wondered if he was going to dive in after them.

"You're a very unusual man."

"I'll take that as a good thing." He looked around and saw a bench just ahead. "Let's sit down for a minute."

They sat watching the ducks paddle around the lake for a few minutes. "Are you solving your puzzle?"

"Not yet." He sighed a little. "I will, though."

"Somehow, I don't doubt that." Allie watched him for a moment. Since the fleeting glance he'd made at her breasts at the bistro, she hadn't seen him even notice her body again. "If this is too personal, I understand, but are you dating anyone?"

"Me? Oh, no! Most women think I'm really as crazy as my CO thinks I am."

Allie could see that happening. It was easy to confuse crazy and eccentric. "Do they? Are you always like you are today?"

"No, I'm really not. I'm just really wrapped up in this puzzle."

She picked up a small twig from next to her on the bench and began twisting and flexing it in her hands. "Is that why you seem a little, I don't know, flighty?"

"Yeah, it is." He smiled at her. "I should apologize for that, too. It's a miracle you haven't had your bodyguards spirit you away by now."

"Not really, Harry." She played with the twig.

His eyes watched her twisting and bending the small green twig, and Allie saw them narrow. He reached for the branch. "May I?" He took the twig and flexed it a few times, then twisted it, bending it into a circle. He almost whispered. "Mobius strip."

"What?"

"A Mobius strip. That's the answer!" He stood suddenly and pulled her to her feet. "The code is a textual Mobius strip in five dimensions! Of course! I have to go!" He hugged her, and Allie's heart skipped a beat. "Thanks!" He turned and ran for the exit. He stopped and turned back to her. "Call me!" He was out of sight in moments.

Allie stood alone and tried to get her heart to slow down. The brief, fleeting hug had hit her with an unexpected wave of desire to kiss the amazing longhaired man. When she managed to compose herself, she turned for home, puzzling over the encounter.

* * * *

Harry walked into Devon's office at 1643 and tossed a data card on his desk. "Here you go."

"What's this?"

"The new Arupian code, all cracked and ready to go."

Devon smiled slowly. "Your excursion helped, I guess."

"Yeah, it did. A girl I had lunch and took a walk with was even more help."

"A girl, eh? Anyone I know?"

"Almost certainly."

Devon watched his underling for a moment. "OK, keep your damn secrets."

"I plan to." Harry nodded at the data card. "You should get that to the readers. I'm going home."

Devon could only shake his head as the crazy man left his office.

* * * *

Damon was staring up the corridor at the guards around Allie's parents' suite when she opened the door. He turned to look at her, and his smile faded from his face. His jaw swung open. "Wow."

Allie wore a short black dress that was low cut on top and high cut on the bottom. "How is this?"

"You're staggeringly beautiful."

"Thanks." They reached the Café without Damon walking into the bulkhead, but he kept watching her.

After ordering their drinks, Damon took her hand. "How was your day?"

"Good." She frowned a little. "I met the strangest man, though."

"Anyone I know?"

"Maybe. Harry Douglas. He works in the Intelligence Office."

"I don't think I know anyone there. You said he was strange."

"Yeah." She thought about her encounter with Harry for a moment. He'd made her laugh, and he'd been so relaxed with her. She was not sure what to think of him. "He's very smart, but he's, well, strange. Maybe eccentric is better word. And he has hair to his shoulders and a beard."

"Really? Is he a civilian contractor?"

"Nope, he's a JG."

Damon smiled. "Had to be Fleet."

"I've seen some shaggy Marines around here, too."

"Just the security types and not real Marines."

She laughed. "Are you going to tell Ike Payne she's not a real Marine?"

"Do I look like I want my ass kicked?"

"No, I guess not." Allie sipped at her drink. "Anyway, Harry is interesting. He was trying to solve some puzzle, and we shared a table at lunch." She grinned. "He knew I was a princess right from the start."

"You know how to make a guy feel good."

"You have no idea how well I know how to make a guy feel good."

Damon sat staring at her. "What?"

She smiled at him over her glass. "I know exactly how to make a guy a feel good." Despite the encounter with Harry, Allie wanted Damon. She'd been willing to hold her passions at bay last night because he was so nervous, but she didn't think she could do that again.

Their dinner came, and Damon avoided the subject. Rebecca, another simulated human, was the only server The Imperial Café had ever had. A tall redhead, most men found her attractive. She also had eight hundred years of practice fending off passes and could lift a shuttlecraft with one arm.

"Allie, I wanted to ask how your moms and dad are doing. They haven't been in for more than a month."

"Daddy's just been really busy with all this war stuff going on, I guess."

"I remember the first night Jim and Janelle came here." Rebecca laughed, looking around the bar. "Marilyn had all the stops pulled out flirting with your dad, but he shut her down."

"I've heard that story, too. I would have loved to have seen that!"

"Yeah, they were both ready to clear off a table, but I think he and Janelle didn't entertain the multiple marriage idea yet. A couple of nights later, Marilyn and your dad made up for it, though. It seemed that Marilyn has been your dad's favorite ever since."

"Seems that way, but there really isn't much difference in how he loves my moms."

"No, I guess that's true. He loves all four of them. Even for me, it's easy to see that." Rebecca looked around the club for a moment. "I have to go, but tell your folks I said hello." She left, off for another table.

Damon frowned a little. "Something just occurred to me...I guess I've known for as long as I can remember that your folks are in a multiple marriage, but how does your father love more than one woman?"

She smiled over her fork at him. "Haven't you ever wondered what it would be like to have four women in your bed?" Allie knew she was flirting, but she couldn't stop.

"Four? No, not really."

"Just two, then?"

"I think every man has that fantasy."

"Yeah, they do, but you're missing the same thing that most men miss about what my moms and my dad, and most of my brothers and sisters, have. It's not about sex at all. It's about love. My folks hate the term multiple marriage and prefer to call what they have a *polyamorous* marriage."

Damon looked puzzled. "What's poly—whatever you said?"

"Polyamorous, as in many loves. My moms and daddy are all in love with one another." She shrugged. "If you want to get technical, my moms are all bisexual."

"Is it always one man and several women in your family?"

"No, but that is probably about half of the marriages. My brother Jimmy is gay, and he's in a single marriage, and my sister Claire is in a single pairing with Zach. My oldest sister Rose is married to two men, and my brother Stewart is married to three women and two men."

"Maybe I don't understand." Damon thought for a minute. "I can't see how anyone can love more than one person that deeply."

"Daddy and mom didn't understand until they met Tanya and Marilyn. Then Paige came along a little later. I'm not sure I can explain it, though." She smiled. "I have to find one person to fall in love with before I can find a second." The electric feeling she had said that she might have found him.

Damon laughed a little. "You said your moms are bisexual. What about the two men your sister is married to?"

"Yeah, Bob and Charlie are bisexual, but my brother Stewart and his two husbands are all three straight, and so are their three wives."

"This could get complicated just trying to figure out who it's safe to sleep with."

Allie laughed heartily. "Yeah, it could! It's easier if you take sex out of the equation, though. It's about love, not sex."

"Maybe I'll never understand."

"You never know."

"So, what about you? Will you have a polyamorous marriage?" He pronounced the word carefully.

"Maybe." She smiled. "Like I said, I have to find one person first."

* * * *

As they danced, he nuzzled her hair. "You smell great, Allie."

"Thanks. I borrowed this perfume from my mom." She was glad her face was against his chest, so he didn't see her reaction to his touch. The feeling of him holding her in his arms was intense. Allie had the urge to pull him to the floor with her and chew his shirt off.

"No, not the perfume, although that's nice, too. I mean you, you smell great."

Her cheeks warmed. She felt good in his arms, safe and wanted. "Last night, I really came here to meet someone who wasn't in the military."

"Sorry to disappoint you."

"You haven't." They'd been dancing for four songs, and one that Allie recognized came on. It was the one her dad and Marilyn thought of as being their song, even though she didn't know the name of it. "Damon, do you know what this song is?"

"Yeah. It's *Nights in White Satin* by a band called The Moody Blues."

The music was full of heavy drum and bass beats, pounding to a rhythmic pulse. The soloist sang about how he loved someone. As the music reached a climax, Allie had contained herself as long as she could. Strong muscles lurked under his uniform. His arms around her as they danced, pulling her against him, made her want to touch his bare skin. The soft scent of his perspiration was in her nose, driving her to wonder how he would taste as she ran her tongue over his skin. She leaned back in his arms, her eyes half-closed, and parted her lips slightly. Damon responded, pulling her to him, pressing his lips to hers as his tongue probed her mouth. They kissed through the last two minutes of the song as it changed to poetry and orchestrations. As the song ended and their lips parted, Allie's eyes opened slowly and she looked deeply into his eyes. "Let's get out of here."

* * * *

Allie managed to keep her hands off Damon as they walked to her suite, but as soon as they entered her cabin, she grabbed his neck and pressed her face to his, almost painfully so. Her hands ran over his shirt, feeling the strong muscles of his chest, heaving with his heavy breathing. His hands ran up and down her back, firmly caressing her shoulders as he hugged her body to his. They stumbled to the center of the sitting room still locked in their embrace. Allie tore at his shirt hungrily, ripping the buttons from the material. As she struggled to pull the shirt from him, she could see his rippled abdomen and well-defined masculine shape, the smell of his sweat, pungent and spicy, driving her passions. She pulled her lips from his and licked his chest, tasting the musky excitement in his chemistry.

Damon's hands moved on her back, and he pulled the zipper of her dress down. The little black dress slipped from her shoulders and fell to the floor, making a soft black cloud around her ankles. She never wore a bra, and her breasts flushed with excitement, her nipples hard and firm in expectation. While last night, Damon seemed to make a conscious effort not to look at her breasts, now he didn't seem able to pull his eyes away from them. His voice was soft and reverent as his eyes drifted over her near-naked body.

"My God, Allie. You're amazing."

Her heart melted at his compliments but not just his words. Anyone could say words, and she had heard a lot of them, but the tenderness and raw emotions she saw in his eyes and on his face excited her and pushed her forward.

"Come with me." Stepping over her discarded dress, she led him to the sofa where she removed the high heels she wore. She tugged at his belt and pants, undoing them and letting them fall around his feet. They stood together in their underwear and kissed again, exploring each other's mouths deeply with their tongues, tasting each other. Allie's pulse pounded in her head. She could hear the rush of the blood in her ears as their mouths writhed together. The sheen of sweat on their bodies made his chest slip delightfully over her breasts.

After several minutes, she pulled away from his lips and pushed him gently to the sofa. Kneeling next him, she kissed him again, her hands running over the hot flesh of his chest. His hands tentatively moved to her breasts, and Allie's pulse hammering in her head. When his fingers brushed over her rigid nipples, she twitched and pressed her lips to his harder. Her hand moved slowly down his chest to the washboard muscles of his stomach. The sinuous ridges trembled slightly under her touch. His body was deliciously firm. Damon kissed across her face and nibbled at her neck and ear. Waves of shocks moved through her as her hand slipped lower. His cock, long and hard, strained at his briefs. Gripping the rigid shaft in her fist, she pulled and stroked, feeling him twitch and jump to her touch.

Damon's breath was like fire on the skin of her neck. His tongue flashed in and out of her ear, causing her to shudder. Allie's hand ran down and cupped his balls, hard and hot and swollen, and she tugged at his briefs, working them from him. Her hand again gripped his dick, hard as steel, and she slowly stroked his length.

His lips moved from her ear, kissing down her neck, and he slowly circled her nipple with his hot, wet tongue. She could feel the spreading wetness in her panties and the cramping desire in her groin as his attentions drove her passions higher and higher with each fleeting flick of his tongue. Allie could hear her own moans escaping her lips as her head lolled back, her hair falling down her back. She squeezed the stiff shaft in her hand and pumped rapidly over the full length, burning for his touch, longing to take his cock into her body.

Damon suddenly stood, sweeping her into his arms, biceps bulging. He knelt on the floor and gently lowered her to lie in front of him. She looked up into his eyes as he slowly pulled her panties from her, sliding them down her legs and over her feet. As he moved to kneel between her spread legs, she saw the look on his face, not of blind lust, not of wanting just any woman, but a look of blind passion meant only for her. He slowly lifted her legs and entered her core, his cock sliding effortlessly into her flowing pussy. He leaned and kissed her as he began to thrust firmly and rhythmically into her, impaling her with his hardness. As they kissed and he thrust fully into her, Allie's hips met his every onslaught, gyrating and pressing to get just one more millimeter of penetration.

Their lips still locked, their hands moving over each other, their thrusting increased in tempo, bouncing harder and harder together as they neared climax. Allie could sense her own orgasm closing on her, crawling through the semidarkness to reach her. The tempo of the song of passion increased to a crescendo, and he made a final, powerful thrust just as her orgasm hit her.

They grunted and moaned together, their lips still locked together despite the risk of biting each other. Their hips slammed fiercely against one another, Allie pinned to the floor by his impetus, and she writhed in her orgasmic seizure under him. Through the shuddering fog of her climax, she could feel the heat of their bodies. Her mind raced around the pounding of her pulse. The intensity of the orgasm was like none before.

Slowly, the driving force receded, and their lips slipped apart. She nuzzled against his neck as they trembled together in their embrace. His ragged breathing blew like a hot desert wind across her face, and it felt wonderful.

He carefully lifted his body from her and rolled to the side, leaving his arm across her stomach. "You didn't have to move."

"I don't want to squash you."

She laughed as his fingers gently tickled her belly. "You won't." Allie rolled to her side to face him. "I'm almost afraid to talk. I don't want you to vanish into thin air."

"Unless you want me to leave, I don't plan to go anywhere."

"No, I want you to stay." Allie stared into his eyes. She could see the glow of adoration on his face, and the knowledge that she was the target of his strong feelings made her heart race faster. "I've never done this before, Damon."

He frowned a little. "You're...um, you were a virgin?"

She laughed. "No. I mean I've never had sex with someone on the second date before."

"I'm sorry." He was still frowning.

She pressed her fingers to his lips. "No, don't be sorry. I'm not."

His frown faded to a soft smile. "Now, it's my turn to be afraid to talk."

"You don't need to talk." She leaned and kissed him. As their kiss intensified, their bodies moved together, sliding across the carpet, until they touched fully. The faint stirrings in the half-erect cock pressed against her triggered a tingling response in her. Damon again suddenly pulled away and moved to his knees, lifting her effortlessly in his powerful arms. He turned and sat her on the sofa. Without a word, he moved to kneel between her knees and lifted her legs to place them over his shoulders, his hard tongue suddenly plunging into her wet cunt.

Allie jerked with the bolt of pleasure that shot through her. Her hands moved to his head, running through the close-cropped blonde hair, pulling his face to her slit. His tongue plunged deep into her core and flicked firmly over and around her hard clit. He licked her pussy and his fingers dug deeply into her hips, pulling her against his darting tongue. His lips closed around her clit, sucking it firmly into his mouth where his tongue played around the swollen button, causing Allie to scream incoherently and thrash on the sofa, her arms flailing wide and her hands grabbing the material.

His hand moved slowly from her hip, and his fingers slipped into her soaked pussy, probing her and stroking her cervix. Her hips thrust against his face and hand. The second wave of her climax drew near. She grabbed his head, forcing his face into her. Screaming his name loudly enough that her parents would have heard if not for the sound damping fields, she thrashed in her climax, slamming his face into her flowing pussy as he sucked harder on her clit, causing wave after wave of her orgasm to pound her like some unspeakably towering tsunami crashing to the shore.

She jerked spasmodically when he released her clit from her mouth with a slight popping sound and lowered her legs to the floor. She managed a weak smile. "Wow."

"Yeah." He crawled to sit beside her on the sofa and slipped those strong arms around her again, cuddling her until her tremors subsided.

Allie turned in his arms to face him and pressed her lips to his again. The scent and taste of her own juices mixed with his perspiration was heady in her nose and on her tongue. She kissed over his face, savoring the spicy sweetness of his skin, licking his lips. Allie kissed down to his neck and chest, the hard muscles quivering slightly. As she slipped to kneel before him, she licked the sinewy ridges of his stomach. She could feel his hard cock nestled between her breasts. With a burst of longing, she moved and impaled her mouth on his dick, swallowing his full length into her throat, causing Damon to twitch violently, his hips thrusting up to meet her mouth. Pulling his shaft from her mouth, she licked his balls, then the full length of his cock, her tongue swirling around the head. She nibbled gently at the glans as his hands moved to brush over her hair.

As her lips slipped over the head of his cock again, he held her head and gently pumped his dick in her mouth, never forcing himself into her. Allie sucked firmly on the stiff dick in her mouth. As she flicked her tongue around the bulbous head, he trembled and she heard him softly speak her name. Closing her mouth firmly on him, she pumped his staff in her mouth and down her throat. His hands held her head, his touch soft and gentle, only guiding, never forcing. Her own wetness flowed again and she reached with her hand to rub her clit as she sucked Damon's cock.

Damon's body suddenly went rigid under her. Allie slipped the head of his cock out so she held the glans between her lips. He gave a jerking thrust and his cum exploded in her mouth, like lava flowing from a volcano, hot and sticky, salty-sweet. She sucked firmly on his pulsing dick, draining him fully. When the steaming stream ebbed, she gave the head of his cock a final, gentle kiss and moved to sit beside him. She cuddled to his chest, and his arm slipped protectively around her shoulders. Her emotions were awash with the swirling changes she felt. She thought she had been in love before, but this was different, more intense. Allie had never had sex so soon after meeting a man, but that didn't matter to her. She could feel how good and how right Damon was for her.

He nuzzled her hair. "I think that it's my turn to say wow."

She kissed his neck. "Will you stay the night with me?"

"I'd love to."

She stood and took his hand. They showered and lay together in bed. They woke one another several times in the night and made love again, but they mostly slept in each other's arms.

Chapter 3

Damage

After they'd made love in the shower and shared breakfast, Allie kissed Damon goodbye at the door of her suite. "Have a good day. I'll see you this afternoon."

"You too, Allie." He kissed her again and turned to leave. He almost ran over Marilyn and Janelle as Marilyn reached for the doorbell. "My Ladies." He practically ran down the hall.

Allie stood at the door in her robe. "Um, hi, moms."

Marilyn smiled slowly. "Making new friends?"

"Yeah." Allie arranged her robe to cover her right breast where Damon had fondled it before he left.

"Allie, your father will shit." Janelle at least smiled.

"He'll get over it." Marilyn looked in the sitting room. "Can we come in, or do you have someone else in there?"

"Oh, sure."

After they had all sat at the dining room table, Janelle sipped at her coffee. "So, are you in love?"

"Maybe."

"Lust is good." Janelle elbowed Marilyn. "Well, it is!"

"I didn't say it wasn't, but you know how Jim gets."

"Mom, the word you're looking for is weird."

Marilyn laughed. "Yeah, that's Jim when it comes to his daughters. Just keep things a little discreet, Allie."

"I'll try."

* * * *

Damon put his assault team through a practice operation on the holographic simulator. The simulation of an urban environment with hostiles emplaced in the eight to ten story buildings along the street had all the look and feel of reality. His team moved down the street, systematically drawing fire from an emplacement, neutralizing it, then moving on to the next and clearing the buildings as they went.

They had just cleared a building and prepared to move out for the next target. Damon heard Gabe in the communications headset. "Alpha squad on point, heads up for mortar fire."

Damon stepped out from cover just a split second before the team moved out, and a bolt of red hostile laser fire stabbed out from the building across the street and touched his body armor. The simulator's computer announced dispassionately that he was now dead. Damon sagged in on himself and walked to the dead man's bench at the side of the action, throwing his helmet against the wall.

When Gabe and the corporals had secured the rest of the simulation, with no further losses, he came to sit beside Damon. "What the fuck was that about?"

"I'm just not thinking too clearly today, Gabe."

"Gee, do you really think so?"

Damon laughed. "Yeah, I do."

"You know better than that shit."

Damon looked at Gabe. Over two hundred years old, he'd been a Marine for 191 years. "You're a good officer, one of the best I've seen, but you need to get your head out of your ass or some fur ball will shoot it off. What's wrong?"

"Nothing's wrong."

The older man watched Damon for a moment. "Man, don't tell me that it's that little piece of ass from the bar the other night."

"She's not a piece of ass."

"Shit, Damon! She was cute, yeah, but she's either not worth dying for or she's worth not dying for."

"What?"

Gabe thought for a moment. "I'm just an old fart jarhead, but you're a young man. Listen, if she's just a piece of ass that you're going to fuck for a while and get a little head from, she's not worth dying for because your head is fucked over. On the other hand, if she's something special to you, then she's worth coming home to, and you need to get your shit together so you don't die out there."

"I see your point."

"You need to think about these kids, too." He nodded at the lance corporals and PFCs gathering their gear. "They look up to you. They're Marines, but they're also kids. If they see you all fucked in the head, they'll lose confidence in you. That's how officers get shot in the back."

"That's comforting."

"Maybe, maybe not. Like I said, I'm just a knuckle-dragger, so what do I know? Just get your shit together, Damon. I do not want to carry you home in a body bag."

* * * *

Harry always thought that one of the big perks of working in Intelligence was that he had nearly unlimited access to the computers and databases. He even knew who killed John Kennedy. He used the computer to locate Allie. He planned to meet her at the University and take her to lunch. Devon came to his cubicle with Commander Dalton. "Harry, glad we caught you."

"Oh, hi, Devon. I mean Lieutenant. Commander Dalton."

Dalton sat in the chair next to Harry's desk. "Douglas, I just wanted to tell you well done for cracking that newest code."

"Thank you, Sir. It was nothing once I figured out what they had done."

"Maybe it was nothing, son. Most people would be staring at that for weeks."

Harry glanced at the location display. She was still at the school. "Well, thank you again, Sir, but I have a lunch date."

"We don't want to keep you, then." Dalton stood. "Thanks again, Lieutenant."

Dalton left as Henson watched him. "Harry, you're going to piss him off one day."

"Maybe, but I have to go." He left the Intelligence Office and ran to the University.

* * * *

Allie wasn't nearly as frustrated with her students today. The class discussed a string of sex scandals that had rocked the American Presidency at the end of the twenty-first century, and the kids all paid better attention. Sex sells. She gathered her notes and tried to decide where to go for lunch as she left the University. She stopped and looked towards the mall, thinking the deli might be a good choice.

"Hi, Allie."

She turned. Harry walked up to her, smiling a lopsided grin. Much to her dismay, her heart sped up, and she found herself smiling in response. "What are you doing here?"

"Do you want the truth or the standard line?"

"Let's try the truth first."

"I came to take you to lunch for helping me with my puzzle yesterday."

"No thanks are needed. I really didn't do anything."

"Sure you did. You let me think, and then you played with that twig."

"That was all coincidence."

"Don't you believe in serendipity? Synchronicity?"

"Maybe."

"How about fate?"

"Of course."

"Everyone has to believe something, Allie. I believe I'd like to buy you lunch. You pick."

"I can't talk you out of this, can I?"

"Not in a million years." He smiled a little. "Based on the stare you gave the mall, I'd guess the deli for lunch."

"Damn, you're good."

"You have no idea." He took her hand and wrapped her arm around his. The tingle that shot up her arm from his touch whipped into her shoulders and shook her spine. It finally stopped when it hit her shoes. "Come on. The wonderful world of deli meats awaits!"

As they ate, Harry's banter flowed easily and smoothly. The flight of ideas he'd shown yesterday was gone, although he would still frequently change topics. "You seem more relaxed today, Harry."

"I am. The puzzle is solved, my reputation as a genius is intact, and my CO isn't going to shove me out an airlock." He considered her face for a moment. "That wasn't really me yesterday, Allie. I tend to get so wrapped up in problems that everything else fades a bit in importance."

"That's all right. It was actually fun." She smiled at him. "You're funny and can make me laugh."

"Is that funny as in ha-ha or funny as in needing a white coat that ties in the back?"

"Funny ha-ha." She giggled and folded her arms across her chest to hide her jutting nipples. "That's what I mean."

"I'll take that as a good thing. Tell me, my princess, are you seeing anyone? I know you're not married, and you told me you weren't engaged."

"Well, yeah, I am seeing someone."

"Anyone I might know?"

"Maybe. He's a Marine."

"Oh, probably not then." He flipped his hair with his hand. "Marines don't care for me a lot."

"I wonder why?" She paused for a moment. "It's a very new relationship, just a day or two. Who knows how things will go, though."

"You can never tell, Allie. I'm not trying to move in on anyone's territory here."

She smiled again. "So you're not making a play for me?"

"I never said that."

"But you did say yesterday you weren't trying to get in my pants."

"No, I didn't. I said that you're pretty, and I wasn't saying that to get in your pants. I never said I wasn't trying to get in your pants."

She blinked at him. "My mistake."

"That's OK." He looked at her plate. "Are you going to eat that pickle?"

"No, I guess not. Help yourself."

"Thanks." Harry snagged the pickle spear from her plate and licked it slowly. Allie knew her lips parted as she watched his tongue swirl around the pickle. She looked down at her plate quickly, hoping he didn't catch her stare. "I love dill pickles."

"That's an interesting way you have of eating them." Allie couldn't decide if she needed to be here or not. It felt wrong, but she didn't want to leave.

"You think so?" He smiled at her over the pickle. "Are you going out with your new flame tonight?"

She knew he was flirting with her, and she liked it. She also saw something familiar from her relations with Tanya and Claire. Harry never said anything he didn't mean to say. "I don't know yet. Are you asking me out?"

"Like I said, I'm not trying to move in on anyone's territory."

"Was that a yes or a no? I know you answered me, but I can't pull the answer out of that response." Despite her uncertainty, she wanted him to say yes.

"It was neither. You could say it was a maybe."

"There you go again, making me laugh! Then I suppose my answer will have to be maybe."

"I can accept that." He finished the pickle and took a handful of paper scraps from his pocket. After rummaging through them for a moment, he finally dropped one on the table and wrote with his pen. "Here you go." He handed the paper to her.

"Your intercom number?"

"Yeah. Call me when you decide what you're going to do."

She was way off balance. She studied the wadded scrap of paper with his intercom number written on it, along with a lot of other numbers and doodles, and knew she should give it back to him. Instead, she folded it and tucked it into her briefcase. "OK, but what if I decide not to go out with you?"

"That would be your loss as well as mine, Allie. I think we'd be good together."

"You're nothing if not direct." His calm, matter-of-fact manner, and his confidence were exciting. She knew she shouldn't, not with Damon in her life, but she couldn't help herself. The feelings nagged at her. The longhaired man across the table fascinated her.

"And entertaining," he said.

"Right. Do you have another puzzle to solve today?"

"Not today. I get to go back and stare at the cubicle walls."

"No more walks around the lake?"

"Sadly, no. If I could, I'd ask you to go along and chase rabbits with me again."

Allie really wasn't sure why, but she called Q on her implant. She was treading on dangerous ground, but she couldn't resist the pull. "There, now you're off duty for the afternoon. Orders of Admiral Q." She smiled. "Being a princess has certain perks."

"I see that. Shall we go, then?"

"Absolutely."

As they walked around the lake on the OD, Harry didn't chase the wildlife. "Tell me, why did you arrange for this little outing?"

"I'm not really sure, Harry." Allie wasn't sure at all, other than she knew Harry made her laugh and made her feel good. She could forget about the world around her while he talked. "I guess I like to be around you."

"That's a good thing. By the way, what time does your boyfriend get off? Duty, that is."

She laughed despite herself. "About 1630 or so. Why?"

He shrugged. "I just wondered how much time I have to convince you that you have the wrong guy."

"Really? You don't act like you're trying to romance me, Harry."

"I'm not. Instead of all the fake romance and other things that a guy will do to get in a woman's pants, I'm trying to show you the real me, not some fictitious fantasy of the perfect man, or at least the perfect man most women imagine. I'm not perfect. You should know that right up front."

"That sounds a little pessimistic."

"Maybe. I'll tell you right now that I'd love to sleep with you. I won't do that by lying to you about what and who I am, though."

Allie stared at him for a moment, his openness again slapping her in the face in a very pleasant way. "An honest man! What will they think of next?" She was trying to be funny, but she doubted it came off that well. She shouldn't be pursuing this line of conversation, and she knew full well why. "Harry, what exactly are you doing?"

"You mean with you? I'm not really sure. Yeah, I'd like to get in your pants. What man who likes women wouldn't? I guess I'm mostly just wanting to get to know you and you to know me without all the fluff and crap getting in the way."

"Women like a little romance."

"Of course you do. You may not know it, but men like a little romance, too. But would you like lies and fake romance, or would you prefer the truth that will lead to real romance?"

"Well, when you put it like that..."

"Exactly." He stared at her face for a moment. "Let me guess at a few things. You said you've been in this new relationship just a day or two. He's been all cuddly and romantic, and you slept with him last night."

She wondered if Harry was crazy and psychic. "That's really none of your business."

"No, it's not, but that's what happened. Allie, what do you really know about him? The first thing you did yesterday was pull my file from the computers to learn about me. Have you looked at his file? I'll bet money you haven't. And I know why. Because he's romantic and swept you off your feet."

She couldn't deny the facts he pulled up. That didn't mean she had to like them. "Are you going somewhere with this?" She should walk away. Now.

"Yeah, I am. You should go out with me. You already know the real me. I won't tell you I love you just to fuck you, and I won't deny that I'd like to fuck you. If we hit it off and something does grow, then we're ahead in the game. If not, what have we lost?"

Allie's laugh sounded uncomfortable, even to her. "We'll see."

"Finally! We're getting someplace! You've got my number. You can call me when you've thought about things a little more." He smiled. "In the meantime, we've got rabbits to chase. Come on!" He pulled her, laughing, into the woods where they chased the wildlife until 1600 when Allie went home.

* * * *

Allie didn't hear the doorbell until its second ring. She stood from her ruminations on the sofa and opened the door. Damon stood there smiling.

She moved aside as he entered.

"What's wrong?" he asked.

"Oh, I was just thinking about a lot of things."

He studied her for a few moments. "I guess I should get to what I need to tell you. We're having some night operations on the OD this evening. I probably won't be free until after midnight. I'm sorry."

She shook herself out of her reverie. "That's all right." Despite Damon standing in front of her, she kept thinking about Harry.

"I could come by after that."

She thought for a moment. "No, that might not be good tonight."

"Oh. Yeah, I, um, guess that was a little uncomfortable with your mothers this morning."

"Yeah, it was."

"OK, Allie. Can I call you in the morning?"

She smiled at him. "I'd like that, yeah."

After Damon had left, Allie sat cursing herself. She didn't know why, but the things Harry had said bothered her. She liked Damon and was intensely attracted to him. She was sure he felt the same way. Maybe not love, yet, but the feeling could grow as time passed. She pulled the scrap of paper from her briefcase and planned to call Harry to scream at him. She dialed half of the number four times, hanging up and starting over. She threw the paper on the coffee table and slumped back in the chair.

How dare he! Making her doubt herself and even her own feelings! Allie knew Harry said exactly what he meant to say and planned to make this happen in her head. The arrogant son of a bitch made this happen! She grabbed the paper and dialed all but the last number before she hung up again. On the other hand, maybe he did her a favor. If Damon was playing a game just to bed her, maybe Harry was right, and she had picked the wrong man. Allie wasn't sure if she needed to slap Harry senseless or kiss him. Maybe she needed to just forget about him.

She picked up the paper and dialed all the numbers this time.

"Hello?"

Her heart raced. "Harry, this is Allie."

"Hi, there. What's up?"

"It turns out that I'm free tonight. I thought we could have a couple of drinks."

"Sounds good to me. Anywhere in particular?"

"Yeah, let's meet at the Dog and Pony Show in about thirty minutes."

"Allie, you know that's a gay bar, right?"

"Yeah. That cuts down on the number of guys hitting on me."

"All right, Princess. That's less competition for me, then. See you in thirty minutes. Bye." He hung up without waiting for an answer.

* * * *

Harry waited outside the door to the bar.

"Why are you standing out here?"

"I wanted to make sure I didn't miss you. What happened that you're free tonight?"

"Let's get a seat and we'll talk." He held the door for her, and they went to a table. After their drinks came, Allie took a large swallow of her vodka. She needed to nerve herself for being this close to him. "To make a long story short, Damon had duty tonight at the last minute."

"I hope I didn't cause any problems with the things I said. Sometimes my mouth gets way ahead of my brain."

"I seriously doubt that. I will tell you that I've been thinking a lot about what you said."

"Is that good or bad?"

"I'm not sure myself. Let me ask you a question. Why shouldn't I think that the things you said aren't just another more original way to get into my pants?"

"Maybe you should think that way, because I can't see any reason for you not to." He smiled over his drink. "Other than I'm telling you that it's not."

"That's a lot of consolation."

* * * *

Admiral Q was getting ready to leave the bridge for the evening when the science officer got his attention.

"Sir, I'm seeing a strange wave-like pattern in the subspace fields." Q looked over the officer's shoulder. "See, Sir? It looks a little like the bow wave of a cloaked ship, but there's none of the other spatial distortions."

Q watched the rhythmic waves on the scanners for a few moments. "Run a neutrino emissions scan, please."

"Yes, Sir." The science officer played his controls. The neutrinos were off the scale.

Q spun from the Science station. "Battle stations! Collision alert!" He glanced back at the displays for a moment. "Clear and seal the OD!" Alarms rang through the ship. "Helm, hard to port, maximum impulse power!"

Boone swung hard to port as her huge drives generated more than seventy thousand Gs. Airtight doors throughout the ship closed as medical and damage control teams moved to their ready stations. All weapons systems were armed, but there was no target for them to fire on. Just when enough time had elapsed that it seemed things would be all right, the aft overhead screens flashed as something huge, slow moving, and invisible slammed into the defensive shields and Harbison Field.

The Harbison Field worked by absorbing and storing energy, then radiating it away in another direction. If too much energy came into the Field too fast, or if there was no place to radiate the energy, the stored power would be released inwards toward the ship. As the Field heated up through the visible spectrum from only red hot, through the yellows, to the green, on into blue, and finally to white, things got worse.

Completely overwhelmed by the object, the deflector shields collapsed with no detectable change to the impact of the invisible attacker. The Field went from its normal black, the same temperature as the surrounding space, to white in microseconds. The object slammed through and impacted the Observation Deck dome, crushing it to dust.

* * * *

Allie stared at Harry, watching him casually playing with his hair, when the battle stations alarm screamed. *Boone* shook like a dog drying itself, and a deafening explosion came from somewhere forward. The artificial gravity wavered for a few moments. Allie was thrown from her chair. Harry tried to catch her but he fell himself. He grabbed her and pinned her to the floor, covering her with his body, arms and legs spread wide to prevent them from rolling. Allie tried to link in with her implant to see what was happening, but the computer didn't respond.

When the shaking stopped, Harry rolled from atop her. "Are you all right?"

"Yeah, what happened?"

"I don't know. Try to get to your family's Safe Room. I've got to go." Harry hesitated a moment. He kissed her lips gently, not more than a peck, and despite the dire situation they were in, she tingled in response to the casual touch. "Be careful," he said and then ran from the pandemonium of the club.

* * * *

The Bridge Talker held an interesting position. Only used when massive damage from battle or accidents affected the ship, the Bridge Talker gave no orders and took no initiative, only repeating words given to him by others. He had no command and no authority, but the words he parroted controlled the ship.

"Preliminary damage report, Sir. There's a full breach of the OD dome and full decompression in that area. Airtight doors are holding, but door twenty-six is leaking." The Talker listened to his headset. "Casualties show 143 dead, 271 injured, and 482 missing."

"Thank you." Q glanced around the bridge as teams worked to get Boone brought back to life. Most systems were only marginal and several, including the drives, had gone fully offline. His intercom buzzed. "Bridge, Q."

"Admiral, Ike Payne here. I have the entire royal family accounted for and secured except Admiral Reeves. She's in medical with the injured."

"Well done, Sergeant. Any injuries?"

"Nothing serious, just some bumps and bruises. Empress Marilyn is asking about the status of the zoo."

"Unknown, Sergeant. We have no operative sensors or personnel in that area yet."

"Understood. My people are securing the corridors and beginning search and rescue ops to support medical."

"Very well. Thank you, Sergeant." He cleared the intercom.

The Bridge Talker frowned. "Sir, we're getting reports of a Marine battalion on the OD for a training exercise."

"A full battalion?"

"Yes, Sir."

Q frowned. A full battalion of 256 people in the impact area had little chance of survival. "Very well." He clicked the intercom. "Sergeant Payne, what would be the chances of Marine in combat gear surviving on the OD?"

She hesitated. "Not great, Sir. If they made it to cover from the heat and fireball, their armor and oxygen would keep them alive for about two hours."

"Thank you." He clicked off and turned to the Bridge Talker. "I want rescue teams on the OD in twenty minutes looking for those Marines." He walked to the science station. "Can we scan the OD for life signs yet?"

"No, Sir. We may have some sensors operating in thirty minutes but certainly no sooner."

Q frowned. "Launch a shuttlecraft to do sensor surveys."

"Aye, aye, Sir."

* * * *

"Ike, what was that about the OD?"

"We think there may have been a battalion of Marines in there doing an exercise, Allie. The OD is fully decompressed."

Allie's knees unhinged. Her eyes stung and her vision blurred. Ike grabbed her arm and helped her to a chair. "You OK?"

"There are Marines in there. Damon Hyde said he took his team there."

"I know him." Ike thought for a moment. "I don't know what's going on, but it doesn't look good for anyone to have survived there."

"Yeah." Allie took a deep breath. She wiped her eyes then pointed at Ike's handheld data terminal. "What about Intelligence?"

"No damage there. The staff is helping where needed."

"Thanks, Ike." Allie fought the temptation to chew her nails.

* * * *

Seventy-two minutes had passed since the impact. Q had called a staff meeting in the Ready Room. "Damage reports."

The Chief Engineer was on the intercom. "We have full decompression on the Observation Deck, but all airtight doors are secure and holding. The zoo appears to have sealed. We can see movement inside, so we assume that's OK. We're at least twelve hours from having the drives online, but everything else is at least operational."

"Thank you. Casualties?"

Claire looked up from her notes. "We have 206 confirmed dead, 348 injured, and 513 missing. That's counting the 187 Marines we're still looking for. Probably half of the injured won't make it."

Q sighed. "Thank you, Doctor. Science and Weapons, what's your best guess on what happened?"

"It looks like it was a slow moving cloaked asteroid, Sir. The diameter was about two kilometers, and the speed was around ten kilometers per second. We think we have a way to detect them in the future worked out, Sir."

"Very well. Weapons, can we shoot these things between now and when the drives are online?"

"Yes, Sir. Weapons are in good shape other than the forward port torpedo tube is bent. We should have that operational in two hours or less."

"Very good. Does anyone know the status of the search parties?"

Claire spoke up again. "They're moving as fast as they can, but there's so much debris, they have to go slowly. Sensors aren't much use, either, because of the debris, and there's a lot of leaking energy messing things up as well." She glanced at her watch. "I figure any survivors have about forty-five minutes of oxygen left."

"All right. Let's try to move faster without killing anyone else. Dismissed."

* * * *

When the computers came back online, Allie linked in and checked the casualty lists. She found Damon's name listed as missing. Harry's name wasn't on any list.

Janelle watched as Allie used the implant. "Any word?"

"No, Mom, nothing."

Before the computers were online, Allie had asked Ike about Damon and Harry several times, and Janelle had overheard. "Allie, who's this Harry person you asked about? Another friend?"

"Yeah. He works in Intelligence."

Janelle waited, but Allie didn't say any more.

* * * *

Everyone now called it a recovery operation, and Harry had gone to the OD to assist. It had been ninety-five minutes since the impact, and Harry crawled through the remains of the park. He thought he was somewhere around where the lake once was, but he wasn't sure because none of the familiar landmarks remained. The operations on the OD had recovered only bodies so far. Harry had pulled eleven out himself. He wondered what a cryptologist was doing in this situation.

He squeezed under some debris from the dome, awash in sweat despite the environmental controls of his suit, when the life sensor chirped. Harry studied the readout for a moment and then tapped the communicator with his tongue. "This is unit eighty-three. I have possible life signs nineteen meters from my present position, bearing zero-six-niner."

"Copy, unit eighty-three, nineteen meters on bearing zero-six-niner."

Harry began crawling in that direction.

The going was slow. Harry had to use his handheld laser to cut through debris as he went. He wondered casually about the device running out of power. He wondered more than casually about the laser overheating and exploding in his hand. As he cut through a girder that blocked his way, the steel suddenly twisted as the metal melted, slamming against his helmet and knocking him backwards in the tiny crawl space. As the section of structural material above Harry's head sagged under the load, it pressed down, pinning Harry to the deck. His oxygen tanks stopped it from crushing him.

The grinding weight of the debris above him slowly crushed not only him but his tanks as well. The creaking of the metal as his tanks flattened was lost to the hard vacuum of the open OD, but Harry knew, even if he couldn't hear it, that it was happening. The only question was if the tanks would rupture before the ever-increasing pressure blew out the regulator and imploded him under several metric tonnes of air pressure.

"Control, this is unit eighty-three. Do you copy?" There was no reply. Harry tongued the controls. There wasn't even static on the receiver. The beam hitting his helmet had smashed the communicator.

He had never considered himself to be brave, but Harry didn't feel afraid. He felt more resigned than anything else. His left arm was pinned beneath his body, but his right remained free. He pulled the flashlight from his belt and looked around him. About three meters ahead of him was the door to one of the service areas for the lake, closed and intact. He wondered if some of the Marines might have made it inside, and that was what the sensors had seen. He wondered if it made any difference.

He shut off the light and lay in the darkness, resigned to the fact that his name would soon be on the list of the dead. As his mind began to do free association, as it always did, he thought about Allie. He wasn't sure if she made it to safety, but he suspected she had. He wondered if one of the bodies he'd pulled out might have been her Marine. Damon was his name, she'd told him. Harry let a small smile come to his face as he thought that Damon might be in the service area just ahead of him.

As his mind simply ran freely, Harry realized that he wasn't ready to die, at least not without a fight. While Allie thought she belonged to this Damon guy, Harry knew she didn't. Allie didn't know it yet, but she belonged to him. He'd finally encountered a woman not only attractive and funny, but who was his intellectual equal. Not being one to be modest, Harry knew that was a very rare combination.

He stretched out his right arm for the laser, but it was just beyond his grasp. He stretched, straining his body. He could feel a heavy weight on his ribs, squeezing the air from his lungs, but he grimaced with the pain and reached farther. His fingertips just touched the laser. Harry took a deep breath and lunged as much as he could, his hand gripping at the same time, and the laser scooted towards him a little, then his fingers gripped it.

He turned the laser to full power. It would give him, at best, a seven second burst at that setting. Pointing the laser upward at the debris piled on top of him, Harry pulled the trigger. The searing red beam shot up into the junk, and white-hot molten bits of metal and plastic rained down around him as the laser ate its way through the target.

The weight on his chest suddenly released as the debris over his head shifted, and he crawled like a mad spider for the door. He studied the outside of the door for a moment and wondered how to get anyone inside out when he had no communicator and no oxygen. Harry saw some of the lighter debris on the deck beginning to move, being blown by a rush of air. Engineering had managed to get the OD under pressure. He grabbed the door and pulled, feeling the strain cause a screaming pain in his left ribs. He took a deep breath and heaved with all his strength. The door opened halfway.

A big blond man, nearly a head taller than Harry, fell through the open door into his arms. Dried blood on the man's face left trails from his nose, ears, and the corners of his eyes, the sure signs of decompression. Harry felt the man's neck and found a pulse, weak and rapid, but it was there. The man's eyes flickered open, and they were the bright red of arterial blood.

"Get my people."

Harry glanced into the service area and saw at least a hundred Marines. Most moved, but they were clearly dazed and lacking direction. When he looked back, the Marine was unconscious again.

Harry laid the big man on the deck and looked at his chest. The name stripe on his battle armor read *HYDE, D.*

Harry pulled his laser out and began to flash the beam on low power. As he flicked the laser on and off trying to attract attention, he reached for his visor, remembering he was under pressure again. The visor was about halfway open when the regulator failed, flooding his suit with six tonnes of air pressure.

The last thing Harry saw was the lower edge of the helmet shooting by his eyes as the pressure blew it from his suit. The rest was lost to darkness.

Chapter 4

Recovery

Boone remained at battle stations to support emergency operations, and Allie remained stuck in the Safe Room. Ike listened intently to her communicator for a few minutes before coming to sit next to Allie. "I have some news."

Allie inhaled deeply. "OK."

"Douglas found a bunch of Marines in the wreckage on the OD and managed to get them out." Ike smiled a little. "One of them is Lieutenant Hyde. I don't have any details other than Douglas and Hyde are both alive and in sickbay now."

A wave of relief swept over Allie. The wave didn't have either man's name written on it, though. It had both names. "How are they?"

"I don't know. The rescue teams told me that the Marines all have decompression injuries and that something went wrong with Douglas' suit and he went over-pressure." Ike listened to her communicator for a moment. "Anyway, they're both listed as injured right now."

Allie nodded. "When can I get out of here?"

"We're still at battle stations."

"That's not what I asked you."

Ike sighed. "Damn it. You're going to get me busted one of these days." A slow smile came to her face. "If I turned my back and you weren't here after, I don't have anyone to send after you right now."

"You're the best, Ike."

* * * *

Harry woke slowly. He opened his eyes. At least he made the movement to open his eyes, but he couldn't see anything other than darkness. His left arm wouldn't move. When he tried, something pulled across his chest. He reached up with his right arm for his face.

"Just relax. You're in sickbay, and you're fine."

"Allie?" His voice sounded rough and dry, even to him.

"Yeah, it's me."

"Are you all right?"

"Yes, I'm fine. Are you having any pain? I can call the nurse over."

"No, I'm OK. Why can't I see?"

"You had some pressure damage to your eyes and they're bandaged. Claire said your eyes would heal in a day or two."

"That's good." Harry moved his hand for his head again. "Who's Claire?"

Allie took his hand. "Just relax. Claire, Admiral Reeves. She's my sister."

"Nothing like a little nepotism, I guess."

He heard Allie's laugh, and it sounded wonderful, like music. "There you go making me laugh again."

He heard her shift about before she said softly, "That room you found had 134 people inside, and a lot of them, including Damon Hyde, would have died if not for you."

Harry nodded. "He didn't look good when I found him. How is he?"

"He's got some decompression damage, but it looks like he'll make it."

He heard her pause for a moment and wished he could see her face. "Looks like you're a bit of a hero now."

"Not me. I didn't do anything other than damned near getting myself killed."

Another short moment of silence followed. "Maybe."

"When can I get out of here?"

"You're hurt."

"Just get me a cane and a bottle of rum. I'll be fine."

He heard another voice in the mix now. "I see our hero is awake."

"Is that Claire? Um, Admiral Reeves, that is."

"That's me. If my kid sister hasn't told you, you're going to be fine in a few days. The bandages need to stay on your eyes until tomorrow, and the rest will hurt a little, but that's it."

"So, when can I get out of here?"

"That depends. Do you live alone or with someone?"

"Just me and my shadow."

Claire laughed. "In that case, you'll need to stay here until the eye patches come off tomorrow. Blind and alone won't work."

"I could buy a cat."

"You're right, sis, he is funny. Sorry, but that won't do it."

Allie spoke up. "How's Damon?"

"He's still in a drug-induced coma, but he's stable. Why?"

"I can take care of Harry and have him back here tomorrow."

"You don't have to do that, Allie." She still held his hand, and Harry squeezed hers a little. "I can stay here."

"Well, sis, that's fine medically, so you two can work it out. Just let me know." He felt Claire pat his left hand. "I'll see you a little later, Harry."

* * * *

Harry tried to argue, but Allie would have none of it, and she soon pushed him along in a wheelchair. "You realize I'm at your mercy since I can't see."

"Yep, so just sit back and enjoy the ride."

As she pushed the chair through the door, Allie saw Harry sniff the air. "This is your cabin, isn't it?"

"Yeah. Does it stink?"

"No, it smells like you."

She couldn't help a little shiver. "I'll take that as a compliment. Do you need to lie down?"

"No, but this contraption is really uncomfortable."

"All right." She pushed the wheelchair to the sofa. "Let me help you." Allie got him sitting down. "Need any pillows or maybe a blanket?"

"No, I'm fine other than not knowing where I am."

"That's fair." She pushed the wheelchair aside and sat down next to him. Being close to him felt heady. She shouldn't be feeling this way. She was so grateful he was alive. "You're in my suite sitting on my sofa."

"That sounds pretty possessive to me, Allie."

"Maybe it is." Her laugh came so easily. So did the guilt over the fact that Damon lay in sickbay while she flirted with Harry.

"What time is it, anyway?"

She checked her watch. "It's 0345."

"No wonder I'm tired."

"Let me take you to bed. Claire gave me some sleeping pills for you to take."

He smiled. "Damn it."

"What?"

"You want to take me to bed and I'm blind, have my ribs taped up, one arm is useless, and I hurt all over. On top of that, you want to drug me!"

A chill shot through her body. "You're being silly."

"I guess I am. I can sleep here on the sofa."

"Bullshit."

"What?"

"Bullshit. You'll sleep in the bed."

"It's *your* sofa but *the* bed?"

"Sounds that way, doesn't it?"

"Allie, all kidding aside, you sleep in your bed and I'll sleep right here."

"Nope. You'll sleep in the bed and I'll sleep in the chair by the bed if you need anything."

"Just to cut through to the point, I have no chance of winning this argument, do I?"

"Not a one. Come on, let's get you to bed."

She helped him to the wheelchair. "I guess we should have just done this when we came in."

"No problem. Um, Harry, do you need the bathroom?"

"Not just now, but we could make a date of it."

"Silly." Allie helped him lie down and gave him a sleeping pill. "Comfortable?"

"Yeah, a lot more than you will be in a chair."

"Maybe." Allie watched him for a moment, his head moving slowly, trying to locate her voice. She had the urge to hug him again, but she managed to fight it off. She also had the urge to join him in the bed. "Thanks Harry."

"For what?"

"First, for protecting me at the bar. Second, for helping all those people on the OD. You could have died." She sat down on the bed beside him.

"I guess you're welcome, but it really wasn't anything. Trying to keep things from falling on you seemed like the right thing to do. Helping on the OD is just my job."

The casual way that he dismissed his actions attracted her even more. He wasn't being modest or coy, but honestly didn't see it as an issue. "Maybe, but thanks anyway." Allie leaned and kissed his lips softly, far less passionately than she would have liked. "Now, try to sleep."

* * * *

Harry woke to the smell of something wonderful. The wonderful smell was something other than Allie, too, even though her delicious scent pervaded the room and clung to the bedclothes.

He needed the bathroom and managed to get himself sitting on the side of the bed. Harry thought he could make it on his own until he realized he had no idea how to get to the bathroom. He sighed. "Allie!"

He heard her run to the bedroom. "Are you OK?"

"Um, yeah, I just need the bathroom and I have no idea where it is."

"Ah! No problem. Let me get your chair."

"I can walk, I think."

"OK." She helped him walk to the bathroom.

"I think I can handle it from here."

"I'm not modest."

"Maybe I am."

She didn't answer for a moment. Harry wondered what she was thinking. "All right, but I'll be right out here."

"You won't peek?"

"No, I won't peek." He heard the door close.

Afterward, Allie helped him to the dining room. They had a small argument about how he would eat. It ended when Allie insisted on feeding him. She said it would speed things up.

"What time is it?" he sighed.

"It's 1230."

"When do I get these bandages off my eyes?"

"Like Claire said, tomorrow."

"Oh. She meant tomorrow as in tomorrow and not tomorrow as in after a while."

"Exactly."

"Have you heard anything about what's-his-name?"

"Damon. Yeah, I talked to Claire. He's holding his own."

"That's good." He thought for a moment and decided to broach the subject. "I'm really glad for that. I still think you've picked the wrong guy, but I can tell you like him."

She hesitated, and he wished again that he could see her face. "I won't deny that I like him," she spoke carefully, "but I haven't picked anyone yet." She shoved his mouth full of hash browns.

Harry had to talk around the potatoes to keep her from having enough time to get her balance again. He could feel himself slipping into attack mode as he tried to sway her from Damon to himself. "That's good, too." He swallowed. "That means I still have a chance to change your mind."

"There's nothing to change. I haven't picked anyone. Yeah, I like Damon, and I'm worried about him because he's hurt. I like you, and I'm worried about you, too."

"Besides, you're here taking care of me."

"Right." She crammed eggs in his mouth this time. "Just relax and focus on getting well."

"My eyes are covered. I can't focus on anything."

* * * *

While Harry tried to talk Claire into removing bandages from his eyes, Allie went to see Damon.

The pulmonologist checked Damon's lungs. He'd suffered damage from decompression when the dome shattered. "When he's stronger, we'll replace his left lung. I'm not sure about the right yet, Princess."

"But he'll make it, right?"

"I think so, yes. All things considered, he's doing fairly well."

A knot of tension between her shoulders relaxed a little. He would be all right with time. As she watched him sleeping in his drug-induced coma, Allie wondered how she would deal with her feelings. She didn't think she loved Damon, not yet anyway, but she had a strong attraction to him. At least as strong as what she had for Harry. She decided that, for now, she needed to focus on getting Damon back on his feet. A pang of guilt hit her as she thought about Harry staying with her while she took care of him. She wondered what Damon's reaction to that would be. Allie sat at Damon's bedside for thirty minutes before going out to where Harry sat in the waiting room.

"I see you lost that argument." He looked a little pitiful with his eyes bandaged, his head swaying around like in a breeze. She wanted to hug him, and only part of the desire centered on being attracted to him. She wanted to protect and care for him.

"Yeah, I did." Gauze still covered his eyes. "She's pretty tough."

"Just like all the girls in my family."

"Now there's good news."

"What do you mean?"

"That gives me something to look forward to for the next few hundred years."

Allie smiled a little thinking about spending a lifetime with Harry. The suddenness of the thought shocked her, and she shut the line down quickly. "You're getting the cart a little ahead of the horse, aren't you?"

"No, I don't think so."

Allie pushed the wheelchair into the corridor as she headed for her suite. "Sometimes you scare me, Harry."

"I feel like people are staring at me."

"How can you tell?"

"I don't know. Are they?"

"No, not really anymore than they would anyone being pushed down the corridor in a wheelchair."

When they reached her suite, Allie helped him to the sofa. "Just remember, you're completely at my mercy right now." Her heart quickened as she thought of the handcuffs on the bed frame.

"I could think of worse things. By the way, you said that I scare you sometimes. Why?"

"You remind of my mom. You seem to know what I'm going to say before I do sometimes." Allie frowned a little. "And you also know exactly what to say to press my buttons." He could also press her buttons in the right order.

"I won't apologize for either of those things."

"No, I'm not expecting or asking for that. It's just a little strange sometimes." Her smile returned. "You seem a little envious of Damon."

"Not me. That's one of the deadly sins, you know."

"Deadly sins?"

"Yeah. I guess you didn't go to Sunday school too much. The seven deadly sins are sins that earn you eternal damnation unless you confess. They were usually said to be pride, envy, gluttony, lust, anger, greed, and sloth."

"Sloth? As in tree sloth?"

Harry laughed. "No, sloth as in being lazy."

"Oh." Allie smiled. "A few of those sound like fun."

"You bet they are, and that's why the church didn't want people doing them. Most priests today more or less ignore the concept."

"Which one is your favorite?"

"I'm not sure I have a favorite. I think I'm guilty of all but two of them."

She wondered if his list included lust. She definitely felt lust right now. "Five out of seven ain't bad."

"True. Do I need to save you a seat by the fire?"

"Probably. I think I'm six out of seven."

"Who are you envious of?"

"How do you know envy is the extra one I have that you don't?"

"How do you know I don't have envy on my list?"

"I can't really see you as being envious of anyone, Harry."

"You're right. Envy isn't on my list."

"I envy a few people, I guess. You, mom, and Claire are three of them. You're all so smart."

"No more than you. Maybe we know certain things in our specialty that you don't know, but you know things that we don't know. Everyone has something to learn from everyone else."

His compliments again made her shiver. Maybe she had picked the wrong man. "Maybe we do. What do I know that you can learn from me?"

"How to show people that you care about them would be the big one on my list."

"Maybe I don't understand."

He seemed to think for a minute. Allie wished she could see his eyes. The way they twinkled when he thought stirred her in ways that made her want him. "I guess I sometimes have a problem showing people how much I care about them. I'm not sure if I lack the words or just how to express that emotion." He frowned a little. "Maybe it's emotion in general I have problems with."

"A preposition is a terrible thing to end a sentence with."

He laughed. "OK. Maybe it's emotion in general I have problems with, Allie."

"That's better. I think you do fine. You've made it very clear that you care about me."

"I've been working at that one, though."

Allie considered him for a moment, sitting on the sofa, his eyes bandaged. Taped to his chest, his left arm supported both the broken ribs and the dislocated shoulder. Scrapes from the friction of the weight that had settled on him and bruises covered a good part of the left side of his torso. The urge to hold him to her breasts nearly overwhelmed her. It would be wrong to cheat on Damon. "Can I ask you a question and get a straight answer?"

"I always give you straight answers."

"OK, how about one that's simple enough for me to understand and not wrapped in a puzzle?"

"All right."

"You know I'm seeing Damon, so why are you chasing me?"

"Let me see if I can boil this down and, as you say, extract it from the puzzle." Harry sat silently for more than a minute. "Allie, I can't really explain why, because I don't know, but you're very attractive to me, and I'm not talking about physically. Yeah, you're very pretty, but it's something else, something more. I know you're seeing Damon, but I think you can do much better."

The simple words that he found her attractive caused Allie to tremble with excitement. She knew the feelings she had didn't belong in her heart and the thoughts definitely didn't belong in her mind, but she couldn't stop them. "In a word, you, right?"

"Yeah, that's it in a nutshell."

"Why would you make a better choice?" This was like encouraging a used spaceship salesman to make his pitch.

"I can't answer that because I don't know Damon. I just know I'm the best for you, and that's what you deserve."

Allie laughed a little. "Never had a problem with your self image, have you?" His confidence topped the list of his good features.

"Not a bit, no." His lips curled into a grin. "Don't you want the best?"

"Of course I do, but isn't that my call?" Now she tried to talk herself out of buying the spacecraft.

"Sure, but you need to have all the facts to make that call."

"So you're just giving me facts, then?"

"That's right. After all, have I even come close to trying to seduce you?"

Allie tensed. In many ways, she wished he would try to seduce her. She knew he wouldn't have to try very hard. In other ways, she was glad he didn't try. She held on to her commitment to Damon by only the thinnest of threads. "Well, no."

"And have I even told you a half-truth, let alone a lie?"

"Not that I know of."

"I'd give my left...Um, my eyeteeth to sleep with you, Allie, but I won't lie to you or pretend any feelings to do that."

"Are you saying Damon lied or pretended his feelings?"

"I don't know him, so how can I make that judgment? All I'm saying is men do that, often enough it makes me almost ashamed that I'm a man." Harry's head leaned to one side. "I'll bet that he's acted all macho with you, too, and then said he did that to cover the fact he's afraid of you."

"Are you trying to break us up?"

"I just want you to consider all the options."

"I told you before, women like romance."

"I know, but we're not talking about romance right now. We're talking about being real."

"What if it is real, Harry?"

"Do you want my honest opinion, even though I don't know Damon?"

"I'd like to hear that."

"I think he is being real with you. I think he cares a lot for you. Maybe he's a little afraid of you because he does care about you. I also think his own psyche is making him do the macho things because he feels that fear and doesn't like the way it makes him feel. He's a Marine and he's supposed to be all tough and hard, but he can't make that work when he's with you."

Allie shook her head. "I don't know now if you're saying he's trying to get laid or he's falling in love."

"Both, I'd think." Harry shrugged his shoulders as much as the bandages would allow. "I think he started off wanting to get laid, then he fell for you."

"What about you, Harry?"

"Oh, I fell for you first." He smiled. "Now I want to get laid."

Allie had to fight not to shake so much that he would feel it through the sofa. Her heart, as much as it might be wrong, tried to leap from her chest. "That's one thing I like about you. You're direct, at least when you want to be direct." Allie watched him for a second. "Are you having any pain or anything?"

"No, I feel pretty good, actually."

"That's good." Allie paused a moment. Her mind had moved down a road it shouldn't travel. Allie swore at herself for even considering taking him to bed. "Harry, why aren't you married? You strike me as the marrying kind."

He laughed. "Maybe I am. Other than to say that I haven't found the right girl, I'm not sure I have an answer to that question."

"I can accept that."

"What about you?"

"Really, the same answer applies."

"All right. Tell me about what's it like to be a princess."

"In some ways, it's good, but in others it can be a pain in the ass." She considered for a moment. "A lot of men are scared of my father and won't even look at me."

"That's their loss and my gain, then."

"Maybe."

"Yeah." He fell silent for a time. "I wish I could see."

"Hush for now. You will soon enough."

* * * *

When Allie reached sickbay to see Damon, she bumped into her sister in the hallway. "Hi, Claire. How's Damon doing today?"

"He's good." Claire smiled. "He's awake."

The knot in her shoulders relaxed a little more. With Harry back on duty and now Damon awake, she could relax a little. The knot didn't fade completely, though. The conflict in her between the two men still troubled her deeply. "That's great!"

"Yeah, it is. His new lung is doing well. The other damage from the decompression is healing, too. He should be out of here in a few days." Claire smiled at her. "Go on and see him. He's been asking about you."

Allie went to his room and peeked in. He seemed to be sleeping, but when she pushed the door open to enter, his eyes opened.

He smiled. "Hi. Are you OK?"

Claire telling her that he was awake was one thing. Seeing him awake made it real. "I'm fine." She leaned to kiss his forehead. His lips looked dry and chapped, almost painful. "How are you feeling?"

"A little tired, mostly." He scratched at his chest. "This incision itches, too." He stared at her.

She twisted her lips into a pout. "My poor baby." She kissed her fingers and pressed them to his lips.

He chuckled softly. "I can't remember much about what happened."

"I think that's normal." She took his hand. "What *do* you remember?"

"We were on the OD doing the exercise when the collision alarm went off." He shivered a little. "I saw the seal lights on the doors cycle, so we moved for the service areas. The next thing I knew, something hit us."

"Just a second." Allie lowered the side rail on the bed and sat on the edge next to him. When she put her arms around him, the tingles ran through her again. He clearly wasn't in any condition for more than a hug, but she wanted more. "Anything else?"

"Just that someone opened the door a couple of hours later. Then I woke up here." He paused for a moment. "The doctor said that Harrison Douglas found me. Is that the Harry you know?"

"Yeah, it is." Allie tried to avoid looking at his eyes. She worried he would see her feelings there.

Damon sighed. "I see."

She leaned back and moved to kiss him. Despite the chapped lips, they kissed for a long time. Allie held her passions in check, though. She feared she would hurt him. His hands, however, moved over her body, giving her the familiar chills his touch brought to her. She loved the feel of his touch. She rejoiced that he wasn't dead. And she hated herself for her feelings for Harry.

* * * *

Allie played solitaire again. Damon had a treatment in the hyperbaric chamber that would last until morning. Harry had gone back to work, no doubt playing with another puzzle, and wouldn't be off duty until 1630. Her mind wandered as she lost money to the cheating machine. The reunion with Damon had been intense. It hadn't been as intense as she thought it might have been had she not had seeds of doubt in her mind. Harry hadn't actually planted the seeds so much as he had fertilized them.

More than a week had gone by since the attack on *Boone* and repairs were well underway. Admiral Q had pulled *Boone* back from the main battle areas since much of the work required putting men on the hull. *Boone* was close enough to allow providing support to the other ships in the fleet in terms of heavy fire and fighter deployment. There had been no sign of additional asteroid weapons.

Damon's recovery went well and Allie went to see him for a few hours every day. The doctors had replaced his left lung and the right had healed well. The medications accelerated his recovery, and he could walk around sickbay at least a little.

Allie saw Harry daily for lunch or dinner. Harry seemed to have backed off from what she saw as attacks on Damon, but he continued to emphasize to her how he would make a better choice. She fought hard against her attraction for Harry, but the thought of cutting him out of her life made her want to weep. She could not bear the thought of him not being in her life.

She glanced at the clock and saw she needed to get ready to meet Harry at the Café. The computer told her she'd done better at solitaire today, only losing a little more than a hundred thousand credits. She tapped the *PAY* button and shut off the machine to get ready.

As she showered, Allie wondered why she had such mixed emotions about Harry and Damon. She cared for both of them, and she thought she might actually be falling in love with Damon. That was at the very least. She knew she had very similar feelings for Harry. She enjoyed the time she spent with both men. Damon with his boyish machismo and Harry with his almost arrogant intelligence, both had features she liked in men.

She thought for a moment before dressing, returning the tight red dress to the closet and grabbing a dark green pantsuit that fit so tight she had to lie down to zip it fully. Allie dressed and applied her makeup. It occurred to her that in her family of multiple marriages, more than two people in a relationship wasn't even close to being rare. Her parents were a group of five that formed a family. Charlotte had married a man and another woman. Most of her other sisters and brothers shared polyamorous marriages. Allie often wondered about that. Marilyn had told her most mammals weren't monogamous. In fact, monogamy was rare in mammals, being far more common in birds. If that was really the case, Allie wondered why, for most of human civilized history, humans had been monogamous. There were always a few exceptions like the harems of the Arabian cultures and the Mormons, who had changed their name back to Mormons after the Doom Time, but most human civilizations practiced monogamy.

As she considered the history of humanity, Allie realized that monogamy was actually rare. Most human societies recognized marriage as being between two people. For centuries, the definition of marriage was the union of one man and one woman, though that had relaxed over the years to include same-sex couples, but the definition always involved two people. The Mormons, before they changed their names to Later Day Saints, had run afoul of numerous governments because of the belief in and support of polygamy, though they tended to limit the concept to one man and several women. Even with a legally defined marriage as two people, most relationships had more.

How many married people, in the days before multiple marriages became legal, had affairs? In her studies, Allie had read figures as high as eighty percent of all married people had at least one affair. She'd also learned that not all such affairs ended the marriage. Popular on Earth for more than four thousand years, clubs existed where a couple could join and take part in affairs, not always sexual, with partners other than their spouse. History also showed that the ones having affairs outside their marriage weren't always men. Most studies revealed the numbers were about the same for men and women. All Allie's father did when he legalized multiple marriages seven hundred years ago was remove the legal barriers to things that happened anyway.

Allie finished her makeup and touched up her hair. While not all marriages had affairs going on, clearly the majority did. Interestingly, the number of multiple marriages wasn't nearly as great as expected from the number of men and women having affairs. Allie made a fast query of the ship's computers and found that multiple marriages accounted for slightly less than thirty percent of all marriages in the Empire. She knew there must be more people than that having affairs.

She'd never thought much about herself in a multiple marriage. About half of her family had relationships with one man and several women. She grabbed her small purse and headed to meet Harry.

* * * *

Harry had only one idiosyncrasy he considered bad.

It drove him crazy when people were late.

It might have been some game the aristocracy played, thinking that fashionable lateness was somehow good. Allie might really be so disorganized that she could never make it on time. He hoped the latter. If not, that meant that she did it deliberately.

He sat waiting for her at the table he'd found in the Café and checked his watch every thirty seconds or so. She was now seventeen and a half minutes late. He caught himself and stopped drumming at the tabletop with his fingers. That wouldn't look too good. He had already finished half of his bourbon and wondered how many he'd go through before she arrived. Harry knew he had a problem with people who were perennially late, but there was more to this. He looked forward to seeing Allie, and he hated every minute he wasn't with her. When she was late, he lost time he could spend in her company. He bided his time, waiting for her.

Harry didn't have to look when she came into the club. The background noise of conversation dropped noticeably when she walked into the room, every man turning to look at her and most of the women following suit. Allie smiled gently as she walked towards him, crossing the dance floor while her hips swayed slowly. Harry knew his mouth hung open, but that didn't mean he could do anything about the fact. Allie wore an outfit he hadn't seen on her before. For that matter, Harry couldn't recall seeing anything like the outfit before, anywhere. Dark green, more forest green than the emerald of her eyes, it was tight enough that a spray gun could have applied the outfit. It hugged every curve and smooth line of her body, like a second skin.

Allie reached the table and stood. "Well?"

Harry managed to remember that he should hold her chair. "You look, um, great."

As she sat, Allie laughed a little. "Thanks. I wondered if you had brain damage or something."

He sniffed her hair as he held her chair. "You always smell so fresh and clean."

"Thanks, I suppose."

"That's an interesting outfit." The noise level in the nightclub slowly returned to normal.

"I thought it might get your attention."

"It did that, Allie."

"Good. By the way, sorry I'm late."

"Were you? I didn't notice."

"Yeah, I was. Thank you for not noticing, or at least for saying you didn't notice." Rebecca came and took their drink orders, leaving menus behind. "Did you have fun solving puzzles for daddy all day?"

Harry caught himself staring at the tight green paint across her breasts. "Um, actually it was pretty quiet today." He forced his eyes back to hers. "Sorry about that."

Allie sat her menu down and reached across the table to take his hand. "That's OK, Harry. I hoped you'd notice." She sighed a little. "Sometimes, I have the feeling that you don't notice that I'm a woman when you're thinking about something."

"Well, that worked." He laughed, but it sounded nervous. "What about your day? Did you lose more of your father's money?"

"Yeah, but not as much."

"I'll have to teach you the secret to solitaire sometime."

Rebecca took their orders and headed off to the kitchen. "There's a secret?"

"Yeah. You predict, within the limits of probability, what the next card will be, and that let's you decide the best way to play."

Allie laughed. "That'll make daddy happy, too."

"At least his wallet."

"So, when are you going to ask me to dance?"

"Later. I'm having too much fun staring at you right now." His eyes kept trying to see through the tight material.

"I wondered if I had a bug in my hair or something."

"Nope, just enjoying looking at you, that's all." Harry squeezed her hand. "By the way, I wanted to thank you again for taking care of me last week."

"That's all right." She smiled.

"I wonder where things will go when what's-his-name gets out of sickbay in a few days."

"Damon. I don't know, but is there a reason I can't date more than one person at a time?"

Harry felt the frown creep onto his face. "No, I guess not." The idea of sharing her was disturbing, at best. It was just plain wrong at worst. He wanted her for himself.

The uncomfortable silence stretched for a time. The waitress, Rebecca, brought their dinner. Allie reached over the table and took his hand in both of hers. "Harry, you may be the man I want to be with forever. Right now, though, I'm not sure."

"I understand that, even if I don't like it." He knew he wanted her, but not just sexually. Even though women thought him strange, Harry never had a problem getting dates for sex. He wanted Allie. He wanted all of her, body, heart, and soul.

"I can't predict the future, so I can't tell you how things might go."

They ate in silence. Harry had never considered himself a lady's man. Most women found him either arrogant or just plain strange. Allie was different. She was smart, as smart as Harry thought he was, and she didn't find him strange. He liked when she'd find something he said or did funny, and he loved to hear her laugh.

But Allie was also drop-dead gorgeous. Harry wanted to be around her, needed to be around her. He burned with desire for her. Although he could sit for hours just watching her, he could only do that for so long before he gave in to the need to seduce her.

"Are you all right?"

He managed a smile. "Yeah, I'm fine." A real smile spread over his face now. "How about that dance?"

They danced and talked until nearly 2300 before leaving. Harry walked Allie home, her arm feeling natural around his on their way to her door. "Can you come in, Harry?"

His heart lurched. He thought he did a good of job of controlling his desire to grab her and kiss her so far tonight. He knew the façade wouldn't last thirty seconds if he went inside with her. "I don't think that would be a good idea."

"Why not?"

"I'd like to tell you that we could sit and talk, but I don't trust myself that much."

One thing Allie did that Harry found attractive was that she blushed. He knew she was far from innocent, but she still blushed. "If you think that's for the best."

"Yeah, I do. You're involved with Derwood. I don't want you in a bad position."

"Damon." She sighed a little. "You're right, I guess."

"I think so." He brushed his lips across hers and then watched as the door closed.

He stood in the corridor, his body shaking. He said his mantra in his head, but it kept morphing into her name being repeated in a rhythmic chant. Harry's fists balled as he fought to stop himself from ringing the bell. Or maybe just kicking the door in. He wanted her. More than he ever wanted anything. He wasn't sure how long he stood staring at her closed door, but the Marines down the corridor at her father's suite stared at him.

He sighed and gathered all his strength. He managed to walk away.

Chapter 5

Reparations

Allie was on her way to sickbay Sunday morning to meet Damon for his release. She invited Harry, but he declined. No surprises there.

She wondered how she would tell Damon about Harry. For that matter, what would she tell Damon about Harry? Allie considered herself involved with Damon, but clearly, she also felt attraction to Harry. When she'd asked her mother for advice, Janelle had only stared at Allie and replied, "I have no idea. You need to pick one or both."

Allie abandoned the chain of thought as she reached sickbay. Damon insisted on walking home, but Claire, with Allie's help, persuaded him to push the wheelchair so he'd have something to both steady himself and if he needed to sit down.

"You didn't need to come meet me here."

"I know I didn't need to. I wanted to." She wagged her finger at him. "If you get tired, sit down."

"Yes, Ma'am. I know when I'm outranked."

"You'd better."

"Have you heard anything about how the repairs are going?"

"Are you kidding? Between daddy being hypersensitive about his ship and Marilyn getting the zoo, OD, and life support back up fully, that's all I've heard about the last week!" Allie laughed a little. "Actually, things are going pretty well. Q thinks we'll be able to move back to the lines in a day or two, but it's going to take a long time for the trees and all on the OD to get back up to par."

Damon focused on his walking, and they soon reached his cabin. "I can't remember how much of a mess the place is in, but would you like to come in?"

"Yeah, I would. That will let me help you get settled a little, too." The door swished open and Allie followed him inside. While a typical bachelor apartment, it wasn't disgusting. Allie nodded at the picture on the dining nook wall of a woman clad only in a helmet and holding a heavy laser. "Recruiting poster?"

He glanced at the picture. "Sorry about that. I used to hope she'd show up in my command."

"Don't hold your breath."

"No, things didn't turn out that way, but she's still there for, um, motivation."

"Yeah, motivation. Right." She smiled to herself. Every single man she knew had at least one picture similar in theme. She wondered if Q had a naked robot on his wall.

Damon seemed to hesitate a few seconds. The events of the past week must have been fuzzy for him. Allie noticed that he forgot things and often repeated questions. Claire said that was normal and would fade with time. "They told me in sickbay that your friend, um, was it Harvey? Anyway, that he rescued my team."

"Harry. I guess he did, in a way. He crawled through the junk and saw the life signs." She wondered how much of this he should hear from her. "He opened the door to the service area where you had taken shelter."

"Yeah, Harry. They said he got hurt. Nothing too bad, I hope."

"No, he's back on duty now and doing fine. He doesn't think he did anything other than his job." Allie did not want to talk about Harry around Damon. He'd probably see right through her.

"He's the guy with the long hair, right?"

"That's him."

"He may not look like one, but it sounds like he thinks like a Marine."

"Maybe. He wanted me to tell you he's glad you're OK and that he's sorry about those that didn't make it."

Damon nodded. "You've been spending some time with him." It wasn't a question.

She needed to end this conversation. "Yeah, I have. Now I can spend some time with you." She just couldn't think of a way to do that without hurting Damon.

"Allie, we're not exclusive or anything like that."

"I know. That's why I've gone out with Harry a few times for drinks." She paused. "That's all it's been."

"I know how to step aside gracefully."

Like a light bulb turning on, Allie saw where Damon was coming from and where this was going. "Hold on, Damon. No one has asked you to bow out. Is there some rule I don't know that says I can only date one person at a time?" She realized that she'd suggested that she and Harry could date.

"No, of course not. I just thought that..."

"You thought that after making love to me a couple of times, I'd be yours forever." She cursed herself for going on the offensive just because that was easier than facing her feelings.

"No, that's not what I mean."

"Then please explain to me what you do mean."

"I thought that was something special to both of us."

Her anger built, but it now faded as fast as it had come on her. She wondered if her anger had flared to give her a way out. "Of course it was special, and it will always be special. I'm not looking for a dedicated, exclusive relationship right now." She took his hand in hers. The tearing sensation between the two men seemed to rip at her soul. "That doesn't mean that one won't grow. I want to keep seeing you, if that's all right."

"If you want out, just say so."

"The same goes for you, too. And if you want to go out with other people, that's all right with me."

His smile looked a little sad. "OK. So tell me about Harvey."

"Harry. He's a nice man."

"How does he keep the long hair and keep his commission?"

"His CO thinks he's crazy and a genius."

"Is he?"

"There's no doubt Harry is very smart, but he's not crazy. He's eccentric, yeah, but not crazy." Allie smiled at Damon. "Why are we talking about Harry and not about you?"

"I don't know."

"Sizing up the competition?"

"The first thing they taught me in command school was to know my enemy."

"I don't want you to be enemies." Allie didn't think this could be avoided.

"Just a figure of speech, that's all."

Allie studied his face for a moment. She wondered if he'd already read her mind and knew the secret thoughts and feelings she had for Harry. "All right." She leaned and kissed him. "I've missed you."

"I've missed you and a lot more, too. I don't remember much of anything between Thursday and Wednesday."

Allie leaned forward and kissed him again. "How do you feel?"

"I think I feel pretty good." He rubbed at the healing incision on his chest. "Other than this itching."

Allie gave him her best seductive smile. "I have an itch, too."

"Oh."

"Yeah." She leaned to kiss him again, running her hands over his shoulders. Allie felt him, tentatively, responding, his arms moving around her body. "Damon, maybe you should lie down so you can rest."

"I'm fine here."

The brief kiss was all she needed to fire her passions for Damon. Whenever she was with him, she wanted him just as much as the first time they were together. She knew in her heart that Damon was not the wrong choice. She would have been devastated if she'd lost him in the OD decompression. "Let me try that again. Come to bed with me."

"Oh."

They walked together, kissing, to the bedroom. It was in far worse condition than the sitting room in terms of a single man's clutter. Allie waved her hand at the bed. "Will any of that stuff explode if it hits the floor?"

"Sorry. No."

She flipped the blanket to the floor, sweeping the assortment of clothing, military gizmos, and papers to the floor with it. "Now." Allie untied his robe and let it fall to lie around his feet. "Lie down." As Damon lay watching her, Allie undressed and climbed into bed next to him, cuddling close. "Tell me if I do anything that hurts you, OK?"

"Other than leaving?"

"Well, that too." She kissed him, rolling to lie on top of him, pressing her body fully to his. As she swept her tongue deeply into his mouth, Damon's cock pressed against her, hardening more with each passing moment. She missed the taste of his lips.

Every bit as sweet as the first time they kissed, his mouth tasted wonderful to her. Her taste buds wanted to dance and sing in her mouth. His lips, still a little chapped, made a tantalizing blend of rough and smooth with his face. Even in sickbay, as soon as he was able, Damon shaved twice a day.

He didn't use his cologne while in sickbay, but that was all right. Without the pheromone spiked artificial scent, she could smell and taste him without something made in a chemistry set getting in the way. She relished in the flavor of his lips, sweet with salty overtones from his sweat.

As she knew from the first time she saw him, Damon had no fear of hard work. He worked hard with the physical therapy, and he would perspire as he worked out. The dried perspiration mixed with the flavor of his skin to make a delectable blend that made her mouth water with anticipation.

Perhaps, she thought, she smelled the wonderful concoction as much as she tasted it on his mouth and face. His aroma filled her nose. Clean, it spoke to her of his hard work and devotion.

She heard Damon moaning a little, but not moans of pain. He seemed to have missed her as much as she did him, and his sounds were pleasant. As she licked across his lips, his breath came rapidly from his mouth, blowing in a near-pant. The steady, rapid pulsations of his breathing told her as much as anything else that he lived after the attack.

Pulling her mouth from his, Allie moved to sit on his hips, his cock pointing upwards against her mons. Stroking his hardness as she watched his face, Allie smiled gently. "I've missed this, too."

"Yeah, but it's not like we've had a lot of time together."

"We haven't, I guess, but it's enough for me to know how much I care about you." She leaned and licked his nose. "You taste wonderful."

"Thanks." His brow furrowed for a moment. "I should tell you that what made me approach you in the club was how pretty you are."

She leaned and pressed her fingers to his lips. "I know. You hoped to get laid."

"Yeah, I guess so."

"That seemed to have worked well for you."

"Some guys would disagree with that."

Allie frowned. "What do you mean?"

"Yeah, we made love, but I've fallen for you. Some guys would see that as a bad thing."

"I'm not naked in bed with some guys. Is it a bad thing for you?" Concern and excitement both washed over her. She tried to slam the door on the excitement part. In her mind, Harry's foot kept the door ajar.

"No. At least I think that it's a good thing, depending on how the end of the story is written."

"I don't know how the end is written, either." She leaned and kissed him again. "For now, let's write the beginning."

She leaned back, slipping his steely cock into her pussy, feeling the wetness ease the way. She moved slowly, her hips thrusting against him, as she stared into his eyes. Allie couldn't stop the questions in her mind. She caught herself thinking about Harry. She thought she'd managed to keep the questions off her face, and Damon smiled gently back at her as his pelvis lunged to meet her strokes. The physical sensation of their motion together was fantastically pleasurable. Allie pushed hard to reach a climax, but no matter how good Damon's cock felt inside her, she didn't feel herself nearing orgasm. Her mind was elsewhere.

Damon climaxed into her, his body thrashing on the bed under her. Allie moved to lie beside him, her head on his shoulder, her heart torn. "Are you all right?"

"Yeah, just a little short of breath, that's all."

She drew little pictures with her nails on the skin of his stomach. She didn't want to lose Damon, but she couldn't stop thinking about Harry. "That's a good thing, I think."

He laughed a little. "I think so."

Allie cuddled to him, keeping her fingers on his skin, glad that he was alive and with her, but her mind kept wandering.

* * * *

Allie sat staring over dinner at Damon. He returned to limited duty today, four days after his release from sickbay, and he'd done too much. He rubbed his chest often throughout the evening and, when they danced, he just shuffled his feet. "Are you sure you're all right? We can go to sickbay and have you checked over."

"No, I'm OK. I'm just tired."

"Rule number one, Damon. Do not lie to me about your health. Or anything else for that matter."

"I'll be fine. Really."

Allie frowned. "All right, but I'm watching you."

He stared at her for more than a minute. "Allie, what would I have to do for you to go out exclusively with me?"

"Marry me," Allie decided, but she stopped him from answering. "Before you ask, I'll say no, at least right now."

"That's really not what I wanted to hear."

"I know, darling, but that's the truth. I'd rather hurt you a little with the truth than devastate you with a lie."

"I know. Believe it or not, I appreciate that, too."

"I'm glad for that." Allie smiled as she took his hand in hers, caressing the back of it. His hand was large and masculine, like the man. "I'm also glad you're feeling better, but you need to take it easy for a few more days."

"You're right about that." He rubbed his chest again.

"Did you want to leave early tonight?"

"Maybe we should. I need to be at the garrison at 0600, so I need to get to sleep early, too."

"I'll make you a rare offer. If we can stay at my place tonight, I'll drag myself out of bed, and we can have breakfast together." She hesitated a moment. "That is, unless you've cleaned house recently."

"Maybe your place would be better."

"I thought so."

"Yeah. I promise when I get my energy back, I'll clean the place up a little."

She smiled. "You're off the hook."

* * * *

Damon pulled Allie against him as they kissed in the shower. The smooth, soft skin only barely concealed firm muscles lurking beneath. Her lips burned like fire on his, and his hands roamed over her back, squeezing her ass as he pulled her against his hard cock. When he kissed across her face to her neck, Allie leaned her head back, exposing her throat to him as he nibbled gently at the tanned skin.

Her hands slid down his back, kneading the muscles of his back as she moaned softly. Damon kissed around her neck, from ear to ear, his tongue darting over the wet skin as the water rushed down their bodies and made a soft roaring as it splashed and flowed down the walls. Allie turned in his arms and she bent over, grasping the safety bar on the shower, her ass rubbing against his erection. He grasped her hips, slipping his cock into her from behind, ramming his length into her quickly and fully.

"Oh, yes! Yes, babe!" Allie gasped.

Damon thrust into her rapidly, the access she gave him letting him pull his shaft completely from her, and then driving back deeply into her soaked pussy as the warm water streamed across his stomach and down his balls.

He slipped his hand from her hip and rubbed his finger around her anus. "Okay?" he asked softly.

"Yes," she nodded, turning her head around to look at him. He saw the acquiescence on her face, and his finger pressed on the opening a little. When he pushed firmly on her hole, Allie thrust backwards and the full length of his finger slipped into her ass. "Yes! Yes, please!" she gasped again.

The pressure of his finger pushing on his cock through the membranous skin between her ass and cunt forced him closer to climax, but he tried to hold on, wanting Allie to climax with him. When he tried to slow his thrusting, Allie reached back to pull his hips against her. As the urgency of his thrusts increased, she moved her hand to reach between their legs and grasped his balls, rolling them like a magician with billiard balls between her fingers.

Damon took her hand and placed it between her legs. He had to gasp for breath before he could speak. "Cum with me, darling!"

Her hand moved to her clit, and the pressure of her fingers on the base of his cock built as she rubbed quickly. The tip of his finger in her ass would rub over the head of his cock when he rammed his dick into her. Allie turned her head again to look back at him.

"Now! Now!" she cried. Damon slammed his cock into her soaked pussy as it closed around him, threatening to rip his dick from him, and his load shot into her, like water bursting from an overfull hose.

He tried to slip his arms around her waist when he pulled his finger from Allie's ass, but he wasn't sure he could keep himself from falling, let alone her. "I'll try not to fall with us both."

Allie's laugh sent shockwaves through him when it caused her pussy to constrict on his cock. "Let me stand up." She straightened, his cock slipping from her. She turned to face him and slipped her arms around his waist. "Can you breathe any better than I can?"

"I don't think so." He put his arms around her shoulders. He was crazy about her. She felt so good, so right. They belonged together.

* * * *

Harry looked across the table at her and Allie knew something was coming. He had that look he wore when he planned to go on the offensive. "Did you and Dartmouth have a good evening?"

"Damon." Allie sighed. She played with her lunch for a moment. "Yeah, we did, but he's still pretty weak."

"There's good news."

If Harry could be sarcastic, so could she. "He's not so weak that he can't fuck."

Harry's head snapped up from his plate, a piece of his dead cow falling from his fork. The smile he'd tried to hide by looking down at his plate faded when his jaw went slack. "What?"

"You heard me." She had fallen for Damon, and she could, if she allowed herself, fall just as badly for Harry. She knew she had brought this onto herself, but she couldn't stand the attacks they made on each other, competing over her, these two men whom she cared about deeply and couldn't stop herself from seeing.

He looked at her for more than a minute, his eyes going from an unblinking stare to a series of rapid blinks, then back to staring again. "I, um, guess I should say something, but I have no idea what."

"How about that you're sorry for being such an ass about this?"

"I didn't know I was being an ass."

"Yes, you do, Harry. You always know just exactly what you're saying, and you always say exactly what you mean." She sat her fork down, her salad forgotten. "There's no need for all the snide comments. I'm confused enough as it stands. It's not helping your case at all."

He forked the scorched meat into his mouth and added a few of the fried potatoes. He munched slowly as he stared at her, and then finally swallowed. "I guess I have been being a bit of a prick. I guess I'm a little out of control."

"I guess that's one way to put it." She smiled her best smile and found it came very easy for Harry.

"I promise I'll tone things down a little."

"I appreciate that." She decided to change the subject before he became melancholy. "What time do you think you'll get out of the office today?"

"I'm hoping for about 1630, maybe a little earlier."

"That sounds good. Why don't you come to my place and we'll have dinner there tonight?" What was she doing to herself? She wanted the words back almost before they left her lips. She wanted him to say yes.

He frowned a little. "Are you planning to cook?"

"Maybe. Why?"

"I really do love real meat."

She laughed. "Tell you what, we'll both eat the same thing. You'll have your real meat."

"Just how are you going to do that?"

"How long have you been on *Boone*?"

"Three years."

"Then you've probably never had pizza."

"What's pizza?"

"Trust me, you'll love it. This is the only place in the galaxy you can get pizza unless grandma and grandpa have managed to hook the folks on New Scotland on the idea."

"You're not going to tell me, are you?"
"Nope."

* * * *

He'd promised Allie that he wouldn't, but Harry sat in his cubicle, bored out of his mind, considering looking up pizza to find out what she was going to make him eat tonight.

Devon came and leaned on the wall. "Are you busy?"

"Do I look busy?"

"Well, no, but I'm never sure when you're thinking about something important."

"To answer your question, no, I'm not busy. What's up?"

"I need someone to go down to the brig and interview a guy that security thinks is feeding information to the Arupians."

"Devon, I'm not a cop."

"Neither am I, but someone has to do it. I outrank you."

"On one condition."

"What's that?"

"I can leave from there."

"Ah! You have a date tonight, right?"

"Yeah."

"When is she going to make up her mind between you and the jarhead?"

"Damned if I know. She's making me crazy."

"Making?"

Harry laughed. "OK, crazier."

"I don't know what to tell you. I think she's leading one or both of you along."

"Why would she do that? It's not like we can give her money or anything she doesn't already have. That doesn't make sense."

"Maybe just for the fun and challenge. Call it sport if you like."

Harry stared at his boss for a moment. "Shit. You really know how to make me feel better."

"Sorry about that. Your prisoner awaits. I'll see you tomorrow."

The Polyamorous Princess

* * * *

Damon and Gunnery Sergeant Gabe Williams walked out of the brig as a Fleet Lieutenant came in. The JG had long black hair, much longer than regulation, and Gabe gave the man a long look as they passed.

Gabe whispered to Damon, "Jesus! Can you believe what they're letting the Fleet types get away with?"

Damon paused and turned. "Lieutenant, a moment please." The man turned to face him and Damon looked at the name badge on his uniform. "Harrison Douglas. So, you're Harry."

Douglas flipped his hair with his hand. "That's me. Hairy Harry."

Gabe glanced rapidly between the two men. "Damon, we should get back to the garrison."

"No, that's all right." Damon made little secret that he'd like to meet Douglas. He'd also made little secret about not liking the idea of Douglas going out with Allie. "We're all civilized here." He'd hinted that he'd like to kick the crap out of Douglas.

Douglas leaned his head to one side. "Good to see you up and about, Hyde. Allie's pleased about that."

"I should thank you for finding my team. You saved a lot of lives that day, mine included."

"Don't mention it. Just doing my job."

"I guess you were, but thanks anyway. That must have impressed Allie."

Douglas stared for a moment. "Yeah, it did. She was very appreciative."

Before Damon could lunge, Gabe grabbed his arm. "Calm down, son."

Damon could feel the tension stretching in his body. "I can only imagine." He took several deep breaths. "It's pretty clear that you're a hero, but you don't look like most people expect a hero to look."

"I guess I don't. I never saw much point to all that physical stuff." A slow smile came to Douglas' face. "Never made much sense to me when it's easier to think your way out of trouble than to fight your way out."

"It's not often that you see an officer with long hair and a beard."

"No, it's not. Sort of makes me special around here. In a lot of ways."

Gabe still held his arm, but Damon yanked it away now. "I think a woman like Allie can do a lot better than someone who has no respect for authority."

"She seems to disagree with that."

"Come on, let's get out of here." Gabe took Damon's arm again and tried to pull him down the corridor.

"Just a minute." Damon stepped close to Douglas, their noses almost touching. "I think you need to consider your options very carefully, Douglas."

"I think you'll be interested to know that I already have, Hyde."

Damon didn't see what he'd expected to see in the dark brown eyes so close to his. Instead of fear or nervousness, he saw a calm, relaxed mood. "Then you might want to think again." Damon allowed Gabe to drag him away.

* * * *

Harry stood in the corridor for several minutes, letting his meditation calm him and pull him away from a defensive mode. The twenty-six years of tai chi and other eastern martial arts training let him look more confident and calm than he felt. As he said his mantra repeatedly in his head, he knew this relationship had come to a head. If not for Harry's aura of calm confidence and the Sergeant pulling on his arm, Hyde would have started swinging. Despite his training, Harry wasn't at all certain he could have taken the big Marine. In combat of any type, there was a point of no return once the enemy became an overwhelming force. He wouldn't know he'd crossed the point until passed the limit.

He knew this would all eventually come back to Allie, but he and Hyde had to work things out between themselves first. Harry wouldn't say anything to her, and he knew Hyde's macho pride wouldn't let him tell Allie about this incident. Very soon, Harry and Damon Hyde would have to work this out somehow.

Harry sighed and went to interview the prisoner.

* * * *

It turned out that pizza was a huge slice of bread topped with tomato sauce, several other vegetables, cheese, and a wondrous assortment of actual meat. Harry found sausage, some kind of spicy hard salami, and sliced ham in the mix. It was great, and Harry made a pig of himself. "What did you call this salami again?" He spoke around a mouthful of pizza.

"It's called pepperoni." Allie laughed at him. "I'm really glad you like it."

"This is really good." He eyed the several strips of bread crust Allie had left on her plate. "You're leaving the best part."

"Pizza bones. Too crunchy for my tastes." She seemed to change tack. "Scuttlebutt has it they found a spy today."

"Nope, just a loony, that's all. He thinks the Arupians are talking to him from his drain. He's telling them our secret battle plans by whispering into the sink."

"How much time did you waste on that one?"

"Not too much, I guess." He considered telling her about his encounter with Hyde but stuck to his plans. "What about your day?"

"Just lost more money, taught my class, had lunch with you, and talked to Damon for a while this afternoon."

He wondered if she was fishing. Hyde may have said something to her, but it wasn't very likely. Harry decided to play dumb. "Are you seeing him later tonight?"

"Not that it's really any of your business, but no."

"See? No snide comments."

Allie smiled at him. "Thanks."

"I'm really curious about something." Harry thought for a moment. "Am I wasting my time and yours?"

"I don't know, Harry." She frowned a little. "I want to tell you that you're not, but I am involved with Damon."

"Yeah, you are. You're very special." Harry had been fighting himself all evening to be this close and not touch her. Now, the fight seemed harder. "If I told you I'm happy just being friends, I'd be lying to you."

"I know. I can't tell you what may happen in the future, though." She looked at the partial slice of pizza on his plate. "I spoiled your appetite."

"Not really. I've had six slices besides that." He forced a smile. "I can't promise you I'll stay—friends—with you for too long."

* * * *

Damon sat eating dinner, trying not to look too deeply into Allie's eyes. The echoes of his confrontation with Douglas yesterday still resounded in his head, and he knew he'd been dead wrong. For some reason Damon couldn't seem to grasp, his anger had flared when he talked to Douglas. He knew Allie did nothing more than have dinner, lunch, or maybe a few drinks with Douglas, and their dates, such as they were, hadn't gotten in the way of the time Allie spent with him.

The man had also saved his life along with those of many other Marines. Damon knew he tried to pick a fight with Douglas. Damon was, in many ways, glad that the confrontation hadn't come down to a fight. The calm confidence he'd seen in Douglas' eyes left doubts about Damon's ability to take the smaller man. The exchange could have been cordial, if not friendly, if he hadn't pushed the issue.

The last thing he needed was to drag Allie into the middle of this. She was happy and had made it clear to him that she wasn't ready for an exclusive relationship in terms of seeing others. On the other hand, she wasn't seeing anyone other than Douglas, and she wasn't sleeping with him. Damon didn't like the idea of sharing Allie at any level, but he didn't have any choice. He could threaten to break off their relationship, but that idea had several problems. First, if forced to, he knew that Allie would walk away and straight into Douglas' bed. Second, he couldn't do it. He couldn't walk away and lose her forever.

Allie sat her fork down and looked over the table him. "Are you feeling all right?"

"Yeah, just a little tired is all."

Allie studied his face. "Are you sure that's all?"

"Yeah, that's all." He thought quickly, trying to change the subject. "I didn't know you could cook like this."

"My mom is a great cook and she taught me a little."

"Um, which mom?"

"Oh, yeah! Paige. She started as daddy's assistant, and then became his personal chef. Finally they decided to cut through all the red tape and got married."

"Well, however it evolved, that was great."

"Thanks." She smiled at him for a moment. "Come with me." She took his hand and led him to the bedroom.

* * * *

Allie stood as Damon slipped her robe from her. Letting it fall to the floor, like a green crushed velvet cloud around her feet. "You take my breath away, Allie."

"Let me give it back, then." She pressed her face firmly to his, sucking his tongue into her mouth, as her hands removed his shirt. As she unfastened his pants, Allie could feel the growing firmness in his crotch, and she pushed the garments down his legs until they slid from him. Almost falling in the bed in their embrace, Allie rolled on top of him, and then pulled her lips from his.

As she kissed his chest, Allie tasted the exciting blend made by the cologne he wore and his unique, masculine body chemistry. Damon usually wore a fragrance spiked with a pheromone, and it drove her wild. Even without the alchemy lab additions, Allie knew his flavors and smells could push her over the edge.

She pinned his hard cock to his stomach with her breasts and moved slowly, feeling the drops of pre-cum lubricating the passage. His hands moved gently over her shoulders and head. As she moved lower, nibbling at his stomach, his hands closed on her head and pushed her down, his stiff dick rubbing against her face. With a flick of her tongue, Allie caused him to shake violently, and then she took his hardness deep in her mouth.

As his fingers twisted in her hair, Damon pumped his cock in her mouth, holding her head firmly in place. She sucked as hard as she could, feeling him tremble beneath her. The flavor of his cock mixed with the cologne and his sweat to make a potent blend of sensations in her nose and mouth. Allie wanted to savor the tastes and smells.

When she reached to move his hands from her hair, Damon didn't resist. She nibbled at the head of his cock, causing him to jerk as her teeth bit him gently.

Allie suddenly had the urge to see how far she could push him and gave in. She moved her mouth and tongue quickly on his cock until he shook like an earthquake. When she felt him very near climax, she pulled her mouth from him and moved to lie beside him, not touching his dick again.

He moaned. "Don't stop now, baby."

She managed to hide her smile. "I think I'm done for now."

"That's pretty naughty of you, Allie."

"Yeah, I get that way sometimes."

With no warning, Damon moved in the bed, sweeping her into his arms and turning her to lie facedown across his lap. "You do, eh?" His hand hit her bare ass with a loud pop and Allie jumped. "Bad girl!"

Allie squealed with excited delight as his hand struck her ass again, just hard enough to be erotically painful. "Yes! I'm a bad girl, yes!" His cock pressed hard against her and, her wetness flowed as he spanked her.

As his had hit her ass, his fingers darted between her cheeks. With each swat, one finger slipped into her pussy, and another pressed into her ass.

"Then you need a good spanking."

"Yes! Yes! A good spanking!" The time seemed like both an eternity and only a fleeting moment as he firmly spanked her ass several more times, driving her to a wave of climax, battering her against the stinging rocks of her orgasm. As she squirmed in his lap, she felt the pulsing of his climax spurting from his cock against her stomach and breasts as his spanking slowed.

His hand rested on her stinging ass, gently rubbing her as they both fought for breath. He turned her easily in his strong arms and lifted her like a baby. Damon kissed her forehead softly. "Did I hurt you, darling?"

"Oh, hell, no. I thought you were still weak and tired?" Allie's heart pounded in her head and sweat poured from her body.

He laughed softly. "Me, too." He lowered her to the bed and stretched out next to her, putting his arms around her shoulders.

Allie tried to catch her breath. "Damn it."

"Was that a good damn it or a bad damn it?"

"Good." She kissed his lips. "Very good."

Chapter 6

Conflict

Allie watched Harry. He would fidget with his silverware and napkin, and then glance quickly around the Café. He seemed, for all she could figure, nervous and jumpy, something she'd never seen from him before. "What's wrong?"

"What? Oh, I'm just a little preoccupied this afternoon."

"Like the first time we had lunch?"

"Yeah, I guess like that." Harry gave her a smile, but it looked strained to Allie.

"Maybe we can take another walk after lunch." The excitement of their first meeting stirred her. She loved and hated the feeling.

"I wish I could, but I need to get back to the office."

"Another puzzle?"

"I guess you could say that."

Allie could see on his face he wasn't saying something, but she decided not to pursue. She thought she knew what it was. "Well, at least you could walk me home after lunch."

"Yeah, I can do that."

Harry didn't say much as they ate, and Allie didn't pry. She had her own thoughts drifting through her mind. She'd catch Harry from the corner of her eye staring at her and the look on his face bothered her. She could see him, fighting with himself, a battle raging behind his face, but she wasn't sure if the battle was over saying something to her or over not saying something to her.

They finished lunch with little conversation, just small talk, and Harry walked her to her cabin. At the door, he managed what Allie thought was his first real smile of the day. "Do we have a lunch date tomorrow?"

"Yeah, we do. I'm sorry about dinner, though."

"That's all right." His eyes flicked back and forth between hers several times. "If you get a minute, you can call me."

"I'll try." Allie would never be certain why she did it, knowing it was wrong. She stepped closer to Harry and slipped her arms around his waist, her hands moving to his back. She pulled herself to his body and kissed him. Harry's arms moved around her shoulders and his tongue tentatively moved against her lips, then darted cautiously into her mouth.

He suddenly pulled back, almost pushing her from him. "Allie, I can't do this." He panted heavily.

He had his hands on her shoulders, gripping tightly, and Allie thought it was to keep her at a safe distance. "I'm sorry. I don't know why I did that." Her head pounded with the rush of blood in her ears and tingles fired through her pelvis, along with a slowly spreading wetness.

His short laugh sounded like a bark when it leapt from his lips. "I don't know why either. I have to go." He released her shoulders, paused for a moment just staring at her, and then walked quickly down the corridor.

* * * *

Allie begged off dinner with Damon. She wanted some time alone to think. She sat in her cabin listening to music as she thought about what to do with the situation she'd gotten herself into.

Over the last few days, she'd admitted to herself her attraction and developing feelings for Harry. She'd known all along of her attachment to Damon. The kiss this afternoon with Harry had forced things to a head, however. She needed to make a choice, and she had no idea what choice she would make.

'Torn between two lovers' was what the soloist of the song said, and Allie thought it fit her situation very nicely. She frowned when it came to her that wasn't the case at all. She had one lover and that was Damon. The aborted kiss this afternoon was as close as she'd gotten to taking Harry as a lover, at least in reality. Her fantasies were another matter.

Thankfully, she had refrained from fantasizing about Harry while she'd been in bed with Damon, who satisfied her not only physically but also emotionally. However, Harry had been the subject of more than a few hot dreams and daydreams. She couldn't help it.

Allie was falling hard for Harry. He had the one thing that all the men in her past had lacked, and it was very simple, almost ridiculously so. Harry could make Allie laugh. He didn't have Damon's huge, powerful muscles, but she knew Harry had strength. She'd seen in his personnel file that he was a student of ancient martial arts since age three. He also had won more than a dozen medals in martial arts competitions. As she knew, Harry's true strength wasn't in his muscles, but in his mind. Allie found his intelligence, arrogance and all, attractive. Not only that, he was physically appealing, magnetically so. She wanted him very badly.

Damon, on the other hand, was also devastatingly attractive. Big, burly, tough, and a good dash of boyish charm summed up Damon. He could probably bench press a shuttlecraft, and often lifted Allie with no effort at all. Far from stupid, but Damon wasn't the brightest bulb in the marquee of the Empire. A little shy, Damon didn't seem to like being the center of attention.

Just as he'd been initially attracted to Allie because of her looks, she was realistic enough to know her attraction to him stemmed from the same reasons. His awkwardness with her in those first few hours they spent together had tipped his hand, and she soon found herself attracted to him for more than his body. He would, at times, be very much assertive, but at others, he would give in to her desires. In bed, he tended to let her take the lead. Not for the first time, Allie wondered if he deferred to her because he loved her and wanted her to be happy, or because he didn't want to be assertive for some reason. She wondered what Harry was like in bed.

Decorated twice for bravery in his career, Damon was brave, no question of that, and he had a strong sense of duty and honor. Allie suspected most women would tell her to ditch Harry and grab onto Damon and hold him as tight as she could.

Allie listened to the music for several minutes, just kicking her brain into neutral and coasting for a while. The singer crooned about not wanting to be right for loving someone. Allie wasn't totally certain she knew what love was in the first place. Only twenty-seven years into an effectively immortal life, she hadn't learned much about love. Her sister, Charlotte, had been just over four hundred years old when she met the woman and man she married. Then again, Claire had only been seventeen when she met Zach. Both events were now centuries in the past, and Allie's problems existed here and now.

The problems she'd created impacted all three of them. She'd fallen, if not in love then in lust, with Damon almost on sight. She wanted to sleep with him the first night they'd met. She'd never done that before in her short life. The very next day, she met Harry and had instant attraction to him as well. She should have done something right then to avoid the quandary she had now.

While the singers went on about knowing that, somewhere out there, they knew someone waited for them, Allie knew she had to do something now to fix the mess she'd created. Damon and Harry were both very good men. Neither of them should be strung along the way things were going. The wine seemed to clear her thoughts, now that she'd opened the third bottle. Her logic had been for both men to wait for her while she sorted things out in her own head. That wasn't fair.

Allie's heart tugged painfully as she realized she had to let one man go. Tears slipped down her face as she tried to decide which one.

* * * *

Harry stood outside the garrison offices for nearly ten minutes trying to decide if he really wanted to do this. Their disagreement would soon impact Allie, if it hadn't already, and he wanted to talk to Hyde before it got any worse. He cranked up his nerve a notch and went in. The guard directed him to Hyde's office.

He studied the closed door for a moment. An old-fashioned wooden door, it swung on hinges instead of sliding into the wall when it opened. He saw two bright yellow footprints painted on the deck and a matching yellow square on the door itself with careful lettering explaining, in no uncertain terms, to knock three times inside the square. Harry smiled, placing his feet on the footprints and rapped three times with his knuckles.

"Enter."

Harry opened the door and stepped inside, closing the door behind him. "Good morning, Hyde."

Hyde looked up from the papers on his desk, his face wearing a surprised look. "What are you doing here?"

"We need to talk. Now." Harry took a seat across the desk from Hyde without waiting for an invitation. "We need to talk about Allie."

Hyde carefully set his pen down on the desk and moved a small stack of papers to the side. "I think we need to talk about you."

Harry glanced around the office. Neat and orderly, just what he expected from a jarhead, the office held stark contrast to what Allie had told him about Hyde's cabin being in a constant state of disarray. "Whatever. We do need to talk and get this out in the open."

"Why shouldn't I just beat the shit out of you and be done with it?"

"Several reasons. First, have you thought about how Allie would react to that? Second, you'll wind up in the brig." Harry smiled slowly. "Third, you can't do it." He wondered if he could really back that up. The guy was big.

Hyde's hands pressed palm-down on the desktop. He rolled his chair back from the desk. Harry saw corded muscles through Hyde's shirt. "You're an arrogant bastard."

"Maybe I am, but you're bright enough to know I'm right about the first two and to wonder if I'm right about the third. Just relax."

"I won't pummel you because of what that would do to Allie. As stupid as it may be, she likes you." His eyes narrowed. "As a friend."

"I'm not going to get into semantics with you. All I care about is that Allie not be dragged in the middle of this, and that she not get hurt because of our posturing."

Hyde stared at him for a moment. "I really did mean it when I thanked you for rescuing my team."

"You're welcome. We're all in this war together, and if we don't take care of one another, we're all dead."

Hyde's arms relaxed, the bunched muscles smoothing out. "You're right about that. I told Allie this, but you sure don't look like a Marine, even though you talk like one."

"Can you picture, in even your wildest dreams, me as a Marine?" Harry laughed. "I'm lucky they let me stay in the Fleet!"

"Yeah, you are." Harry glanced around the office again and Hyde followed his gaze. "What are you looking at?"

"Allie told me your cabin looks like the aftermath of a tornado. I'm just trying to reconcile that with this magazine picture of an office."

"She told you that?"

"Yeah, she did." Harry sighed. "You may not believe it, but Allie and I are friends, that's all." He paused deliberately. "For now."

"You're right. I don't believe it." Hyde frowned a little.

"I'll tell you right up front and honestly that I want her to dump you and come to me." Harry smiled. "That would tickle me more than a feather up my ass."

Hyde laughed heartily. "She's right. You are funny."

"Maybe, but that's the truth. Another thing that's the truth is that I want her to be happy."

"I understand that part. I want her to be happy, too." He paused. "As much as I want her to tell you to fuck off, I'll do whatever it takes to make her happy."

"Then we have some common ground other than just Allie."

"I guess we do." Hyde moved his papers around the desk again. "So, what do we do to make sure she's happy?"

"I think the first thing is to not snipe at each other anymore. I'm almost ashamed to tell you some of the things I've said to her about you, trying to get her to come over to me."

Hyde laughed. "Yeah, I've done the same thing trying to get her to stay with me."

"That needs to stop. That puts her in the middle."

"Right. Done deal, then."

Harry swallowed hard. "Next, we both need to agree that this is her choice and not ours." He knew the risk he took. Allie was already with Hyde. It would be a lot easier for her to stay with him than to change men in the middle of a relationship. He wanted her in his bed, but he wanted her to be happy even more.

"Agreed. I need to back off and not be so defensive about her having men friends."

Harry smiled. "Unless she decides otherwise."

Hyde stared at him for a moment. "Do you really think you could beat me in a fight?"

"I don't know." Harry shrugged. "I think I could give you a run for your money."

"Care to test that? For, say, a hundred credits."

"I can do that." Harry checked his watch. "I think we can have a little fun before I meet Allie for lunch."

"Come on." Hyde led him to the garrison's boxing ring where they quickly changed and soon had the gloves on.

Harry stared at the gloves for a moment. "Are we boxing or what?"

"Tell you what, Douglas." Hyde bopped a speed bag with rapid skill, making it rattle like a drum. "Anything you care to try is fair, so long as the same applies for me."

"Sure, why not?" Harry hammered his fists together several times like he'd seen boxers do in the ring. Harry still pounded his fists together when the bell rang. Hyde walked across the ring and hit him in the forehead, knocking Harry to his ass. "I thought we were supposed to shake hands or something!"

"We did that earlier." The Marines surrounding the ring cheered wildly, mostly for Hyde. Harry saw some money changing hands.

Harry climbed to his feet. "Oh, OK. Let's try that again."

Hyde danced around Harry in a circle, his feet moving smoothly and rapidly, fists up in a defensive posture. Harry rested his hands in an easy position at the level of his waist.

"Come on, Douglas! Come and get it!"

"Oh, I will soon enough."

Hyde danced in and threw a left jab that Harry's hands flashed up to block. An instant later, Harry dropped to one knee, the other leg sweeping out and around at the floor level to knock Hyde's feet out from under him.

Hyde's body slammed into the mat with a crash. He laughed as he regained his feet. "So, you do know a little of what you're doing!" He danced in again and Harry hit him with the heel of his hand squarely in the chest, knocking the wind from Hyde.

"Maybe a little, yeah." Harry slapped at Hyde. Soon, Hyde became both startled and angry enough that he charged at Harry, head down like a bull. Harry sidestepped the charge, guiding him into the ropes at the edge of the ring. The bell rang to end the first round.

Harry sat on the stool in his corner smiling at Hyde across the ring. He'd found the man's weakness in that he would get angry and make mistakes. He decided to play with Hyde for another round before putting him to bed. When the bell rang, Harry went on the offensive, jabbing and touching Hyde at any time he pleased, feigning with his feet and legs to keep him off balance.

Harry moved in to tap Hyde's chest, but he found he'd made a fatal mistake, and he'd confused confidence and carelessness. Hyde hit him in the right temple, and despite the head-protector, stars in a wide variety of shapes and colors exploded in his head. His knees unhinged and Harry spiraled to the mat just as the bell rang.

The third round began much sooner than Harry would have liked, his head still a little fuzzy. He decided he needed to end this before Hyde landed another punch as good as the last one. Harry made a leg sweep, but Hyde jumped over the swinging leg, landing a left hook on the way down. He jabbed several times at Harry's head before Harry sidestepped and slipped his arms around Hyde's body, turning as his hip lowered toward the mat. Once in position, Harry spun as his hip jutted upwards and flipped Hyde head over heels with a perfectly executed *O Goshi*.

Hyde slammed into the mat, his breath exploding between his lips. Harry dropped to pin him to the mat, getting low to the floor and high on Hyde's body. Hyde thrust upward with all his strength and flung Harry from him. Staggering, Hyde approached Harry and, as he stood, Hyde hit him in the forehead again. From his position on the mat, Harry swept Hyde's legs from under him and the big man fell to the floor.

They landed on the floor with their heads close together, panting, and both nursing a few cuts. Hyde caught his breath first. "Harry, if you promise not to kill me, I'll settle for a draw."

"If you won't kill me, you've got a deal."

Gabe stormed into the ring. "What the fuck are you two doing in my boxing ring? I should drag you both to your feet and kick your asses from here to next Tuesday!" The cheering crowd seemed to remember something they needed to do and wandered away when the Gunnery

Sergeant showed up.

Harry's head lolled toward Damon. "Isn't he supposed to call us sir or something?"

"He never does." Damon struggled to his knees. "Come on. I'll buy you a drink."

* * * *

Allie sat alone at the deli wondering where Harry was. Harry was never late, but according to her watch, he was now almost fifteen minutes late. She thought about having him located just as he ran into the restaurant. "Sorry I'm late!"

A strip bandage closed a small cut over Harry's left eye, and the left side of his face had the redness of a new bruise. "Harry, what happened to your face?"

"Oh, um, nothing really. Just a little accident."

"Uh-huh." Allie didn't believe him for a moment. "You look like you've been in a fight."

"Yeah, but you should see the other guy!"

Allie laughed despite herself. "If I'm not going to get a straight answer about that, are you at least all right?"

"Never better, Allie."

She sniffed his breath. "Have you been drinking?"

"Yeah, I, um, had a couple of drinks with a, um, friend."

"Before lunch?"

"Yeah, that was the best time to get together." He stared intently at the menu.

"You're a mess." She knew he was hiding something, but Allie decided he'd tell her in good time. After they'd ordered, she watched him for a few moments and decided he was in a good mood. " Are you free for dinner tonight?"

"Yeah, I am, but aren't you having dinner with Damon?"

Allie stared. She could only remember four times he'd gotten Damon's name right. "My plans have changed."

"Sure. Want to meet at the Café?"

"No, how about my place about 1830?"

"OK. I'll be there with bells on."

She giggled. "What does being there with bells on mean, anyway?" She loved it when he made her laugh.

"You're the historian, so you tell me."

"You're being silly again." She stared at the cut on his forehead for a moment before leaning over the table to run her finger over the bandage. "That looks like it hurts."

"Not too bad, but it was worth it."

"You're not going to tell me about how it happened, are you?"

"Nope."

Their lunch arrived and Harry fell to his slab of beef. "What are you going to feed me tonight?"

She smiled demurely. "You never can tell."

He stopped with his fork halfway to his mouth. "Allie, please don't do that."

"What?"

"Smile at me like that." He set his fork down, his lunch seemingly forgotten for a moment. "Between that kiss, or part of a kiss, yesterday, and you smiling at me like that just now, it's almost more than I can stand."

"I'm not sure I know what you mean. I just looked at you."

"Yeah, but it was a come-hither look."

She wondered if it would look strange for her to slap herself. He'd seen the thoughts she tried to conceal right through her smile. "I didn't know I did that. I'm sorry."

"No, it's me. I'm probably reading things into what you're doing. Forget I said anything."

The rest of lunch was small talk, but Harry seemed, somehow, more distant from her. She hated the feeling.

* * * *

When the doorbell rang at precisely 1800, Allie knew it was Damon. He was nearly as persnickety about punctuality as Harry. She opened the door and he hugged her as he came in. "Hi, Allie." He snuggled to her, nuzzling her hair.

"Hi, yourself." She leaned back in his arms and saw he had a small cut on the corner of his mouth. He also had a slight discoloration on his right jaw. "What happened to you?"

"Oh, that." He rubbed at his jaw. "We had a workout for hand-to-hand combat, and things got a little rambunctious. No harm done."

Allie kissed him softly. "As long as you're all right."

He pulled her to him tightly. "How long before dinner?"

"Not that long! Come have a seat and talk to me while I cook."

Damon walked with her to the dining room and glanced into the kitchen. "Are we supposed to eat all that food?"

"Sort of. We have a guest joining us in about thirty minutes." Allie found she couldn't make eye contact with him.

"Please tell me that it's not one of your parents coming to dinner. Please?"

She laughed. "No, nothing like that." She thought this might a chance to distract him. "You haven't met my folks, have you?"

"Who, me? I'm just a grunt. Ike won't let me close to the Emperor on a bet."

"Ike's easy to get along with."

"No, she's not! She's stopped me in the corridor because my belt buckle wasn't as shiny as she thought it should be. Made me do pushups right there, too!"

"Babe, you outrank her."

"No, I most certainly do not! She's a Master Sergeant. Only your dad outranks her, and he'd best not push his luck. Ike Payne can be a real bitch."

Allie managed to keep him fussing about Ike until the doorbell rang at precisely 1830. Damon stood to answer the door.

"Let me get that, Damon." Allie managed to cut him off. She reached the door and paused to get her nerve up. She pressed the open switch.

Harry stood in the corridor with a court jester's hat on his head, eight or more different colors with bells on the ends of long tassels that jingled when he moved. "Hi! I said I'd have bells on!"

The dread in her faded into hysterical laughter. At least until Damon came to see what the ruckus was about.

Damon stopped in his tracks, looking from Harry to Allie. "I wasn't expecting you as our dinner guest."

Harry's smile faltered, but only for only an instant. "I didn't even know we were having a dinner guest."

Both men looked at Allie.

She managed to get her laughter stopped. "I'm sorry." She looked at Harry's hat and it softly jangled when he moved. "That hat!" The men stood patiently as she laughed again, waiting for her to return to the conversation.

Harry looked at Damon for a moment. "How's the jaw?"

"Sore, but I'll live. How about your head?"

"As long as I don't turn my head too quickly, I can walk a straight line."

Allie's laughter faded as she listened to them. "Wait a minute...Did you do that to him?" She looked at Damon while pointing at Harry.

"Yeah, I guess I did."

She turned to face Harry and pointed at Damon. "And that means you did that to him?"

"Yeah, but just so we were even."

"You two were fighting?" Her fury flared suddenly. "You were fucking fighting? You were fighting over me? A damned pissing contest between schoolboys? What in the fuck were you thinking?"

Damon blinked several times. "It's not like..."

"No! Just shut up! I don't want to hear about it, Damon!" She whirled on Harry. "And you! I thought you'd have the brains not to do something like this!" Allie jabbed her thumb over her shoulder, pointing at Damon. "He's a fucking Marine and I expect him to solve everything by fighting, but you, Harry! Do you have your cranium in rectal storage?"

"Allie, give me a chance to answer! It's not what you think. I went to see Damon today and we talked. After that, we just had a little friendly competition in the ring. We fought, yeah, but we didn't have a fight."

"What are you talking about?" She realized she was screaming and paused a moment to calm herself. When Damon opened his mouth, she held her hand in front of his face. She took a few deep breaths. "All right, then. Who won?"

Damon hesitated for a moment before answering. "It was a draw."

"A draw? You beat the shit out of each other and it was a goddamned draw?" Her voice moved to the screaming end of the spectrum again.

"Allie, just calm down." Harry sighed. "We weren't fighting over you."

"Oh, now there's good news! You were just fighting for the hell of it?"

"Um, yeah, sort of." Allie put her hands on her hips and waited for Damon to go on. "We had a hundred credits riding on the fight."

Suddenly, the idea of them fighting, using a hundred-credit bet as an excuse, coupled with the whipped puppy look on Damon's face and Harry's patient, serious look under the jester's hat struck her as funny. She smiled and shook her head. "All right! Come on in the dining room!" The men sat down and waited until Allie joined them with dinner.

* * * *

The dinner conversation was limited to small talk, but by the end, Allie could see that Damon and Harry no longer looked at each other with hostility. While they weren't the best of buddies, they had spent some time together over drinks in Damon's office and became friendly. She wondered if this change would make her coming task easier or harder.

They went to the sitting room as Harry poured wine for them. Allie deliberately snagged one armchair as Harry took the other and Damon sat on the sofa. She didn't want to be next to either of them right now. That would make what she had to do harder. Harry held up his glass of wine. "To the prettiest and funniest woman I know."

Damon raised his glass as well. "Hear, hear."

The two of them drank. Allie decided she had to do something and now was as good a time as any. She cleared her throat. "I wanted you both here tonight so I could talk to you at the same time. I guess I haven't been very fair to either of you." She sipped at her wine for the fortitude. "Damon, you know I care very deeply for you. Since we met, I've done things I've never done before. You can make me feel safe and protected, and your charms are undeniable. I'm falling in love with you."

She paused for a moment. When Damon started to speak, she held her hand up again. "Harry, I care very deeply for you, too. We haven't been intimate, for whatever reason, but that doesn't mean I care any less for you. You make me laugh so I can forget the world around me. In the bar when the attack came, and with what you did on the OD, you proved that you make a damned good protector, too. I could fall in love with you very easily."

Damon looked at Harry for a moment, and then at Allie. "What's this about?"

"Simply that I need to pick one of you and not continue to see the other." She sipped her wine again nervously. "I'm not being fair to you, Damon, because I haven't committed to you fully, and the same applies for you, Harry." She looked at the men several times. "I need to make it clear who I'm going to be with from now on. I should only be with one man."

Harry nodded. "I thought you had something on your mind at lunch."

"I did. I'm leading both of you on right now, and that's not fair to either you." She laughed softly. "Hell, it's not fair to me. We all need to be clear on what the relationships are." Her laughter belied the tears in her eyes and the sadness in her heart.

"Harry and I talked about this today. We're both ready for whatever you decide."

"He's right." Harry picked up his jester's hat and put it on, the bells ringing joyously in the otherwise somber room. "I'm ready for whatever you decide."

A single tear ran down her face. She wiped at it carelessly. "I said I thought I might be falling for both of you, but the fact is that I do love you both."

Harry looked at Damon. "If she dumps us both, how about a date, big boy?"

Damon chuckled. "Works for me."

Allie smiled. "That's what I mean. You're both wonderful men." She sat watching them both, her eyes moving from one to the other. "Choosing is not easy." Her tears came more often now, but she had to go on. She sipped at her wine again, but found little strength there. Looking at the two men waiting for her words, the weight of her decision hit her again. She didn't want to hurt either of them, but she knew making them wait around for her would hurt them both, but going forward would

hurt one of them deeply.
    She took a deep breath.
    "Harry, I'm sorry." She felt her heart breaking.

Chapter 7

Alone

As Allie stared at the two men she cared about, she began to second guess her decision, a road she knew would lead only to more hurt for all three of them. "Harry, I want you as my friend, but that's all that will ever be." She had to force that through her lips.

Harry's head slumped forward, the bells jingling. He managed a sad smile when he looked at Damon. "Looks like you're off the hook and don't have to date me now."

Damon's expression was unreadable. "I guess so, but I'm not as happy about this as I would have been yesterday. Or early this morning, even."

Allie went to sit on the arm of the chair next to Harry and slipped her arm around his shoulders. "I do care about you, Harry." His hair stuck out from under the jester's hat, hanging in his face and hiding his eyes. Allie gently brushed it aside. "Would it help to say I'm sorry?"

He seemed to gather himself a little, taking a deep breath and letting it blow out through his lips. He looked to Damon. "I don't know. I hope Damon won't mind if we have lunch now and then."

"I don't mind, Harry."

Allie touched his stone-cold cheek. "Don't be sad."

"I'm not, not really anyway." He stood. "I guess I should get out of here. You don't need a third wheel hanging around."

Damon came to where Harry stood. "Harry, stop by tomorrow and we'll go another three rounds." He hesitated a moment. "Somehow, a handshake just doesn't cut it." Damon put his arms around Harry and hugged him.

"That's the first time a Marine has ever hugged me." Harry shifted, looking somewhat disconcerted.

Allie watched Harry's eyes for a moment. "Damon, could we have just a minute?"

"Sure." He put his hand on Harry's shoulder. "Call me." He went to the bedroom.

Allie stared into Harry's eyes and saw the pain. "I am sorry, Harry. I truly am."

"Don't be." He shook his head, and the bells jangled. "See? I'm happy." He paused, carefully studying her face. "All I ask is that you not kiss me now like you did yesterday."

"That wouldn't be a good idea at all."

"I still think you're making a mistake." He smiled for a moment before his face took on a serious look. "And, Allie, I'm always here for you, no matter what."

"I know." She smiled. "You're supposed to do something to make me laugh now."

He smiled and shook his bells again, then used a voice that sounded like an old-time carnival barker. "Welcome back, my friends, to the show that never ends!"

Allie laughed. "I needed that." She watched his face again. She had to know that he would be all right. "How about lunch tomorrow? My treat."

"I'll have to check my schedule." They walked to the door and Harry stared at the open button, like it might bite him. "I should go."

"All right." She took his face in her hands. "Harry, are you OK?"

"Of course." His smile spread slowly over his face and the carnival barker made another appearance. "Rest assured you'll get your money's worth, the greatest show in Heaven, Hell, or Earth!"

"You're a mess, Harry." She kissed his lips gently. "Goodnight."

"Goodnight, my princess." He stepped into the hall and watched her face as the door closed.

* * * *

Harry stood staring at the closed door long enough that the guards just up the corridor at the Emperor's suite started to take notice. He considered kicking the door down. She just made the biggest mistake of her life, proof that the aristocracy had no monopoly on common sense.

One of the guards from the Emperor's suite walked down the hall to where Harry stood. "Can I help you with something, Lieutenant?"

Harry turned to the man and smiled a silly grin as the barker appeared again. "Right before your eyes, we'll pull laughter from the skies, and he laughs until he cries, then he dies, then he dies."

"Sir?" The man shifted his weapon in his arms.

"Nothing, Corporal. Nothing at all." Harry turned and walked away.

He wandered around the ship for a while and finally stopped at an old English pub theme bar in the mall called The Pearlie. Quiet and dark, with old music playing softly, Harry knew no one would bother him. Harry ordered a drink and sat in the back thinking. In all his twenty-nine years, he'd never met a woman like Allie. He probably wouldn't ever meet another. That didn't matter, though. Harry thought Allie made a serious mistake in her choice.

As he thought about things, he realized he was angry. He just didn't know whom he should be mad at. It was Allie's choice, so maybe he should go back and yell at her. Damon was another good target for his anger. Knowing what he was up against, he thought he could take Damon this time in short order.

In just a few hours this morning, he'd gotten to know Damon. A good man, Damon wouldn't hurt Allie, but he wasn't the best man she could have. He'd stand by his decision, as he did all his decisions, but what bothered Harry most was her willingness to settle for Damon when Harry knew he was right for her. She settled for second best, and he couldn't accept that. Allie deserves better.

He wondered what he could do to make her see that. Her reaction to the thinly veiled fight over her proved she wouldn't go for that idea a second time. The ale fogged his mind, but he thought the only option was to show her how good he would be for her.

As he sat drinking and thinking, Harry noticed two young Ensigns at the bar watching him. When he glanced at them, they looked away quickly. He went back to his ruminations. He found himself second-guessing the things he'd done over the last couple of weeks with Allie, trying to find where he made his mistake, where he lost her, but he came up dry. He didn't know what he could have done differently to make tonight go a different way.

Maybe, he thought, he should be angry with himself.

The server brought another drink and he drank deeply from the foamy pint of ale, the slight bitterness feeling good on his tongue, and the creamy bubbles tickling his palate. Harry wondered if seeing Allie as a friend, meeting for lunch tomorrow, was really the best thing for him. He wanted to see her, but he wasn't sure of the impact that would have on him emotionally. It might make things worse. Much worse.

Then again, he had to see her. He couldn't live without seeing her. He wondered if he could live with seeing her.

Harry felt the eyes of the Ensigns on him again. When he glanced their way, one of them stood and walked towards his table. A pretty little thing with short red hair and blue eyes walked to his table. She looked about twenty. "Hi, I'm Cathy. Mind if I sit down?"

"Sure, Cathy, be my guest. I'm Harry."

She sat and reached over the table to shake his hand. "Good to meet you, Harry."

He stared at her for a moment. "Your middle name wouldn't happen to be Allison, would it?"

"Well, no." She laughed. "It's Renee."

"Tough luck." He took a large swallow of his beer. "Cathy, I don't want to be rude, so I need to tell you that I'm not really interested. Frankly, I am, as they say, on the rebound, and I'm here to think and, probably, get totally shit-faced. You seem like a nice girl, but I'm certainly not fit company for a nice girl tonight."

She blinked rapidly at him for a moment. "Oh. I'm, uh, sorry to hear that."

"Thanks. Life's a bitch, though."

"My friends all say I'm a good listener."

Harry smiled at her. "I'm sure they're right, too. Like I said, you seem like a nice girl. You should find a nice guy to spend some time with, not a depressed fuck who is going to sit here getting drunk and melancholy."

"Well, I can see you'd rather be alone, so I'll go." She nodded to where her friend watched from the bar. "If you change your mind, just let me know."

"I will. Goodnight."

She frowned at him for a moment. "OK. Goodnight." She left Harry alone.

He sat alone at his table, drinking and thinking, until the bar closed at 0130.

* * * *

He managed to wake up enough to call Devon and say he wouldn't be in to work today because he felt sick. It wasn't really a lie. Harry's head throbbed, and his stomach tried to do back flips inside of him.

It was almost 1100 when he woke up. When he looked around the bed, empty beer bottles were everyplace, and he saw one empty vodka bottle. He managed to take his clothes off earlier, but the mud from his fall in the playground at the mall was all over the bed.

He sat up. The room spun sharply. He thought it went clockwise. "That was a mistake." He fell back on the bed.

As he lay there waiting for the room to slow down a little, he thought about last night. He didn't normally drink that much, but he made up several years of near abstinence in one evening.

He sighed. How stupid could he be? Yeah, he was mad. No, he was royally pissed off.

How could Allie make such a stupid decision? She was the smartest woman he'd ever met, but she still did dumb things. The only explanation was that she just didn't have all of the facts in hand, or she didn't understand them. At least she didn't yet.

And then there was Damon. Harry thought they might actually become friends. The condescending bastard stood there looking smug and making nice. If he could stand up, Harry thought he would find him and beat him to pulp.

While he tried to think, he knew the hangover made his mind fuzzy. He wasn't thinking right, and that was dangerous anytime. Right now, trying to find a way to turn this fiasco around, it was even more dangerous. He remembered thinking last night that Allie reacted poorly to the fight. In the bloodshot light of his hangover, he knew that was right. Beating Damon senseless would probably send her totally to him.

In their parting comments last evening, Harry thought he saw something there, a little spark of feeling in her still holding out for him.

He wondered if this might be some kind of game. Could she be testing him? Did Allie set this up for him to prove to her his worth? Harry shook his head, and the room didn't jerk as bad as it did earlier. He managed to get to his feet and stumbled to the shower. The cool water cleared his head a little, and he thought about that idea.

He had no way to know if she might be testing him. Or Damon. He had to assume that she wasn't doing that.

He wanted to see her, to tell her what a mistake she made. He didn't know how that might work, though. He didn't think he could keep his hands off of her. And that might be what he saw now as the beginning of the end.

He managed over the weeks to keep his hands to himself. He remembered thinking since Allie slept with Damon, any move on his part would push her away. He sighed as the water ran down his face. He added another tick in the column of things he did that carried the label 'stupid'.

Even if not seducing her was stupid before, it was a good idea now. Allie would see any attempt to get her into bed now as an outright attempt to come between her and Damon. She would run, quickly, in the opposite direction.

He smiled a little as he dried himself. Matching wits with Allie could prove interesting. His intellectual equal, she would see right through most attempts to get her attention. He would need to use extreme care.

* * * *

Allie frowned. She called the Intelligence Office and Henson told her that Harry called out sick today. His file said he never missed a day in is twelve year history in the Fleet. She dialed his home number.

After four rings, he answered, voice only. "Hello?"

She paused and even considered hanging up. "Hi."

He didn't answer for a moment. "Hi, Allie."

"Henson said you called out sick today." She didn't know what to say to him. "Are you OK?"

"Yeah, I'm fine. I just needed a day off."

"I know we had a lunch date, but if you're not up to that, it's OK."

Again he didn't answer for a few seconds. "You know, I think that's a good idea." Another short pause came. "I don't want to infect you."

Allie wished she could see him. His voice sounded cold, but she almost expected that to happen. Despite their comments about being friends and having lunch, she understood fully that he probably didn't want to see her. She knew she shouldn't see him.

The temptations would be too great.

"That's all right." She looked for something to say, but nothing seemed neutral. "I hope you feel better."

He chuckled a little. "I'm sure I will." He paused. "Thanks. Bye for now." He hung up.

She stared at the intercom for a time. Maybe she only imagined it, but he sounded hurt.

And she did it.

* * * *

After talking to Allie, no matter how brief the conversation had been, Harry needed to work off some nervous energy. He decided to go to the gym and work out a little.

The exercise made his hangover feel better. His head cleared even more, and his stomach settled down. As he worked through the tai chi forms, he sensed a disturbance in the chi around him.

Violating every rule, he paused for a moment in his motions and looked around. Damon stood at the edge of the mat, wearing his weight lifting suit and a towel tossed over his shoulder.

Damon hesitated. "I didn't mean to interrupt."

Harry completed the form and drifted away from the remainder. "That's OK."

"How are you?"

Harry walked to the edge of the mat and bowed to the dojo. "Does it really matter?"

"Yeah, it does." Damon hesitated. "Everyone is worried about you."

"Sure they are." Harry laughed as he wiped his face with his towel.

"OK. I'm worried about you."

"I'm fine." A sudden fit of anger tried to rise up inside of him. Harry let his mind feel the flow of chi as he said his mantra.

Damon frowned. "All right. I'm not going to push you. I think Allie is worried about you, too."

His anger swamped him. "I can't imagine why." Harry swallowed. "Tell her thanks for taking care of me while I was blind, and thanks for helping me with the puzzle the day we met. Tell her good old Harry is just fucking wonderful. And tell her thanks—" He paused. He wanted to thank her for breaking his heart. Fuck that. His heart had a dent, not a break. "Right now, you need to get the fuck away from me." He stormed off to the showers, leaving Damon standing on the mat.

* * * *

That went well. At least Harry didn't hit him. Damon decided to go to the garrison to shower. Being close to Harry in the locker room would be a serious mistake right now.

In spite of the rivalry for Allie, he'd come to like Harry. As he walked to the garrison, he figured that he and Harry could never be friends, though. Maybe, he thought, in a few months, Harry would forget, or at least learn to cope. He doubted that, somehow.

He knew Allie's decision made him happy. He wondered about her feelings, though. She was attentive and they made love a few times last night, but no matter what he did, she didn't climax. She didn't even fake an orgasm.

She didn't sleep well, either. She tossed and turned in the bed, enough that she woke him up twice. This morning, the sheets were a tangled mass. Allie smiled at all the right times, and she carried on a conversation over breakfast, but he could tell she had other things on her mind.

Right now, the day after effectively dumping Harry, he could let it all slide. Of course she felt bad about what she did. Of course she worried about Harry. After a suitable amount of mourning, if things went on, he would do something. Right now, he didn't know what that might be, but he would do something.

* * * *

He sat in his cubical for a long time just staring at the latest batch of intercepted communications. He couldn't concentrate on them

He had a plan, though.

Actually, it wasn't at all new, just a slight twist on the old plan. He could be Allie's friend. He could even have lunch with her once in a while. Maybe even join her and Damon for dinner now and then.

He was right from the very start. She didn't belong to Damon. She belonged to him. She just didn't know it yet. Nothing had really changed. All he needed to do was let her figure that part out for herself. She might need a little gentle prodding here and there, but he could do that in a way that neither she nor Damon would see as a threat.

This called for care, though. If he pushed too hard, she would back away. If he really pushed too hard, Damon would figure it out and another fight would be sure to start. If he didn't push hard enough, it could take years.

He was ready to wait years for her if he had to, but sooner would be much better than later.

Devon came to his cubicle and leaned against the wall. "Feeling better today?"

"Actually, I am."

"What's new on the relationship front?"

"Oh, she dumped me for the jarhead night before last."

Devon blinked a few times. "I'm sorry to hear that."

"Don't be. It's a temporary thing."

"What?"

"Yeah, we'll be back together soon."

"Why do I feel like I've missed something here?"

"Because you always miss something."

Devon nodded. "All right. You seem pretty chipper for a guy who just got dumped."

"Like I said, it's just a temporary setback."

He shrugged. "OK. By the way, you owe me one."

"For what?"

"Dalton didn't want to approve your leave request for Friday, but I reminded him that he owes you for breaking that last big code."

"Great! Thanks!"

"No worries. What do you have planned?"

"I'm not sure yet, but it will be fun."

He nodded. "Great. I need to get back to work." Henson left him alone in his cubicle.

* * * *

She sat staring at the intercom again. Harry had just invited her and Damon to dinner Friday evening. When she told him that Damon had some things going on and couldn't make dinner, Harry suggested they all meet for lunch. Damon again was busy, so Harry asked her to meet him at the Café.

She expected him to ask her to lunch or dinner soon. Now, nearly two weeks after she told him that she would commit to Damon, this was the first time she heard from him. And he'd bent over backwards to have Damon with them.

She knew Harry well enough to understand that despite his sometimes-flighty behavior, he never did anything without understanding the impact fully. He didn't lack spontaneity, far from that. Even when he did something spontaneous, he understood the impact of every little word and action. Just like Tanya.

She wondered what he thought about this. She shrugged. Harry wanted to show her and Damon that he accepted the situation. That was all.

She frowned at herself, thinking about her reaction when he called. Her heart only now slowed a little, approaching a normal speed. A few trails of sweat ran down her brow, and another bead traced its way down her chest between her breasts.

She thought she'd done pretty well over the last two weeks. She managed to think about Harry only three or four times a day. She only masturbated one or two times while she thought about him. And he only once filled her mind when Damon made love to her.

Her first reaction was to turn him down for lunch. When she called Damon to ask if he could join them, he encouraged her to go, though. If Damon thought going to lunch with Harry was OK, she knew she just was borrowing trouble. Besides, they would be at public place.

She had to keep herself under control, though. Maybe Harry adjusted after two weeks, but she didn't. She made her choice, and now she had to stick to it. She knew she could. It would be hard, yes, but she could do it.

Maybe she wasn't ready to admit to Damon that she loved him, but she recognized the feelings of freefall that gripped her.

* * * *

This might work out. Harry planned to have Allie and Damon join him for dinner Friday evening, but Damon's duty schedule made him drop back to punt. When he suggested lunch, that wouldn't work for Damon either.

He improvised. Allie would meet him Friday at the Café for lunch.

The change from having both of them with him to just Allie alone made little difference. He would be casual and friendly. No suggestions, no pressure. Allie needed to relax so she could think. If he let her think, she would see the error of her ways.

* * * *

Other than staring at her picture, seeing her lovely face in his dreams, and fantasizing while he jacked off, Harry hadn't seen Allie more than twice in two weeks. As she walked toward him across the Café, his heart tried to climb out of his throat. He hoped she would walk slower. It would take some time to get his breathing slowed enough to be able to speak to her.

If anything, and if it was possible, she looked even prettier than in his dreams.

She wore a very conservative pair of jeans and a loose blouse. Thank God for small favors.

She stopped at the table and smiled at him as he stood. He thought she made a move to hug him, but he cut her off and shook her hand. His

The Polyamorous Princess

arm tried to fall off when the jolt hit his shoulder.

"Hi, Harry. How are you?"

"I'm good. I can see you're OK, but how's Damon?"

He held her chair as she sat down, then sat across from her. "He's busy, but good."

They ordered drinks and lunch quickly. "I'm glad to hear that." He chuckled. "Should I even ask about your class?"

When she laughed, his eyes tried to cross. He missed hearing her laugh every day, and seeing the smile that went with it. It wouldn't be long, though. "They have good days and bad days." She smiled. "Mostly bad, though."

"That's what you get for being a teacher."

"I'm not really a teacher. I'm a historian. I just got stuck teaching because no one else can do it."

"You're right about that. I'd love to take one of your classes, just to see if you're as good at teaching as I think you are." He slapped himself mentally. Too much!

"I'm glad someone has faith in me." She laughed. "What have you been up to?"

She didn't seem to notice. "Working, mostly. Your dad has a lot of puzzles for me to solve." He paused. "I can't even imagine how hard it is to be involved with someone like Damon or I. I guess that applies to anyone in the military right now, because we're all so busy."

Allie nodded at him. "Yeah, I do end up sitting alone at home a lot."

"That's too bad. I know that even when I'm home, I spend all my time sleeping so I can get back to work."

"Damon does the same thing." She stared at him for a moment. "Are you seeing anyone?"

This is not where he wanted her to go. The road ahead had about a million landmines, and he only knew where about six of them lay hidden. "No, not really. Not enough time." He smiled and calculated the risk. "Not enough time to see them, and not enough time since you."

She blushed a little. Rebecca bringing lunch gave Allie longer to think than he thought was wise.

Allie smiled. "Well, that's the girl's loss."

"Maybe it is."

They ate in silence, just small talk for a while. After she finished, Allie excused herself.

* * * *

She splashed her face with cold water and stared at herself in the mirror. This was harder than she thought it would be. The old feelings kept coming back, and she kept slapping them down again.

Maybe she couldn't be a friend to Harry, but she wanted to be friends with him. She liked him because he was fun.

Maybe she liked him too much.

In fact, she liked him too much to do anything other than tell him.

She splashed her face again and went back to the table.

* * * *

He smiled as she came back to the table. Her facial expression looked hard and firm, and she walked with a slight stiffness to her motions. She must have decided something when she was in the ladies' room. She sat while he held her chair.

Allie took a deep breath and seemed to square her shoulders a little. "Harry, this isn't going to work."

He frowned a little. "What's that?"

"Seeing you for lunch and things."

He nodded. "Tell me why not."

"It just won't." When she looked up at him, he saw the battle she fought in her eyes. "Maybe the three of us can get together sometimes, but this won't work."

"You may not believe me, but I do understand." He shrugged. "This is more than a little uncomfortable for me, too."

She sat staring at him for a long time. "I'm glad you understand."

He nodded. Harry pulled his credit card from his pocket and ran it through the scanner at the table. "I do. I'll get out of your hair now." He stopped beside her chair. "Call if you need anything." He left without touching her.

As he walked from the club, Harry thought this went perfectly.

Chapter 8

Recovery

In the week since Allie had lunch with him, Harry managed to resist calling her. He and Damon had met for lunch a couple of times in that period. Tonight, they met for a couple of drinks at The Pearlie.

"How's Allie?"

Damon sipped at his ale. "She's OK, I guess."

"That didn't sound too enthusiastic."

"She just seems a little distant. Maybe worried about you."

"She shouldn't be. You know I'm fine." Harry paused. "And so does she." He smiled. "She's not fucking you, is she?"

"Um, not exactly."

"What's that mean?"

"It means that she's going through the motions...Shit! This is none of your business!"

"Probably not, but misery loves company. If I'm not getting any, why should you?" Harry grinned. "Besides, if I can't fuck her, at least I can hear about you fucking her." Despite trying to sound funny, Harry found he really did want to hear about Allie being naked and fucking.

Damon smiled. "If I didn't like you so much, I'd knock your goddamned head off."

"And lose another hundred credits?"

"Well, there is that part, yeah."

"Damn right there is." Harry watched the serving wench delivering drinks at the next table. "She's pretty."

"I hadn't noticed."

"Bullshit, Damon. You're in a committed relationship, but you're not dead."

"I guess that's true." He glanced at the wench as she went by the table.

"You know that Allie is prone to multiple marriages." He had no idea why he brought this up. Harry had less of an idea what to do now that he had.

"If it's in the blood, yeah she is. You won't hear me argue about bringing another woman to bed."

"What if it's another man?"

Damon coughed beer through his nose. "What?"

"Seriously. There's a fifty-fifty chance of that."

"I guess I hadn't thought of that."

"Yeah. She and her family don't think in terms of multiple marriages. They call it a polyamorous marriage."

"She told me that, but maybe I'm too much of a knuckle-dragger to get the idea."

Harry sipped his ale. "I guess it's not an easy concept. The gist is that everyone in the marriage is in love with everyone else. Like any love, that means there's sex, too."

"I guess I can see that. Would the men have sex?"

"Yeah, I'd think so. I think Allie's brother is in a marriage with some other men and they don't have sex."

"Oh, yeah! She told me about him. Three men and three women, but the men only have sex with the women and the women only with the men."

"That's the one. I gather that the others are like her folks, where everyone has sex with everyone else."

"I guess that makes more sense." Damon sipped his drink again.

"Damned if I know. Allie said, and I believe her, that it's not about sex."

"Right. It's about love. I don't know, Harry."

"What?"

"I'm not sure I'd want to share Allie with anyone, man or woman."

"Don't feel bad. I'd feel the same way."

"Don't get all melancholy on me."

"I didn't do anything!"

"No, but you headed that way."

"Maybe." Harry nodded toward the bar. "Want some company?"

Damon followed his gaze to the two Ensigns at the bar. "I'm in that, what did you call it? Committed relationship."

"Yeah, but for me to get lucky, you have to entertain her friend long enough for me to get Cathy out of here. Then dump the other one." Harry grabbed the wench as she went by and told her to get the two girls a drink on him.

"I see what you're up to, Harry."

"What?"

"You'll wait for Allie to kill me and then go to console her."

"Good idea." The Ensigns walked to the table and Harry stood. "Cathy! Good to see you again."

"Hi, Harry. Thanks for the drinks. This is Beth."

"Beth, good to meet you. This strapping young Marine is Damon." Harry held a chair for Cathy.

Damon jumped up suddenly and did the same for Beth. "Um, good to meet you both."

"You seem in a better mood tonight, Harry."

"I am, and I wanted to apologize for being so down before. I didn't mean to be rude, Cathy. I just didn't want to infect you with my black mood."

The four talked for a couple of hours, but Harry noticed Damon at a loss for words most of the time. He persuaded Cathy to go for a walk, leaving Damon holding the bag to get rid of Beth.

* * * *

Damon wasn't used to having a face-to-face meeting with officers much higher than a Lieutenant Colonel or the occasional full bird Colonel. It wasn't unusual when some kind of combat operations were in the planning stages, but he'd heard nothing about any actions coming. If there was a problem with administration, he'd be taking to Captain James or maybe Major Elder to work out the administrative details.

He now sat in Admiral Q's private office with Major General

Dietrich. The last time he talked face-to-face with Dietrich, they planned a covert mission to rescue a Samulian operative from a group of terrorists. The General always handled combat matters personally.

As Fleet Admiral, Q answered only to the Emperor himself. Q seemed to study him for a moment. "General Dietrich tells me that your team is the best we have, Lieutenant. Is that true?"

"Yes, Sir. If you've got a tough job, we're the people to do it right."

"Son, save us the gung-ho speeches." The General relaxed in his chair. "We've got a tough job, and we need to make sure it gets done with a minimum loss of life. Can you do that?"

"Sir, I don't have enough information to answer that, other than to say that we'll get the job done with a minimum loss of Marines. I can't promise you how many of the fur balls might go home in a kitty litter box."

Q leaned on his desk. "This is ultra-secret, Lieutenant. I know that you and Princess Allison are involved, but not even she is to know any of this. Is that perfectly clear?"

"Yes, Sir."

"We have reason to believe there is valuable information about the enemy on the outer moon of Arup. The moon is heavily armed and garrisoned, but we need that information." Q leaned back in his chair and put his feet up on the desk. "We want you to get it."

"What Q isn't saying is that this operation is dangerous and *Boone* won't provide much help. The team and its landing craft going in, getting the information, and getting out is the order of the day." Dietrich sighed. "Like all covert operations, we're looking for a purely voluntary team."

Damon considered saying no, but only for an instant. There was no dishonor in declining these types of missions, but fourteen years of being a Marine plus uncounted years of his family being Marines wouldn't let him refuse. "Understood, General. You've got your team."

Q laughed quietly. "You speak very freely for your team, Hyde."

"Yes, Sir, because I know my people, each and every one of them. They're with this a hundred percent." Damon looked from the Admiral to the General and back again. "If the Empire and Emperor needs us, we're there."

The General looked at Q. "I think he'll do just fine, Q."

"I have to agree with you, Ben." Q put his feet on the floor and leaned over the desk. "Lieutenant, the job is yours. Remember, not a word to anyone, not even your team for now. Ben will get with you for the details very soon."

* * * *

Allie waited for Damon when he got to her cabin. A forest fire of candles she'd set all around the suite met him when he entered. She had turned the lights completely off. Only the flickering of the candlelight illuminated the room. Allie wore her long robe. She signaled the door to close as she slipped her arms around his waist and kissed him softly. "Hi, babe."

"Hi. What's all this about?"

She kissed him again. "I think I owe you a little romance."

"Well, whatever the reason, this is nice."

Allie pulled his face to hers, kissing him passionately. He tasted amazing tonight. "Come on, let's get you changed and showered." She led him to the bedroom and undressed him, touching him as she went. She slipped her robe from her shoulders, tossing it on the bed, and then led Damon to the shower. The warm water ran down her as she soaped his body.

He hugged her gently. "This is great, Allie."

"Yeah, it is." She ran her hands down his chest to massage his hard cock, stroking the full length over and over using the excuse of washing him. She watched his face as she rubbed his balls, the soap making her hands slippery as she rolled them between her fingers.

Damon reached around and grabbed her ass, pulling her towards him. She took his wrists and moved his hands back to her sides. "Not yet."

"Tell me that you're kidding."

"I'm not. Can't you wait to touch me?" She ran her nails up and down his chest, circling his nipples as the water flowed over his skin.

"I'm not sure." He blinked at her several times. "You're so beautiful, Allie."

"I like to hear you say that. Come on. Dinner's waiting." She dried him from head to toe, then held his robe as he slipped into it. Allie took his hand and walked with him to the dinning room. "I just have to grab things from the kitchen." She kissed him, running her tongue deeply into his mouth, tasting him. "Be right back."

They sat across from each other eating and Allie watched him. She could tell he had something other than her on his mind, but she planned to correct that problem very soon. When he'd look up at her, Allie couldn't stop the soft smile that came to her face. The expression on his face said love to her, and she could feel her heart melting.

After dinner, they sat together on the sofa, music playing low, and kissed like a pair of teenagers in the backseat of their parent's car. Allie pulled away from his face, her breath panting and her pulse hammering in her ears. "Damn it."

She could see the boyishness in him, his eyes soft, honest, and trusting. Allie kissed his lips tenderly. She stood and let her robe fall to the floor. She took his hands in hers. "Dance with me." When he stood, Allie pushed the robe from Damon's shoulders and it joined hers on the floor. Kissing him passionately, she slipped her arms around his neck and moved to the music, rubbing against him firmly.

Something about his flavor put her desire in high gear tonight. Allie wasn't sure what it was, at least not exactly. Maybe the mood she created with the candles and the shower fired her passion. She knew it might be the soft music and the wine they shared over dinner. The smell of his skin, a little musky and full of masculine overtones made another good option.

Allie licked his lips, and she knew it was just his taste. Fresh from the shower, he tasted clean and free from perspiration. His cologne had washed down the drain as well. All that she tasted as her tongue fluttered across his face was Damon. The part of her mind that still worked wondered what delightful blend of biochemistry could create such a compound that could whip her into such frenzy. Despite humanity spending all of history searching, no one had yet to create an artificial aphrodisiac able to do what the human body did with no effort at all.

She could feel Damon's erection responding to her, sliding against her body as they danced. Her passions rose, her desire driving her to him. As her tongue darted in his mouth, his hand moved to her neck, pulling her face to his with an almost painful intensity.

They kissed and danced for many minutes, their bodies rubbing together, when he suddenly lifted her in his strong arms and carried her to the armchair, sitting with her in his lap. Still kissing, Damon's hand slipped to the spreading wetness of her pussy. He squeezed her labia together between his fingers and palm, rolling her clit firmly with the actions. His finger darted effortlessly between the lips, plunging deeply into her core, rubbing over her secret places, driving Allie's passions into a tizzy. She tried to wiggle from his embrace to straddle him, but Damon held her fast. He pulled his lips away from hers. "No, babe. Just relax."

She laughed a little. "You expect me to relax?" He only smiled, and then slammed his lips to hers again. Her body shook as a fog of desire fell over mind. His fingers darted in and out of her flowing cunt and across her clit, and Allie writhed in his lap. As Damon slipped a finger into her ass, she jumped with the sudden added pleasure, her eyes flashing open for a moment, but seeing only his closed eyes mere millimeters from hers. His digits worked in her holes as his thumb pressed on her clit, sending quakes of ecstasy through her body.

His arms closed around her and Damon lifted her from his lap a little. His hand slipped from her pussy and ass, and then he slowly guided the head of his stiff cock into her ass. He lowered her slowly onto him, his length gliding smoothly into her. His fingers returned to darting into her cunt, rubbing both her wet pussy and his dick through the thin skin separating them, his thumb again rubbing her clit. Allie's screams of pleasure became inarticulate grunts with her face still locked to his face as she bit his lips and sucked his tongue.

Without warning, Allie's orgasm slammed her between the eyes. She tried to pull her lips from his, not only to scream, but also to avoid biting his tongue off, as Damon plunged it deeply into her mouth. He held her tightly, his kiss feeding her climax, and she could only jerk and shake in his arms as his tongue filled her mouth, his fingers probed her contracting pussy, and his steel-like cock bounced in her ass.

Allie lost count of the number of times he brought her to the edge of orgasm, only to let her slip away again. She had no more of an idea of how many times Damon drove her over the edge. Her body wracked with spasms as she grunted and moaned her screams against his fiery lips as he kissed her continuously for what seemed like hours. He managed not to cum in her ass, but finally, as Allie's latest climax in a long string made her bounce, his body shook violently, and his hot seed exploded into her ass, filling her and squirting around his shaft. As their mutual seizure of love subsided, he allowed Allie to pull her mouth from his, as his softening cock slipped from her ass. She saw his lips red and chapped, probably as red as her own. She managed a weak smile. "Fuck."

"Are you all right?"

"Never better." She kissed the end of his nose. "What brought that on?"

"I don't know." He shrugged a little.

She watched his face for a moment. "Damon, I'm sorry for being so...Whatever I've been the past few weeks."

"No, Allie. Please, never feel sorry for caring about people."

"That's a lot sweeter and a lot more understanding than a big, tough Marine is supposed to act."

"Maybe.

* * * *

Allie's frustration at teaching her class today was doubly high. First, her students seemed stuck on stupid today and couldn't answer even the simplest questions about their assignment. She doubted that most of them even knew their own names today. Second, her ass hurt a little from having Damon's cock fuck her for more than an hour and a half last night. Every time she'd think about her ass being sore, the memories would set off tingles all over her body and she'd lose her place in the lecture.

She finished the lecture and gathered her notes, deciding to go to the Café for lunch. She sighed as she closed her briefcase and resigned herself to having lunch alone today. When she stepped from the lecture hall, Harry almost ran her down. Allie squeaked a small scream of surprise. "Harry!"

"I didn't think I would catch you! At the last minute, I got free for lunch, and I hoped you might be free, too."

She smiled at him broadly, unable to stop the feeling of happiness upon seeing him. "For you, anytime. I planned to go to the Café, if that's all right with you." Despite the tingles in her body, Harry made them more intense. In spite of spending the lest three and a half weeks telling herself this was a bad idea, she liked seeing him.

"Sure!" He held his arm out to her and took the briefcase from her hand. "Shall we go?"

As they walked to the Café, Allie sensed him on edge about something. She decided to wait until they reached the restaurant before broaching the subject and stuck to small talk along the way. "This is a great surprise. I thought I'd have to eat alone today."

"Not if I can help it." They reached the Café and found a table. "You look nice today."

"Thanks." She'd worn an old pair of jeans and a simple blouse. His compliment had its usual effect, making her shiver. Rebecca, the waitress, took their orders. "You act like you've got something on your mind."

"I guess I do. I should know better than to try hiding things from you."

"Yeah, you should. What's up?"

"Nothing I can talk about, I'm afraid. All that cloak and dagger stuff, you know."

She studied him for a moment. "Well, all right. Damon is all nervous about something, too."

"Oh? Did he say what?"

"No, other than to say he couldn't tell me about it."

Harry laughed. "See what you get for hanging around with military types?"

"Yeah, I deserve it. What I don't understand is that I have a higher security clearance than Damon and probably the same as you."

"Nope. I checked and mine is three levels above yours."

She threw her napkin at him. "Ass. If Damon knows, why can't I know?" The genuine laughter Harry always managed to pull from her felt wonderful.

"We don't even know if Damon and I are talking about the same thing."

"That's true. Damn it."

"You'll just have to live without knowing this secret, Allie."

"Do I have to like it?"

"No, not at all."

Allie sipped at her root beer and smiled demurely over the glass at him. "You know I could make you tell me." As soon as she said it, the tingles in her ass and her body returned. She cursed vehemently at herself, too.

"I'd like to think you're wrong, but the fact is, I'm not sure you couldn't."

"You know I'd never do something like that."

"Yeah, damn it to hell."

Allie still laughed as Rebecca brought their lunches. Allie stared at the salad Harry had ordered for a moment. "By the way, what's with the rabbit food?"

"I'm beginning to think that we may all live through this war and I should follow your lead and take better care of myself."

"Really?"

"Yeah." He grinned. "Besides, I have to outlive Damon."

* * * *

After Harry walked her home, Allie sat in her suite wondering about what bothered both him and Damon. Last night, Damon had been a little tense despite the romantic mood she set and the many times they made love throughout the evening. Something was afoot, but Allie didn't know what.

She could deduce a little about the situation. It obviously had something to do with the war and involved both Fleet and the Marines. The fact that Harry had a hand in it meant it probably involved something covert. The combination troubled her.

In a straight out assault, Boone would provide plenty of ground forces, air support, and heavy bombardment. In a covert operation, a small group with little, if any, support would do it all alone. When she queried the ship's computers, Allie found that covert operations actually had a better survival rate than full assaults.

Allie still sat contemplating the goings on when Damon walked through the door. He came up behind her and hugged her, kissing her cheek. "Hi."

"Hi, babe. How did your meetings go?"

"OK, I guess." He fidgeted, shuffling around behind her.

"Come over here and sit with me." He circled the sofa and sat next to her. "I had lunch with Harry and he's as nervous as you are. Can you tell me what's going on?"

He nodded. "Actually, I can, at least a little of it." Q gave permission for him to tell Allie about the mission in general.

Allie stared at him and saw dread on his face. "What's wrong?"

"Nothing, at least not yet." He took a deep breath and let it out slowly through his teeth. "I'm leading a team to one of the Arupian moons to recover some information that we need. Everyone thinks the information is important, but what pushed me over the edge is that Harry thinks it' vital. He's gathered some other information that points to what we're going after."

Her heart dropped into her feet. "A covert operation, then?"

"Yeah. We need to get in and out with a small team."

"How small?"

"Counting me, twelve."

Allie stared. Twelve people made a ridiculously small team. "As I understand it, those moons are heavily guarded." She could feel a rising tide of dread in her.

"Very. Gabe and I are taking two Corporals and eight others. We can do it, Allie."

"I don't know anything about what you do, but that doesn't sound like very fair odds to me." She found her hands shaking and her breath came short.

"But they are good odds." He took her hand in his. "A small team can get in faster than a larger one, and we do a snatch and grab on what we need and have a chance to get out before the heavy stuff shows up."

Allie had a feeling in her stomach that she didn't like. "Damon, I don't want you to do this."

"I know, but I have to do it. My team is the best, and we're the only ones who can do this."

"I didn't tell you not to do it. I just don't want you to do it." She struggled for a minute with the tears that threatened her and won. "So when is this happening?"

"Tomorrow. We leave at 1300."

She sighed. "Tomorrow. Shit."

"I'm sorry I couldn't tell you sooner."

"That's not important." She thought for a moment. "You said Harry thinks it's important."

"Yeah, he does."

"What has he said about the odds?" She didn't really want to know.

"He's not a combat officer."

She pressed on anyway. "That's not what I asked."

Damon smiled. "He said he has no clue."

Her laugh sounded like a bark. "What do you think the odds are?"

"I don't know."

Allie looked deep into his eyes. "Damon, I told you once never lie to me."

"I feel pretty optimistic about it. There are always things that can go wrong, but a small team moving fast is the best chance." He paused for a moment. "If I had to pick a number, we may get a couple of injuries, but not much more than that."

Allie looked at Damon for a long time, tears streaming down her face. "If you die, I'm going to be really pissed off."

Chapter 9

Black Ops

At 0800, Damon put the team of select Marines through a final exercise in the holographic simulator. The team learned today for the first time what their target would be. The two squads under the command of Corporals Harden and Sanchez were sharp, as sharp as knives. Armed to the teeth for the operation, each Marine would carry more than fifty kilos of weaponry and equipment. Gabe came to where Damon watched the team preparing to blow an armored airlock door. "I think they're as ready as they'll ever be, Damon."

"They look good. Well done."

"Thanks." Gabe watched as the door exploded outward from its frame. "How's Allie?"

"Not too good." He checked his watch. "I'm going to spend some time with her before we shove off."

"Good idea." Gabe nodded at the Marines who neutralized a swarm of simulated Arupians who responded to the explosion. "The kids will need some time, too."

"Give it to them." Damon considered the Gunnery Sergeant. "What about you?"

"I'm going to clean my weapon." He smiled. "I got a cat hunt to go to."

* * * *

Damon held. He could feel her in his arms, moving from gentle tears to racking sobs. "Allie, let's sit down." He lifted her in his arms and carried her to the sofa, sitting down next to her. "Everything will be all right."

"I wish I knew that." She wiped at her eyes with her fists. "Damon, I don't feel good about this at all."

"The team is sharp and we're ready. No one else is worried."

"I wish I had your confidence."

"Things will work out."

As he watched, he saw Allie consider something, her brow wrinkled in thought. "If I thought for a moment that it would work, I'd tell you not to go."

"I have to do this." He brushed his hand over her cheek. "This is really important, and I have to do this job, not only for the Empire and your dad, but also for you."

"I know." A small smile came to her face. "You're too fucking gallant for your own good."

"Maybe I am." He kissed her forehead.

"How long will this all take?"

"It's not quite a day transit time each way, so maybe three or four days, but that's variable." He watched her. Her hands trembled. Her eyes darted around the room. "Allie, there's something I want to say to you before I go."

She wiped at her tears. "What's that?"

He took a deep breath, hoping he could get through the words. "I'm in love with you. I think I have been for a long time now."

She stared at him, but her tears slowed a little. "You are?"

"Yeah, I am." He thought about how she made him happy, and how she filled his life and thoughts each and every moment. "If you want the magic words, I love you."

She smiled and hugged his neck tightly. "I'm glad I'm not the only one to feel that way. I'm in love with you, too." She sighed. "This is a fine time to figure this out, though."

She just held him for a time. "How long do we have before you need to go?"

"About two and a half hours."

She nodded her head. "You probably have other plans, but would you mind if we sat here and you hold me?"

"That's just fine with me. In fact, that's fantastic."

She snuggled closer to him. "Thank you."

"Never thank me for loving you."

They cuddled together on the sofa until Damon had to leave at noon. She stood at the door with him. "Remember, you have someone to come home to now."

"I won't forget." He smiled a little as he remembered. "You know, just a day or two after we met, Gabe told me that if you're special to me, I needed to keep my head on tight because you'd be worth coming home to. He's right."

"Smart man." Her tears rolled down her face, and she didn't attempt to even wipe them away. "I love you."

"I love you." Damon blinked back his own tears. "I'll see you in a few days."

"Count on it."

He kissed her lips and hugged her to him. He couldn't think of anything else to say, so he kissed her forehead and left for the hanger deck with his tears only barely at bay.

* * * *

"This is the latest we have on images, maps, and all the rest for the moon." Harry handed the folder to Damon. "Right now, we see about five hundred Arupians at the records facility you're going to, but there are about ten times that many less than ninety minutes away, and they could have fifty thousand cats there in about a day."

"What you're telling me is that we need to get the righteous fuck out of there in a hurry." Damon smiled at him.

"Exactly. Once they know you're there, you're going to have a lot of company in a hurry." Harry considered. "You're the knuckle-dragger, but if they see you on the way in, you're fucked."

"Right." Damon seemed to think for a moment.

"Harry, if this doesn't go the way we hope, make sure Allie's all right, will you?"

"Things are going to be fine so long as you keep your head down. I'll look after her while you're gone, though."

"I'm serious, Harry. If I don't make it back, please take care of her."

Harry felt tears in his eyes, stinging him. He managed to blink them back. He didn't want to think of Damon not coming back. "OK, I'll do that, just to keep you from getting all melancholy." Harry smiled. "That's my gig, remember?"

"Yeah, I remember. Thanks." Gabe and the rest of the team came onto the hanger deck. "Well, looks like my dates are here."

"Looks that way." Harry put on his best silly grin as the landing party surrounded them. "I've heard that rubbing the head of a long-haired Fleet officer is good luck."

Gabe laughed. "We don't need any fucking luck, but we'll take it anyway." He rubbed Harry's head. As the other ten Marines filed by, each repeated the action.

Damon laughed as the procession went by, leaving Harry's hair in more disarray than normal. "Allie's right. You are a mess."

"I guess I am." Harry stood for a moment, watching the Marines gather at the ramp to the landing craft. "Well, you're on." He gave up fighting the impulse and grabbed Damon, hugging him tightly, his rival and yet his friend. "Just get the job done and get back here."

Damon hugged Harry just as tightly. "We will. Thanks for everything."

Harry forced himself to let go of Damon and stepped back. His hand came up to a salute. "Godspeed, Lieutenant."

Damon returned the salute. "Thank you, Lieutenant."

* * * *

Damon approached the waiting team and Gabe shouted, "Officer on deck!"

The team snapped to attention. "As you were. This is it, people. Just like any war, this one comes down to a grunt and a gun. We're going in to get information, but there's a bunch of pussycats waiting to meet us, so we'll all get plenty to kill. Remember your training, and listen to your squad leader, Sergeant Williams, and to me. You will get home alive.

Watch your buddy, watch your back, and watch your ass." He surveyed his team. "All right, let's move out, Hellriders!"

"Hyde's Hellriders! Oohrah!"

Gabe ran up the ramp of the landing craft. "Come on, you apes! Do you want to live forever?"

Damon looked around the hanger deck. Harry stood next to the field control officer and waved. Damon raised his hand and then turned and went up the ramp.

* * * *

Harry watched as the landing craft slipped through the air shield and into space. Damon and his team headed for whatever fate held in store for them. Harry found the cracks in Damon's bravado just before he left troublesome. They both knew that this type of operation had a high probability of success. In and out fast before the enemy even knows you're there, it was hard to get killed. Still, things went wrong in war. He turned and left hanger deck. He wondered how he would handle things if this went terribly wrong.

Over the last few days, since he'd found the message hinting at what secrets the moon might hold, Harry wondered if risking the lives of these twelve brave men and women would be worth the potential it seemed to promise. Harry convinced his mind the risks had justification, but his heart had doubts. Those doubts chewed at him more when he learned Damon would lead the team. Cold, hard facts drove intelligence, not emotions and feelings. The mission would go on, with Damon leading it, and Harry had to cope with his emotions, knowing the facts backed his decisions.

Just like things have always been in war, Harry knew that the objectives held far more importance than the people sent by the commanders to achieve them. Even though Harry had no command training beyond the basics given to all officers, he understood the need to sacrifice a few people to save millions. Q, Dietrich, the Emperor, and other high-level commanders knew it, too. That didn't mean that anyone liked it.

His feelings for Allie made him have reservations. No matter the odds, he worried about the effect Damon's possible death would have on her. She loved Damon and losing him would devastate her. Harry had never turned away from facts, no matter how hard to deal with or understand. Facts made up his trade, and the facts proved Harry liked Damon. He had come to care about Damon. Despite his tough exterior, Damon had a kind, caring streak he tried, not very successfully, to hide.

Since getting to know Damon, Harry found it easy to understand what Allie saw in him, and why she decided to focus on Damon in her life as a lover.

* * * *

Damon slept well on the cutter, as did all the Marines, after taking the sleeping pills the medic passed around. He'd led the team in a few calisthenics to loosen up, and everyone now checked over their gear. Only two hours remained before landing.

The plan called for the cloaked landing craft to drop the team about five kilometers from the objective, a records facility in the center of a small crater on the moon. The landing craft would then lift off and go to a long-period orbit of the moon on autopilot. After meeting the objective, they would recall the landing craft. Then back to *Boone*.

Simple enough on paper, the problem came in that between the LZ and the objective was five klicks of airless lunar landscape and five hundred Arupian troops. Arupians had descended from a desert-dwelling cat. Huge, most well over 250 centimeters and massing a staggering 200 kilograms, they easily occupied the space of two men. Covered with blue-gray fur except for the palms of their hands, around their eyes, around their Chinese-fan-like ears, and their short stubby tail, Arupians looked like big Russian Blue cats. The blue-gray skin not covered by the fur looked like suede. Their oval eyes, like an Earthly cat's but turned on its side, ran the gamut of possibilities of colors. The most frightening part from a combat view was that Arupians had claws. The fingers had dagger-like retractable claws, each five centimeters long and sharp enough to shred human flesh. With the muscle of a fully-grown Arupian warrior behind the claws, they could puncture body armor.

Damon absently cleaned his automatic grenade-launching rifle as he wondered about Allie. He hoped she had adapted a little to his absence. He could count on Harry to look after her, though.

Harry. An interesting man, nothing less than brilliant, Harry was about as eccentric as a person could get without being crazy. Damon knew Harry loved Allie at least as much as he himself did, but he knew he could trust Harry around her and not worry about Harry making a move. Not while he was alive. He and Harry had become far too close in the last couple of months for that kind of thing to happen. Damon had several worries about Allie, though. She loved Harry, despite her insistence that they were only friends. How much she loved Harry was open to speculation, but she had picked Damon, so that counted for something.

He finished assembling the AGLR and loaded the weapon with 12-millimeter explosive rounds and grenades. He trusted Allie and knew she wouldn't change her mind.

* * * *

"Five minutes to LZ, Admiral."

Q nodded to the Science Officer. "Thank you. Weapons, are you seeing any indication the Arupians have seen the landing craft?"

"No, Sir. No unusual ship movement and no unusual messages are being sent from the moon."

"Please maintain surveillance." His command chair intercom buzzed. "Bridge, Q."

"Jim here. How are we looking?"

"Everything is nominal so far. We assume the cloaking device is hiding the landing craft, since the Arupians haven't reacted to its presence."

"Good. How long before they land?"

Q glanced at his display. "Just more than three minutes."

"Very well. Keep me posted."

"Yes, Sir." He closed the link. "Weapons, any change?"

"No, Sir. The Arupians are acting like they don't see them."

"Let's hope our luck holds."

* * * *

The landing craft came in fast and hard. No finesse to this landing, just getting on the ground in one piece. Gabe screamed above the roar of the atmosphere rushing around the hull. "All right, people! Sixty seconds to LZ! Move out by the numbers and secure the area. Kill anything with more than pubic hair on its body! Watch your back and your buddy's back! Remember, you are His Majesty's Marines!"

"Oohrah!"

Gabe looked at him. Damon stood up, holding on to the safety strapping. "Look sharp and stay alive! Today we make history!" Damon slapped Gabe's helmet. "Come, you apes! Do you want to live forever?"

The landing craft hit the ground hard and the back wall dropped away. Twelve Marines swarmed out like Labrinian killer bees, darting left and right to cover the LZ. The landing craft, now on automatic control, lifted off and moved away into the black, star-studded sky. Both Corporals reported the area secured. Gabe turned to Damon. "It's party time."

"Yeah." He tongued the communicator to contact the entire team. "Now the fun begins. Five klicks due east of us is the record center and five hundred fur balls. Don't get greedy, people. That gives each of us at least forty kitty cats. Move 'em out, Gunny."

"Aye, aye, Sir." Gabe smiled. "All right, move out! Alpha squad, take the point!"

* * * *

"Landing craft moving to parking orbit, Sir." The Weapons Officer studied the sensors carefully. "No alarming activity, Admiral."

"Very well." Q allowed himself a small smile. He used his neural implant to link to the Emperor. "Jim, they're on the ground and the landing craft is clear."

"Now, we wait."

"Yes, Sir. Princess Allison asked me to call her when they landed. Would you prefer to do that?"

"No, you'd better call her. I think she's pissed off at me."

"Very well."

"Thanks, Q."

Q cleared the link to Jim and connected to Allie. "Princess, the landing craft has moved to its parking orbit, so they are on the ground."

"Thanks, Q. We won't hear anything until the call for the landing craft now."

"That's right."

"Thanks, and please let me know if you learn anything new."

"I will, Princess."

* * * *

Harry came by for a few minutes that morning to check on her. He said he promised Damon he would do that.

"They're on the ground." Allie sighed and turned to Harry. "I guess this is the dangerous part."

"Yeah, but it's also the part that Marines are trained for and are very good at doing."

"I suppose. Thanks for stopping by." She found herself pleased by his caring.

"You're welcome." Harry looked at the large candle she left burning on the coffee table. "What's that?"

"Many years ago, women would leave a candle or lamp burning in the window when their men went off to war." She smiled a little. "That way, her man can find his way home in the dark."

Harry nodded. "I think I understand."

"I wish I understood why he has to do this."

"It's a matter of numbers, Allie." Harry paused. "I'm not a combat officer, but I know that if we went in to get the information with a full assault, a lot of people, human and Arupian, would die. Also, the Arupians would probably scuttle and destroy the information before we got our hands on it."

"But a small team can't fight."

"Yeah, they can. The idea is for them to fight as little as possible, though. Get in before anyone knows they're even there. Grab the documents, then run like hell." He sighed. "It probably doesn't make sense to you as a civilian, but these kinds of operations work, and they work well."

She could see the logic. Hide and sneak around instead of going in with guns blazing. Her heart didn't like the idea, though. "Harry, when I asked him, Damon gave me a song and dance number about the odds. What do you think?"

He shrugged. "Like I said, I'm not a combat officer. Dietrich said that he expects everyone to come back, maybe a few minor injuries."

"I didn't ask about what Dietrich thinks."

"No, I guess you didn't. My gut tells me that he's right, though." He smiled. "To use the vernacular of the military, I have a high degree of confidence about the mission."

"Thanks for making me laugh." She thought for a moment. "Aren't you worried at all about this?"

"If I said I wasn't, I'd be lying to you. Yeah, I'm nervous. You know the things that can go wrong in any situation, but we can't dwell on that too much. We need to focus on the facts and what's really happening, not on what our paranoia tells us might happen."

Harry was right. She let her fears get away from her. "All right."

He fell silent for a moment and Allie could almost see him thinking. "Listen, there's no chance of any word for at least a couple of hours, so how about if we get you something to eat?"

"I guess I am hungry." She'd only picked at her dinner last night and breakfast this morning. "Can we just get something and eat here?"

"Sure." He smiled at her. "How about some Chinese fried cat?"

She smiled. "Thanks, Harry. You can always get me to laugh."

* * * *

In just over an hour, the team had reached the inner perimeter of the Arupian record center. They'd found the sensor grid Harry told them they would find, and disarmed the detectors. At least Damon assumed they'd disarmed it. No fur balls came to meet them. They now stood forty meters from an airlock. They saw no guards. Damon jumped when Gabe spoke in the communicator. "Baker squad, move out."

Five warriors moved across the distance to the door and stood watch as the others joined them. Damon entered the codes Harry provided. The airlock eased open. The team went through in one cycle. Once under pressure, they shut off their oxygen and opened their helmets. The team moved along the corridors, following the red line on a map Harry had drawn from the information in his messages. At a junction, Gabe pulled his mirror from his vest and peeked around the corner. He pulled back quickly. Holding up five fingers, he pointed to Sanchez. Damon nodded and held up three fingers. He ticked them off. When he lowered the last, the twelve Marines sprang around the corner and fired at five Arupians in the corridor.

Caught by surprise, the five Arupians soon lay dead. Damon glanced at the carnage. "All right, we've got maybe ten minutes. We move fast from here on in! We're going to have company!"

The Marines went down the corridor at a run as alarms began to wail.

Chapter 10

Lost and Found

Twenty-nine Arupians had the team pinned down outside the very room where they had just found the documents. The medic tended two wounded Marines, and Damon tried to think of an option. A burst of heavy fire hit the back of his armor. He spun in midair as he fell and saw two fur balls coming up from behind them. He pumped a close-quarters nuclear grenade at the pair as he shouted into the communicator. "We've got company from aft!"

Gabe turned and poured fire into the smoke left behind by the grenade while the others concentrated on the main firefight. "We have to get out of here!"

"Right! Fall back!"

The Marines began to work their way backward down the corridor, dragging the wounded with them.

* * * *

Allie couldn't concentrate on either lunch or conversation. She tried, but her mind focused on the small outer moon of Arup, trying to see events unfolding there. She didn't have much luck.

"Allie? Are you listening?"

"What? Oh, I'm sorry."

"That's OK, but are you all right?"

"I don't know."

"It's not a very good answer, but I can accept it."

"How much longer will this take do you think?" The team landed almost four hours ago.

"I don't know."

A smile slowly came to Allie's face. "I guess I deserved that one."

"Maybe." Harry took her hand in his. "We'll know something when we know something."

"Yeah, that's true."

* * * *

Q sat watching the screens on the bridge. More than four hours had passed since the team landed, and no word had come from them, but Arupian ships moved in alarming ways toward the moon. He had a feeling in his biosynthetic stomach that he should move *Boone* towards the moon. That would probably be suicide for the team and, perhaps, *Boone*.

The Weapons Officer stared intently at his instruments. "Sir, the landing craft is moving out of orbit."

Q relaxed a little. "Thank you." He called Jim, then Allie on the implant. "Princess, they have recalled the landing craft."

"Oh, my God! When will we know if they're all right?"

"Not until tomorrow. They will maintain radio silence."

Allie sighed. "OK, Q. Thanks." She cleared the link.

Q waited the thirteen minutes it took the landing craft to reach the surface and watched as it lifted off again.

"Sir, there's something wrong." The weapons officer used his controls. "The landing craft is accelerating at two hundred Gs." He tapped keys on his console. "At this rate, they'll run out of fuel just over halfway here."

"Understood." Q considered for a moment. "Maintain radio silence with regards to the landing craft. No course change."

Forty minutes later, the communications officer spoke up. "Admiral, the landing craft is hailing us."

Q sighed. No sense in not answering. "On speaker, please." The communications officer nodded. "Landing craft delta seven, this is *Boone*."

"*Boone*! This is Corporal Harden commanding. We need immediate evac, repeat, we need immediate evac! We have five injuries, all severe, and two in grave condition."

"Stand by." Q turned to the helmsman. "I want a minimum time course to the landing craft now, execute when ready." He pressed the switch for the landing craft. "We're on our way." He returned the conversation to the communications officer.

"Sir, ETA to landing craft is thirty-six minutes."

"Thank you. Weapons, what do we have for company?"

"I have eleven Arupian battle cruisers closing on the landing craft. Best ETA is thirty-eight minutes."

"Continue to monitor." Q called Jim back and advised him. After he finished, he started to call Allie, but thought better of it. He thumbed the intercom and called Harry. "Lieutenant Douglas, report to the bridge on the double." He heard Allie in the background asking if she could come, but Harry told her to stay put.

Harry came on the bridge about five minutes later. "Reporting as ordered, Sir."

Q waved to the leftmost of the three lower command chairs. "Mr. Douglas, we have a problem. First, the team is on their way back. I should say we are on the way to get them. They called a mayday with extensive injuries, and Corporal Harden is commanding."

"Where's Damon Hyde—um, Sir?"

"Unknown, but our first priority is the information." Q thumbed the communications link. "Corporal Harden, this is Admiral Q. Did you obtain your objective?"

"Affirmative, Sir. Objective obtained."

Q looked his question at Harry. "Emily, this is Harry. Tell me what the first two characters look like."

The Emperor walked onto the bridge and stood quietly to the side listening.

Harden paused for a long time. "The first one looks like an upside down R and the second looks like a bird with four legs."

Harry nodded. "Q here, Corporal. Well done. What is the status of your team?"

"Bad, Sir. Sergeant Williams is near death, as is Sanchez. The others will make it if sickbay can get them soon enough."

"What about Mr. Hyde?"

"He's not here, Sir. He made us leave without him while he covered us."

Q saw the blood leave Harry's face. "Very well, Corporal." Q checked his status display. "Our ETA is twenty minutes. Please get things arranged, and we'll transport you to sickbay as soon as we're in range."

"Yes, Sir. We'll be ready."

He closed the intercom. "Mr. Douglas, I'm sorry about Mr. Hyde."

Harry only nodded, his face white.

The Emperor slumped in the command chair next to Harry. "I am not looking forward to talking to Allie, but I guess I have to."

"Jim, I can talk to her. My order sent him on this mission."

Harry looked from Q to the Emperor. "Your Majesty, Admiral, I think I should talk to her."

"You may be right." Jim stared at the forward screen for a moment. "Harry, what do you need to do to get that information decoded?"

"I'll have to look at it, Sir."

"I know you've got your hands full, but it needs to happen fast. This has already cost the life of one good man."

"Yes, Sir. I'll need permission for Allie to see it so I can work on the decryption and stay with her at the same time."

Jim waved his hand. "Done. Somebody log that."

Harry stood up. "I need to go see Allie. Just have that information brought to me as soon as possible and I'll get on it. Pardon my French, Sirs, but this is really fucked up." Q and the Emperor watched as Harry left the bridge, walking slowly, his shoulders hunched like an old man.

* * * *

Harry moved slowly on the short walk to Allie's cabin. Hot tears scalded his face, but he didn't know how to stop them. It was like a part of him had died, a deep loss that tore at him. Allie would be devastated. Harry stopped far enough away from the door that it didn't open at his approach. He tried to get his tears under control, but he didn't feel like he had much luck. He knew he had a time limit, so he bolstered himself as much as he could, and then stepped to the door.

Allie watched the candle, and she turned when he entered. "What was...?" She froze in place, watching Harry's face. He came and knelt next to her. Her hand moved in slow motion to her face and covered her mouth. "Oh, my God."

"Allie, Damon didn't make it back. He's not on the landing craft."

She had both hands over her mouth now, her eyes wide and full of tears. Her voice trembled as she spoke in a whisper. "No, Harry. No."

Harry gave up trying to stop his tears and let them run down his face in waves. "I'm so sorry."

"No! They're wrong! No! This isn't happening!"

He took her shoulders in his hands. "It's OK. I'm here with you."

She wailed, collapsing into his arms, her body wracked by wave after wave of sobs like high tide. "This isn't possible! He said this was safe!"

"I'm not a command or combat officer, but I know that sometimes things go horribly wrong. We won't know much more until we get the landing craft back and can talk to them. If you want me to stay with you, I can. They'll bring the information the team captured to me soon and I need to look at that."

She sobbed for a time. "Could you stay for a while? I don't want to be alone." She paused. "Yeah, if you don't work on that stuff, this is all for nothing."

"I think Damon would want us to make use of the information."

"Yeah." She leaned in his arms crying for thirty minutes until the doorbell rang. When Harry answered it, two armed Marines gave him a folder marked *Ultra-Secret*. The guards took up positions in the corridor as Harry closed the door. He sat back down next to Allie. "Is that it?"

He thumbed through the information. "Yeah, this is it." He sat the folder down and hugged her. "Damon did exactly what we needed done. I'm proud of him."

"Me, too."

* * * *

Three days after the team's return, Allie still found herself breaking down into fits of tears, but she had to talk to Gabe. He improved in sickbay, but Sanchez had died of his wounds. Claire listed the other five injured Marines as stable.

Allie tapped lightly on the door of Gabe's room and looked inside. He looked up at her. "Allie."

She came and sat by the side of his bed and took his hand. "How are you feeling?"

"I'm OK. What about you?"

"I'll get there."

"I'm sure you're proud of him. If not for Damon, the entire team would have died, and we wouldn't have the papers."

"I am proud, but of all of you. So is my dad."

"We just did our job, that's all."

"You talk like Damon."

"I guess all of us grunts sound alike."

"Yeah." Allie paused for a moment. "What happened?"

"Well, we got in with only a small problem, but we needed to get out fast. The fur balls pinned us down and we took a couple of minor casualties there. We fell back, and they got us in crossfire. They beat us up bad there, too. Sanchez got hit there." He seemed to relive the battle as he spoke.

"That's OK, Gabe."

"No, you need to know this and it's probably good for me to talk about it." He took a deep breath. "All of a sudden, we had cats all over the place and I took a hit. The next thing I know, Damon grabbed my AGLR and yelled to Harden to evac immediately and not to wait for him. He charged out front and started firing with both hands. That bought the time we needed for Harden to get us all out of there to the landing craft." He had a tear in the corner of his eye. Allie took a tissue and patted it dry. "Thanks. We waited until the fur balls started to pour out the door, then we had to go."

"I'm happy the rest got out of there."

"We wouldn't have if not for Damon." He smiled a little. "He's a genuine hero, Allie."

"He'd say he just did his job."

"Maybe he would. All I know is that he's my hero."

Allie checked her watch. Her fifteen-minute visiting period had ended. "I need to go so you can rest. Thanks for telling me that."

"You're welcome, Allie." Another tear snaked its way down his face. "I'm sorry."

"Don't be." She leaned and kissed him softly. "Get some rest."

* * * *

She'd left Harry at her cabin working on the Arupian documents. He'd wanted to come with her, but she insisted he stay and work. He finally relented. He'd not left her side since word that Damon hadn't lived reached her, even going so far as to sleep on the floor next to her bed so he would be there when she woke up screaming, the imaginary last battle for Damon raging in her dreams. Allie didn't think Harry had taken Damon's death very well himself. She'd catch Harry crying as he worked on the encoded papers, his persistence dogged because he felt he owed that to Damon.

She went into the suite and found him just where she'd left him at the dining room table, papers all over. "Any luck?"

"Not really. How's Gabe?"

"He's feeling better, but still weak. Claire said he'll be fine in a week or so."

"That's good. Did he tell you anything?"

"Yeah." Allie told the story to Harry.

"Gabe's right. He's a bona fide hero."

"I guess so." She watched him as he kept working while he talked. She reached over and pulled the pencil from his hand. "Look at me." He turned his head, a questioning expression on his face. "I can make you stop working, but I can't make you stop thinking about that, but please stop, just for a minute."

"All right." He blinked at her. "What's wrong?"

"Thank you for being here for me. I wouldn't have made it this long without you."

"None are needed, but thank you for helping me get through this, too."

"You're welcome." She took his cheeks in her hands. "You're a special man."

* * * *

Harry wore his dress uniform for the first time since he could remember. He sat next to Allie, dressed in black, on the hanger deck, only six chairs from the Emperor. Two caskets draped with the flag of the Empire, one holding the remains of Corporal Sanchez and the other empty, sat near the bulkhead. Father Gonzales, the ship's Padre, said the Requiem Mass for Sanchez and Damon. Harry believed Allie had stopped sobbing because she'd used up all her tears in the last six days. He wanted to cry, but the tears wouldn't come.

Harry had no use for religion. Based purely on speculation and faith, Harry found the faith blind and misguided. He knew, however, they buried, at least symbolically, the best friend Harry ever had. He and Damon hadn't known each other very long, but they had hit it off immediately, even with the rivalry for Allie between them. Perhaps, he thought, the love they both had for Allie brought them together so quickly and easily. Maybe simple compatibility played a part. Harry didn't understand the reasons, but they really didn't matter.

He gave a quick glance at Allie and could see that she took comfort in what the Padre said, no matter if she believed it or not. A routine check of Damon's record found no next of kin and no known living relatives, his parents and siblings having died several years ago in an accident. Allie's father had declared her as the next of kin.

The Padre finished the Mass. The honor guard, led by Corporal Harden, carefully folded the flags from the caskets. Harden took the flag from Damon's casket. She marched sharply to stand in front of Allie and handed the folded flag to her. "A grateful Empire offers its sympathy on your loss." Harden slowly saluted, and then returned to her place at the head of the caskets. Her voice was soft for a Marine, but it carried well on the hanger deck. "Ship's company, attention." Everyone stood. "Ship's company, present arms." Harry, along with every other officer, including the Emperor, dressed in his jet-black Lord Admiral of the Fleet uniform, saluted. A pair of buglers, far down the hanger deck, played taps. The air curtain activated and the caskets slipped silently into space.

The last strains of taps reverberated in the cavernous space. "Ship's company, order arms. Dismissed."

* * * *

Allie stopped as they walked into her cabin. She held the folded flag in her arms, cradling it like a small child. She stared at the candle she kept burning on the table and sighed.

When she walked to the table, she knelt beside it. She sighed. "I love you, Damon."

She blew out the candle and watched the thin trail of smoke as the ventilator sucked it away.

* * * *

Allie and Harry sat in her suite sipping wine. Sometimes they'd talk about Damon, but mostly, they kept their thoughts to themselves. She carried the flag, neatly folded, with her everywhere she went. Harry watched her as she went to the bathroom, carrying the flag, and then returned to the table with it in her hands. "Are you doing all right, Allie?"

"Yeah, I think I am actually."

"That's good." The doorbell rang. "I'll get that."

Her father stood at the door, still in his uniform, the neck pulled open. "Hi, Harry. May I come in?"

"Sure, Sir."

Jim went to the dining room and sat down at the table next to Allie. "Little one, I know you're still mad at me."

She had, in her initial grief, been angry with her father. She'd actually been really pissed off at him. "No, Daddy. I'm not mad anymore. You and Q had to do this, and you couldn't have known it would go wrong like this."

"I am sorry, though. He gave his life for what he believed in. Good men do that sometimes."

"Yeah, he did."

"I didn't think you'd want a big public deal made over this, but if I'm wrong, we can do it that way." Jim reached in his coat pocket and pulled out a small box. "I hate to give out posthumous medals, but Damon earned this."

Allie opened the box and it contained the Imperial Medal of Honor. Allie knew the Empire had awarded only 271 medals in its 3,685-year history. Now 272. "Daddy..."

"No arguments, little one. He saved ten people directly and who knows how many indirectly." The Emperor had a lopsided grin he wore often and he smiled that grin now. "Maybe Harry knows."

"Not yet, Sir, but I will."

Allie looked at the medal and felt both the tears and the smile on her face. She looked up at her father. "Daddy, this is so wonderful."

"Like I said, he deserves it, and so does Corporal Sanchez. Everyone else is getting the Fleet Cross." He smiled at his daughter for a moment. "Allie, I'll go now." He kissed her forehead and went to the door, letting himself out.

"Harry, did you know this would happen?"

"No, not really. There are always decorations involved in these situations."

"What's wrong?" Harry looked like he might cry.

"This isn't going to sound the way I mean it, but I feel as bad as I did when you dumped me."

"I never dumped you, but it's OK." She lifted her glass of wine. "We can have a small wake, if you don't get as drunk as the last time."

"Do I look stupid?"

"No, you don't. Why don't you forget about your work for the rest of the afternoon and evening, and we'll sit here having some drinks while we talk about Damon?"

"That sounds like an excellent idea to me."

They started drinking in earnest about 1600. By 1830, Allie knew she was shit-faced. They talked about their brief relationship with Damon. While they both cried a lot, they laughed even more. As the evening wore on, Allie saw that they had far more good times with Damon than bad ones. They celebrated his life, not mourned his death.

Harry had just finished telling her about the fight he and Damon had. They laughed hysterically at the idea of two grown men having a pissing contest when the schoolteacher turned her back, when Harry became very serious. "Allie, this may sound strange, but I think I could have loved Damon."

"That's not strange. Good friends are supposed to love each other, silly!"

"No. I mean really loved, as in fall in love with kind of love."

"That's still not strange. Remember I'm up to my armpits in gay and bi brothers and in-laws."

"Oh, yeah. Say, how many siblings do you have, anyway?"

"Um, 141 counting myself."

"And you say I don't give straight answers! You don't count yourself among your siblings!"

"Oh!" She giggled and fell on her side.

"Good thing you're on the floor already!"

"Yeah! You can't fall off the floor!"

"Not unless the gravity fails."

Allie managed to sit up and stop giggling. "You're smart. How did we stay on the ground before they passed the law of gravity?"

"They made it retroactive."

She fell over again. "I like that!"

"Wait! You've got 140 brothers and sisters?"

"Yep." She decided to stay on her side.

"That's, um, 35 kids per mother, not counting you. Shit, your dad is one busy guy!"

"That's over seven hundred years."

"Still..." His brow furrowed as he tried to do the simple math in his head. "That's a lot of fucking, anyway you look at it."

"Not really. If you figure he had to fuck each mom five times to get them pregnant, that means daddy only got laid once a year."

"That's terrible!"

"That explains why he gets so irritable sometimes!" Allie rolled around on the floor laughing. "Are you as drunk as I am?"

"Maybe more."

"Wait here. I need to change." She struggled to her feet and staggered to the bedroom. She kept laughing while she undressed and put on her robe, and then managed to stumble back to the sitting room. She did a little turn, almost falling. "How's this?"

"That looks soft." He touched the material near her knee. "It is soft."

She managed to sit down on the floor. "Just like me."

"Yeah." He frowned for a minute. "I don't have a robe."

"Go get one."

"No, I don't own one."

"Oh. I guess you'll have to go naked, then."

"There's an idea." He grinned. "Ever play strip poker?"

"Oh, no! After what you showed me with solitaire, I am not playing cards with you!"

"Chicken shit."

"No, smart shit." They finished the drinks they had, and then changed over to soft drinks. She tried to speak, but only made a series of false starts.

"What's wrong? You're not going to puke or anything, are you?"

"No." She sighed. "I miss him."

"So do I." Harry took a deep breath. "Allie, as much as I have always wanted you for mine, I know you care about Damon. I can't tell you how sorry I am about this."

She nodded. She figured out about a month after she made her choice that Harry still pursued her. He hadn't pushed, though. "Thank you." She didn't know what else to say to him right now.

* * * *

Eight days after they buried Damon, Harry thought Allie was all right to leave alone most of the time. He stayed at his quarters and went to work everyday. He would stop by in the evenings for a couple of hours to check on her. A big part of that he also wanted to be close to her.

She went back to work, too. Now more than three weeks after Damon's death, she was back to fussing about her students almost daily.

Harry sat on the sofa trying to figure out a way to kick his own ass. He still wanted Allie. He *really* wanted her. Something in him wouldn't let him do anything about the want.

He considered the feelings he had about Damon. Space was a

dangerous place and things went wrong. He'd lost friends before, even in combat. This case seemed different, somehow, and he couldn't put his finger on exactly how or why. In some ways, Harry had many of the feelings for Damon that he had for Allie.

As he sat thinking about Damon, Harry looked at the neatly folded flag on the coffee table. Allie had finally stopped carrying it around with her. He studied the smooth twists and turns the flag had in its folds as the image of the Marines carefully folding it played through his mind. He could see each precise flip of the cloth as it moved. He stared for a time and the familiar eureka feeling came over him.

He carried the data from the raid with him everywhere so he could work on it if an idea hit him. He ran to the dinning room table and started working with the encryption, following its twists and turns in his head, as he folded the data over and under, just like the flag.

Allie came back from the bedroom. "What are you doing?"

He smiled up at her. "I've got it!"

Chapter 11

Findings

The crowd in her suite befuddled Allie. Harry, Lieutenant Henson, Commander Dalton, Q, and her father sat around the dining room table, all talking at the same time.

Harry looked frustrated. "Wait! Shut up! Sirs!"

The table fell silent. Her dad smiled. "OK, Harry, we're all listening."

"Sorry, Sir. This is exactly what it looks like. The Arupians are building a..." He hesitated for a moment. "I guess they're building a doomsday weapon."

"Can you tell the nature of the weapon, or what their intended target is?" Q thought for a moment. "Particularly the target."

"Not really, Admiral." Harry pointed to a series of squiggles on the documents. "This tells me that it's something to do with a star, but nothing more. There's more here that's in a different, multi-layer code that I haven't got yet."

Dalton had made it clear he didn't like being here. He didn't want Allie anywhere around this information. He didn't like Q and the Emperor here looking over his shoulder. "Are you sure the information is there, Douglas?" He seemed to blame Harry for what he saw as a serious breech of protocol.

"No, Sir. For all I know right now, that's a recipe for Arupian brownies."

Dalton's face turned red.

Her dad gave him an amused look. "Harry, this is pretty important."

"I know, Sir. I'd like to work on it, but I get a little distracted with all these people around."

Jim laughed, throwing his head back. "All right! We can take a hint, even as veiled as that one." He looked around the table. "OK, folks. Let's move 'em out so he can get his work done." He herded Dalton and Q out.

Devon and Harry watched them go. "Harry, I told you that you'd piss him off one day."

Allie laughed. "I think that day is today."

Harry shrugged. "Maybe, but I don't really care. I'm not here to make him happy."

"That's true, but he's the one who decides when to promote you." Devon sighed. "You're not very good with the political side of the military."

"I'm not very good with the military side of the military."

Allie stared at Devon, flicking her eyes toward the door. He smiled. "All right, I can take a hint, too. Harry, call me if you need anything. Bye." He left the suite.

"Well, I think you've got them all pissed off except daddy."

"Looks that way, doesn't it?"

"You really should try to get along better if you want to succeed in the Fleet. It's pretty political, you know."

"I know, but this is a temporary gig."

"Temporary? What is it that you want to do?"

"Be a successful gigolo."

"Oh, my God!" Allie laughed and sat down. "The scary part is that you may be serious!"

"I am serious." He grinned at her. "Say, you've got money."

"Yeah, I do, but you don't know what you'll need to do for me to be a kept man." Allie already had a long list in her mind.

"That's true. Maybe we'd best not go there right now."

* * * *

It took four days, but Harry decoded the rest of the document, and while the new parts didn't hide a recipe for Arupian brownies, they didn't give him the information he needed.

Allie invited Harry to take a break from his work and watch a movie with her tonight. He sat next to her on the sofa. The old movie she borrowed from her mom was a 2-D space horror flick about a tough woman stuck on a spaceship with a killer alien. The woman reminded Allie of Ike. The movie even had something like Marines and many firefights with the alien.

The movie reached a climax with the alien jumping out to kill the heroine. Allie screamed and almost landed in Harry's lap as she grabbed his hand with her nails. "Sorry about that!" The heroine got away.

"That's the most fun I've had in months."

She punched his arm. "Silly."

When the movie ended, Harry turned to face her. "Didn't your mom say there are four of these?"

"Yeah, but I don't think my heart or your hand could take three more."

He flexed his hand, marks from her nails on the palm. "Yeah, you're right."

Harry reached up and put his hand on the back of her neck, pulling her face to his tightly. His other arm slipped around her side as her own arms wrapped around him.

Even though he caught her off guard, she responded, her heart hammering in her chest. His tongue moved in her mouth, almost like he counted her teeth as he explored her. He tasted delightful, his saliva mixing with hers. His lips moved slickly over her mouth, and then slipped to caress her face.

Her hands ran over his back as they kissed, and her fingers traced the taut muscles of his back and shoulders as they flexed, holding and squeezing her.

When Harry rubbed his face against hers while they kissed, his beard made a soft cushion between them. The short curly hair almost tickled in its slow movements over her face. Her hands ran through his hair, and it slipped softly through her fingers. Sometimes, a lock would become entwined around her finger, and she flexed her hands so not to pull his hair.

His hair spilled onto her face, and she smelled the clean scent of the shampoo mixed with the heady aroma of his body. The blend made a delightful combination of sweet spices as it filled her nose and mind.

His cologne was like nothing she ever smelled before. It has clean scent, like a blend of spices filling a kitchen as someone baked a cake. Cinnamon and nutmeg seemed a part of the mix, but there were other smells she couldn't identify through the haze that filled her mind. She also thought it smelled of the sea, a clean, fresh ocean beating on the shore.

Where his hands touched her neck and back, the warmth of his touch gave her goose bumps. His hand around her neck held her tightly to him, and she knew that, even if she wanted to, she couldn't pull away without his consent.

The kiss lasted for many minutes, and Allie moved to kneel next to him on the sofa, her lips never leaving his.

Allie's pulse pounded in her head and heat flushed her face when their lips finally parted. "Tell me that you're not going to push me away again."

His answer came when he pushed her back on the sofa, lying on top of her and kissing her face and neck. Harry's breath burned against her ear as he licked her canal, sending hot shivers through her. She ran her hands through his long hair as he kissed her neck, pulling him to her.

His teeth bit gently at the skin of her neck and the swelling in his pants pressed against her.

He panted. "I want you."

When he moved to look into her eyes, Allie saw both tenderness and lust there. He stood and took her hand, pulling her to her feet. When they reached the bedroom, Harry wordlessly undressed her. "You look exactly like I've dreamed you would. Like an angel, everything I've ever imagined."

"Thank you." She removed his uniform, letting his pants fall to the floor. He put his arms around her waist, pressing their bodies together as his erect cock slipped against her stomach. Still kissing deeply, they eased to the bed where Harry laid her on her back and kissed down her face and chest to her breasts. His tongue swirled around her nipples and he sucked them gently into his mouth, biting gently as Allie shook like an earthquake.

"Roll over." He helped her roll to her stomach and straddled her hips. His hands moved over her back in long, slow motions, firmly massaging her muscles from her shoulders to her ass. His fingers dug into her flesh, sometimes almost painfully and others he barely touched her. Both motions sent chills through her and she moaned softly. He pressed firmly on her spine. "Is that too hard?"

"No, not at all. That feels wonderful."

His hands kneaded her shoulders and neck like a roll of dough. She groaned. Harry laughed softly, and his hard cock bounced against her ass. He ran his fingernails down the middle of her back, causing Allie to wiggle and giggle. "That tickles!"

"No, this tickles." He grabbed her ribs and tickled her ferociously.

Allie screamed loud enough that her folks would have heard her if not for the sound dampening fields. She bucked, nearly flinging Harry to the side of the bed. "Stop! You're killing me!"

Harry managed to catch himself before he fell off the bed. "Now, I know how to get your attention!"

"Oh, my God! I'm so ticklish!" Allie managed to catch her breath and crawled down the bed. Her heart raced and her desire drove a heat through her pelvis. She kissed Harry's nose. "You always have my attention."

Harry smiled softly at her. "I know that feeling." He sat up and slipped his arms around her, pulling her to him. When he pulled his lips from hers, Allie wanted more. "I'm afraid this is a dream and I'll wake up."

Her heart raced again, threatening to jump from her chest. "It's not a real dream, just a dream come true." She crawled to straddle his hips and kissed him.

Harry lifted her gently as he hugged her, and he slipped his hardness deep into her core, slowly lowering her to his lap. They kissed as they rocked together, his steely hardness penetrating her gently as they moved. Allie expected their first session to come wild and hard, but the gentleness with which he touched her drove her passions to a level she'd never known before. His hands ran over her back and sides and around to caress the curve of her breasts. His tongue and lips writhed against hers firmly, but not hurting. His gentle, rocking thrusts filled her completely, but his touch made a tender, caring expression of his feelings for her.

Her orgasm crept up on her through the forest of passion they shared, and it suddenly pounced on her. Her body seized with the sudden pleasure. Her spasms were so intense that she barely noticed when Harry's fingers fell to her hips and pulled her against him, his hips thrusting as his steaming cum exploding deep inside her.

They hugged as their shivers and shakes faded. Allie kissed him, feeling his cock softening inside her. Allie smiled her best seductive smile at him. "This was all tender and romantic, but if you think you're done, you have another thing coming."

"Oh, really?" He lifted her from his lap and laid her back on the bed, kissing her breasts. "Sorry, but your boobs have always fascinated me."

"This is not a time to be silly."

"I'm not." He kissed and mouthed her breast, nearly sucking the entire thing into his mouth. He kissed her breasts again, and then eased his way to lie between her spread legs, licking her thighs slowly, sending tingles through her as his tongue gently tickled her flesh. Without warning, he plunged his tongue between her lips, deep into her pussy. He fucked her repeatedly with his hard tongue, his hands spreading her labia as he licked from her soaked cunt to her clit, flicking stiffly over her swollen clit as she moaned and pulled his head against her.

"Yes, Harry!" He licked from her wet pussy down and circled her anus with his tongue, pressing against the opening firmly. He pressed harder, and the tip of his tongue slipped effortlessly into her ass. She moaned with the sensation. His fingers had found their way to run deeply inside her cunt, spreading the flowing juices over her lips and thighs. His thumb rubbed firmly on her clit and she could feel her climax creeping at her again.

His probing fingers and tongue pushed her over the edge, and Allie's hips began to thrust against him, her legs wrapping around his head and neck, forcing them tighter into her. Her screams came as nothing more than incoherent bursts of vocalizations and her body vibrated the bed.

As her tremors faded, Harry slipped his fingers from her pussy and his tongue from her ass. He kissed up her stomach and lay beside her. He kissed her cheek. "Hi."

Her breathing still came as a rapid pant. "You could hurt a girl that way."

"Sorry."

"You won't hear me complain." The sweet, heady smell of his sweat mixed with her juices on his face woke Allie's arousal again.

"Good." He kissed her cheek again.

"Why are you kissing my cheek when my lips are right here?" Allie pressed her face to his, plunging her tongue deeply into his mouth. In the split second before her eyes closed, Allie saw the surprised look on Harry's face. She rolled on top of him, pinning his rigid dick between the lips of her wet cunt and his stomach, her hips gyrating slowly as his hardness rubbed her clit. Allie pulled her lips from his and kissed his neck, biting the skin gently, and then began to suck his nipples, flicking her tongue over them as he twitched under her. She kissed down his stomach, feeling his hard cock between her breasts.

Reaching his cock, Allie slowly licked the full length, still able to taste her own juices there. Her juice mingled with his cum from when they fucked, and the small dribble of pre-cum on the purple head of his dick made a delicious combination of musky aromas and spicy flavors. Her tongue flicked over the head of his cock as she swallowed him fully, Harry's body jerking in a spasm of pleasure.

She bobbed her head as she swallowed his staff from tip to base, sucking firmly and drawing her pleasure from the writhing reactions she would elicit from Harry. Allie grabbed his balls, rolling them through her fingers like a magician with billiard balls, squeezing gently as the hot, hard orbs moved freely to her touch. She pulled his cock from her throat, biting the tip between her teeth and swirling her tongue around the head, causing Harry to thrash and moan on the bed.

His body stiffened as his shaking increased and his climax almost caught her by surprise. His hot salty-sweet cum surged into her mouth and filled her cheeks. He screamed senselessly, the only intelligible sound being her name. She sucked and swallowed his seed, his body bucking as she ran her tongue around his pulsing head. She gave his softening cock one final kiss before crawling up to lay beside him.

"And you said I could hurt you. Damn!"

"Is that a good damn or a bad damn?"

"Very good." He sighed. "You're like every man's dream."

"Hardly, but I like being your dream."

* * * *

"We just don't have the information in any of the stuff we have now."

Jim sighed and leaned back in his chair, putting his feet on the desk. "So how do we get the information, Harry?"

"I think the Arupians are using low power transmitters to get commands from the planet to small, fast ships, who then carry it to the fleet." Harry brushed his hair from his eyes. "That's why we've seen such a drop in communications since the raid on the moon. They know we can read their mail."

Dalton slapped his palm on the desk with a loud pop. "There's no evidence to support that, Douglas! You're talking out your ass!"

"Commander, you need to relax and consider the possibility." Q ran his hand through his hair, a habit he'd picked up from the Emperor over the seven hundred years they'd known each other. "Mr. Douglas has proven very sensitive to what the Arupians are doing."

"No, he's guessing and lucky at it, Admiral."

Jim cleared his throat. Harry smiled to himself thinking that if you learned nothing else serving on *Boone*, when the Emperor had something to say, you listened. Carefully. "That's enough. Dalton, you are way the fuck out of line." He turned to Devon. "Mr. Henson, I understand that you and Mr. Douglas are the lead people on this work?"

"Well, I suppose, Sir, but it's mostly Harry."

"Close enough. Effective now, Lieutenants Henson and Douglas will report directly to Admiral Q." The Emperor looked at Dalton and Harry saw a cold hardness in his eyes he never expected the friendly man could have. "We don't need political bullshit in the way of this. You're dismissed, Commander."

Dalton huffed but left the office without comment. Devon looked at Harry. "I told you that you'd piss him off."

"Yeah, and we have to go back and work for him."

Jim laughed. "Maybe. Q, is there a way we can check Harry's idea without looking like we're doing that?"

"Perhaps. It really depends on how small the hypothetical ships are. I think we could see anything down to the size of a shuttlecraft."

"OK, make it happen. Also, we need to find offices for these two."

"I'll take care of that, Jim. Anything else right now?"

"No, I think that does it. Take Mr. Henson with you to find some office space. I need to talk to Harry."

"Yes, Sir."

Jim watched Q and Devon close the big wooden doors. "I think you and I should talk, Harry."

"About what, Sir?"

"First, call me Jim. All that Sir stuff makes me nervous. In a word, Allie."

"OK, Jim. She's doing a lot better now. She has a few bad times, but she's getting there." Almost five weeks had passed since Damon's funeral.

"I know that. I meant you and Allie."

"Oh. If I didn't know better, I'd swear that you're asking me what my intentions are toward your daughter." Harry smiled easily but he couldn't shake the feeling that he sat across the desk from the most powerful man in the galaxy. Jim could have him tossed out an airlock and no one would ever know.

"I guess I am, in a way. You should know that I'm very protective about my daughters." The hard coldness returned to Jim's eyes. "If I think for a moment that you're taking advantage of her, I'll kill you myself."

Harry blinked. His Majesty James the First, by Grace of God Emperor to Mankind had just threatened his life. He could, Harry knew, also make good on the threat. "Jim, I'm not taking advantage of her. I care about Allie."

"That's good. Who knows if you'll be together forever, but don't play games with her feelings."

"I'd never do that."

"We'll see how that goes. Meanwhile, you're right and she is doing better. What about you?"

"Me?"

"Yes, you. Allie said she thought you took it as hard as she did. I understand you and Damon had become pretty close."

"I guess we did, but I'm doing all right."

Jim stared at him for a moment. "You should never try to lie to a seven hundred year old man."

Harry wondered if Jim could read his mind. "I guess you're right."

"Yeah, I'm always right." Jim's lopsided grin slipped to his face. "Except when I'm arguing with my wives." He considered Harry for a moment, something like a bug under a magnifying glass. "You fell in love with Damon, didn't you?"

"Maybe I did. I'm not sure. I'm not used to thinking that way about a man."

"Well, there's not much I can do about that, and my concern is with Allie. You'll have to work out the rest of your feelings for yourself."

"I guess I will, Jim."

* * * *

Allie had lunch with her moms for the first time in nearly two months, and it felt good to go out with the girls. Janelle elbowed her. "So, tell us about Harry."

"Mom, he's great. I've never known anyone like him, not even Damon."

"Allie, don't do that." Marilyn struggled with a piece of grilled salmon, trying to get it on her fork.

"What's that, mom?"

She gave up and used her fingers. "Compare the two."

Paige patted Allie's hand. "She's right. That's a road to heartache."

"M-Marilyn, use your f-f-fork, p-please." Tanya shook her head. "I've t-tried for 2,700 years t-to teach her t-to use a f-fork."

"You're right about that. Harry is Harry and Damon is Damon."

"Yes, they are." Marilyn snaked a piece of fish on her fork. "So, other than being great, how is he?"

Allie smiled. "He's tender and loving, but he can be tough when he wants to."

"No, Allie. I meant how is he in bed?"

"Marilyn!" Paige blushed and hid her face. Janelle rolled her eyes. Tanya didn't react at all.

Allie smiled at the sensations they'd shared. Harry seemed to know when she wanted soft and tender, or when she desired hard and a little rough. "Well, if you must know, he's fantastic. It's like he can read my mind and knows what kind of mood I'm in. He can be all cuddly like a big teddy bear, or he'll grab my hair and take me like a caveman."

Janelle laughed. "You spent too much time with Marilyn growing up."

Paige somehow managed not to choke. "God! You're all degenerates!"

"Who t-tied up Jim the other n-night and called us so w-we c-c-could all take t-turns?"

Paige smiled. "Um, yeah. There was that."

Allie laughed. She enjoyed being with her moms. They all looked and acted more like her sisters than her mothers. "You four are a mess!"

Janelle pushed her plate aside. "Maybe we are, Allie. Is Harry the one?"

"I really think so, mom."

* * * *

Allie met Harry at the door and slipped into his arms before it closed. "Hi, honey." She kissed him softly. "You're home."

"Hi. Why do I feel like Ward Cleaver?"

"Who?"

"Never mind. How did lunch with the moms go?"

"We had a wonderful time."

"That's good." He kissed her.

"What about your meeting with daddy?"

"Well, other than him almost firing my boss and threatening my life, it went good."

"What?" She laughed. "He didn't."

"Yeah he did. Both of them."

"That's my daddy. Come on, I've got dinner for us."

"Why the rush?"

"I don't want it to get cold. Come on."

After dinner, they helped each other change and went to the sitting room. "Let's sit on the floor."

"Well, OK, but you may have to help me up later."

"I will."

They chatted over dinner for a while, talking mostly about the war. Harry smiled at her. "I'm wondering if dinner is over or not."

"Yeah, I think so. Why?"

He reached out and grabbed her arms, pushing her to the floor. He moved to straddle her hips and pulled her robe open. "Because I want you. Right here. Right now." Harry ripped his robe open and shrugged it from his shoulders. He moved to lie on her, and his hard cock slid into her pussy as her excitement built rapidly to a blazing passion. She reached to put her arms around his neck, but he pinned them to the floor beside her head as he pumped rapidly into her, feeling the rough texture of the carpet against her ass.

His eyes stared into hers as he fucked her, his dick hitting the back of her now flowing cunt with each powerful thrust. "Harry, yes! Fuck me! Harder!" He thrust into her over and over again, the forcefulness of his taking her driving her raging passions as much as his cock's probing of her pussy.

Pinned to the floor by his hands holding her arms and his urgent pounding against her hips, Allie squirmed as her orgasm took her. Through her excitement and building climax, Allie wondered what he would do if she told him to stop. In one way, she hoped he would stop if she told him, because he loved her so much that he could control his passion. In another, she hoped that he couldn't stop because he wanted her so much. Allie didn't want him to stop.

Just as the first strike of orgasm hit her, Harry gave a mighty shove that moved her ass across the floor, and his cum shot into her cunt. He grunted and pumped into her, trying to gain just another millimeter of penetration.

He released her arms and Allie hugged him to her, finally tasting his lips. They kissed while their bodies trembled. His soft cock slipped from her. She looked up into his eyes and smiled. "Wow."

"I didn't hurt you, did I? I kind of lost control there."

"No, you didn't hurt me."

"That's good, because your dad would have me spaced."

"He'd have to send me with you."
As they kissed again, the battle stations alarm wailed.

Chapter 12

Attack

Allie sat in the safe room with her family, and no one would tell her why the ship went to battle stations. When she asked him, her father only shrugged. "I don't know, little one. This is all Q's call and he's busy."

Allie kicked the table and almost broke her toe to remind her she wore her slippers. "Ike, what's happening?"

"I don't know, Princess." Ike smiled at her. "All I know is that I'm supposed to keep you here until we secure from battle stations."

She went to the communications console and tried to call Harry. He didn't answer. Allie couldn't decide if she was more worried, scared, or just plain pissed off. Finally, her dad got the look people had when communicating via implant. Allie waited until his expression returned to normal. "Daddy?"

"Relax. Just another of the cloaked asteroids and we dodged that just fine. Q is just making sure there aren't any other surprises out there."

"Thank God!" She hesitated for a moment. "Daddy, is there a way to get Harry a different battle station other than search and rescue?"

Jim took her hand and led her to the sofa, sitting Allie between himself and her mother. "You know I can't do that. I can't show him any favoritism." He shrugged. "If you were married, maybe we could do something, but right now, he has his station and that's all there is to it."

"Doesn't Q make those assignments or something?"

"Technically, yeah, he approves them. He has no clue where every JG on this ship is assigned any more than I do."

Janelle took Allie's hand. "You're talking about putting Q and your dad in a bad position."

"I know, Mom. I just worry about him. I can't go through the last few months all over again."

Jim glanced at Janelle. "I know." He ran his hand through his hair. "Let me talk to Q and see what we can do, OK?"

"Will you, Daddy? Really?"

"Yeah. You know I can't say no to any of you kids and make it stick."

Marilyn giggled from where she watched on the other sofa. "You're a pushover, baby."

"Looks that way, doesn't it?"

* * * *

Allie paced the sitting room waiting for Harry to come back from his battle station. She threw her arms around his neck when he came in the door, and the tears came through in her voice. "I'm sorry. I'm worried about you."

"It's all right." His arms felt good around her shoulders. "Everyone, including us, is just fine."

"Yeah." She paused for a moment. "Would you hold me?"

"Of course! Come on." He led her to the bedroom where he carefully removed her robe and eased her to the bed. After undressing, he lay down next to her and slipped his arms around her body, pulling her close to him. "Better?"

"Yeah." She snuggled in close to his chest, her fingers twirling the hair. "I talked to daddy."

"About what?"

"He's going to get you transferred to something safer as your battle station."

"That's not needed."

"Yeah, it is, for my mental health. I can't do another loss."

"I know the feeling. If that will make you feel better, I guess it's OK with me."

"It will make me feel better." She wiggled up a little and kissed him. "I love you."

"I love you. More than I can believe it's possible to love anyone."

Her hand moved down his chest to reach his cock and found it fully erect. "Seems that battle excites you." She stroked his stiff dick slowly, running her hands over the head, the drops of pre-cum making her hand slippery.

He twitched. "No, you excite me." He turned suddenly and rolled on top of her. "I want you."

"I'm yours."

"No, you're not." He kissed rapidly down her chest and abdomen, spreading her legs, and began to lick her thighs, biting gently. Allie's pussy flowed with her excitement as Harry's fingers pinched her clit, sending a blast of pleasure through her. His tongue plunged into her slit, spreading her lips and licking deeply into her core, and his free hand came up to finger her cunt as his thumb pressed against her anus.

As his fingers rolled her clit and his tongue darted in her cunt, Harry pushed slightly. His thumb slipped inside her ass, causing her to jerk with pleasure. His fingers replaced his tongue probing her pussy, rubbing the thin skin between her ass and pussy between thumb and finger, his tongue swirling around her clit. Allie thrashed on the bed, grabbing his head. "Harry! Yes, honey! Oh, God!" Harry slipped his digits from her and moved to kiss her. The tangy sweetness of her juices on his face, mingled with the saltiness of his sweat made an aromatic mix in her mouth and nose, sending shivers through her as she relished the heady blend. The head of his cock pressed urgently against her asshole. "Yes! Fuck my ass!"

With a gentle push, the bulbous head of his dick slipped into her anal vestibule, causing Allie's eyes to open wide with the slightly painful pleasure. Slowly at first, Harry thrust against her, Allie moving her hips to meet his lunges, and his shaft moved fully in her ass. He pulled his lips from hers and looked into her eyes. "I can't last long."

"Please, honey! Fill my ass with your cum!" In less than a minute, Harry's eyes closed, his face wrinkled with a pleasurable seizure, and he gave a last mighty thrust. His cock throbbed and spasmodically jerked inside her, its hot load of cum erupting deep in her ass. "Yes, yes! That's it! Give me all you've got!"

His jerking slowed and his cock slipped silently from her ass. He panted heavily. "I'm sorry."

"For what?"

"You didn't climax."

Allie kissed his lips softly. "You don't have to make me cum for me to know you love me."

"It doesn't seem right." He rolled from on top of her.

"It does to me." She kissed him again. "If you feel better about it, you owe me one."

He laughed softly. "That's a deal."

* * * *

Harry and Devon sat in their new office located just off the bridge. Harry liked the location. He'd more or less moved in with Allie and her cabin lay less than three minutes away. He didn't need to get out of bed until 0750 to make it to his office by 0800. He and Allie spent a lot of time in bed, too.

Sometimes he wondered if she was a nymphomaniac. Allie seemed ready for anything and everything at any moment. Harry had never known a woman like that before. Though she hadn't said anything about them or used them, he'd found the restraints and handcuffs attached to the bed frame one morning while making the bed. He wondered what more lay in her closet.

"Harry? Are you listening?"

"What? No, not really."

"I can see that." Devon dropped a stack of printouts on the desk. "Q has confirmed that your little ships are darting back and forth from Arup to their fleet."

"I knew they were there." Harry glanced through the printouts. "I wonder how we find out what they're carrying."

"Got me. You're the genius."

"That's what they tell me." He pushed the printouts aside. "We need that information."

"OK, should we just call and ask them for it?"

"Smart ass. I wonder if the communications people could build something that could tap into the transmissions from here."

"I don't know. Empress Paige is the expert, and maybe you can talk to her about it."

"Yeah. That's a good idea."

* * * *

"Let me get this straight. You want to detect a radio a signal designed to reach from the planet to low orbit, say about two hundred kilometers, and you want to do that from more than a billion kilometers away?" Paige laughed. "They're right. You're crazy."

"That's not the question. I know I'm crazy." Allie planted an elbow in his ribs. "The question is can you do it?"

"We're not talking about sticking a coat hanger on the back of the tri-v set to get a better picture, Harry." Paige's eyes focused on the distance. "The signal strength falls with the inverse square of the distance. Over the distance you're talking about, the losses are tremendous."

Allie blinked. "Mom, why can't you just amplify the signal?"

"It's not that simple. As the signal fades, it gets deeper into the noise. Simple amplification will amplify the noise along with the signal, so we don't gain anything. We need to get the signal out of the noise."

Harry nodded. "I understand the problem, and I know what you mean. Can you do it?"

"Maybe. I'll need to get with Tanya and see how much of the ship's brain I can use for signal processing." Paige frowned. "If we can get enough computer power, and if we can get a big enough antenna out there, we might be able to do it, but I won't promise anything."

"All right." Harry grinned. "While I know his orders don't apply to you, your husband said that this has top priority." Allie elbowed him again.

"Damned right his orders don't apply to me!" Paige wiggled her hand where a huge diamond ring rested on her finger. "This outranks the Emperor."

* * * *

Allie smiled up into Harry's eyes through the afterglow of their lovemaking. "Why do I feel so safe with you?"

"I don't know, but I'm glad that you do." His face took on a wry smile. "Do you trust me?"

"Of course I do. Why?"

He moved to sit straddling her hips. "I've wondered about something."

"You're talking in puzzles again. What?"

He leaned like he planned to kiss her, but grabbed her arms and quickly used the handcuffs at the head of the bed to secure them over her head. "Why you have these on your bed."

Dual waves of nervousness and excitement swept over her body, reawakening the throbbing in her wet pussy. "I guess the correct answer would be that they're there for you." A smile spread slowly over her face. "Master."

"Good answer." He stood and walked to the foot of the bed. Taking her left ankle, Harry moved her leg to the corner of the bed where the shackle waited. Allie tried to pull her leg away, offering a token resistance, but Harry pulled her leg firmly and attached the leg iron. The strength in his hands and arms surprised Allie. Always gentle with her, he made it clear she couldn't fight him and win. He moved to her right leg, and Allie put up genuine resistance. Without any hint of harming her, he easily restrained her leg to the bed. Allie lay spread-eagle on the bed, totally at his mercy. "Now that's better."

The forceful tenderness had Allie's desire in high gear. She eagerly awaited his commands. "Yes, my master."

He sat on the bed near her hips, facing her, and his fingers moved to her soaked slit. His fingers ran slickly inside her, plunging deep into her pussy, as his thumb pressed against her clit. Allie's eyes tried to close. "No, keep your eyes open and your mouth shut."

She obediently opened her eyes and nodded her head. As his fingers darted across the folds of her lips, her eyes locked to his. She could see his gentle smile. As he played with her clit and cunt, Allie fought the strong urge to moan. Harry pulled his hand away and leaned to the bedside table. He retrieved a large bottle of lubricant and her dildo. Greasing the dildo and his hands thoroughly, Harry slipped the vibrator into her pussy with the switch set to high speed. Her excited anticipation built as his fingers swirled around her anus, pressing at the tight opening.

He carefully slipped his fingers into her ass, causing Allie to tremble and quake.

The finger in her ass soon had a mate as a second finger probed her. The dildo and his fingers pressed together through the wall between her cunt and ass. Allie kept her eyes open and mouth shut, as he commanded her. His free hand moved to pinch her labia together, rolling and squeezing her clit, driving her closer and closer to the brink of her orgasm.

As the first waves came on her, Harry pulled his hands and the vibrator away. Allie, despite his admonition, let a slight squeal escape her lips. Her heart pounded in her head, and her pulse raced madly. Sweat poured from her body with the excitement he stoked and she longed to beg him to continue.

Silently, Harry dropped the dildo on the bed and moved to kneel beside her head. His cock, hard and long, almost touched her face. She could see drops of pre-cum running over the swollen head. The smell of his cum, mixed with her juices, was strong in her nose, a sweet musky odor with a tinge of saltiness. Allie lunged her head, trying to lick the end of his dick to get the sweet taste in her mouth, but Harry dodged back, easily avoiding her. "No, no. You can have this when I give it to you." He shook his cock in her face with his hand. "Close your mouth."

Allie did as he commanded. Harry grasped his hard dick and rubbed the head across her lips, the droplet's of his fluid moistening her lips. As he rubbed his cock across her chin, Allie chanced darting her tongue to her lips to lick away the moisture. The taste made her body shake with desire to have his full cock in her mouth, spurting its hot liquid onto her tongue.

He pressed the swollen head of his cock against her lips and Allie parted them slightly. Harry again pulled back. "No, keep your mouth shut." She dutifully closed her lips. He again rubbed his dick against her mouth and the head pushed her lips aside. The purple head slipped between her teeth and lips, running into her cheek. Allie fought to not open her mouth to swallow his shaft, her eyes on his face. He pumped slowly, his cock moving in and out of her cheek. Harry shook. "Now! Open your mouth!" Allie snapped her mouth open, and his cock shuddered as his cum squirted from his dick. "Fuck, yes! Suck me!"

Allie closed her mouth around his throbbing dick, his cum filling her mouth with its hot, sticky sweetness. His balls, slick with sweat bounced against her cheek and she the passionate scent of the man filled her head. His harsh gasps and forceful thrusting faded to a series of grunts and twitches as she drained him.

He paused for a moment, sweat rolling from his face and chest, before moving to lie between her spread legs. Harry slowly licked her clit, sucking it into his mouth at times. Allie's orgasm hadn't receded far when he pulled the toy and his fingers from her and it moved rapidly at her again. The juices from her cunt that Harry's tongue failed to lap up flowed down her slit to her ass, creating a wet spot on the sheets.

Even before her orgasm began, Allie thrashed on the bed, the bonds on her arms and legs limiting her movements. His tongue darted over her hard clit and his hand had found its way to run two fingers each into her ass and pussy. Her arms longed to pull his face tighter to her cunt, and her legs ached to wrap around his neck. If Harry pulled away now, Allie knew she had to find a way to break the ties that held her, taking him by force if she had to.

Allie's head suddenly filled with a billion flashbulbs going at the same time. The flash nearly blinded her, and her back arched high from the bed as the full force of her orgasm hit. Unable to control her voice and eyes any longer, Allie screamed, but only incoherent sounds came from her lips. Her eyes clenched in the wake of the shuddering frenzy that seized her body. Her hands and feet supporting her, Allie's body hovered over the bed. Harry's hand and mouth continued to drive her forward.

After what seemed an eternity in her mind, Allie collapsed back onto the bed, soaked in sweat and her juices flowing from her pussy. Harry moved to lie beside her. "Hi."

"Shit. Are you trying to kill me?"

"Never." He kissed her softly. "Let me get you free." He moved to free her hands and feet, and then cuddled her close to him. Allie still had waves of shivers running through her.

"If I thought I could move, I'd be all over you."

"Promises, promises."

Allie laughed. "You always make me laugh."

****

"I count sixty-three battle cruisers and seven attack carriers, Sir. Closing at HS layer three with an engagement ETA of four minutes."

"Understood." Q considered. The fighters would be in harms way, but with that many ships closing, he had to buy some time. "Please launch all Cobras."

The weapons officer worked his console. "Cobra launch in ninety seconds." The tiny Cobras, one-man fighters that weren't much more than a huge impulse drive with weapons stuck all over and a cockpit added as an afterthought. Fast, hard to hit targets that could inflict tremendous damage, the made an important part of *Boone's* arsenal. More than a hundred thousand Gs of acceleration made the Cobras nimble, but they had no shielding and one hit would neutralize them. *Boone* carried 250 Cobras and the pilots went out on essentially a suicide mission to protect *Boone*. "Cobras away, Sir. Engagement in 140 seconds."

"Thank you. Arm all weapons, shields to full power. Shunt hyperspace power to the Field."

"Aye, aye, Sir. All hands at battle stations. All airtight doors closed and sealed."

"Is the royal family secured?"

"Sergeant Payne reports that they are, Sir."

"Very well." Q watched the dots closing on Boone's location and the swarm of Cobras forming a protective eggshell around her. "Weapons, you are authorized to fire at will."

"Aye, aye, Sir. Understand authorized to fire at will. Engagement in thirty seconds."

"Thank you. Helmsman, slave the helm to the fire control console."

"Aye, aye, Sir."

Q watched as the weapons officer counted down to engagement range.

****

Space battles are beautiful sights. The lasers and other light-based weapons stab out in a range of colors covering the visible spectrum, throwing exawatts of energy at their targets as they hit targets as small as a centimeter square from ten million kilometers away. The galvanic torpedoes blaze through space and, on impact, their multi-terawatt load of energy bursting on the target. The pulses of energy from the blasters carry ten billion electron volts and can blow through any normal matter in seconds. The disruptors cause the very atomic structure of the target to fall apart.

The sights are beautiful from a distance. There are no sounds in space, but the effects on the target are dramatic. Being up close and personal with a space battle is never a good idea.

The energy pouring into the protective field of the target runs its temperature higher and higher as the energy is stored, its color reflecting the rise as it runs up the spectrum from black to red, on to yellow, then into the blues and purples. The field will then flash to white and collapse. The collapsing field radiates the stored energy outward to space, and inward towards the ship. When the field fails, ships die.

From a distance, the dangers aren't apparent, and the battle looks pretty. Huge swollen balloons are the ships in their fields. The balloons, tied together by brightly colored strings of light and looking like a refugee collection from a carnival, float through space as the ships try to outlast one another before their fields fail.

Boone's weapons fired on targets as the Cobras darted among the many Arupian ships, firing and taking their toll. Arupian fighters, launched by the carriers, engaged the Cobras, but the Cobras badly outclassed the Arupians. Q watched his status display and counted only five Cobras lost so far, a much smaller number than he had feared. The battle was still young.

The failure of an Arupian battle cruiser's field made a bright flash to port. Q didn't even bother to scan for survivors. The battle seemed to move in slow motion as Q reflected on the ancient movies Jim and the Empresses seemed addicted to. In the films, the battles raged in high speed, the destruction of ships taking only moments. Then again, the movies also had sounds in space. The reality was much slower, but far more destructive of ships and of life.

Q saw a flicker in the corner of his eye and turned to the Harbison Field monitor. He saw a few flecks of green in the otherwise orange temperature display. "Engineering, why do we have hot spots?"

"Some of their fighters are carrying small high energy lasers, Sir. I think they're trying to burn holes in us instead of overloading the field."

Q frowned. "Weapons?"

"I think that's right, Sir." The young lieutenant turned to face Q. "I think they mean to board us."

"Bridge to security."

"Security, Payne here."

"Sergeant, we have reason to believe the Arupians may attempt to board *Boone*. Please be ready."

"Understood, Admiral."

Q cleared the link and watched as the green spots became less numerous and moved up to blue.

Marines in full armor and battle gear moved rapidly through *Boone* to designated areas designed to allow maximum coverage with minimal manpower. They waited for word of intruders.

* * * *

Corporal Jack Ingram commanded the team in sector delta thirty-five, just off the OD. His communicator crackled. "Jack, Ike here. Things are getting hot in your area. Stay alert."

"Copy. We're ready."

Jack watched the corridors, his team cautious and anxious to kick some cat ass. The fur balls had killed too many Marines without paying the price. Jack and his team stood ready to settle the score. The announcement from the bridge rang in his headphones. "We have field breech in sector delta thirty-three. Repeating, field breech in sector delta thirty-three."

"Move out!" Jack his twenty-three Marines ran for the area of the breech, only two corridors forward of their station.

The hull blew away as the Arupian warriors set off charges and poured through the hole into Boone. Jack and his team began firing, the rapid rattling of the automatic weapons lost in the vacuum. Close-quarters nuclear grenades whizzed through the air and blew out bulkheads as the fight raged. Jack stood to fire and several heavy rounds from the fur balls slammed his chest, the body armor saving him. As he fell backwards, he returned fire. The cat that shot him wouldn't shoot any more Marines. He needed a head to do that. More Arupians poured into Boone, as fast as the Marines could kill them, but a flash from outside announced that a Cobra picked the fur ball's landing craft from the hull. The stream of kitties ended. Fifty more Marines led by Ike came around the corner, and the rest of the Arupians went down in moments.

"Damn it, Ike! We had them!"

Ike slapped his helmet. "You fucking knuckle-dragger! You can't have all the fun!"

"I could if you'd been a little slower." A private called to say that they had ninety-eight dead cats. "Only a few more billion to go."

"Yeah, let's get 'em." Ike looked at the hole in the hull. "Get some engineers up here to seal that and stay on your toes."

* * * *

Harry wondered if the change in his battle station offered any improvement. He stood in the hanger deck dressed in a fire-resistant suit waiting to put out burning Cobras.

He'd heard of several attempts by the Arupians to board Boone, but the Marines had repelled the attacks so far. He had heard of only minor injuries and light damage on the communicator.

The collision alarms wailed and the bridge talker spoke on the intercom. "Hanger deck, hanger deck! Brace for collision! Hostile craft closing!"

Harry and the other firefighters held their position behind the blast shield. He saw the Arupian landing craft move through the Harbison Field, most of its energy being absorbed. It hit the air curtains and slammed into the deck, bouncing once before ramming the bulkhead.

The doors fell open and twenty Arupian warriors scrambled off the crippled ship. The Marines were on the way, but the people here now had to buy some time. Harry flipped his fire suit helmet from his head and went to meet the first fur ball to come his way.

The Arupian snarled as Harry approached, the Arupian version of a grin. He holstered his weapon and swatted at Harry with his platter-sized paw, claws extended. Harry sidestepped the swat, grabbing the huge arm and twisting. As the cat fell forward and sidewise, Harry kicked. He felt ribs crack in the cat's chest as his foot met fur. The Arupian fell to the deck.

Harry glanced up and saw the remaining nineteen kitties wouldn't fall for this trick. He dove behind a large crate as they opened fire on him. He covered himself as best he could. Now he had to wait for the Marines to rescue him.

Chapter 13

Messages

The Arupians fired on Harry with both energy and projectile weapons. Hiding behind the nearly impenetrable blast shield of the hanger deck, his comrades seemed safe enough. Harry had only a plastic box as cover. The lasers melted the plastic where they hit, causing flaming globs to drop around him. He managed to dodge the bigger blobs. The projectile weapons shattered and shredded the plastic, spraying Harry with flying shards. His fire suit offered some protection, but cuts dug into his face from the flying debris. Harry hunkered down and waited for help.

He glanced toward the blast shield, and one of the men waved and pointed frantically towards the Arupians. Harry risked a fast peek around the edge of the box. An Arupian warrior approached with a wicked knife in his paw. He was very close now. Harry rolled to his right, away from the approaching fur ball. He crouched on the balls of his feet. His legs like coiled springs, Harry prepared himself to move quickly.

Harry cleared his mind. The sounds of the weapons firing faded from his attention, as did the shouting of both Arupian and human fighters. His mantra echoed in his head as he calmed and steadied himself. The familiar quiet of total awareness settled around him, pervading his mind. He could see, in his mind's eye, the approaching cat. Harry saw the Arupian shifting the knife in his paw to get a better grip. Like he could read the mind of the attacker, Harry sensed the nervousness the kitten had. The warrior knew he approached an enemy who had dropped a full-grown Arupian once already today.

A small smile spread across Harry's face as the fur ball neared the end of the crate. Harry knew the smile on his face reflected the joy of combat.

The Arupian peeked around the end of the crate and Harry sprang into action. The energy his mantra had stored in his muscles struck out in a bolt, directed at the hapless warrior. Harry grabbed the wrist of the kitty, twisting and spinning. The satisfying snap in the bones of the cat's arm caused the knife to clatter to the deck. Harry only vaguely saw the combined look of surprise and pain on the warrior's face. Harry pulled, and the Arupian spun behind the crate. The energy of his chi built.

He struck out and up with a single blow, the heel of his right hand striking the Arupian in the chin. The warrior's head snapped backward and Harry heard a loud pop. The Arupian went limp as his head lolled on a fractured neck, and he collapsed to the deck. The cat didn't move.

Harry instinctively dropped to a relaxed fighting posture, waiting for more attackers. He didn't wait long.

The doors of the hanger deck opened, and two hundred armored Marines swept inside, led by Ike Payne and a Corporal Harry didn't know. The Arupians watched Harry and didn't see the Marines until two-thirds of their numbers lay dead. Ike made short work of the remaining cats.

* * * *

Allie paced the waiting room in sickbay. She had walked out of the safe room against the orders of both her father and the Corporal that Ike had left in command. She had little information at this point.

Claire came from the treatment areas and Allie ran to her. "How is he?"

"He's fine. Just relax."

"I want to see him. Now."

"The nurses are cleaning his wounds. It will be about ten minutes." Claire turned to leave.

Allie grabbed Claire's arm. "No. Now."

"Maybe you didn't understand me." Claire's eyes narrowed. "He has a few cuts, nothing that even needs sutures. You can see him in about ten minutes when we throw him out of sickbay to make room for people who need to be here."

"I want to see him." Allie was firm, but she fought tears. She thought she had a reasonable grip on her control, at least for right now.

"Allie, you got by with walking out on daddy because he's a pushover for us girls." Claire had been an Admiral for more than six hundred years. The officer attitude now showed. "You got by with walking out on the guards because they didn't want to restrain you. You're in my sickbay now, and as one sister to another, I'll kick your ass clean into next Tuesday if you fuck with me. Do I make myself clear?"

Allie's tears broke through her forced bravado, streaming down her face in huge waves of sobs. "I'm scared!"

"I know you are." Claire put her arms around her sister. "He really is OK. Just a few little cuts that we could probably not treat at all." Claire laughed. "If we don't treat them, that might scar that handsome face of his, though."

"He's really all right?"

"Yes, he is." Claire sighed. "I'm sorry I went off on you. I don't like people coming into my sickbay trying to throw their weight around."

Allie's tears slowed, but a few still ran quietly down her face. She didn't know if more were coming or not. She cried because she worried that Harry might be seriously injured. Now she wanted to cry because he wasn't seriously injured. "I'm sorry, too."

The nurse came from the treatment area. "We're all done with him, Claire."

"Thanks." Claire held Allie at arm's length. "OK, sis. Go back there, kiss him, and get him the hell out of my sickbay. He's in room seven."

"Thanks. I'll get him out of your hair."

Claire kissed her forehead. "Good." She headed off to another case someplace in sickbay.

Allie went to the treatment room and found Harry sitting in the chair reading a magazine. He had several cuts on his face, some with strip bandages closing them. He looked up as she entered. "Hi. What are you doing here?"

Allie hugged him and knelt at his feet. "Are you OK?"

"I'm fine, but you didn't answer me."

"I came to make sure you're all right." Her shakes faded, now that she had seen him. "I'm worried about you."

"None the worse for wear." He laughed a little. "I think Damon beat me worse than the cats did."

She leaned and kissed him softly. She smelled and tasted the perspiration on his face when her lips touched his. It hit her, causing a wave of desire to run across her. "I think you're right."

"You need to get back to the safe room."

"Are you coming with me?"

"No, I have to get back. The Cobras are still out."

"Can I come with you?"

Harry laughed. "No, you can't! Go back to the safe room and relax."

"Yeah, right." Allie hugged him again. She made no move to let go.

He kissed her hair.

As they embraced, Ike stormed into the treatment room. "What the fuck is this?"

"I think we're both in trouble."

Allie only sighed. "Yeah, we are."

Ike pulled her helmet from her head, her hair a rat's nest. "Yeah, you're both in deep shit." She pointed at Allie. "I don't know if I should kick the Corporal's ass for letting you leave, or your ass for leaving! For now, you will get the righteous fuck back to the safe room, even if I have to have you clapped in irons to make it happen!" She pointed at Harry. "And you will get your sorry ass back to the fucking hanger deck!"

Harry frowned. "Why are Sergeants always yelling at me?"

"Because you, Sir, are a fuck up!" Ike turned to four of the privates who had came with her. "You four make certain the Princess gets to the safe room. Make certain that she stays there." She looked back to Allie, her face hard. "Do whatever is needed to keep her there."

"All right, Ike, I'll go." Allie hugged Harry again. "Be careful, OK?"

"You know I will." He kissed her.

* * * *

Ike walked part of the way to hanger deck with Harry. He thought he saw a smile on her face. "I wanted to tell you that deal with the Arupians was pretty impressive."

"Just doing my job."

"Maybe. I know a handful of jarheads that might be able to take down an Arupian in hand-to-hand combat."

"Just lucky, that's all."

"Lucky, yeah." Ike paused a moment. "Where did you learn to do that? What I heard about is nothing they teach in the Fleet training."

"I've had a little martial arts training."

"A little?"

"Yeah, just a little." They reached the point where Ike needed to turn for the Security Office. "Thanks for taking care of Allie."

"Just doing my job."

Harry laughed. "I guess I deserved that."

* * * *

The last fourteen Arupian ships ran away. "Helm, pursue the remaining carrier. Weapons, you may destroy that ship when in range." The helmsman played her controls. The weapons officer only grinned as the Arupian attack carrier exploded into flickering fireworks. Q smiled. "Recall the Cobras." His smile faded to a frown. "Losses on Cobras?"

"Forty-two, Sir."

"Thank you." Q considered. "Pull us back twenty million kilometers, and secure from battle stations."

"Aye, aye, Sir." *Boone* moved away from the field of battle.

Crews made minor repairs around the ship. No reports of major damage came in beyond the holes the Arupians punched in their failed boarding attempts. A few weapons had overheated from firing so long. The only deaths reported were the forty-two Cobra pilots. The reports showed only minor injuries. Overall, Boone destroyed fifty-seven ships of the Arupian line. From a military point of view, Q was happy with the outcome, but he stoically mourned the loss of his forty-two shipmates.

* * * *

As he secured his gear from battle stations, his communicator chirped. "Douglas."

"Harry are you all right did you get hurt again where are you when will you be home?"

"Allie, take a deep breath and relax! I'm fine! I'll be back to your cabin in maybe fifteen minutes."

"Are you sure you're OK?"

"Yes, I'm sure. Are you all right, other than in hysterics?"

He could hear her panting in the communicator. "Yes, honey, I'm fine. Please get home soon?"

"I will." She sounded like a scared little girl. "I'll be there as soon as I can." He cleared the link and finished stowing his gear.

While he walked to Allie's cabin, he saw only moderate activity around the ship as engineers checked systems and repaired anything they found damaged. The battle hadn't made Harry too nervous. He knew Boone could handle almost anything the Arupians had, other than another asteroid. He also knew Allie would be fine. The safe room for the royal family could survive, in stasis, almost anything short of an antimatter globule or a black hole. He reached Allie's suite and the door opened. She almost knocked him down when she dove into his arms.

"Harry! You're OK!"

"Yeah, I told you that, remember?"

She cried and had her head buried in his shoulder. "Yeah." Harry stepped forward with her in his arms enough so the door would close. She sniffed. "I was scared."

"I know, but everything's all right now."

"I can't do that twice."

"You won't have to."

* * * *

Allie cuddled to Harry's chest as they sat on the sofa listening to music. She wanted to touch him, to feel he was real and not gone.

Harry sniffed. "I should take a shower."

"No, stay here, please."

"I'm sweaty, and I smell like a goat!"

"No, you smell wonderful." Allie could smell the salty musk of his sweat on his clothes and body. Cooked in the chemistry lab of his body, Allie's mind processed the aroma into meaning he had protected her. Her mind knew he fought not only for her, but also for everyone on *Boone*, himself, and the Empire. All that mattered to her was the part about him protecting her. She inhaled deeply, the scent only slightly stirring her sexually. A wave of love and tenderness swept over her mind.

"That's a little crazy." He squeezed her shoulders.

"Maybe. I don't know if you can understand or not." She sniffed again. "I feel safe right now. I can feel in my heart and mind that you'll always protect me."

Harry chuckled. "They say that olfactory stimulation is the most intense."

"Don't get all clinical with me while I'm trying to be mushy."

"Sorry."

She cuddled closer.

He sighed. "The only thing that scared me with the Arupians was that I might lose you."

She laughed softly. "A big tough man isn't supposed to say that."

"Maybe, but it did. Maybe it's my male brain and the limitations that come with that, but I don't think I can put into words how much I care about you."

Allie sighed and tried to get closer. "You just did put it into words."

He seemed to pull away from his tenderness. "I know you said you like it, but I need to shower. I stink!"

"All right. You probably feel gritty, too. Come on." She held his hand as they went to the shower, and then helped him undress. As they stood under the warm cascading water, Allie licked his chest, tasting the amazing blend she had only smelled before. The salty taste sent shivers through her body. She wanted more.

"I didn't think anything would feel better than the water on my back, but I was wrong."

She smiled up into his eyes. Allie licked his chest and neck, her tongue savoring the heady combination of his body's alchemy that spoke to her heart of courage, intelligence, love, and passion. She wanted to taste Harry, to eat him up, feeling the wonderful caring and desire to protect her that his flavor spoke to her about. She reached the shower controls and shut off the water.

Harry frowned. "What are you doing?"

"I'm not really sure." She licked his chest, swirling her tongue around his nipples. Her hands pulled his body to her face as she kissed and sucked his skin, tasting him, wanting to get as much of the sweet flavor of love as she could from his body. Standing on her toes, Allie licked and kissed his face and neck. Her lips caressed the smooth texture of his beard, sucking the perspiration from the slick black hair. His hard cock pressed against her stomach, but Allie became lost in the desire to lick every inch of his body so she wouldn't miss even a single molecule of his flavor. She moved to his side, licking his shoulder. She lifted his arm in her hands, and kissed the full length, licking around and between his fingers before sucking his fingers into her mouth. "God, you taste great..."

Harry laughed a little nervously. "Um, OK. You won't hear me complain."

Allie stepped to stand behind him. Her tongue flicked up and down his back and across his broad shoulders. The water that had ran across his back made his taste less strong, but Allie could still feel the tingles it sent over her tongue. He wiggled slightly as she licked the edge of his back near his ribs. Allie's thoughts of love and protection drove her forward. She knelt on the shower floor, her mouth moving up and down the back of his legs. When she licked the back of his knees, Harry quivered.

Allie's breathing became rapid, and she could feel her heart hammering in her chest. Her pulse pounded in her ears. She could only whisper softly. "Turn around for me."

Harry turned. She licked from his feet, up his legs, until she reached his thighs. The water hadn't diluted the taste of his chemistry here, and the flavor was strong again. She knelt, holding the head of his cock in her hand, and licked his hard shaft. The intensity of the flavor hit her hard. Allie swirled her tongue around the head of his dick where his chemistry had added a few drops of pre-cum to the mixture. Her tongue thrilled at the taste. Holding the base of his cock firmly in her fist, she slipped the swollen head into her mouth, then down her throat. Harry shivered as her head bobbed over his length.

As she sucked and licked his cock, Allie knew that she wanted to taste his cum. Thoughts of the pleasure that would bring Harry were far from her mind, blinded by the overwhelming desire to taste him. Her mouth worked over his length, her tongue swirling around his cock as she sucked him. Harry reached back to grab the safety rail in the shower to balance against his shaking. His shaking intensified, and his hips thrust gently against her face. He moaned loudly. "Oh, my God! Yes, Allie!"

His cum erupted into her mouth, hot and sticky, its salty sweetness mixing with the flavors of his body as Allie sucked harder, draining him. She continued to lick the pulsing head of his dick as his hips bucked and his body shook.

Allie licked up his chest as she stood, gathering the small beads of new sweat that formed there. She kissed his lips gently. "You still taste great."

His breath came fast and rapid, causing his voice to sound choppy. "And you call me crazy." He managed a weak smile as his hands came from the rail to hold her.

* * * *

"Any idea what any of this means?"

Harry moved a few of the papers around on the conference table. He and Devon took over the ready room so they could spread the thousands of documents they found on the crashed Arupian landing craft on the big table. "Not really anything we don't know now. All old news."

"So, there's nothing here we need?"

"Not really." Harry moved the papers again. "Just copies of old orders and such."

"Damn it." Devon tossed his pen on the table. "We need a break on this. Has Empress Paige come up with any ideas?"

"Not yet. She said she needs to know the frequencies, or at least a small range, the cats are using. That will let her optimize the system."

Devon smiled. "I still think we should call the kitties and ask them."

"Yeah, right." Harry thought for a minute. "I'm going for a walk." He dropped his pen on the table and left.

He thought about going home, but Allie distracted him enough when he only thought about her. He thought about her all the time. He knew his male brain lacked the capacity really to express love, but he wanted to try. If he didn't concentrate, the only thing that came to mind to express his love for Allie was to have sex with her. Another man would understand that. Harry knew a woman didn't really understand that a man expressed his love for her through sex. At least he didn't think women understood that.

He didn't even notice the people he passed as he walked *Boone's* corridors. He wondered about the different ways men and women viewed love and intimacy. He tried to cuddle and hold Allie, to talk to her and call her cute little names. He talked baby talk to her regularly. Even though he didn't know what it was, he even called her 'pookums' a few times. She did the same for him. Well, not the 'pookums' thing. In his mind, no matter how hard that he tried, Harry believed he really showed her his love only when they had sex.

He smiled a little. He had entertained thoughts that Allie might be a nymphomaniac. He knew now he was mistaken. Allie knew exactly the differences in how they viewed love. She understood fully that Harry needed to make love to her to show his love. That was why she always seemed ready for sex. She also understood that he would hold her, giving her what she saw as an expression of love, at any time. He wondered if Allie actually knew these things consciously, or if she just followed her instincts. Harry knew it didn't really matter.

He thought he understood, within the limits of his male mind, what Allie saw as an expression of love. She wanted him to cuddle and hold her. She liked him to touch her, not in a sexual way, but in a tender, loving way. She liked him to stare into her eyes. He thought what she liked most of all was for him to talk to her. He laughed as he thought she probably liked to hear him stammer around trying to tell her how much he loved her.

He popped out of his revelry and saw that his feet had carried him to the hanger deck. He went in and saw the Arupian ship resting against the bulkhead where it crashed. The guards waved him through the security perimeter, and Harry went aboard the ship.

As he sat in the copilot's chair, Harry studied the control panel. Fluent in written and spoken Arupian, he could read the console. He knew nothing about flying a spacecraft, so most of the controls meant nothing. In the middle of the console, between the pilot and copilot, rested the communications board. He flicked the power on and watched the lights come to life. The heads up display floated in three dimensions before his face. Harry noticed a control marked with a series of squiggles, the Arupian equivalent of *HISTORY*. He pressed the button.

A list of numbers appeared in the display. Each number had the form of three digits, a period, and three more digits. He stared at the list for a moment before the hair on the back of his neck stood up. These numbers are frequencies.

* * * *

"All of the frequencies are between 135 and 155 megahertz." Paige wrote something on her handheld data terminal. "That would be prefect for ground to low orbit and ship to ship communications at low power. You don't need any fancy equipment of any kind to make it work."

Allie held his arm tightly. Since the battle, she seemed to want to touch him all the time. "Does that help us?"

"I think so, Harry. The equipment to do this would be simple stuff the Arupians probably had on hand." Paige smiled. "I think they're counting on the low power as the only measure needed to keep us from listening to them."

"So when can we get started?"

"Today. The hardest thing will be building the antenna. It needs to be big, and it needs to be in free space so nothing interferes with it." She wrote on the data terminal again. "Maybe a week tops to get that part up and running. Tanya said she can give me plenty of computer power, so that's not a problem."

Harry and Allie left as Paige mumbled something about cryogenic encapsulation of the ultra-low noise amplifiers.

* * * *

Paige decided on two antennas instead of one. The antennas took shape over the next five days. Huge structures, nearly as long and as wide as *Boone*, the antennas were mostly empty space. The artificers welded and bolted long tubes and lengths of stiff wire together into a spider web of intricate straight lines and right angles. Each antenna had several small impulse motors to keep the antenna pointed in the right direction, and a guidance system controlled the motors. The two antennas were placed several thousand kilometers apart to allow the computers to combine the received signals using a system Paige called an interferometer. All Allie knew was that her mom said it would let them hear the signals better.

Paige appropriated a conference room near the hanger deck for her work with the special receivers. The place looked like the lab of a mad scientist from some of the old movies Allie's parents seemed so fond of. Large vats with wires and cables running from them boiled with white vapor venting from fittings. Huge coils of wire arced with tiny bolts of lightening. The smell of ozone hung heavy in the air.

Allie watched her mother move among the equipment. She reached to touch one of the coils of wire. Paige grabbed her arm. "Don't touch that!"

"It's not smoking or anything." Allie pulled her hand away from the coil.

"Just because it's not on fire doesn't mean it won't hurt you." Paige picked up a heavily insulated metal rod. She moved it toward the coil. A loud snapping sound accompanied a bright flash of electricity. "See?"

"Oh." Paige sat the rod down and looked around the room with her hands on her hips. She smiled and looked satisfied with her creation. "Mom, can I talk to you?"

"Sure." Paige pulled up a lab stool and sat next to Allie. "What's on your mind?"

"In a word, Harry."

Her mother smiled. "He should be on your mind."

"Well, yeah, but I'm worried about him. He's spending a lot of time on this war. I'm afraid he's getting a little burned out." Allie smiled. "You're the only mom I have who is really in the Fleet."

Paige held the rank of Rear Admiral. "I guess I am. Little one, we're all stressed with the war, especially your father. Now you have Harry to worry about, too." Paige paused for a moment. "If you want my opinion, he's the best chance we have to win this."

"That's what I mean. He's trying to do this alone."

"Yeah, men do that a lot." She smiled. "Just look at your dad."

"Yeah. Harry does the same things, too. He reminds of daddy in that respect." Allie sighed. "Mom, how can I help him?"

"That's the easy part. Harry, just like your father, will push himself too hard. Yeah, he wants to serve the Empire and its people, but he's doing most of it for you. He's just trying to protect you." Paige took her hand. "The best thing you can do for him is to just love him. Let him know that you appreciate what he's doing for you. Never, ever let him forget for a single second that he's the center of your universe."

"That sounds too simple."

"It is simple, but men are pretty simple minded, bless their hearts."

Allie laughed. "I guess that's true."

"Yeah, it is." Paige released Allie's hand and stretched. "I need to go check the antenna. Just support him and be there for him."

* * * *

Allie stood next to Harry, her arm around his, as they watched Paige activate the system. The soft hiss of static filled the room as the receivers came to life. Paige listened to her headset and played the controls in the crude panel in front of her. Allie smiled as she thought the panel looked like something a hobbyist would have cobbled together in his garage.

Paige moved a control for the antenna comparator. A sudden burst of high-pitched whining screamed from the speakers. Paige twisted the volume control and the sound softened. She pulled her headphones from her ears and smiled at Harry. "Data tones. We've got them."

* * * *

Harry sat at the dining room table with a stack of printouts from the data Paige's radio had received. He said that the data had only light encryption. It seemed Paige had been right about the Arupians relying on the low power to hide the messages.

Allie tried to leave him alone to work. She found herself going to the kitchen after things about every fifteen minutes. On the way there or back, she would touch his shoulder or kiss him briefly. She knew she was disturbing him, but she couldn't help herself. She wanted to touch him.

During one such visit, Allie rested her hand on his shoulder. Harry put his hand on hers. He looked at the squiggles of Arupian text for a moment. He tensed. "What's wrong?"

"Oh, my God."

"What?"

"Allie, they're going to destroy this system. And Earth."

* * * *

The meeting in Jim's office was small. Harry was the lowest ranking officer there, and the next lowest was Major General Dietrich. Jim had his feet up on the desk. "So, this is similar to what the Samulians did in the New England system seven hundred years ago."

"Only in that they both involve black holes." Harry gathered his thoughts. "The Samulians found a way to contain a black hole in a gravity generator they could control. That let them effectively turn the black hole on and off. The difference is that the Samulians made it work with a quantum black hole of planetary mass. The ones that the Arupians have are much larger. As near as I can tell, and I'm no physicist, these are just about of solar mass."

Q wasn't a physicist either, but his positronic brain had tremendous speed and power. "If such a black hole would be dropped into a star, the resulting collapse and energy release would sterilize the system."

Jim rocked slowly. "Right. What I would call a bad day." He stared at the bulkhead for a few minutes. "When will these things be ready, Harry?"

"Near as I can tell, about ten days, maybe two weeks."

"And they plan to launch one to Sol system and Earth, then use the other in this system?"

"Right."

Jim rocked for a moment. "Ben, what are our options?"

Dietrich thought for a moment. "Only two that I can see. We either sterilize this system, or we go after the weapons."

"I was afraid you'd say that. What would be the losses on going after the cat toys?"

"I'd guess maybe thirty or forty percent. The fur balls will be eager to protect them."

"Right." Jim continued to stare at the walls.

"Jim, there may be a problem going in after the weapons." Q looked at Dietrich for a moment. "I think Ben is right. The Arupians will defend the weapons heavily. I also think they'll set the device off if we attack."

Harry nodded. "The messages sound desperate. I think the Admiral is right."

"That still leaves us with the same options." Dietrich sighed. "The only change would be that we send a small team in to neutralize the weapons instead of a full out assault to destroy them."

"I think we'd have the same problem sterilizing this system, too." Jim looked back to the group at his desk. "What would stop them from setting the thing off while we're attacking?"

Q shrugged. "Nothing. I think you're right."

"Yeah. That leaves us with one chance. A small team to neutralize the threat of the weapon." Jim inhaled deeply. "Harry, is there any indication in those messages that they plan to give us an ultimatum?"

"No, nothing that I saw."

"That's fucking great."

Q hesitated. "Jim, in light of this new threat, I think *Boone* needs to withdraw."

"I understand what you're saying, Q. The answer is no. I'm staying right here."

"What about sending your wives and children away?"

Jim laughed heartily. "Do you want to make that suggestion to them? I'm sure not going to do that!"

Q smiled. "Right."

"OK. We have a few days to decide what to do, and a few more days to get ready to do what we decide." Jim put his feet on the floor. "Ben, you work on plans. Coordinate with Q, and Harry will get you the information you need. Harry, you keep reading the mail. Q, you work on what ships we need to keep here, and get the rest out of this system before the Arupians have a chance to set this thing off. Also. Come up with a way to detect if they launch towards Sol system. Dismissed."

Chapter 14

Plans

The workload almost overwhelmed him. Since Paige had the receivers working, he had a nearly endless stream of documents he needed to decode and read. He delegated much of the work to other intelligence staff members, but he still had more than three hundred pages a day he needed to look at himself.

His efforts gleaned valuable information. The Arupians had built a base on the inner moon of the planet, and they built their weapons at that base. He gathered a few details about the black holes that the physicists found interesting. The base for building the weapons seemed heavily guarded, as Dietrich predicted, and well protected by automatic weapon systems and alarms.

Harry also refined his estimate of when the weapons would be ready. He believed they had six or seven days before the Arupians would have the weapons ready for deployment. He confirmed that the cats didn't plan to give any warning to *Boone* before they used the weapon in their own system. No ultimatum, just total destruction.

The plan for a small force to attempt to neutralize the weapon moved forward. Harry gave Dietrich the information about the moon and weapon as he decoded the pages. In addition to the construction base, the moon had other installations including a number of conventional weapon emplacements, a repair center for ships, and a prison.

Harry found several messages of a more political nature. Instead of talking about the weapon or the battle plan, the Arupian government seemed concerned about riots, protests, and general discontent among their own people. Harry read these messages to say that the Arupian people weren't as much behind the war as the government wanted it to seem. Harry doubted that the people knew anything about the plans of their government to kill them all.

His communicator chirped. "Douglas."

"Hi."

"Hi, Allie."

"What time do you think you might be home?"

"Why? Do you have a guy in there you need to get rid of before I come home and kill him?"

She laughed. "No, silly! I hoped we could go to the Café for dinner tonight."

He checked his watch. It was 1715. "Yeah, that sounds good to me." Harry's eyes hurt and he rubbed them. "Give me fifteen minutes, and I'll be there."

* * * *

Allie always felt good in his arms, but since Harry's actions on the hanger deck, it somehow got even better. She never thought of Harry as being a physical person. Her thoughts of his strength had always been more in terms of his mental abilities. Harry killed an Arupian soldier with one blow, and left another with a dislocated shoulder and five broken ribs. He obviously had secrets she hadn't learned yet. Allie knew she wanted to spend the rest of eternity learning about him.

As they danced, Harry's hands moved softly over her back, holding her close to his chest. His ability to read her moods fascinated Allie. At times, Harry could be tender and gentle, treating her like a little girl. Others, he could be aggressive and forceful. He always seemed to know what her mood wanted at the moment. The female soloist sang about being someone's lady and the recipient of the song being her man. Allie sighed as she prayed she would always be Harry's lady, and he would always be her man.

When the song ended, they walked to their table holding hands. She sat down as he held her chair. He leaned to kiss her cheek and smelled her hair. "I remember that first day you took me to your cabin."

"Yeah. I thought my suite smelled bad."

He laughed. "Not at all. It smells like you, all sweet, fresh, and innocent. Don't ask me what innocent smells like, because the best answer I could give would be that it smells like you."

"Innocent isn't a smell." She smiled over her wine glass. "Besides, if you think I'm innocent, you haven't been paying attention."

"Allison Jenkins! Are you flirting with me?"

"Not exactly."

"What then?"

"I'm trying to seduce you."

"Oh."

She slipped her shoe off and moved her leg to rest her heel on the chair between his legs. Her toes wiggled against his crotch. "Should I stop?"

"I never said that." He smiled at her. "But you're going to make it hard for me to walk."

"My goal is to make something hard for you."

"Oh."

Allie laughed. "Am I making you uncomfortable?"

"No, not really. You're right, though."

"I'm always right." She wiggled her toes and Harry jumped. "What am I right about this time?"

"That whole innocent thing is way off base."

"Maybe. I wish the OD was open." A large section of the observation deck was for adults only. The area had no banned activities. The trees and grass still needed replacing, so the OD remained closed to visitors.

"Yeah. So much for public displays of affection."

A thought slowly came to Allie's mind. The smile came to her face much faster. "Finish your drink."

"Why?"

"Come on. Let's get out of here."

Harry looked puzzled, but he tossed off his beer and they left the club. As they walked to the elevator, Allie held his arm and bumped her hip against his. While they waited for the elevator to arrive, Allie kissed him, running her tongue deep into his mouth, her hands straying through his long hair as she pulled his face to her. Allie's excitement built and she could tell from the swelling in Harry's pants that he followed suit.

Just as the doors opened on the empty elevator car, Allie whispered in Harry's ear. "I forgot to wear panties." Harry blinked at her as she pulled him into the car. The doors closed. She pressed the *STOP* button. "I want you." She rubbed his cock through his pants.

Allie undid his pants and let them fall to the floor. After stroking his cock for a moment, Allie turned and leaned with her hands on the rail in the elevator. She lifted her skirt to her hips. "Now." She looked back at Harry and saw a silly smile on his face. He moved in behind her, and his stiff dick slide smoothly into her pussy.

They moved together slowly, and his cock slipped completely from her before he plunged back into her flowing cunt. He held firmly to her hips as he bucked against her, causing Allie to fight to keep her feet. As he thrust with more urgency, Allie reached over and started the elevator moving again.

Harry froze in mid thrust. "What are you doing?"

Allie stifled a giggle. "We're playing elevator roulette, that's all."

"What if someone catches us?"

"That's the idea." Allie tingled at the thought that someone might catch them. Maybe even her folks. "Don't stop."

Harry moved again, slowly at first. In moments, his raging hardness filled her, sliding quickly in her pussy. "This is crazy!"

"Yeah."

As they neared their stop, Harry thrust mightily into her, and his cum spurted inside her. Harry had just buttoned his pants as the door opened. He didn't move to leave the car. "That was, um, fun."

"I thought so."

He hesitated. "Want to do it again?"

"Yeah!"

They played elevator roulette for three hours before finally going home.

People caught them only twice.

* * * *

Harry woke up at 0530 and couldn't get back to sleep. Allie cuddled to his side, a gentle smile on her face. She snored quietly. A small trail of drool ran down her cheek. Her hair looked like a grenade had sprayed it in every possible direction.

She was beautiful.

Harry sat in the semidarkness and watched her sleeping. He knew this was the love of his life resting in his arms. She was the person he wanted to be with for the rest of his life.

Harry knew Allie was the most beautiful woman he had ever seen. Her physical beauty was second to none. It was her soul that held her true beauty, though. He could feel her caring when she looked at him. Her touch would send him into frenzy. Her smile could melt his heart. When she kissed him, Harry could feel his heart try to leap from his chest. He knew he had found true love and true happiness.

Allie had once told him that she thought he was the marrying kind. Maybe he was, because he wanted to marry Allie.

His mind wandered. He could see her, dressed in a long white wedding dress. As the strains of the wedding march played, he saw her walking towards him. He thrilled as, in his imagination, her father placed Allie's hand in his. His mind played the sounds of the wedding ceremony in his head, and he could see gentle tears on her smiling face through the veil.

As he raised her veil to kiss his new bride, Harry saw the twinkle of happiness in her eyes. In his daydream, he could taste her lips as they shared their first married kiss.

His mind seemed to fast-forward. He sat beside Allie's head as she gave birth to their first child. The details of his imagination even told him it would be a girl. The baby they held between them had the honey blonde hair and the bright emerald green eyes of her mother. They cuddled their baby together and talked quietly about love and life. They talked of being together for all eternity.

Again, his mind sprang into the future. He and Allie sat in the church as their daughter took her husband. He looked like a fine man, a Marine, and he stood proudly beside Harry's baby. When they turned to face the congregation, Harry saw that his daughter looked exactly like Allie, down to the last detail.

Her new husband was Damon Hyde.

* * * *

Ben watched the young Lieutenant sitting across the desk from him. Ben needed someone to lead the assault on the Arupian base, but his best man had died two months ago. He had to settle for second-best now. "Tell me, Draper, what makes you think you can do this?"

"Mostly because we have to do it, Sir." Draper frowned for a moment. "General, we have to do this. My team and I are ready, and we can get the job done."

"I know we have to do it." The General leaned back in his chair. "And it has to work. If not, we're probably all dead. We just don't know it yet." He thought the young man might be able to pull this off, if he lived long enough.

"Yes, Sir."

Dietrich considered the man facing him for a moment. "All right. The job is yours." He pulled a folder from his desk drawer. "Here are the diagrams and maps that we have so far. Douglas is working on getting more details for you, and that will continue up until you leave."

Draper thumbed through the dossier. "Sir, some of these protective systems around the base look pretty sophisticated."

"They are that. Do you have a technician in mind that you think can defeat them?"

"I don't know, General." He read a few paragraphs of Harry's reports. "I'll have to set this up in the simulator so we can practice."

"Very well. You'll have only one landing craft, and it will carry a cloak. You have a hard limit of 125 people on your team. Choose wisely, Lieutenant."

* * * *

Allie watched Harry as he worked at the dining room table. He had papers spread all over the table's surface, plus more in the chair next to him. He hadn't spoke for more than an hour. He also had only nibbled at the pizza they shared for dinner. Allie worried about him. He slept only a few hours a night and would go all day without eating. His eyes had dark circles around them, and he looked to have lost weight.

When she came to stand behind him, he didn't react to her presence. "Harry?"

He looked around, as if seeing her for the first time. "Oh, sorry."

"That's all right." Allie leaned and hugged him from behind. "Why don't you take a break?"

He rubbed his eyes, stretching his back and neck. He put his hands on her arms. "I wish I could."

Allie considered making him take a break. One thing that stayed her hand was that she wasn't at all certain she could. She had never seen him this distracted or absorbed. She wondered if she would be able to seduce him right now. Allie smiled to herself as she thought she might be protecting her own ego against failure. "Believe it or not, I do understand." She kissed his neck. "I know you're doing this for me."

"I guess I am." He stared at his papers. "I don't want to ruin my macho image, but I can't let anything happen to you." He pulled her arm and sat her in his lap. "Maybe it's some bit of leftover evolution, but I can't help myself. I have to protect you."

She saw a look of mixed emotions on his face. There was tenderness and caring there. Allie could see fear in his eyes, not a fear of death, but a fear of failure and loss. His desire to protect her touched her deeply, far down in her soul, but the expression on his face went farther. The urge to cuddle him to her, to hold him and make his fears subside, swept over her. Maybe she simply reacted to having a man willing to give up everything for her safety and happiness. Allie hugged his neck and kissed his cheek. "I know."

He sighed. "I need to get back to work."

Allie let her best seductive smile slip to her face. "I could sit on your lap while you work."

"Yeah, that would work well." He chuckled. "Maybe I should pass on that."

"All right. I'll let you get by with that for now." She kissed his nose. "I'll take a rain check." As she stood, the doorbell rang. "I'll get that."

When Allie opened the door, Devon almost ran her down on his way to the table. "Harry, one of the coders just brought this to me." He handed Harry a printout.

Harry read for a moment. "When did we get this?"

"In today's batch of recordings." Devon fidgeted. "What do you think this means?"

"Pretty simple. They have a prisoner who isn't cooperating too well with them."

"Yeah. Me, too." Devon cleared some papers from a chair and sat down. "I already asked Admiral Q, and we don't know of any prisoners held by the Arupians."

Allie stood behind Harry, her hands on his shoulders. "Could it be a Cobra pilot?"

"Maybe." Harry hadn't looked away from the printout. "We can't be certain that the missing ships and pilots were destroyed." He worked the data terminal. He stared at the original Arupian code that went with the printout. "Devon, do we have anyone else missing and presumed dead?"

"Several people from the OD and Lieutenant Hyde."

Allie's breath quickened. "Damon?"

Harry nodded slowly. "I don't know. What we do know is that the Arupians have a human prisoner at the prison."

"Then we have to go after him!" Her excitement roared.

"That may not be possible." Devon looked at Harry for a moment. "The weapon has to be top priority. The Marine idea of never leaving a man behind is good sentiment, but we can't risk the big target to rescue one person." He sighed. "It may or may not be Hyde."

"I know that." Allie paced behind Harry. "We can't just sit back and do nothing."

Harry wouldn't look at her. "We have no choice." He sighed. "We can't go after this person."

Allie stopped pacing and stared at him. For the briefest of moments, a thought flashed through her mind that Harry didn't want to rescue Damon. Things settled the way he wanted them, and bringing Damon into the mix would upset Harry's plans. Repulsion gripped her. The idea that Harry might do that didn't repulse her. Her own thoughts and doubts of Harry did that. She pushed the thoughts deep away inside her mind. "We have to do something."

"Yeah." Harry rubbed his eyes again. "I just don't know what." He stared at the printout for a moment. "Devon, we need to keep this between us for now."

* * * *

"Two days before the mission is not a good time to learn about this, Mr. Douglas."

Harry and Q sat alone in the Admiral's office. "No, Sir, it's not. I just learned of this myself yesterday."

"Are you certain about this information? We have no reason to believe that the Arupians have captured anyone."

"You have to define certain. I'm certain they have, or least had when this message was sent, a human prisoner."

Q sat the printout aside. "You think that it's Lieutenant Hyde?"

"I can't imagine it being anyone else." Harry gathered his thoughts. "We have ninety-seven people listed as missing. Forty-two are Cobra pilots from the last battle." Space battles left few, if any, survivors. "Fifty-four are from the asteroid impact on the OD. The remaining one is Damon Hyde."

Q nodded. "I can see your logic. That doesn't change things, however."

"No, Sir."

"Have you mentioned this to General Dietrich?"

"No, Sir. The only people who know about this outside of this room are Lieutenant Henson and Allie."

"Very well." Q watched him for a moment. "Why do I feel like you're about to spell some plan out for me that will make this all work?"

Harry shrugged. "I'd like to, Admiral. Right now, I have an idea cooking, but it's not done yet."

"Time is not our friend, Mr. Douglas."

"That's for sure." Something bounced loose in his head, an idea that tickled his mind. "Sir, can you give me five hours to work on this?"

Q frowned. "The assault team is practicing on the holographic simulator for the mission as planned. Are you thinking of changing that mission?"

"Maybe I am, Sir." Harry decided to play his cards. "If the mission fails, we're all dead. Even if it succeeds, the team may be dead. If we can make a rescue attempt without shifting the odds of the overall mission, I think we should do that."

A smile slowly came to Q's face. "The Fleet isn't supposed to be gung-ho on getting back missing people."

"No, Sir, I guess we're not. I still think it's the right thing to do."

"Perhaps." Q considered him for a moment. "If we knew this person wasn't Mr. Hyde, would you be so eager to go after the prisoner?"

Harry asked himself that very question many times over the last twelve hours. "I want to tell you that I would, but I'm not sure. My job is to deal with the facts, Admiral, and keep my emotions out of the equations. Honestly, I think I've failed at that, at least to a degree. The only answer I can give you is that I want to go after this person, no matter who it is. The fact that it may be Damon makes me want to do that even more."

Q nodded. "Very well. Five hours. Be back here at 1530 with your plan. We'll discuss it with General Dietrich."

* * * *

Allie came up behind him and kissed his ear, her tongue flicking around his lobe. Harry sighed. "Love, I really can't do that right now."

"Are you telling me to stop?" She licked up his neck from his shoulder.

"No, I guess not, but I'm a little busy. I have to get this done for a meeting in two hours."

"This will only take a few minutes."

Harry laughed. "Gee, thanks for the vote of confidence!"

"That's not what I meant to say!"

"I know." He turned in the chair and pulled her to stand in front of him. He kissed her stomach through her blouse. "I just have a lot to do and no time to do it."

"It's been that way for almost a week now."

"Yeah." He thought back and a pang of guilt hit him for not spending more time with her. In his mind, Harry knew that the time he spent away from her now would give them more time in the future. He thought of it like a bank for time. That didn't really change that he had neglected her. "Allie, I know you're excited about maybe finding Damon. I don't want you to get your hopes up too much." He waved at the papers on the table. "There are several billion things that can wrong with this, and it may not even be him."

Allie stared down at him for a moment. "Here." She moved his arms and sat in his lap. "I know that, but I think what's really on your mind is what happens to us if things go right and it is him."

A pain shot through him, and his heart fell into his feet. "Yeah, that has crossed my mind."

"I know it has." She hugged him.

"Is this where the but, Harry part comes in?"

"No. I'll be thrilled if Damon is alive, and I'll be happy to see him. It's you I want to stay with."

"Are you sure?"

"I've never been more certain of anything. I won't try to deny that I love Damon." She smiled at him. "I'm your lady, and you are my man."

His heart danced its way up his legs from his feet. Once back in his chest, it raced. He heard the pounding of his pulse in his ears. A knot of tension that had rested between his shoulders for nearly a week dissolved into relaxation. His male brain struggled with the feelings. Holding her close to him, Allie sitting in his lap, he felt excitement, but not a sexual excitement. Harry smiled to himself, thinking that this was love. At some point that his brain had missed, Harry moved from pure lust to true love. He'd completely missed the transition. "I don't know what to say."

"I have no doubt of that." She kissed his nose. "I'll let you get back to work."

* * * *

General Dietrich blinked at Harry. "Let me get this straight. You want to change everything, two days before we land, to raid a prison for someone who may or may not even be there?"

"No, Sir. I know the person is there. I just don't know who it is." Harry smiled. "I'll bet you credits to donuts that it's Damon Hyde."

"Shit."

Lieutenant Draper joined the meeting. "General, this is a Marine we're talking about. We can't leave him there."

"This is terrible timing. Draper, your team has spent four days practicing for a particular mission. Now we're changing that."

"Yes, Sir. It's not that different, though." Draper glanced at Harry. "Mr. Douglas has shown me the new assault plan, and it's basically the same."

Q held up his hand. "Let's all have a look at the proposed plan."

Harry spread several maps on the desk. "They built the new base around the old prison, like adding a room to a house." He pointed to the map. "The original plan had the team entering here, about nine hundred meters from the objective. The team would have to pass this garrison to reach the objective." He pointed again. "Now, the team will enter here, going through the prison. That takes the distance to the object to about sixteen hundred meters, but they bypass the garrison, coming in here, behind the Arupians." Harry smiled. "I'll bet the prison guards will give them less trouble than the garrison guards, too."

Dietrich pointed to a pair of heavy weapon emplacements near the entrance to the prison. "What about these big guns?"

"I think those are abandoned, Sir." Harry pulled a few pictures from his folder. "See? There have been no changes or activity there for two weeks."

The General looked like he'd swallowed a frog. He must have swallowed it only halfway, because he worked his mouth like the frog kicked in his throat. "Shit." He finished swallowing the frog. "I don't care who that is in there, Marine or Fleet, we can't just leave them there to rot."

Harry thought he saw a small smile play across Q's face. "Ben, this is your call."

"Draper, what problems do you see in the changes?"

"The biggest would be these sensor arrays, here." He pointed to an area just inside the entrance. "Also, we have the cell doors to deal with. We don't want to use explosives unless we have no choice. The team technicians would need to get up to speed on how to bypass all of this, and that will be cutting things close."

"All right, we can get them the time." Dietrich sighed. "Can you do it?"

"I think so, Sir."

Dietrich nodded. "OK, we'll go this way."

Chapter 15

Assault

Rich Draper watched the technicians working the simulation Harry set up for the sensors, alarms, and cell doors. They hadn't done very well. The number of possible security variations coupled with the ambiguity of the information Harry had to work with left the technicians in a position they had never been trained to handle. So far, in sixty-one tries, the technicians had succeeded only nine times.

Rich knew the techs were the best available. He couldn't blame them for having problems solving Arupian puzzles at a glance. They could all read Arupian, at least enough to read the control panels, but they couldn't think like an Arupian. That was the problem. To solve the puzzles quickly, as quickly as the team would need them solved, the techs needed to think like an Arupian.

He watched as the simulator's computer announced that the techs were all dead. "OK, let's try it again, people." He reset the computer for another try.

* * * *

Q had breakfast with Jim and his wives. The morning briefings happened routinely, even if they didn't happen every day. He had laid out the generalities of Harry's plan.

Paige poked at her omelet. "I'm not a combat officer, but this sounds crazy to me."

"It might be crazy enough to work, though." Marilyn ate her hash browns with her fingers.

Jim ate quickly. He had cut his hand yesterday and his nanites needed extra fuel to repair the damage. He had three omelets and as much bacon as the others put together. "Crazier things have happened."

Q smiled remembering an inexperienced Commander taking a team of a hundred Marines to secure an entire planet against the Samulian Empire seven hundred years ago. "Yes, they have, and you did them."

"I suppose I have." Jim tossed off his seventh glass of orange juice. "How is the team doing?"

"Fairly well, other than the technicians having problems with the sensor systems."

Tanya glared at Marilyn for eating with her fingers. "That's g-going to b-b-be key to this. If they can't g-get through undetected, it's all over." Even though she wasn't Fleet, Tanya had spent the last 2,800 years around the Fleet. She knew more about Fleet operations than most Admirals.

"They understand that." Q waited while the steward took his empty plate.

Jim nibbled on another slice of toast. "How is Ben feeling about this one, Q?"

"He's nervous, but I think he has faith in the success."

"I'll bet he's not as nervous as I am." Jim chewed thoughtfully. "I'm worried about the problems the techs are having. Like Tanya said, no matter what else happens, if they can't get in undetected, we're fucked."

"Watch your mouth. There are ladies present." Marilyn wiped up the last of her egg on her finger and slowly licked it clean. Jim stared at her.

Q laughed. "Maybe I should leave."

"Marilyn, s-stop that! W-w-we're at the b-breakfast table, for God's s-s-sake!"

"That's never stopped her before!" Paige had the giggles as she watched Marilyn's seductiveness and Tanya's irritation.

"I'm going from here to check with Draper and see how things are going." Q checked his watch. "The operation begins in thirty-one hours."

Jim pulled his eyes away from Marilyn. "Right. What's the plan to get them there?"

"Classic diversion, actually. *Boone* will make a high speed run at the planet, shooting anything that moves. As we pass the moon, we'll drop the landing craft. *Boone* will fire a few shots at the moon to make things look good, but our prime target will be a nuclear power plant just outside the capitol on the planet."

Jim nodded. "Good. Just going to let the landing craft fall to the surface?"

"As much as possible, yes. The landing craft has a cloak as well. We hope the Arupians will be so busy watching *Boone* that they'll miss the landing craft. We'll also continue to hit targets on the planet for a few hours afterwards, just to keep the defenders busy and distracted."

Paige thought for a moment. "We know enough about their communications systems now that we can play merry hell with them."

Q smiled. "That would add nicely to the general confusion."

"I'll get with the communications department right after breakfast."

"Very well." Q checked his watch again. "I should go check on Draper. Paige, please let me know when you have the communications interference ready. Thank you for breakfast." Q left, headed for the holographic simulator.

* * * *

Harry came to bed at 0515. He had tried to be quiet, but Allie woke when he climbed into bed next to her. She put her arms around him, and he fell asleep in minutes.

She looked at the clock. It was 0830. Allie considered waking him but decided against it. He hadn't slept well for the last week.

As she held Harry, she wondered about her feelings and how she would react if this nebulous prisoner actually was Damon. She wanted to stay with Harry, but she couldn't deny that she and Damon shared something very special. Allie still loved Damon, but she knew now it had been a different love from what she and Harry now had for each other.

She had no regrets about either her love for Damon or for Harry. She wondered, as she had at the time, if she had really made the right choice by picking Damon. Thinking back to that time, and looking at the last two months as well, she knew that, even after knowing her for only a couple of weeks and never having been intimate, Harry loved her so much that he was willing to give her up to make her happy.

Harry mumbled in his sleep, and he moved in jerky fits at times. Watching his eyes in the dim nightlights, Allie could see them moving behind his lids. She kissed his forehead softly.

She knew he felt responsible for the dead and injured from the first team. This team, much larger, weighed on his mind just as much. Allie could sense in Harry the stress of possibly sending them to die. He'd told her several times that he had no choices, however. He also had the weight of knowing that, if his plan failed, *Boone* would probably be just as dead.

Allie found herself talking to Harry, just like he was awake. "I wish I could do something to make this all easier for you, but I don't know what that might be." She smiled to herself, and decided she should stop talking out loud. Then again, what difference did it make? "Thank you for taking care of me. Thank you for caring about me the way you do. I know you're the man I want to be with, and I want to feel you near me forever. No matter what."

She held him to her and his sleep quieted, like he had waited for her to speak to him. He slept until 1030.

* * * *

Harry's head still had cobwebs when he reached Admiral Q's office at 1200. He thought he'd actually rested. When he woke, Allie was awake holding him, still in the last position he could remember before he fell asleep.

Q roused Harry from his thoughts. "We have a problem, Lieutenant."

Harry yawned. "Sorry, Sir. What sort of problem?"

Q nodded at Draper. "I hate to admit this, especially to the Fleet, but the techs are just too dumb to solve the problems you say they'll be up against."

Dietrich laughed a little. "Actually, they don't have the skills needed. They were never trained for this, and we don't have a year to train them."

Harry nodded as he stifled another yawn. "So, how can I help?"

"Mr. Douglas, is there a way you can give the technicians more information?" Q paused for a moment. "Perhaps get precise details on what they will be up against?"

"No, not really. A lot of the information you're asking for isn't in the messages we have." Harry shrugged. "Not really too surprising. After all, we don't routinely transmit the security codes to open the brig cells back to Earth. We're not really being secretive, there's just no need for that."

"Understood. We need something for the technicians to work with, something concrete."

"Yeah, I can see where this would be a bit much for a technician."

Q nodded. "If we can't give the team a bit more of an edge, I can't see any choice other than to go back to our original plan. If possible, they can go after the prisoner after the main objective has been completed."

"Just a minute, Admiral. If we do that, we'll likely not be able to rescue the prisoner." Harry could almost feel the chance slipping away from him. "We can do this in one order, but not the other. We have to get the prisoner first, then knock out the weapons."

Dietrich sighed. "If the team can't get inside, we won't be able to do either one."

"Harry, if there's a way to make this work, we'll listen." Q glanced at Dietrich and Draper. "We want to get that person out, but we must take out the weapons."

"Yeah." Jim joining the meeting interrupted Harry's thoughts.

"I'm not used to meetings that aren't in my office." Jim smiled as he sat down. "Actually, this is kind of nice."

"Thanks for coming, Jim." Q watched Harry for a moment. "We've already filled in Harry on the problems."

"I see." Jim sat down next to him. "We want to do this, not just because it might be Damon. Any member of the Fleet or Marines deserves the same consideration. It's up to you to tell us how to do it."

The answer came to him quickly, but Harry didn't care for it that much. He looked for another answer, but couldn't find one. "Actually, it's pretty simple and, at least to me, obvious."

Draper looked puzzled. "What?"

"I go with you to solve the puzzles."

Jim and Q barely reacted. Harry marked up most of that to their ages. Draper's mouth swung open. Dietrich chuckled. "You're not even a Fleet combat officer."

"No, Sir, I'm not. I can take care of myself, though."

"Harry, have you ever even fired a heavy weapon?" Draper looked amused.

"No, the things scare me." Harry grinned. "I don't even like hand weapons."

"This is great!" Dietrich had moved from chuckles to mild laughter. "I can't condone this, Q."

Q shrugged. "We asked him to give us an option, Ben. I think he's done that. I doubt there is anyone aboard *Boone* better qualified to do what we need."

Jim cleared his throat. "Harry, are you really sure about this?"

"Yes, I am. Since this is all my idea, don't I actually have an obligation to do everything possible to make it work?" Harry looked to Q. "I think I should go, but it's your call, Admiral."

Q leaned back in his chair. "I can't pass the buck on this one other than to ask Ben what impact this will have on the composition of the team."

"If I may, General." Draper thought for a moment. "There's a good argument that I'll lose a fighter by taking you along, Harry. Then again, after what you did on the hanger deck, we all know that's not true. I will lose a gun, though. I think I can live with that tradeoff."

Dietrich nodded. "If Mr. Draper is good to go, I'm behind him all the way."

Q looked at Jim. "Hey, don't ask me. I'm just the Emperor."

"Right." Q laughed. "Very well. You'll join the team, Mr. Douglas. Coordinate with Mr. Draper on your gear and other details."

Harry wondered what he had gotten himself into now.

* * * *

Jim stopped Harry as they left Q's office. "Walk with me." As they moved down the corridor, Jim tried to get his thoughts in order. "Having lived with her mother for seven hundred years, I can tell you that Allie is not going to be very amused by this."

"No, she won't." Harry looked confused. "What choice do I have?"

"None that I see. I'm just saying that she won't be happy."

"What would you do in my place?"

Jim laughed. "You should make that past tense. I've been in these situations. To make a long story short, I made the same decision you made, went home, told Janelle and the others, and then took my lumps."

"So, I just need to face her anger?"

"That's right." Jim smiled for a moment. "Even today, it sometimes amazes me that my wives aren't sisters, they're so much alike. Cut from the same mold, Allie is just like them. She won't yell and scream. She'll give you the silent tear treatment. After a while, she'll beg you not to go. Then she'll pout." He laughed. "By the way, she's just like her mother, and is very good at pouting. In maybe four or five hours, she'll come around. Actually, that's not right. She'll know right up front that you have to do this. She'll just admit to herself that she knows that. She'll still cry. Then she'll do the thing that I still don't understand."

"What's that?"

"She'll ask you right up front, one time, not to go."

Harry frowned. "That's the hard part."

"Yeah it is. The tears and the silent treatment are easy to deal with. Even if she screamed like Paige, that's pretty easy, too." Jim thought about the time he went to Samulus and Janelle didn't want him to go. "She'll put her arms around your neck and look at you with those amazing green eyes of hers. She'll ask you softly to stay with her, where it's safe." Jim shuddered a little. "It's really hard to say no to that."

"I can see that." Harry walked in silence for a moment. "But it's not safe here. I need to make it safe for her. I'm the only one who can do that."

"Precisely." Jim smiled. "At least that's what I always tell Janelle."

"How's that working for you?"

"She hasn't killed me yet."

Harry laughed. "I guess that's a plus."

"Yeah." Jim pondered for a moment. "I once told you that if you ever hurt Allie, I'd kill you. I take that back. You're going home now, and you're going to hurt her. I won't kill you for that." They stopped at the door of Jim's office. "You're going to hurt her because you love her."

"That sounds crazy. Even to me."

Jim laughed. "I guess it does."

* * * *

Rich checked him out in the body armor and the Marine version of the environment suit. Harry also had a rundown on the hand weapons and the AGLR1915 rifle. The automatic grenade-launching rifle is a huge, bulky weapon. It could fire 12-millimeter explosive projectiles at six hundred rounds per minute in fully automatic mode. It also could fire up to twenty-four close-quarters nuclear grenades. The weapon kicked like a sledgehammer to the shoulder, and the recoil could spin a man from his feet. Rich was finally satisfied Harry wouldn't kill himself with his own equipment.

Harry stood outside the door of Allie's suite for a few minutes, trying to nerve himself for the coming storm. According to Jim, it would be more ice than fire. He remembered the last time he'd stood here working up the courage to face her with bad news. The similarities struck him. The last time, Harry nerved himself to tell her that Damon was dead. Now, he nerved himself to tell her that he would probably soon be dead.

He stepped forward, and the door obediently swished open.

* * * *

Allie came from the kitchen when she heard the door. She hugged Harry. "Hi. You're a little earlier than I expected, so you have time to change before the pizza gets here."

Harry hugged her tightly, but he made no move to kiss her. "OK. Be back in a minute." He squeezed her again before going to the bedroom.

Allie watched him leave and wondered what he had on his mind. Over the time they had been together, she had learned to read his moods. Harry clearly had something on his mind, but it wasn't the same as the last week. He was tense, and that worried her. The tension in his body was different, somehow, from that of the past week. Allie couldn't put her finger on the difference, though. She gathered the pizza and drinks, and then went to meet him in the sitting room.

When he returned, he sat down next to her on the floor. Only then did he kiss her, not much more than a peck on her lips. She studied him for a moment. "What's up?"

His eyes darted around the room for a moment. "I guess this is something that I need to come right out and say." He took a deep breath. "I'm going with the team to the moon."

Allie's heart almost stopped. Her breath froze in her throat as she tried to swallow, but her mouth had gone instantly dry. She stared at him, her eyes wide, as her mind searched for some meaning to his words that she had missed at first. "What did you say?"

He took her hand in his, and Allie knew it must have felt cold and limp. "I have to go with the assault team. There are problems they can't handle. Without me, the rescue won't work."

"What about the attack on the weapons?"

"They can probably handle that part, but then we'll lose Damon."

Tears ran on her face, but she saw no point in wiping them away. "Then they take out the weapons."

"No. We have to rescue Damon, too. If they take out the weapon first, there's no chance to get Damon. If we rescue him first, we can still take out the weapon."

"Harry, we don't even know that it is Damon."

"No, not for certain, not based on the facts." A sad smile came to his face. "I can feel it in my gut. It *is* Damon."

"I can't lose you."

"I don't want that to happen, but if this fails, we're all lost. You, me, Damon, and everyone on *Boone* are all lost. For all I know, we'll lose everyone on Earth, too."

Allie tried to calm herself. She could feel panic and hysteria closing on her. She didn't know what argument to make to him. Harry's mind normally ran on logic and facts, but he seemed to ignore that now. "The weapons are top priority, so you don't need to go."

"Yes, I do." He sighed. "I owe this to him."

"I doubt Damon would see it that way." Allie brushed absently at the tears gathering on her chin as they ran down her face. "And what about the things you owe me?"

"I know. The biggest thing I owe you is a chance to live. I need to make sure that you're safe."

"I don't want to live without you." As soon as she said it, Allie knew it sounded flippant, a cliché, but the few words described her feelings to perfection.

"Don't say that, Allie." He moved to hug her, but Allie pulled away.

"I'm trying really hard not to scream at you right now." Allie's hysteria, barely contained, morphed into anger, also barely contained. "What are you thinking? There's at least even money the prisoner isn't Damon. You're leaving me, and you may die. Yes, we may all die anyway, but if we do, I want to die in your arms! What in the fuck are you thinking?"

Harry sagged a little. "I'm not sure I can explain this in a way that will make sense to anyone other than me. I'm not sure I really understand it myself." He stared at the bulkhead for a moment, his eyes focused on something only he could see, far out in space. "Your dad asked me one time if I've fallen in love with Damon. I told him that I'm not used to thinking that way, especially about a man, so I didn't really have an answer for him. Now that I've had time to think, maybe I have."

"You're not making any sense."

"Maybe I'm not." His eyes returned to the here and now, and he looked deeply into her eyes. "I love you, Allie. I think I always have, even before we met. I love Damon, too. I thought my own guilt and grief caused me to misunderstand, and I saw those feelings as love. I've never pretended to understand the polyamorous relationships your family is so fond of because I don't understand how a person can love, really love, more than one person. I still don't understand, but I know it's possible now, because I love you, and I love Damon."

Allie stared for a moment. "I thought you were being metaphorical before."

"So did I."

"This day is just full of fucking good news. First, you tell me you're going off to die over some mixed up sense of wanting to protect me. Now you're telling me that you're in love with someone else." Allie sighed. "Anything else you want to throw at me just for fun?"

"I'm not doing or saying any of this to hurt you. Only to protect you and tell the truth, try to explain why I have to go with the team."

Allie sat silently, trying to control her anger, and get her mind under control. She knew that Harry had feelings for Damon, but this made it official. "Believe it or not, I understand that. I'm just a little off balance right now. Maybe a lot off balance."

"I can see how that would happen." Harry managed a small smile. "So, aren't you going to try to talk me out of going? Please?"

Despite herself, Allie laughed. "I love it when you make me laugh." She sighed. "No, mostly because I know it won't work."

"I like making you laugh. You're right, though. I have to do this."

"Yeah." She sighed as a wave of remorse came over her for dodging his hug earlier. "Come here." She hugged him tightly. "All I ask is that you come back to me."

"That's my top priority once we get there. To get the job done, and come back to you."

"When do you have to leave?" Allie's anger had gone, leaving sadness behind.

"Everything starts happening at 1400 tomorrow. We'll drop at about 1440 or so."

"Shit. That soon?"

"Yeah." He ran his hands over her back, pulling her to him.

"What do you need to do to get ready?"

"Just show up. My paperwork is all ready, and they don't trust me with a gun."

Allie laughed again. "I can't blame them for that." Her tears had slowed to a trickle now. "So, you're mine until tomorrow?"

* * * *

They spent the night cuddled together. They never had sex, but they made love all night. Allie held Harry as he slept, having taken the sleeping pill Claire gave to the team. He needed to rest for the mission.

Her mind wandered around. The feelings Harry had expressed for Damon were neither new nor surprising. He'd hinted around at the idea for a long time, but he had never actually said that he had fallen in love. Allie wondered how she felt about that. Her first thought had to be hurt and angry, but that wasn't fair. She loved Damon, too. She knew she didn't love Damon as much as she loved Harry. Allie also believed that

Harry loved her more than he loved Damon.

Then again, she knew all of this could be an exercise in futility. Odds are, the prisoner wasn't even Damon. The odds are also such that Harry probably wouldn't come back, with the prisoner or not. In a few days, she'd be exactly as she had been for the last twenty-seven years, save the last few months. Alone.

The clock said it was 1030. In about three hours, Harry would be gone. He'd fallen asleep about 0300, but she decided to let him rest.

Allie expected him to want to have sex, but he only wanted to hold her, to touch her. It had taken her a little time to understand that there are many ways to make love. Their kisses and hugs had never moved to cross the bridge to sex, but it was lovemaking none-the-less. Allie smiled, as she finally understood the love that Harry had for her.

He had, somehow in his primitive male brain, made the jump from having sex to making love. Her tears returned as she realized that he had to face death to make that jump.

* * * *

"Harry, time to wake up."

He heard Allie, but she sounded very far away. He opened his eyes, and she smiled into his face. Her eyes were red and puffy. "What time is it?"

"It's 1145. We need to get you ready."

"Yeah." Harry stretched. "How long have you been awake?"

"A while now. I let you sleep."

"Thanks. I'll probably need it."

"Yeah." As he watched, the smile faded from her face. "I want to ask you something."

"Anything."

"Would you change your mind? Stay here with me?"

"I can't, Allie."

"I know." A single tear rolled from her right eye, across the bridge of her nose. "If you could, would you do that?"

"If I could, I'd like nothing better."

Her smile returned slowly. "That's all I wanted to hear." She kissed him softly. "Come on, let's get you up."

They shared a shower, always touching, and Allie wouldn't let him do anything for himself. Her gentle smile never faltered, but Harry saw a few tears now and then. After she dried and dressed him, Allie held his hand as they went to have lunch together. It surprised him that she let him feed himself.

They sat together, touching and holding each other, for the remaining time. They talked very little. Harry found himself pleased and satisfied with the contact. He hugged her tightly. Harry checked his watch. "I should go."

"Yeah. There's just one more thing that I want to say."

"There are a lot of things I want to say." Harry smiled. "I just don't know how."

"I can relate to that." Allie's smile again drifted from her face. "Come back to me, Harry."

"I promise."

"No, don't promise. You may not be able to keep that promise to me. Just do it."

He hugged her tightly as tears welled in his eyes. "I will." They walked to the door where they hugged again. Harry kissed her passionately. "I love you, Allie."

"I love you, too."

He smiled at her. "I'll see you a little later."

"You'd better."

He left the suite, on his way to the hanger deck.

* * * *

Q took a deep breath. "Please take *Boone* to battle stations."

"Battle stations, aye." Alarms hooted throughout the ship.

Q checked his status board. The landing craft was ready to deploy at a moment's notice. They would play a good deal of the coming run by the seat of their pants, and there was no plan set in concrete for when to make the drop. "Engineering, systems status check."

"All systems are at full operational status, Sir."

"Thank you." If they lost the drives or any defensive systems, things could get ugly in a hurry. "Helm, do you have your attack course plotted?"

"Yes, Sir. We'll move toward the planet at full impulse power. We'll slow down a little at each of the moons to give us a chance to fire a few shots, and so we can drop the landing craft. Then we'll whip around Arup to fire on the planet itself."

"Very well. Communications, do we have Lady Paige's interference system online?"

"Yes, Sir. Ready to activate on your orders."

Q nodded. He thought for a moment. "Helm, what will the drop speed be?"

"Assuming things go as planned, we'll be within two one-millionths of light speed." The helmsman checked her display. "That will leave the landing craft with only six thousand meters per second of leeway before it comes apart."

"Understood." Q thought for a moment. They might need to help the landing craft stay in one piece.

The weapons officer flicked a switch on his console. "All hands at battle stations, Admiral."

"Thank you." He checked the status board again, and then clicked the intercom. "Bridge to Draper."

"Draper here, Sir."

"Is your team ready?"

"Yes, Sir. We're good to go."

"Things may get a little bumpy when we drop you. Make sure your pilots are ready."

"Understood, Admiral."

"Very well." Q paused for a moment. He couldn't think of any inspired words a commanding officer should say at a time like this. "Godspeed, Mr. Draper."

"Thank you, Sir. We'll see you soon." Draper closed the link.

Q made a final check of the status board. "All right. Helmsman, you may execute your course. Weapons, you may fire at will."

A duet of "Yes, Sir" answered him. As *Boone's* huge impulse drives ran up to full thrust, accelerating at nearly 100,000 Gs, Q's biosynthetic heart sped up.

"Sir, we have enemy movement." The weapons officer watched his display. "I have 180 seconds to engagement."

"Noted. Helm, hold your course."

"Yes, Sir."

He watched as the Arupian battle cruisers closed on *Boone's* projected position. "Communications, activate the interference device."

Q thought he heard joy in the officer's voice. "Aye, aye, Sir."

Paige's device wasn't a jamming system. Instead, it sent random commands gleaned from Harry's decoded messages to the Arupian fleet. The system also encrypted the commands using the keys Harry had found. Q thought the idea for the device smacked of sheer genius.

The weapons officer laughed. "Sir, it must be working! The cats are all but running into each other trying to follow the commands! The downside is that they are so disorganized now, I can't tell when, or even if, we'll engage them."

Q allowed himself a small smile. "Very good. Keep an eye on them. Helm, ETA to drop point, please."

"Ninety seconds, Sir. No change in projected speed."

Q thought for a moment, his positronic brain working the math of his idea a million times faster than a real brain could have done. "Weapons, when we drop the landing craft, I want a 75,000 G push against their velocity from the tractor beams."

"Sir? That will be tricky at best."

"Understood. Make it happen, Mr. Robinson."

"Yes, Sir."

He clicked the intercom. "Mr. Draper, *Boone* will be using the tractor beam to kill a good part of your velocity on drop."

"Understood." Draper paused. "Sir, the pilot asks that you send the vectors to him."

"Copy." Q tapped a button on his status board. "You should have the details. We have forty-five seconds until drop."

"Understood, Admiral."

"Be ready, Mr. Draper." Q closed the intercom. If the idea to push against the landing craft went wrong, it would go terribly wrong, crushing the small ship. Q's plan effectively called to pinch the ship between its own velocity and the tractor beams, putting enormous stress on the hull of the small ship.

"Fifteen seconds to drop, Sir."

Q watched as the helmsman counted down to dropping the landing craft. The weapons officer stood by the tractor beams.

"Drop in three, two, one, mark!"

Chapter 16

Cats!

Shaking violently, the landing craft dropped through the Harbison Field and into space. Harry's heart twitched as they passed through the Field. The Field absorbed energy, including electrical and kinetic energy, and tried to stop the hearts of the team as they transited the Field boundary. In an instant, the effect passed.

Moving faster than small ships like the landing craft should at launch, the ship pitched and rolled. The artificial gravity held, but the ship bounced roughly. The tractor beam from *Boone* stabbed through space to push against the landing craft's velocity. Gently at first, the push rapidly built to more than three-fourths of the acceleration *Boone* gave the ship when they dropped the team.

The landing craft moved so close to light speed that Harry would need to set his watch later. Caught between their own velocity and the tremendous force of the tractor beam, the landing craft creaked with the stress. From his seat, Harry could see the pilots fighting for control. The tractor beam cut off, and the ship lurched, the artificial gravity reacting sluggishly. Harry and the Marines bounced in their landing chairs, the straps biting into their skin.

"Mr. Draper, we're free and beginning our descent." The pilots had better control now.

"Acknowledged." Rich looked at the team. "All right, people. We have eighteen minutes to the LZ. On touchdown, I want a smooth deployment by the numbers. Secure the area, and watch your back."

Harry watched the young Marines. He saw maybe thirty women, but most were young men. Combat, Harry thought, is a young man's game.

He saw no fear on the faces of the team. He wondered if they really had no fear, or if their training just let them hide the fear. Any normal person would feel fear. Harry felt fear.

He watched the mission clock. *Boone* had dropped the landing craft only eight minutes ago, and there was another ten to fall before landing. In the radio silence between the landing craft and *Boone*, Harry wondered what *Boone* did now. The chatter of the communications systems told Harry that Paige's device had a tremendous impact on the Arupian fleet. The battle cruisers communicated by voice, and Harry heard the confusion in the voices of the commanders.

Boone should be firing on Arup by now. Since the pilots of the landing craft said nothing, Harry assumed no Arupian ships came after them. Between the cloak and the confusion, the Arupians gave all their attention to *Boone*. *Boone* must have been out of range because the moon's defensive batteries ceased fire. Harry hoped the battery crews didn't look around too carefully for more targets.

"Four minutes to LZ, Lieutenant."

"Understood. Get your gear check finalized, people!" Draper smiled. "It's show time!"

As Harry finished checking his environment suit, he realized that while none of the Marines looked frightened, most looked eager. That he could understand. In his years of martial arts competition, he always looked forward to the fight. His mantra sang in his head as he calmed himself.

His thoughts wandered to Allie, now alone on *Boone*. Her family would be with her now in the Safe Room, as *Boone* threw hell's own fire at the planet. He believed his separation would be easier than hers. He'd be too busy in a few minutes to ruminate. Allie would have no such diversion to keep her mind occupied.

Jim had been right. Harry going on this mission hurt her. The fact that he hurt her because he loved her didn't make it any easier, and the idea still sounded crazy. Jim had been right about another thing, too. When Allie looked into his eyes this morning and asked him to stay with her, saying no was the hardest thing Harry had ever done.

The ship vibrated as the thrusters of the landing craft ran up to power. "Sixty seconds to LZ, Sir."

"Acknowledged." Draper unbuckled his harness and got to his feet, holding the safety straps against the buffeting. "One minute! Lock and load!"

"Oohrah!"

The sound of soldiers ramming magazines into the AGLR and clicks of releasing safeties filled the cabin. The five Marines carrying the heavy lasers unplugged from the ship's power source, and the weapons buzzed as they came to life. Harry could smell the eager sweat of the men and women around him as they prepared for what lie ahead. An electric feeling of anticipation swept through the cabin as the pilot counted down to landing.

"LZ in three, two, one, and mark!" The landing craft hit the ground hard, then thrust downward to pin itself down, preventing any bouncing. The big doors on the back and sides of the ship opened to make ramps to the lunar surface, and 124 Marines swarmed out, looking for targets of opportunity.

Harry followed them.

* * * *

Too busy with the battle to watch the landing craft, the Weapons Officer turned that duty over to the Science Officer. "Sir, the landing craft is at the LZ."

"Thank you, Mr. Proffer." Q clicked the intercom and called the Safe Room. "Jim, the team has landed."

"Any sign the Arupians know the team is there?"

"Not that we can see. Paige's device has them confused right now, so the commanders have been busy."

"Good." Jim hesitated for a moment. "Keep me posted."

"Will do." Q closed the link. "Weapons, range to primary target."

"Engagement in thirty seconds, Sir." So far, Boone met little resistance from the Arupian fleet. The ground and satellite defenses would present more opposition.

"Very well. You are authorized to return fire to any target and to fire on the primary target at will."

"Authorized to return fire and fire on primary target at will, aye."

Q checked his status board. All systems displayed green. He watched as the Weapons Officer locked his systems on target. The blue-green laser fire from the satellite defenses came first. *Boone's* blasters lashed out to touch the tiny automated orbital platforms. It took very little energy to vaporize the unshielded targets.

The ground weapons presented bigger problems, being shielded and able to bring more firepower to bear on *Boone*. Pulses of energy, each in the petawatt range, slammed into the Harbison Field. The Field absorbed the energy, transferred it to the side of *Boone* facing away from the planet, and radiated it away into space. The Field facing the planet moved to the dull yellow range, while the opposite side moved to red, the color of a dwarf star. No Arupian ships came to pour extra energy into the Field, and Q calculated *Boone* could handle several hours of the fire.

Boone's weapons struck out at the ground targets, but Q saw the Weapons Officer studying his display. "Admiral, I have a battery located in the middle of a civilian population center." He played his controls. "I'm not sure I can take it out without collateral damage."

"How hot is that target?"

"We're getting a lot of fire from there, Sir. We'll have to fly right over it to reach the power plant."

Q's anger flared. The Arupians put a weapon emplacement in the middle of a populated city, hoping *Boone* wouldn't fire on civilians. An old trick, as old as warfare itself, and Q understood what he should do. If the enemy preferred to put their people at risk, then the decision was theirs. The human emotions built in to his positronic brain, along with nearly 1,800 years of living with humans, made Q hesitate. He fought this war against the Arupian government, not the Arupian people. "How much collateral damage?"

"Outside of the weapon emplacement itself, I see us taking out two square kilometers of city. Based on average population density estimates, there would be about 2,100 people in the area, Sir."

Q thought, but only for an instant. "Not acceptable. Do not fire on that target. Divert full power to the Field and deflectors as we pass over."

"Do not fire on the weapon emplacement, aye." The Weapons Officer clicked switches. "Full power to Field and shields."

"Beginning attack run on primary target, Sir." The helmsman moved the controls. "We'll be in range in twenty seconds."

Fire from the ground emplacements intensified, and the Field heated to indigo on the planet-facing side. The cool side moved up to green.

Boone screamed through the upper atmosphere at more than two hundred kilometers per second, 750 times faster than sound. The friction added more energy to the Field, and Q watched the displays as the color moved to a uniform violet. With no cool places to radiate the energy, the Field stored the heat. Someplace, deep inside *Boone's* Harbison Field generators, the temperature of a pinpoint of neutron star matter approached infinity.

The ship flashed over the battery and, moments later, the disruptors fired on the nuclear power plant. The sensors revealed a blinding flash of white light and the typical mushroom cloud as the fusion pile of the reactor failed. "Science, radiation readings from that plant?"

"Looks like a clean plant, Sir." The officer used his sensor arrays. "No predicted collateral damages."

"Very well. Helm, get us out of here to cool space." The Field showed bright violet with flecks of white appearing.

"Aye, aye, Sir." The helmsman didn't try anything fancy. A simple tangential thrust to the curve of the planet, whipping *Boone* back to free space.

* * * *

As the team moved toward the prison, Harry felt guilty. He should be thinking about Allie, but his thoughts kept turning to Damon. He reminded himself that the prisoner might not even be Damon. Harry believed the normal thing to worry about would be Damon stealing Allie from him. Harry didn't worry about that, though. He laughed to himself when he thought that Damon might steal him from Allie.

Harry adjusted the temperature on his environment suit. It was a little cold. He hated environment suits. Isolation suit always seemed a better name for them. He couldn't feel anything through them, and they limited his movements. His breathing, the puffing of the regulator, and the chatter on the communicator made up the sounds he could hear. The air filters removed all scents, leaving only the crisp, ozone tinged smell of pure air. Humans evolved to live using a precise balance of nitrogen, oxygen, and a fraction of other gases. The suit met those needs. The suit left emotional needs hanging. Gone were the scents of other people. Harry couldn't even smell himself in the suit. On Earth, the aroma of thirty billion people living there now, plus the countless billions who came before, filled the nose and stimulated the mind. The very smell of Earth said to a human that it was home. The environment suit was a plastic bag with a man inside.

Harry jumped when Draper spoke in his communicator. "Harry, we need you up front." He moved up the team to where Draper and two technicians stood at the control panel for the prison airlock. "This is encoded."

Harry studied the panel for a moment. A series of different sized circles, arranged in an odd geometric pattern, made up the panel. A large circle formed the center, while six smaller circles rested at various distances around the perimeter. "This is the Arupian solar system." He pointed at the smaller circles. "Six planets around a star." Harry thought for a moment. "What are they trying to tell us?"

"Damned if I know." Draper shifted his AGLR in his hands. "We need to move, Harry."

"Right." Harry thought about what he knew of Arupian astronomy. It wasn't much. He pulled his data terminal from his vest and looked at the information there. In one of those strange coincidences of science that made Harry wonder if God might really exist, astronomers found centuries ago that the planets in the Arupian system existed in an odd relationship. The ratio of the orbital periods could be expressed as a string of numbers. Not just any numbers, but one, three, five, seven, eleven, and thirteen—the first six prime numbers. Harry smiled. "Rich, if you listed the planets in this system, would you start at the sun, working your way out, or would you start at the outer-most planet and work your way in to the sun?"

Draper frowned. "We don't have time for this."

"Yeah, we do. Which way?"

"From the sun out."

"Me too." Harry tapped the first circle from the sun once. The second circle he pressed three times. Arup, the third, he pressed five times. He worked his way out to the sixth circle, pressing it thirteen times. The airlock opened slowly, puffs of dust blown by the residual air inside.

* * * *

Boone withdrew from the planet to return to the parking orbits near the edge of the system. Once secured from battle stations, Ike let Allie and her family leave the Safe Room. She went to the coffee shop on the mall and sat watching the few people venturing out to shop. Trying to distract her mind from dwelling on Harry and the mission, she watched the people.

Boone made up an interesting community. Only about two-thirds of the people on *Boone* were military. The rest were civilians, either contractors or family of the crew. In a way, it reminded her of a fixed military base, where the worlds of military life and civilian rules crammed together. Conflict between the two different lifestyles often arose.

An hour after a battle, only forty minutes after securing from battle stations, and people shopped for clothes. The civilians took the attitude that life goes on. The military personnel, in contrast, worked getting *Boone* ready for the next battle.

Allie sipped at her coffee. A group of children came by with their mother. Laughing and running, several of the kids stopped at the fountain to toss in a few coins. Allie wondered what they wished for. She had two wishes. She wished first for Harry to come home safely. Second, she wished him to bring Damon back.

As she sat thinking, Allie couldn't help remembering the impromptu wake she and Harry held for Damon just over two months ago. She wondered if she might need to do that again, alone this time. A few slow tears moved down her face.

She finished her coffee and walked to the fountain. She tossed two one-credit coins in before going home.

* * * *

The team encountered only four prison guards as they made their way to the cellblock. All four lay dead in the wake of the Marines. Harry looked at the control panel for the cells. Several rows of switches and lights bore labels with cell numbers. The switches were marked with the simple labels *LOCKED* and *UNLOCKED*. The lights had the equally simple marking of *LOCKED*. A small plastic guard over each switch prevented accidentally throwing the toggle. All the switches rested in the *LOCKED* position, and all the lights shown brightly.

The hair on Harry's neck tried to stand on end. It couldn't be this easy. He pointed at the console. "Rich, this scares the living shit out of me."

"Why? Can't the cats have done something the easy way? We just find the right cell and open the door."

"Arupians like puzzles. Cats are even more curious than primates." Harry shook his head. "We're missing something here."

Draper shrugged. "What do I know about puzzles? Let's go find the prisoner and spring him."

"It doesn't make sense." Harry stroked his beard for a moment. "One person could release all the prisoners from here, and no one would know." He thought for a time. "Let's go see if we can find the prisoner."

The cells occupied two corridors, fifty cells on each. A technician stopped at the first cell. "Mr. Douglas, look here." A small keypad with eighteen keys rested in a recess in the wall next to each door. The doors held no windows and only a marking for the cell number.

Draper sighed. "This is great. How do we find the one prisoner we're looking for?"

Harry stared at the keypad. "There must be a list back in the control room." He ran his fingers over the keys gingerly. "Eighteen?"

"I can count."

"Why not sixteen?"

"What are you talking about?"

"Number base systems. Humans use base ten numbers because we have ten fingers, just like Arupians. Base two and its binary multiples like four, eight, and sixteen are used for data and technology." Each key bore a single letter of the Arupian alphabet. "Eighteen? I could even understand twenty. One for each finger and toe."

"Sir, Arupians don't have twenty fingers and toes." Harry looked at the technician as he spoke. "They have four digits on each hand and foot, plus two dewclaw digits on the paws."

Harry smiled slowly. "Eighteen...Of course! Just one more layer of the onionskin security!"

Draper looked from Harry to the tech, then back again. "So, what do we do with this information?"

"I have no idea. Yet." Harry went back to the control room. "There must be a book in here with the list of prisoners. There's no computer display, so they have it written down."

The team tore through the control room, opening drawers, looking at everything on the desks and consoles. "Sir?" A PFC held up a ledger book. Harry took it from him.

"This is it." He read quickly. A smile came to his face. "Here, in cell twenty-one." His smile faded. "No name, just says human and two numbers."

"What now?" Draper fidgeted.

"We enter one or both of these numbers on the keypad outside cell twenty-one and flip the switch here. The question is in what order we do that." Harry rubbed his beard again.

"We need to get moving. The longer we're here playing these mind games, the more likely we'll be found."

"If we fuck this up, every kitten in the place will come visiting." Harry thought for a moment. "My gut tells me that we enter the first number, in base eighteen, on the keypad. Then we flip the switch, then we enter the second number."

"Is that anything more than a guess?"

"Yeah." Harry smiled. "It's an educated guess."

"That's fucking great."

"I thought so." Harry gave the technician instructions to stay at the control panel. "Come on, Rich." They went to cell twenty-one. Harry read the numbers, then pressed the keys.

The tech called. "Sir, the light is flashing now."

"Good! Flip the switch."

"Done, Mr. Douglas. The light is still blinking."

Harry glanced at Draper. "Well, then." He entered the second number.

"Sir? The light just went off."

"Bingo!"

Draper and a Corporal pulled on the door. Damon stood from the Spartan bunk.

* * * *

Allie ate dinner with her parents. The same ages-old seating assignments still amused her. She tried all afternoon to somehow read Harry's mind from a hundred million kilometers away, but she had no luck. Her father often showed flashes of precognition or other psychic abilities, and her younger sister, Miranda, seemed to have inherited the ability somewhat. All Allie seemed to have inherited was her mother's green eyes.

Her father's cut hand now healed, accelerated by the nanites, he ate normally tonight. "Paige, Q wanted me to tell you again how well your communications surprise worked against the Arupians."

"That makes nine times he's commented on that." Paige smiled. "I'm glad it helped, though."

"I think he likes you." Marilyn ate her peas one at a time, with her fingers.

"Shut up, beanpole." The top of Paige's head came only to the level of Marilyn's breasts. She had called Marilyn beanpole since they met seven hundred years ago. "Besides, since Zach fell for Claire, no guy has had a crush on me."

"That w-w-was seven hundred years ago." Tanya glared at Marilyn. "W-w-would you p-please stop that?"

Allie liked the banter between her mothers, but she found it distracting tonight. Her thoughts were very far away. "Daddy, when do you think we'll know anything?"

He shrugged and sat down his fork. "Hard to say, but I wouldn't think it will be too long." He thought for a moment. "We'll see something before we hear anything, though. When they set off the gizmo your mom built to whip the black holes off to the tenth dimension, it should make quite a splash on the sensors."

Tanya nodded. "Yeah, I love st-string physics."

"You're driving the physicists crazy, though." Janelle laughed. Allie wondered if her own eyes lit up like that when she laughed. "There's one of the hyperspace theorists who claims he can prove that you can't even build the gizmo you built."

"Too late now." Marilyn licked a strip of crabmeat from her fingers, her tongue moving slowly around the tip. She smiled at Jim.

Jim stared at Marilyn. "Um, anyway..." He looked at Allie. "I'd think soon."

Allie laughed at her parents despite her worries. "You four are a mess!"

"Maybe we are, little one, but we're your mess." Her father pushed his plate aside and waved his empty wine glass at the steward. "How are you holding up?"

"I think I'm OK." Allie hadn't cried for more than an hour now. "I'm worried, but something inside is telling me he's all right."

"That's just fine, then. I guess I should tell you that I'm not feeling anything about the outcome of this."

"That's all right. Maybe if Miranda were here, she'd feel something."

"You never know." Her father sat silently for a moment. "You seem to have a penchant for picking brave men to hang around with."

"That's your fault. I'm used to being around brave men."

"Brave? Me? Hardly!" He laughed heartily. "I'm just too stupid to stay out of trouble, and then I'm lucky enough to get out later."

"Maybe." Allie hesitated for a moment. "Do you think Q would let me hang around on the bridge?"

"I won't tell you not to ask him, but I can promise you he won't."

Janelle waited as the steward picked up her plate. "That wouldn't be a good idea, Allie." She glanced at Jim. "Things can get busy up there, and you'll just be in the way."

"You're right, Mom. I'll just go home and wait for the call."

* * * *

Harry ran into the cell and hugged Damon to him. He had lost mass, and his hair needed a trim. "I don't know what to say!"

Damon squeezed Harry, but his arms seemed weak. "Is it really you? You're not some mind game the fur balls are playing with me?"

"No, it's me." Harry held Damon out at arm's length. "Are you all right?"

"I think so." He tugged at his torn uniform. It fitted him like a sack, baggy and loose. "I guess I could use a few kilos, though."

Draper came up behind Harry. "Damon, good to see you. Let's get a medic to give you a quick check." The medic came and used his scanners. Rich pulled an MRE ration from his pack, and handed that and his canteen to Damon.

"Thanks." Damon looked at the men and women in his cell and standing in the corridor. "This had to be your idea, Harry."

"At least in part. We were in the neighborhood and thought we'd drop by."

"Yeah." Damon wolfed the MRE and drank deeply from the water. "How's Allie?"

"She's OK, but we'll talk later."

The medic put his scanners away. "Other than some dehydration and a little malnourished, you're in good shape, Lieutenant." Two men came in with battle armor and an AGLR.

"Let me fill you in on what's happening." As Damon dressed in the armor, Rich spelled out the mission to him. Harry added a few things here and there, and Damon soon had the picture.

Damon picked up the AGLR, spinning it in his hands with a practiced flair as he checked the magazines. "God, this feels good." He smiled at Draper. "So, what's next?"

"We take out the cat toys, then we get the righteous fuck out of here. We'll need to figure some way to cram you on the landing craft, though."

Harry laughed. "I'll sit on his lap."

* * * *

The team moved quietly through the prison, encountering six more guards. The team dispatched the guards quickly and silently. Harry believed that from here on out, things would get harder. They stood at the door from the prison into the newer base.

Rich watched his scanner. "OK, looks clear on the other side. Open it." The technician triggered the door and it rolled open. Squads moved into the corridor, covering the rest of the team as they came through. Draper pointed. "This way, three hundred meters."

Harry stayed close to Damon, but they talked little, and then only about the here and now. Harry felt good close to the man. He wondered only briefly about the electric tingle that went through him when the cell door opened and he saw Damon. Harry still didn't have it clear in his own mind how he felt about Damon, and he didn't have time now to explore the feelings.

They reached the door to the lab where Harry's intelligence reports said the work on the black holes went on. A Corporal tried his scanner. "No readings, Sir."

Harry nodded. "The room is shielded."

Draper nodded. "OK, should we knock first?"

A feral snarl spread over Damon's face. "Fuck no."

"Good enough." Rich nodded to the Sergeant.

Harry had a bad feeling about this. "Um, guys, wait. There are pussy cats in there."

"I sure fucking hope so." Damon still snarled. His voice held no humor.

"No, I mean there are lots of cats in there."

"How you know that?" Draper held his hand up, stopping the Sergeant from opening the door.

"You'll think I'm crazy."

Damon chuckled. "We already think that."

"Right." He sighed. "I can feel them. That's not right. I can feel their chi, their life energy, if you like that better."

"You're right. We think you're crazy." Rich nudged Damon.

"Maybe I am, but the place is working alive with them."

Damon thought for a moment. "Rich, we'll go in fast and hard. All the front people with blast shields." He smiled. "It's your command. Sorry."

"That's OK. I like the idea."

"Guys, wait. Somebody without a tail is going to get killed that way." Harry thought, but only for a moment. He turned suddenly. He pressed the open switch on the door. No one a chance to do anything other than diving for cover as Harry walked into the room.

He found himself alone with about three hundred Arupians.

* * * *

Allie paced her suite. Something was wrong, but she couldn't say what. Things were fine a few moments ago. She worried about Harry, wondering if he'd found Damon, then, like a brick between the eyes, a foreboding fear hit her.

She had never shown any of her father's ability for, as he puts it, feeling things. She couldn't deny that she felt something now.

The feeling told her that someone just did something stupid. Probably Harry.

* * * *

The Arupians turned as one person. Weapons came up, all pointed at him, but none fired. Harry raised his hands over his head, fingers spread wide. He spoke in perfect Arupian. "Hi, guys! What's new?"

The cats stared at him in disbelief. One with an officer's uniform growled at him. "How did you get in here?"

Harry walked slowly toward the officer. None of the cats stopped him, seeming happy in their shocked state of watching an unarmed human stroll into their midst. He lifted his right foot from the floor and swiveled it at the ankle. "I walked."

The officer took a step forward, drawing his arm back to swat at Harry. He took one too many steps forward.

Harry kicked out and up, jumping as he did. "Now, guys!" His foot connected with the officer's chin, a head and a half above Harry's own. The cat's mouth snapped closed, his teeth slamming together with a loud click. The last third of his tongue dropped to the floor.

The team swept into the room as the Arupians stared at the human who just knocked out their commander. Few of the rounds fired came from the Arupians.

The technicians located the containers holding the black holes in stasis fields. They worked to rig the gizmo.

Marines had the habit of hitting each other's helmets. Hard. Damon walked up to him and hit Harry's head with his palm. Harry didn't wear his helmet. The blow to the side of his head staggered him. "What the fuck was that, Harry?"

He rubbed the side of his head. "Damn! That hurt!" A spot on Harry's head went numb from the blow.

"And you thought three hundred kittens opening fire on you wouldn't hurt?" Damon's face glowed red. A large vein pulsed in his neck. "That was fucking stupid!"

"It worked." The feeling came back in his head. It hurt worse now.

"So did the raid on New Scotland, but that was a stupid idea, too!"

"I get the point."

"I doubt that you do!" Damon hugged him. Harry found it easy and natural to hug back. "If I didn't think you'd kick my ass, I'd kick yours."

The hug also felt good. Not the hug of two comrades-in-arms, or even of two friends. "Sorry, but it seemed like a good idea at the time."

Draper stood nearby, and a Corporal came to whisper in his ear. Rich tapped Harry's shoulder. "I hate to break up this touching moment, but the techs need your help with the gizmo."

The three men walked to where the technicians worked. Damon frowned. "What's this thing do, anyway?"

Harry shrugged. "All I know is that it's supposed to stuff the black holes, stasis fields and all, into one of the eleven string dimensions. Don't ask me how it does that, though. Most of the physicists on *Boone* say they don't even understand the basics of the theory."

"It won't take us with it?"

"Damned if I know."

"That's comforting."

"Yeah, I thought so, too." Harry helped the techs with the translation of the Arupian text on the stasis fields. "Tanya said we need to get at least five hundred meters from this thing before it goes off. I wonder what the energy pulse is going to do to my balls."

"You two are real bundles of joy, aren't you?" Rich listened to his communicator. "No one's coming to check on the shots fired."

"We try. Maybe they didn't hear it." Damon reloaded his AGLR.

Harry stood up from the stasis field generators. "We can hope."

The technician Corporal came to Draper. "Mr. Draper, I think we're ready to go."

The intercom on one of the desks buzzed. Harry stared for a moment at the blinking light that accompanied the insistent buzzing. "Would someone like to get the phone?"

"Fuck that." Damon fired his AGLR. The explosive projectile shattered the intercom into a million pieces. "Time to go!"

"Set the gizmo for a three minute delay." The techs moved to carry out Draper's orders. "Let's move!"

The team ran for the landing craft waiting outside.

Chapter 17

The Paladins

The team encountered the first of the Arupian warriors just before the door back to the prison. Sixty fur balls from the garrison met them. The AGLR dropped easily into place in Damon's arms. Its recoil bounced familiarly against his chest.

He always fought his enemies with compassion. War wasn't personal. It was about ideals of governments, not the individual soldiers. Damon read in command school that a pre-Doom Time General once said something about the idea of war is not to die for your country. The idea was to get the other poor dumb bastard to die for his country. Damon couldn't remember the General's name now.

A snarling smile spread on his face as he killed fur balls. The killing brought him a joy he'd never experienced before. His captors managed to burn out the compassion he' had for the Arupian warriors. They beat him and starved him. They used several types of torture, all trying to get him to tell them about *Boone* and her structure. Damon knew they planned another assault on the ship, trying to gain entry.

As the rounds spit from his weapon, Damon hated his lack of emotion for the dying cats. He didn't know how to regain his compassion for creatures that so carelessly mistreated him.

Harry stood behind him, and Damon could feel Harry's hand clutching the straps of his armor. Not surprisingly, Harry carried no weapon. Damon knew he preferred to use his hands and feet as weapons. Other than range, Harry's body made at least as deadly a weapon as the AGLR Damon fired.

As he killed indiscriminately, Damon wondered about Harry's

comment that they would talk later about Allie. Damon suspected that Harry and Allie might even be married by now.

He also wondered about Harry. He said the team needed him to solve puzzles for them, but he believed there must be more to Harry leaving Allie behind to go on this mission. He had known Rich Draper for three years. Damon understood him being there. Harry must have other motivations. Damon admitted being happier to see Harry than Rich. The friendship he shared with Harry was, somehow, more.

Harry yanked down on the back of his armor. "Duck!"

Trained reflexes reacted instantly to the command, and Damon ducked. As he turned, he saw a group of three Arupians behind the team at a cross corridor. Harry made a smooth motion, pulling a star-shaped disk from his vest. He threw the disk with a backhand motion. It buried itself five centimeters deep in the skull of one attacker. The other two pulled back, followed by a grenade Damon sent after them. "Thanks."

"The bill is in the mail."

* * * *

"Admiral! We have a string dimensional pulse!"

Q tried to walk to the science station, but he almost ran. He watched the ripples the sensors detected move across the fabric of space-time. "Can you find a point source?"

"Yes, Sir." The officer used the sensor arrays spread over *Boone's* hull to triangulate and refine the readings. "On the inner moon, Sir." He smiled. "At the base."

Q allowed himself a very uncharacteristic whoop of joy. "Monitor and observe for any sign of the black holes in normal space."

"Yes, Sir."

Q went back to his command chair and used the intercom. "Jim, we have the pulse of Tanya's gizmo activating. We're scanning for the black holes now."

"Fantastic! Let me know as soon as you confirm the black holes are gone. Any news on the team?"

"Negative. The landing craft hasn't moved yet."

"Very well. Keep me posted." Jim paused. "I'll call Allie."

The Polyamorous Princess

"Very well." Q closed the link.

* * * *

"All we know is that they set off the gizmo." Allie tried to get her breathing under control. Her racing heart wouldn't show through the intercom. "Nothing on the landing craft, then?"

Her father sighed. "No, little one. As soon as they lift off, we'll go after them at maximum speed."

"All right. You'll let know when that happens?"

"Yes, I will. Try to relax a little."

"Yeah, right!" Allie closed the link.

The fearful feeling from earlier faded almost as quickly as it came. She knew things were better now, but Harry still had a long way to go before being home safely.

* * * *

The team pushed the Arupians back to reach the door to the prison. Now, they fell back as they moved for the exit. Harry still stood behind Damon as the staccato of rapid-fire weapons filled the air.

Draper screamed above the din. "They know where we're going! We need to move faster!"

Damon ducked into the cross corridor to reload. "Right. What do we have in terms of casualties?"

"Twelve minor injuries, one serious, and one dead."

Harry looked at the two big Marines. "You're right, Rich. We need to move before they cut us off." He glanced at his watch. "The gizmo will go off in a minute, too. I think we're far enough away."

"I hope so." Damon peeked around the corner. He fired and picked off a fur ball.

Suddenly, the universe tried to turn inside out. The atoms of Harry's body tried to fall apart as the gizmo flexed the fabric of space and time in directions it shouldn't go in this dimension. Spatial distortions slammed across the battleground. Harry actually saw the twelve-millimeter slug leaving the muzzle of Damon's rifle. It changed shape from a smooth bullet to a glob of lead covered in plastic explosive. It then morphed into something like a pencil, slowly moving broadside to its target. The universe then snapped back to what men thought of, in their mundane experience, as normal. Harry assumed the bullet returned to normal as well since the Arupian target now lacked a head.

Humans came back to the normal universe quickly. The Arupians didn't fare as well. The ones not already dead rolled on the floor, holding their heads and mewing.

Rich smiled. "Come on! This is our chance!"

Damon sighed. Harry thought he probably wanted to stay and finish off the cats. Harry pulled on Damon's armor. "Let's go."

"Yeah." He watched the helpless Arupians for a moment before turning to trot down the corridor.

At a cross corridor, Harry was the last to pass. Halfway through the intersection, heavy fire from his right slammed his body armor. He fell and rolled. Coming to his feet, the chi of four Arupians approached his position. He dropped into his fighting stance and readied himself.

A fist closed tightly in his hair, yanking him back from the intersection. "What in the fuck are you doing? You are not going to die on me!" Damon threw him against the wall, and then pulled his visor down. Stepping into the corridor, Damon spit fire from his rifle at the warriors. In seconds, he lifted the visor. "You Fleet types need to leave the fighting to the Marines." He put his arm around Harry's shoulder. "Come on."

Harry slipped his arm around Damon's waist, and they walked quickly to the airlock.

* * * *

"We have landing craft movement, Admiral."

Q smiled. "Very well. Helm, get me a minimum time course to intercept. Weapons, take us to battle stations. Scan for any enemy ships. You are authorized to fire on any ship in range."

The helmsman worked her navigation console. "Minimum time

course plotted and laid in, Sir. ETA to intercept is twenty-two minutes."
"Engage."
"Aye, aye, Sir." *Boone* leapt ahead at 90,000 Gs.
"Scanning Arupian ships, Sir. None are moving for the landing craft or us currently." The Weapons Officer smiled. "All weapons armed and tracking. Understand clear to fire on any enemy ship."
"Thank you." Q thumbed the intercom and advised Jim the team was on its way home.

* * * *

Allie didn't think she could be happy just hugging and kissing Harry when he stepped off the landing craft. She knew her dad would react badly to her jumping Harry's bones on the hanger deck. She really didn't care too much.

She tossed another outfit on the bed. It didn't seem right for meeting him. It joined the three already there. "Fuck this." She left for hanger deck wearing her jeans.

Boone was at battle stations, but she didn't care that she didn't bother to go to the Safe Room. She'd kick Ike's ass if she tried to force her to go there. Her father didn't even try to get her to come to the Safe Room.

The eerie quiet on the hanger deck unsettled her. The crew stored the other ships out of the way, ready for what Q said might be a hasty recovery of the landing craft under enemy fire. So far, everyone told Allie that the Arupian ships seemed reluctant to engage *Boone*.

A medical team stood by, with Claire leading them. Allie went to her. "Hi, sis."

Claire smiled at her. "I see you beat Daddy up about being here instead of the Safe Room."

"Not really." Allie smiled. "He knows better."

"Yeah, he does. Any word yet?"

"No, not yet. Have you heard about any injuries?"

"No, we're just standing by if we're needed."

Allie nodded. "I hope he's all right."

"Me too. I hope they're all OK."

"Yeah." Allie watched her older sister. "Claire, do you ever get used to the waiting?"

"I'm not used to it after seven hundred years." She sighed. "Every time Zach goes off to some planet to meet with unfriendly people, my heart falls into my feet. Even diplomacy can go terribly wrong."

Years ago, her father had been shot while on Samulus. Only the nanites saved his life. "Yeah, I guess it can."

"This isn't just a friend or an acquaintance we're talking about. I can see how you look at Harry, and the way you feel about him is all over your face."

"I didn't think it showed that much."

Claire laughed. "It does."

"If he's hurt..."

"Relax. If he's hurt, I'm right here."

"I'll try. Relaxation is pretty scarce right now."

"I know."

* * * *

Boone and the landing craft maintained radio silence. No enemy ships came within range, and the recovery of the team would be a routine landing. Q turned to the Communication Officer. "Please hail the landing craft."

"On speaker, Sir."

"Landing craft alpha three, this is Boone."

"Alpha three here, Sir."

"You are clear for routine landing at the pleasure of the hanger master. No hostile ships in range."

"Understood, Sir."

"Can you say the condition of your team?"

"Yes, Sir. We have one dead and two serious injuries. We have another seventeen minor injuries."

"Very well. Medical is standing by." Q smiled a little. "My compliments to Lieutenants Draper and Douglas. Welcome home."

* * * *

The Hanger Master's amplified voice rang through the hanger deck. "Now hear this, now hear this! Routine recovery of landing craft alpha three in sixty seconds. Medical teams, we have reports of two serious injuries and seventeen minor injuries. All hands, standby for recovery operations."

A knot bigger than the landing craft rested in Allie's stomach. She watched through the battle glass windows of the blast shield as the landing craft pulled alongside *Boone*. The Landing Signal Officer waved the ship aboard, and the landing craft eased its way onto hanger deck. The LSO gave the signal for touchdown, then power off. Boatswain mates swarmed around the small craft, securing it to the deck and making the weapons safe. The doors opened, and Claire went aboard with the medical team. Allie wanted to run to the ship, to find Harry. She knew her place, though. She fidgeted as she waited.

Soon, some of the Marines came off the ship, whooping and giving one another the high-five. Claire and several of the medical team came off with a woman on a gurney. Claire had opened the woman's chest and held the Marine's heart in her hand, squeezing rhythmically as they ran for sickbay. The medical team carried more people from the landing craft. None of the people looked like Harry. Allie's breath panted in her lungs.

A gurney came off the small ship with a person covered by a sheet. Allie didn't want to look, but she forced herself. She saw red hair sticking out from under the sheet.

More Marines filed off, all enlisted and noncommissioned officers. Rich Draper followed them. Allie ran to the foot of the ramp, just as Harry came out. His arm locked around Damon's waist, they both laughed until they saw her.

Warm tears streamed down her face and around the broad smile. She ran up the ramp and jumped onto Harry's chest, her legs wrapping around his hips. Her pulse pounded as her happy tears flowed freely. "Oh my God!"

Harry kissed her. Hard. His arms closed around her. He eased her to the ramp. "Miss me?"

"Yeah." She turned to Damon. "You're all right." She knew she should say more, but the words wouldn't come.

"That's what they tell me." Damon looked at Harry. "Is this what we needed to talk about?"

"Yeah, I guess it is."

Damon nodded. "No worries."

Allie smiled at him. "I'm afraid to touch you again." After a moment, she hugged him tightly. "It's like you're back from the dead." The familiar quickening of her breath and heart as his arms, still strong, but much thinner now, held her tightly to his chest flooded into her body. When she touched his ribs through his shirt, the skinny, bumpy sensation saddened her.

"Not exactly, but I am back."

Harry put his arms around both of them. "Together again."

* * * *

Harry and Allie walked him to sickbay for his check up. The nurse said it would take about an hour. Damon made them leave. They made a date at the Café for dinner in five hours.

As he sat waiting his turn with the doctor, Damon tried to get his mind around what just happened. He didn't think about his time as a prisoner or the mission they just completed. He tried to get a grip on the fact that Harry and Allie made a couple now.

He couldn't deny that. After the hug she shared with him on hanger deck, Allie never left Harry's side. Damon also saw that she always touched him. Damon looked for it, but he found no anger. He also didn't find any hurt. He smiled at himself when he thought that logic said this would happen. Fleet had officially declared him dead. Damon knew that romance between Allie and Harry would bloom when he vanished. He wanted that to happen so Allie wouldn't be alone.

Logic be damned, he found he knew he was happy for them. He sensed the love and happiness between them. As Harry told him what seemed like a lifetime ago now, the only thing that mattered was Allie and her happiness. Damon smiled thinking about his friends, now lovers, and felt privileged that he could be a part of that.

He sat smiling when Claire called him into the treatment room. She looked him up a down several times. "You just keep coming back to my sickbay."

"Seems that way, Admiral."

She did a physical exam and so many scans that he lost count. "Looks like the medic was right. You're a little dehydrated and need to eat better, but you're in good shape." Claire watched him for a moment. "I'd like you to see a psychiatrist, though. You've been through a traumatic time."

"If you think that's best, no problems for me."

"Good." Claire watched him again. He wasn't used to dealing with seven hundred year-old women with nearly superhuman intelligence. He felt like she watched him under a magnifying glass. "Anything else you want to talk about right now? A few things have changed since you left us."

He laughed. "Yeah, I guess they have." He understood doctor-patient confidentiality, but this was Allie's sister. "Is Allie happy?"

"She seems happy. I'm not saying she didn't seem happy before."

Damon nodded. "What about Harry?"

Claire shrugged. "I don't know. He doesn't seem depressed."

"Maybe I should talk to the shrink about this."

"I think that would be a good idea." Claire looked at the readouts again. "OK, you need to eat, and make sure you drink plenty of water. Get some rest, and you can return to duty in a week."

"Thanks, Admiral." Damon stood. "I guess I need to find some clothes that fit, too."

* * * *

As they danced, Damon holding her in his arms, Allie still tingled at his touch. Guilt also weighed on her mind. "I'm sorry."

"There's nothing to be sorry about." He leaned back and looked into her eyes. "I really am OK with things."

She became lost in his eyes. This was even more wrong than when she first found herself attracted to Harry. "I guess I feel like I owe you an explanation."

"All you owe me is another dance later."

She laughed. "I can do that." Allie wanted to explain to him why she and Harry were together, why things couldn't go back to how they were before. "I hope you know that I never lied to you about my feelings."

"I know that, just like I never lied to you about mine." He shrugged a little. "I won't lie to you now. My feelings for you haven't changed."

"It's hard to believe, but mine haven't changed, either."

"You love Harry more than you love me." He chuckled. "I can't think of a better man than Harry. He's the best."

"He said the same thing about you."

"I can see that happening." Allie moved to look into his eyes. She moved her face towards his. "Allie, don't. It's not right."

She sighed, thankful that he found the strength she lacked. "You're right about that."

"I think so." He hugged her tightly. "Come on. Let's get back." They walked back to where Harry waited at the table. After holding her chair, Damon excused himself for a moment.

Harry watched her for a moment. "Are you OK?"

"Maybe. I think so." Allie blinked against the tears trying to well up in her eyes. "He doesn't want to hear what has happened."

"He knows what happened. He doesn't care to hear why. Or at least he doesn't want to hear you explain why it happened."

"Yeah, that's it." She watched her drink for a moment, but it offered no answers. "I thought he was dead."

"We all did." Harry took her hand. "Allie, you didn't cheat on him."

A wave of attraction swept over her as Harry said exactly the right thing again, saying nothing more, and nothing less, than he intended to say. "I think that's it. I feel like I cheated on him. Maybe we both did."

"I doubt he feels that way."

"Probably not." She sighed. "I think he's still in love with me."

"I can't read his mind, so I don't know how to answer that." Harry shrugged. "If I were him, I know I'd still be in love with you."

Damon returned to the table. "You two looked awfully serious. Anything I should know?"

Harry laughed. "Probably. It was all about you."

Allie listened to the music for a moment. The song about a woman with two lovers played again. "Let's go home so we can talk in private."

Harry and Damon exchanged a glance. Harry patted her hand. "OK, if that's what you want."

They walked to her suite, Allie holding Harry's arm in hers. They sat on the floor in the sitting room, and Harry ordered a bottle of wine. He poured for them.

Damon lifted his glass to Harry. "You're making a habit of rescuing me, but I appreciate it. I truly do."

"My pleasure." Harry sipped at his wine.

"I'm glad you thought of this, Allie." Damon took a deep breath. "I'm so happy for both of you. As much as I hate to admit it, I'm glad you're together."

Harry sat his glass down. "Bullshit."

"What?"

"You heard me. Remember, I've been where you're at now. Honestly, you're handling it better than I did, too." Harry glanced at her for a moment, then back to Damon. "Allie asked an interesting question awhile ago. Are you still in love with her?"

Damon blinked at Harry. "Yeah, I am. As far as my handling this better than you did is concerned, the night is yet young."

"I'm not as good as telling when someone isn't being honest as your folks, but I think I'm pretty good." Harry looked at her. "You're still in love with Damon, too."

Allie didn't want to be in this position, but Harry's directness, the very thing she found most attractive in him, put her here. "As much as I ever was." She squeezed Harry's hand. "That doesn't change anything between you and me, though."

"Again, bullshit." He sighed. "Of course it changes things. It has to. Like it or not, my friends, we are a threesome."

Damon's eyes narrowed. "What?"

"Yeah. Allie, your family is big into the polyamorous relationships. This should be old hat for you, at least in terms of thinking about it."

She rode a runaway train, moving too fast to comprehend what was happening. "What are you suggesting?"

"OK, this gets complicated, so stay with me." Harry took a deep breath. "Allie, you love me, but you also love Damon. Damon and I both love you. Damon once told me that he wouldn't be inclined to share you. Honestly, I'm not either. We need to consider the reality we have here."

He shrugged. "If you're not happy, Allie, we'll both lose you. I said I wasn't crazy about sharing you, but with the right person, I could do it and be happy about the situation." He smiled. "Damon is the right person."

She looked at Damon. He wore an amused smile on his face as he stared at Harry. She looked back at Harry. "Are you crazy?"

"Probably, but that's not the issue."

"This isn't something that you decide over a glass of wine!"

"Why not? Your dad, mom, and Marilyn made the decision over drinks."

Her eyes narrowed. "How do you know that?"

"I have nearly full access to the computers. Besides, I'm a monkey, and I'm curious."

"That was different anyway."

Harry laughed. "Let's see...Your dad met your mom on Earth's moon, and they fell in love at first sight. A few days later, he met Marilyn, and that was lust at first sight, at the very least. A week later, they became a threesome. Nine days later, Tanya made it four. As I recall, Paige joined the merry-go-round about a year after that." Harry squeezed her hand. "Other than a little minor issues with the times involved, tell me how that's different."

Allie looked to Damon. "Aren't you going to help me?"

He shrugged. "Other than to say that you're right that Harry is crazy, no. I'm not ashamed or afraid to admit that I love you, Allie. I think Harry is onto something here that would be workable if, that is, you would be happy. I want you happy, and that's the most important part about all this for me."

"You were both too close to mom's gizmo when it went off." She thought while the two men laughed. "You both need to think about this. Daddy, my moms, and my brothers and sisters who are in polyamorous relationships all spend a lot of time talking about the intensity. We're not talking about a little three-way sex here. I don't want that, and it sure won't make me happy, since you're both so concerned about that. We're talking about love."

Harry smiled. "We do understand that, Allie. I think the question is if having both Damon and I would make you happy."

Allie tossed off her wine. "I need something stronger, but I'll drink until I'm drunk. The last thing I need is to be shit-faced trying to think about this."

"I don't believe that thinking is the answer." Damon refilled her glass from the wine bottle. "How do you feel about the idea?"

"Thanks." She sipped. "I don't know. I love you both, but if I had to pick just one of you, it would be Harry. That's a very close thing, though."

"Just like your dad and Marilyn." Damon smiled.

"Yeah. Just like that."

Damon looked at Harry. "May I?"

"Be my guest."

Damon stood and turned the music up a little. He held his hand out to Allie. "Dance with me?"

She took his hand. "Sure, why not?"

Allie could feel the old electric tingles spread through her as they moved to the music. The earlier shock of his lost weight no longer distracted her so much. Damon held her close, his head snuggled to her hair. Unlike the earlier scent of his unwashed body, he smelled clean and fresh now, but his aroma came through to her brain. It stirred memories of the time they shared.

She thought about the things he and Harry said. In some ways, it made sense. She loved both men, and they both loved her. Harry and Damon no longer saw each other as rivals. They hadn't since before Damon left for the first mission. She stifled a laugh as she thought that they saw one another as comrades now. If nothing more, they shared the basis of a multiple marriage. Allie didn't think she really wanted that, though. She wanted the whole thing, a full-blown polyamorous relationship where everyone loved everyone else, just like her parents.

Harry said in the last week that he believed he loved Damon. She wondered what Damon thought about that.

Allie didn't hear Harry move, but she found herself sandwiched between him and Damon. Harry whispered in her ear. "Is this OK?"

"Yeah, but a little unexpected."

Damon touched his lips briefly to hers, and Allie jerked from the quivers it sent through her. "Sorry."

She smiled softly. "Don't be. You always have that effect on me."

"What about me?" When she turned her head to look at him, Harry kissed her. Her mind melted into a fog of desire.

"Oh, yeah." As the three danced together, Allie turned to face first one, and then the other. As she moved face to face with one of them, she would kiss him while the other man nuzzled her head and neck from behind.

The things Harry said made more sense with each passing minute. Allie knew it could just be her rising passions, but her mind understood the logic of it all. Without the solution the men laid out, at least one of them would be hurt, the way she hurt Harry not so long ago.

Allie's pulse raced. She had never been with two other people at the same time, and intense excitement built in her. The four firm hands running over her body, caressing her through her clothes, stirred her passions to levels she never knew existed.

Before leaving for the Café, Harry trimmed his beard. He always used some old aftershave with a spicy aroma, and she could taste it on her lips as she kissed and licked his face. Allie often teased Harry about the old brand, but it tasted so delicious, she wanted him to bathe in the stuff now.

She turned to face Damon, and his lips pressed to hers, his tongue moving deeply in her mouth, tickling her cheeks and gums. He had gotten a shave and a haircut. His hair was back to his normal crew cut. She ran her hands over his head, the stubble of his blonde hair feeling rough and soft at the same time. The barber used one of the more modern colognes on Damon. The taste wasn't as intense as Harry's, but the aroma held traces of pheromones that spoke directly to Allie's pleasure centers with promises of passion.

As Harry rubbed against her back, his cock pressed firmly against her ass. His hands slipped around her hips, and he unzipped her pants. He worked them, and soon the pants and her panties rested in a heap around her ankles.

As Harry manipulated Allie's pants, Damon's hands slowly unbuttoned her blouse. Harry slipped it back from her shoulders, tossing it to the armchair. She stood naked, sandwiched between the men she knew she loved.

Damon moved to lift her, but Harry put his hand on Damon's arm. "Let me. You're still weak." Harry lifted her in his arms and carried her to the bedroom. He sat her softly on the bed.

Allie heard only the drumming of her heart in her ears. Sweat poured from her skin, and goose bumps raced across her flesh. She tried to slow her breathing, in through her nose and out through her mouth, as the men undressed by the bedside. They stood side by side, their shoulders almost touching.

Different men with different professions, Harry and Damon's bodies appeared equally different. Even having lost a fifth of his mass, Damon's shoulders were broad and strong. Hard and resilient, the muscles of his abdomen would make a good anvil. His chest rippled, pectorals flexing delightfully, as he removed his shirt.

Harry had few of the big, bulging muscles, but the strength still showed. When he stretched, Allie saw the lean sinews turn to steel bands as they flexed.

She had seen both men nude before, but this was very different. The two together made her stare. As they stood beside the bed, Allie saw that, while different, they both were delicious, and her mouth watered. As a pair, the sight nearly overwhelmed her. The familiar electric jolts went through her when with one of them became stronger than the pulses of energy *Boone* could throw at its targets. The energy hit her repeatedly, pushing her passions and senses ever higher.

They crawled onto the bed with her, Harry to her right and Damon to her left. The hot masculine flesh pressing against her body made her shiver with anticipation. Damon's smooth face moved to rub against her shoulder and neck, the touch driving her wild. Harry's soft beard tickled her cheek, then slipped down to stroke her neck, causing her to squirm in response.

Allie wanted to speak. Something in her mind told her she should say something to them. Speak, perhaps, of lust, desire, passion, and love. Her breath came too short to allow her to do more than softly moan. Her heart told her that she needed to say nothing to the men. They knew she loved and wanted them.

Her senses in high gear, Allie could smell the two men, far beyond the simple artificial fragrances they wore. Each man's unique and enchanting scent caused her head to reel. She could sense Harry's calm confidence, somehow, in the salty smell of his perspiration. Damon's musky aroma spoke to her of devotion and honor. Revved up by her senses and passions, Allie's mind couldn't put the pieces together, but it didn't matter.

The men kissed her. First one, and then the other pressed his lips to hers.

When Harry kissed her, his beard tickled her lips and face a little. His soft hair fell against her cheek, and it moved softly as his mouth ranged over her face. The delightful taste of his spicy cologne made her mouth water nearly as much the sweet flavor if his saliva as his tongue darted about in her move with urgent force.

As Damon replaced Harry's lips with his, she sensed the light pheromones he wore beating against the pleasure centers of her brain. The hint of pheromones only accentuated his scent. Even after his ordeal, the musky aroma of the big man flamed in her nose, driving her passions higher.

Harry's lips again met hers, and he moaned softly as she sucked his tongue. His lips smacked quietly as he kissed her.

When Harry pulled away, she lunged after him, but Damon's lips intercepted hers. His tongue moved slowly in her mouth, probing and touching her in every possible place. His saliva ran freely into her mouth, and the sweet passions of want followed his flavor.

Two strong hands moved over her breasts, gently squeezing and caressing them. The fingers would softly roll and pinch her nipples, causing her to moan and writhe. Harry's lips slipped around her hard right nipple, sucking gently as Damon's mouth moved to her left where he tenderly nibbled at the stiffness their touch created.

The hands moved across her stomach slowly to stroke her thighs. Allie parted her legs, and the hands moved again to rub teasingly over her mons, the fingers tugging gently at the small patch of blonde hair there. Her mind running wild, Allie wasn't sure whose hand moved first, but fingers slipped into her pussy, probing her gently, as the two sets of lips continued to tease her nipples.

Her hands moved over the heads of her lovers. The right hand slipped through long black hair, the strands wrapping around her fingers, and then sliding free again. The left hand ran over short blonde hair, the stubble flicking tantalizingly between her fingers.

She gasped when the lips pulled from her breasts, and the men kissed down her stomach and sides. Each man moved to straddle her legs, Harry still on the right, and they spread her legs wider. They kissed her thighs, licking slowly to where their fingers still plunged into her. Damon licked her clit, a flickering pass of his wet tongue, and Allie jumped with the shocking wave of pleasure. Harry repeated the move, and she jerked again.

The men took turns licking her clit, and then removed their probing fingers from her cunt. Their tongues darted deep into her soaked pussy, and Allie's orgasm closed on her. Her back arched on the bed, and she shook uncontrollably.

Harry and Damon moved slightly, and both of them licked her at the same time. Suddenly, a billion suns seemed to explode in her head, the blinding flash causing her to scream with the passion of her climax. Her body thrashed as they continued to tongue her pussy. Allie pulled their heads tighter to her, her fingers twisted in Harry's long hair and grappling for a grip in Damon's short hair.

She collapsed back onto the bed, her chest pounding as sweat poured from her body. She twitched and jerked as her men crawled back up the bed to lie next to her, cuddling her close on both sides. Allie again wanted to speak, but her panting allowed her only to smile at them.

Neither man spoke, but only held her tightly as her shaking faded to tremors, then subsided. She kissed Harry, and then turned to kiss Damon. Looking from one man to the other, Allie smiled at them. "I love you. Both of you."

Chapter 18

Peace

"Terms? You're kidding." Jim sat at the end of the large conference table in his formal office. Admirals Q and Zach Reeves sat to either side of him. A hundred fully armed Marines under the direct command of Ike Payne also filled the room, most aiming their weapons at the Arupian President, and the two officials with him, who sat at the other end of the table.

The electronic translator did a good job with the work, but the Arupian language sounded like a catfight. "We are here to discuss terms of surrender."

Jim shifted in his throne. He didn't like sitting here because it didn't fit with the more relaxed image he preferred. "All right. The terms are simple. You surrender with no conditions, and I won't blast this system into glittering slag." Jim sighed. "Zach, tell them what's going to happen."

"As the Emperor said, it's pretty simple. The Emperor will appoint a military governor. Your government will be dissolved, and some officials may stand trial for crimes against the Arupian people." Zach smiled. "A new constitution and government based on the Imperial democracy will be put into place. Arup will then be a part of the Empire of Mankind."

The three Arupians spoke among themselves. One of them switched off the translator. Normal Arupian conversation sounded like a catfight. Three Arupians in a heated discussion sounded like a major feline war, with nuclear weapons. Jim's patience wore thin. Only in the meeting for three hours, the Arupian President's arrogant attitude pushed Jim's good nature.

The Arupians turned the translator on again. "The idea of a military government is not acceptable."

Jim ran his hand through his hair. He knew his frustration showed. "OK, this is getting out of hand. I'm done playing nice with you." Jim stepped down from the throne and walked to the far end of the table. Ike moved, placing her body between him and the Arupians. "It's OK, Ike." She stepped back, but he heard the safety of her rifle click. Jim pulled the chair next to the official to the President's right from under the desk and sat down. "We have a problem here. The problem is that you seem to have the idea you have some say in this. Make no mistake about it. You have no say at all. What Admiral Reeves outlined is what will happen."

"Then the fighting will continue."

"Yeah, I guess it will." Jim glanced down the table. "Admiral Q, how long to destroy the remaining Arupian ships?"

"Less than twelve hours, Sir. Probably closer to eight."

Jim turned back to the President. "The fighting will go on, but for a very short time." He sighed. "I don't want to destroy your fleet. We'll just have to rebuild it later. I certainly don't want to kill a lot of civilians in ground actions. Our problems aren't theirs. If you leave me no choice, I'll do both."

"Are you threatening me?"

Jim smiled. "Yeah, I am."

He hadn't learned to read Arupian facial expressions and other nonverbal queues very well, but Jim saw the whiskers twitching on the President's face. The Arupian made flickering glances at his two officials. "I would receive immunity from prosecution?"

"Nope. I will give you immunity from a death sentence, and, if convicted of any crimes, you'll do your sentence at a prison out of the Arupian system."

The official between Jim and the President snarled something the machine translated as *chicken shit*. The President seemed to relax a little. "Very well. We have a deal." He paused. "Your Majesty."

* * * *

Allie woke to the smell of something wonderful, and it didn't smell like Harry or Damon. She was alone in the bed. The thoughts about the night the three shared made her smile. They also made her body tingle with a shiver of happiness. She found her robe and stumbled to the dining room.

Harry sat at the table, while Damon looked like an alchemist in his lab as he worked in the kitchen.

Harry turned as she entered. "Morning, beautiful." He stood, coming to hug her. He kissed her softly. "How did you sleep?"

Allie found it interesting that she still had any tingles left to make her quiver. She spent the entire night tingling. "Wonderfully." She kissed him again.

Damon came from the kitchen. "Only time for a quickie! I have waffles cooking!" He kissed her briefly but deeply before going back to his work.

Allie sat as Harry held a chair for her. "I didn't know you could cook."

"I can't, but I can follow directions."

Harry leaned and whispered in her ear. "Claire said she could cure food poisoning."

Allie laughed. "Shut up! He's trying to be sweet!"

Damon brought a bowl of whipped cream for the table. He also sat a cup of coffee in front of her. "I hope you like Irish cream." He pointed at Harry. "Your coffee will get something special if you don't get off my shit about cooking."

Harry smiled. "I think I like it when you're being all domestic." He nudged Allie. "Gives me more time with our lady."

"Uh-huh." Damon went back to the kitchen. "Oh! Allie, get some whipped cream for your coffee, too."

"I will." She lifted a dollop of the fluffy white peaks on her fingers and dropped it in her cup. She then licked the rest from her fingers while she watched Harry.

"Damn it."

"Yeah. We need get more of this stuff."

Damon returned with three huge waffles and a bowl of strawberries. "Are you two doing something nasty with the whipped cream?"

"Not without you." Harry sniffed the waffle. "This smells great."

"Thanks. Dig in!"

Allie glanced at her watch. "I can't believe I slept until almost noon."

Harry put a mound of whipped cream on his waffle twice as thick as the waffle itself. "We had a long night."

Damon chuckled. "I guess we did." He chewed for a moment, and then swallowed. "Allie, I'm not trying to pressure you, but how do you feel?"

"Satisfied. Very, very satisfied." She giggled. "Sorry, I couldn't pass up a straight line like that one."

"Humor is my gig, remember?" Harry poked her hand with the handle of his fork. "I think what he means is if you're happy with the direction this relationship took last night."

She thought for a moment as she ate. "I wish you would both stop worrying only about my happiness. For this to work, we all should be happy." She sat down her fork and took their hands. "I love you both, and I want you to be happy. I also want me to be happy."

"You didn't answer the question." Damon squeezed her hand. "While this is all new to me, and I have no idea what I'm doing, I'm happy."

Harry nodded. "I agree with all that."

"Then we're all happy." Allie decided to attack her questions about how her men felt about each other head on. "I want to tell you that what I want isn't a multiple marriage." She saw the look passing between the men. "I grew up in a home with polyamory, and the love that fills my home is amazing. Daddy and my moms are all in love with one another, and that love spills over to the kids. Everywhere I look, there's love. That's what I want for myself and my family."

Damon sighed. "Family...That's a powerful word."

"You know it." Harry thought for a moment. "Is that where we're going?"

"I hope so." Allie smiled at them. "Pretty scary stuff for most guys I know."

"Not really. I don't recall ever actually telling you, but my family is all dead." Damon blinked a time or two. "They died in an accident about nine years ago."

"No, you never told me, but we found out when you..." Allie

frowned. "Well, when we thought you were dead." She stood and went to the bookcase, taking down a triangular container. She handed the box to Damon. "I guess we need to decide what to do with this."

"This is more than a little creepy." Damon looked through the glass front at the neatly folded flag. He took the smaller box from the top. "What's this?"

Harry glanced at Allie for a moment. "Oh, that. We sort of forgot to tell you about that in all the excitement."

Damon opened the box that held the Imperial Medal of Honor. He stared. "You forgot about this?"

"Yeah, we did." Harry grinned. "Congratulations."

* * * *

Damon, Harry, and Rich Draper stood at rigid attention before Jim in his formal office. Allie, her moms, Q, and General Dietrich all stood to the side of Jim. Jim wore his Lord Admiral of the Fleet uniform. He didn't like the uniform any more than he liked his throne, but for a different reason. The uniform made him itch.

Jim smiled a lopsided grin that most people in the Empire would recognize. "Gentlemen, I hate these formal affairs, but we have to do this one. I'll keep this short so you can get back to relaxing." He glanced at Allie. "Or whatever it is that you're doing." He moved to stand in front of Rich. "Lieutenant Draper, I'd like to offer my personal thanks and congratulations on a job well done. Things haven't changed in the more than 4,500 years that the Marines have been around. When we have a tough job that needs doing, people like me still send in the Marines." Jim pinned the Fleet Cross on Rich's chest. He then took a small box from the steward, and pinned the bars of a Captain on Rich's shoulders. Jim slowly saluted. "Congratulation, Captain Draper."

"Thank you, Sir." Rich returned the salute.

Jim stepped to Harry. "Lieutenant Douglas." He smiled. "Harry. The best term I've heard to describe you is one that Stu Dayton called me about 650 years ago. You're crazy as a bedbug. Be that as it may, well done." He placed the Fleet Cross on Harry's chest, and then pinned the insignia of a Lieutenant Commander on his shoulders. Jim saluted.

"Congratulations, Lieutenant Commander Douglas."

Harry returned the salute. "Thank you, Sir."

Jim moved to Damon. "Lieutenant Hyde. I'm afraid I have no medals or promotions that can change the things you have endured. Only time will make things right again." Jim pinned the Captain's bars on Damon's shoulders. "For now, all I can really offer is the appreciation of the Empire and myself for your sacrifice." Jim smiled as he saluted. "Welcome back, Captain Hyde."

"Thank you, Sir." Damon saluted.

Jim lowered his hand, and then walked back to the small podium. "Gentlemen, the three of you aren't really here just to represent yourselves. You represent the many men and women who serve the Empire. You each have the best qualities of those people. It's you and your comrades who make the Empire great. And it's people like you who make the Empire safe for us all." Jim smiled. "I'm proud to call you my shipmates." He saluted.

* * * *

"Claire told me I shouldn't drink." Damon tossed off his beer and waved at the serving wench for another.

"Hell, a few drinks won't kill you." Harry signaled for another drink, too. He smiled. "It's a little strange, Allie not with us."

"Maybe, but we need some guy time, too." The wench brought their drinks. Damon watched as she walked away. "You know, she's not as cute as the last time we were here."

"No, she's not." Harry considered. "Actually, she never was all that cute."

"Nope." Damon took a large swallow of beer. "That tastes great."

Harry laughed. "After eating cat food for two months, I'd think anything that didn't taste like ocean fish would taste good."

"You've got that right!" Damon thought for a moment. "Is it just me, or is it a bit strange that our promotions jumped two or more ranks?"

"He's the Emperor and Lord Admiral." Harry shrugged. "He can do what he wants."

"Yeah, he can. Including having us both spaced."

"I guess he can." He told Damon the story of Jim threatening him. "I think he wouldn't hesitate a second if he thinks we're hurting Allie or taking advantage of her."

"I believe you're right." Damon smiled. "I know you can kick my ass, but if you hurt her, you're going for a walk outside."

"That's good. If I do something that stupid, please toss me off the ship."

"Only if you give me the same treatment."

"That's a deal." Harry sipped at his beer. "So, do you think this is going to work?"

"I can't see why not. We both love her, and she loves both of us."

"Yeah, but that's not what Allie wants."

"No, it's not."

Harry smiled. "Would it make things easier if I told you that I've fallen for you?"

Damon laughed. "I don't know. It's hard not to fall for someone who saved your life. Twice."

"Maybe, but that doesn't explain how I feel about you."

"Maternal instincts?" Damon smiled over his glass at him.

Harry laughed. "That could be it, yeah."

Cathy and Beth walked to their table. "Hi, Harry. Damon."

Harry glanced at Damon for a moment. "Hi. How are you girls tonight?"

"We're good. We thought maybe you'd like some company."

"We wouldn't mind the company, but I need to tell you that's all we're looking for."

Cathy blinked for a moment. "Oh. Are you, um, involved?"

"Yeah, I guess that's one way to put it."

Cathy smiled a little. "Thanks for telling us." She glanced at Beth for a moment. "We'll leave you two to talk, then." She and Beth made their goodbyes and left the table.

Damon smiled. "I guess that makes it official."

"What's that?"

"That you and I are involved."

"Aren't we?"

Damon smiled again. He put his hand on Harry's. "Yeah, we are."

* * * *

Allie stared at Harry and Damon when they came home, hugging each other, laughing hysterically. "You two are drunk."

"Maybe a little, but not much." Harry let go of Damon long enough to hug her. When he kissed her, his tongue plunge deeply into her mouth, setting off shivers all the way to her toes. "See? We're not drunk."

Allie laughed as she looked at Damon. "What about you?"

"Me? I'm drunk." He kissed her, dipping her low to the deck before lifting her back to standing.

"I may have to get you both drunk more often." She slowed her breathing. "Let's get something for dinner."

Damon frowned. "We're not hungry."

Harry smiled. "Except for you."

A wave of desire swept over her as her heart raced in her chest. "I, um, see."

"Come on." Damon took her hand, leading her to the bathroom. The men slowly undressed her, touching her body and giving her chills.

They helped each other to undress before Damon bent to lift her. Harry frowned a little. "Don't hurt yourself." He turned on the shower. Damon carried her into the cascading water, and then eased her back to her feet.

Four strong hands moved over her body, soaping and caressing as they went. One set large, with a few calluses from gripping powerful weapons for control. One set smaller, with smooth skin.

Allie tingled as Damon lifted her hair to kiss down her back. Her breath came short as Harry pressed his lips to hers. The mix of the only warm water flowing down her face with Harry's hot lips on hers made a scrumptious feeling sweep over her.

Harry's hardness pressed to her as they kissed deeply. She moved her legs, wrapping them around Harry's hips and lifting herself onto him. His cock slipped into her pussy, causing her to quiver with the delight of his deep penetration.

As she moved slowly on Harry's dick, Damon's erection pressed against her as he stepped behind her. With a gentle push, his cock slid slowly into her ass. She gasped as her eyes opened. She saw only Harry's closed eyes, millimeters from hers.

Passion rushed through her body as her hips, suspended by her legs wrapped tightly around Harry, thrust back and forth. Harry's dick ran deeper into her cunt on each forward thrust, and Damon's cock slid farther into her ass when she thrust backward. The pounding of her pulse in her ears drowned the gentle rush of the water as it ran down her body and the shower walls.

Pulling her lips from Harry's, she turned her head sharply, and Damon met her move, his lips pressing to hers, his tongue darting wildly in her mouth. The sensation caught her by surprise. When they kissed, Damon often moved his tongue slowly in her mouth, but now he moved urgently. The tip of his tongue flicked against hers as he kissed her, and the change in him made her want to kiss both men at the same time.

She imagined their tongues both dancing in her mouth together, filling her mouth with the amazing melding of their flavors.

Harry's hands, sandwiched between her and Damon, moved to rub her back and Damon's chest. Harry leaned to lick her ear, sucking the lobe into his mouth with gentle nibbles of love.

Damon's hands moved from her hips to grasp her thighs, lifting her body from Harry's. Harry pulled his hard cock from her pussy, and then kissed down her neck to her rigid nipples, swirling around them with his tongue, sucking them firmly.

As Damon held her from behind, her legs spread wide while he fucked her ass, Allie's body jerked with his thrusts. Harry knelt before her, his mouth pressed to her pussy. He sucked her hard clit between his lips. As he ran his tongue back, Harry reached to rub her clit with his fingers, and his tongue plunged deep into her pussy.

Allie's tongue dueled with Damon's as they kissed, his taste flowing across her tongue and into her mouth. She wanted all he could give her. Harry's fingers and tongue caused her twitch and jump, making Damon's cock run firmly into her ass, triggering more jerking.

Her orgasm came suddenly. When her body tensed, Harry held her clit gently between his teeth, his tongue flicking frantically over her. Damon bounced her up and down on his cock. Fearing that she might bite him, Allie pulled her mouth from Damon's. She thrashed in his arms, screaming incoherently as wave after wave of her climax seized her. She bucked against her orgasm, feeling her juices flowing freely as Harry sucked and licked her.

Damon trembled. He moaned loudly as his cock pulsed in her ass. The hot fluid erupting from his dick squirted deeply into her as he jerked and rocked unsteadily on his feet. Harry stood and put his arms around them both, steadying them. He carefully lifted Allie from Damon's softening cock, and then lowered her to her feet.

Allie clung to Harry's chest while Damon clung to her back. She smiled a little. "My God."

Harry laughed gently. "If he could talk, Damon would say the same thing."

Allie smiled and kissed Harry deeply. She reached down to grab his hard cock, pumping him slowly. As she knelt before Harry and licked his dick, Damon stepped back under the flowing water from the showerhead. He watched as she sucked Harry's cock, slowly rubbing his dick with soapy hands.

Harry ran his fingers through her hair as she held his cock and licked his balls. When she licked up his length to flick her tongue around the head, Allie tasted the salty sweetness of the pre-cum glistening there. She sucked him firmly, and then slipped his shaft down her throat until she could lick his balls.

Allie watched Damon from the corner of her eye as she sucked Harry. His cock and balls covered by soap bubbles, he stared as Harry's dick moved in and out of her mouth. His hands worked his balls and cock, sliding slowly up and down his length.

Sucking Harry and watching Damon playing with his cock, Allie's pussy got wetter. Pulses of electricity moved through her body, making her quiver. When she licked her lips between deep swallows of Harry's dick, she could taste the beads of sweat on her upper lip.

As if he came from nowhere, Damon suddenly stood beside Harry, his cock pressing against her cheek. Allie pulled her mouth from Harry to run Damon's dick deeply down her throat. She grasped the men's cocks in her fists, pressing the heads together. She licked the swollen glans, flicking her tongue over them rapidly. The men trembled before her.

Damon and Harry moved closer together, their cocks jutting at her face as she cupped their balls in her hands. Licking and sucking the two dicks before her, Allie tasted the mixture of the two men's perspiration. The flavor mingled with the sparkling drops of fluid on the tips of their cocks. The scent of the three bodies pressed so close nearly overwhelmed her, speaking of passion, desire, and love.

Allie grasped the hard cocks again, pumping rapidly as she sucked first one then the other into her mouth to tease the head with her tongue. She nibbled tenderly at the glans of the two men, feeling them jerk in response.

They brushed their hands over her hair as she sucked them. She slipped Harry's cock into her mouth, and Damon's strong hands pressed her head toward Harry, until his dick slid fully down her throat. Damon gripped her hair and pumped her head back and forth on Harry's cock. She moved to take Damon's hardness between her lips, and Harry's hands pushed her mouth farther down Damon's shaft.

The cocks in her mouth and the firm hands on her head drove Allie to the edge. Kneeling before her lovers, sensing the pleasure they took from her, made her passions rage. A tingling started far down in her brain, building slowly to encompass her entire body as her orgasm made a second appearance. She pumped rapidly on the men's dicks, feeling their hips thrusting in response.

As the first waves of her orgasm reached her fully, Harry's body jerked. Allie sucked his cock into her mouth just as his cum exploded from him. His hips bucking, he filled her mouth with his hot sweetness as his cock in her mouth prevented her from screaming with her climax.

Still pumping his cock, Damon moaned, and his cum spurted onto her cheek and across her mouth where Harry's dick still filled her lips. She pulled her mouth from Harry to lick Damon's cum running down her face. She sucked rapidly on Damon's cock to get all his salty fluid she could in her mouth. As Damon thrashed in his climax, Harry trembled before her.

The remarkable combination of their cum thrilled her palette, the sweetly salty flavors blending. Mixed with their perspiration, the concoction made her heart skip a beat as she hungrily savored the flavors.

When Damon's flow ebbed, Allie kissed the two cocks softening before her eyes, and then stood. She kissed them both softly.

When their trembles eased, the men soaped her and themselves all over again, their hands keeping her passions from fading with the shakiness. They rinsed one another, and then made her stand by helplessly as they dried her gently.

After leading her to the bed, they lie down beside her, Harry again on her right, and cuddled her between them.

Allie wanted to kiss them both at the same time, the way she sucked their cocks at the same time. She knew she needed to work on the mechanics of that. She settled for turning her head to kiss them one at a time. "You two drive me wild."

Damon rested his hand protectively over her stomach. "I'll take that as a good thing."

"I mean it as a good thing."

Harry's hand moved to rest protectively on Damon's. "A very good thing."

Damon chuckled.

Allie looked at him. "What?"

"Oh, nothing. I don't want to ruin the moment."

"As long as it's you, I don't see what you could do to ruin the moment."

"Remember when I said that this whole polyamorous thing could get complicated just trying to keep straight who you can sleep with?" She nodded. "Well, I think Harry is short a turn at bat." Harry laughed hysterically as Allie giggled. Damon blushed. "I told you I like baseball."

She kissed his nose. "You didn't ruin the moment, but I've never heard it put quite that way before."

Harry managed to quell his laugh. "Me too, but if anyone is keeping score..."

"Shut up, Harry."

"Yes, ma'am."

Allie smiled. "Two men calling me Mistress...That has possibilities."

Damon chuckled. "Yikes! We may be in trouble, Harry."

"Good trouble, but trouble none the less."

Damon's hand slipped from under Harry's to massage her breast.

"Speaking of good."

"Yeah." Harry massaged her other breast.

Allie sighed. "That's nice...You two are going to kill me with kindness, but I love it." She kissed them both. "And I love you."

Damon slipped his hand to her pussy, his fingers twirling around her clit. "I love you, too."

Harry kissed her breast. "I love you both."

Damon leaned across her chest and kissed Harry's lips. "I love you."

Chapter 19

Directions

Allie watched as Damon and Harry kissed while leaning over her body. They continued to touch her, but otherwise seemed absorbed in each other. Shivers ran through her body as the men she loved showed their love for one another. Harry's hand moved to Damon's neck, and he pulled Damon closer to him.

The excitement of watching them sent sparkling tingles of electricity passing through her, but there was much more. Alone with either of them, she always burned with passion and desire. In the times they shared as a threesome, Allie found a new level of desire and passion. Passion and desire now, but she sensed something new in the mix. As she watched them kissing, hands running over each other's heads and still touching her, Allie could cut the love in the air with a knife.

Afraid that moving would break the spell, Allie lay still, watching. She risked moving her hands to touch them both gently. Both men jumped like her fingertips shocked them when she softly ran her hands over their backs.

Several minutes passed before Harry slowly leaned away from Damon. He smiled. "Damn it."

Damon's eyes held a softness Allie recognized from the first kiss she shared with him. "Yeah." Damon tuned to Allie, and he leaned to kiss her. "We didn't mean to ignore you."

Allie's breath blew rapidly through her lips as she panted. "You didn't." Turning her head to face Harry, Allie smiled at him. "You're supposed to say something funny about now, I think."

"I can't think of anything funny to say right now."

Allie's excitement that built as she watched the men kissing finally broke over the top. "Good." She pushed Harry to his back, and then rolled to straddle his hips, facing his feet. His hard cock slipped easily into her wet cunt. As she rocked slowly on his dick, Damon moved to kneel between Harry's legs.

Damon leaned to lick her clit as Harry's cock moved in her. Allie leaned far back, placing her hands on Harry's shoulders as he supported her back with his hands, rubbing her back firmly.

Allie closed her eyes and moaned softly. Her hips gyrated on Harry's hardness, and the head of his cock pressed against her cervix as she moved. Damon's tongue moved to plunge into her pussy along with Harry's dick, sending quakes of passion through her body.

When she opened her eyes, Allie saw Damon licking the shaft of Harry's cock as she moved. The vision pushed her farther, her mind awash in desire.

Moving suddenly, Allie pulled herself from Harry's cock and moved to kneel beside Damon. She kissed him deeply before licking Harry's cock. The taste of her pussy strong and sweet on Harry's shaft, Damon's tongue joined hers. Together, they licked and kissed Harry's hardness.

Her eyes closed, Allie could only feel Damon as his lips slipped over the head of the cock they sucked, slipping it deeply into his mouth. Allie reached down to grasp Damon's cock, finding it hard, a slick coating of pre-cum on the head. Licking the shaft of Harry's cock and his balls and feeling Damon's lips wrapped around the head, Allie stroked Damon's dick repeatedly.

Harry's growing moans and thrusting hips told her that he neared climax. Allie whispered in Damon's ear. "Share with me, please."

Damon's lips came from Harry's head with a pop, and they both licked the head rapidly until Harry's hips bucked wildly on the bed and his cum shot from his cock, splashing over their faces. Allie kissed Damon as they licked frantically to gather the salty sweetness from the others' face.

After licking Harry's cock clean of the last trails of cum, Allie and Damon moved to lie beside him, cuddling him between them. The three shared soft kisses as Harry's trembles subsided.

Allie touched his chin with her fingers, turning his face to her. She kissed Harry deeply. "Are you all right?"

His breathing slowed to a rapid rising and falling of his chest. "Never better."

She kissed his nose, and then leaned across Harry's chest to kiss Damon. "What about you?"

"Great."

The men moved to put her between them again, strong hands holding her. They cuddled and talked together for a long time. Allie drifted off to sleep feeling warm, safe, and loved.

* * * *

The clean up of the remaining Arupian forces went well. Even without knowing of the truce now in place, most of the Arupian ships seemed happy to surrender. Most of the ships had some degree of damage. By human standards, many would be considered not spaceworthy.

The ground forces presented bigger problems. More rested and healthier than the space forces, many of the Arupian warriors seemed reluctant to surrender, even after Q made them aware of the truce.

Even with the token resistance of the Arupian ground forces, the clean up proceeded, with only a small number of minor injuries to humans and Arupians. Overall, Q believed the operation went well so far.

He smiled at the idea that Jim had bigger problems to cope with. Jim still needed to create the military government. Jim also still needed to find a lord to take over the civilian government and oversee the creation of a home rule democracy. Jim told Q at the breakfast briefing that his first choice for lord turned down the assignment because he wouldn't be available for nearly a year.

"Admiral, we have an Arupian carrier signally surrender." The Weapons Officer checked her sensors. "Their offensive and defensive systems are fully offline."

Q chuckled to himself. "Very well. Tell them to stand by and we'll have someone there as soon as we can to accept their surrender." He looked to the officer from the JAG office assigned to bridge. The man sat at the Press Officer's station. "How long before you can have someone there?"

"Maybe two or three hours, Sir."

With more surrenders than they could handle, Q understood the pressure on the JAG officer. Q nodded and turned back to the Weapons Officer. "Send some Marines and a medical team."

"Yes, Sir."

* * * *

"Jonas, you have to help me out here!"

"Jim, I hear what you're saying, but I can't walk out on what I'm doing here in the Chelsea system."

Jonas Remslure held the official Imperial title of Floating Lord. Rebuilding planetary governments that needed rebuilding, his job sounded simple on the surface. Of the four hundred or so Floating Lords, Jonas definitely came out as the pick of the litter. Intelligent, personable, tough, and compassionate, Jonas offered more than three hundred years experience doing the things that Arup needed done. Jim ran his hand through his hair. "I know that. How long will it take you to get free from Chelsea?"

"Like I've told you several dozen times now, about a year. Maybe eleven months."

Jim didn't like military governments, even when he held the military governor position. They smacked of a totalitarian dictatorship, and the people lacked any hint of home rule. He didn't really care for the limited-time appointed off-world lord system, either. Both removed government from the hands of the people of the planet. He didn't have a choice, though. In shambles, the Arupian government couldn't meet the needs of the people. The planet's infrastructure suffered severe damage in the war. Food and water supplies, as well as the sanitary services, existed as someone's idea of a bad joke. "Jonas, I really need you here. You're the best man for the job."

"If you order me to Arup, I'll be on the next ship, but you need to ask yourself how many people in Chelsea system will die because we're not meeting our obligations here."

"I wish you wouldn't have said that." Jim sighed. "I know you won't yank my chain, but what's the best hope for you to get free sooner than a year?"

"That is my best estimate." He shrugged as Jim watched him through the hyperspace link. "If everything goes perfect, no problems at all, I might be out of here in nine months. Maybe."

Jim thought. His pattern for the last seven hundred years for these situations remained the same. He sent in a military governor to rebuild most of the infrastructure. With only one person making decisions, the military model worked best for that task. With Marines to back up the decisions, the process became very efficient. After that, Jim appointed a lord, usually an off-world person, to a limited term of eighteen months or so. The lord set up the new constitution and government with help from a temporary elected council of the people. The people would then elect a permanent council, and Jim would appoint a new, permanent lord, from the planet's population. He saw no need to change now. The damage to the infrastructure of Arup would take months to repair. Maybe the military government could drag out for a year. Jim outlined his idea for Jonas. The military governor would rule for a year, until Jonas came in from Chelsea. "That's a long time for a military government, though."

"It is that." Jonas stared blankly at the screen for a moment. "If the damage is as bad as the briefing you sent says it is, then it will take a year to fix. You'll need someone as governor that you trust, though." He smiled. "I doubt you'll get Zach to sit out there in the armpit of the galaxy for a year."

Jim laughed. "Oh, I can get Zach to do it, but Claire and her mothers will kill me."

* * * *

Damon sat next to Allie and across from Harry at the table, holding their hands. Feeling better than he did a week ago, and having gained back more than a kilo of his mass, he felt eager to go back on duty tomorrow. He watched the two people he loved as they watched him.

Just three months ago, he would have never believed he could love one person, let alone two, especially when one of them was a man. As he watched them, Damon knew the things Allie told him when they came here on their first official date were true. He couldn't remember the exact words she used, but he knew that what the three of them shared was about love, not sex. Love knew no boundaries about gender, age, or appearance. Of course, when love existed as it did between them, sex made up a big part of the love.

He smiled as he thought about last night. He and Allie met Harry at The Pearlie for drinks. Allie casually announced that she would spend the night with her parents so he and Harry could be alone. Over the last week, each man spent one night alone with Allie while the other stayed away for the night, so Damon didn't find the idea for him and Harry to have some time together unusual. Harry argued a little, but Allie would hear none of it. She walked them to her cabin, what they all now thought of as home, kissed them gently, and then left them alone.

Never having been alone with another man before, Damon's nerves chewed at him. Then again, this past week marked his first threesome and several other firsts. He watched Harry closely. True to his form, Harry gave away nothing more than he intended, so Damon didn't know if this was all new for him or not.

Their lovemaking came easily and naturally. He missed feeling Allie's soft arms and skin touching him, but the strength of Harry's arms was fantastic, giving him shivers very like those she gave him. The passion of the kisses he shared with Harry came even closer to what he and Allie shared. As he kissed Harry, Damon saw what Allie found so attractive.

Damon shivered a little remembering the way Harry's aftershave filled his nose as they kissed. The aroma held a powerful spice component, and made his mouth water even now. The flavor was like a bite of a warm cake, fresh from the oven, and like a child, he wanted more.

He recalled his sighs and moans as they kissed, and how they mixed with the sounds of their lips smacking, as they slipped apart for a moment before pressing tightly together again.

The driving, forceful desire that Harry's kiss made shoot through his body caused Damon to shake all the way to his toes. As they kissed, their hands moved over each other, and the chills shook him like an earthquake. The heat from Harry's hands nearly burned him through his clothes.

As they touched each other, Harry's muscles rippled through his shirt. Damon worked out regularly and that gave him highly defined muscles. Harry only rarely went to the gym to lift weights, but he practiced what he called tai chi several times a day, a dance-like exercise that gave him strong firm muscles without the definition of a body builder. The bands under Harry's skin flexed and hardened like steel cords as he moved.

They soon tore at each other's clothing. Falling to the floor, they explored one another with their hands and mouths. Harry's cock pressed to his stomach as they rolled about. The flavor of Harry's sweat sang on Damon's lips as he kissed and licked his way to the dick that pressed against him moments before. Allie tried to teach him to swallow Harry's cock fully, but Damon had yet to master the skill. He licked and sucked the swollen head. The scent of Harry's body tickled his nose as he did the things for Harry that he liked Allie to do for him. Harry's moans and writing told Damon that Harry liked them, too.

Harry suddenly grasped his shoulders and rolled Damon to his back. Harry's lessons from Allie seemed to have gone better. Harry swallowed his cock to the base, his lips touching Damon's balls. Harry's tongue flicked over the head of his cock, swirling and probing, between deep runs down his throat.

Harry reached into what Allie called the toy drawer of the end table and pulled out a tube of lubricant. He poured the glistening fluid over his hand and gently rubbed it liberally around Damon's ass. Other than physical exams, Damon always thought of his ass as a one-way street, but Harry gently massaged him, relaxing the muscles and Damon's trepidations. With a slight push, Harry slipped his finger deep inside Damon. There was no pain and, as Harry worked his hand, another finger moved into him. Harry's fingers curved upward to point at the base of his hard cock. Harry rubbed inside him, and waves of pleasure swept over him.

Harry slipped the fingers from his ass, and then applied the lubricant to his cock. He lifted Damon's legs high and guided the head of his dick into Damon's ass. Demon shivered now, thinking about the tender gentleness with which Harry entered him. Harry's climax came quickly, filling Damon with his cum.

They spent the night napping, waking to make love, and then sleeping again as they cuddled together. This morning, Allie joined them for breakfast. She smiled at them both, after kissing them good morning, then commented on how happy they looked.

Damon knew he was happy.

"Are you OK?"

Allie's question jarred him back to the here and now. "Sorry. Just thinking."

Harry laughed. "Go back to thinking, then. We're going to dance." He held Allie's chair as she stood, and then both of his lovers kissed his cheeks before they went to the dance floor.

Damon sat watching them dance, a gentle smile on his face.

* * * *

As she sat down, Allie studied Damon's face. She giggled a little. "I don't know what you're thinking about, but that's a goofy grin on your face."

Harry kissed her cheek and took his chair. "I planned to let that pass, but she's right."

Damon shrugged. "I guess the short answer is that I'm thinking about you two."

Allie squeezed Harry's hand as she smiled. "Harry hasn't stolen you from me, has he?"

"Oh, no! Never!"

"Just the way it should be." She grinned.

"Yeah, but I know there's a hierarchy to this polyamorous thing." Damon smiled.

"Don't be silly."

Harry frowned a little. "Maybe he's right." He thought for a moment. "If I had to pick just one of you, it would be you, Allie."

"That's what I mean." Damon's smile never faded. "I feel the same way. I'd pick you over Harry in a heartbeat."

Harry nodded. "You already said that you would pick me, too."

Allie didn't think she liked the direction this conversation headed in. She didn't want to get into a debate about how much they love one another. "I guess I did."

Harry sighed. "The thing is, I'd fight to the death not to make that choice." He took Damon's hand in his. "I love you both, and I want you both."

"Exactly!" Damon's smile broadened. "I'll be greedy, too. I want both of you."

Allie laughed. "You have no idea how happy that makes me."

"I think we do." Harry leaned over and hugged her. "You were right, and all of us need to feel happy. I can only speak for my own happiness."

Damon hugged her, too. "I can't say how happy I am any better than Harry already put things."

Allie's heart pounded and sang in her chest. Somehow, with no conscious work, a love affair evolved into what her parents shared. The very thing she always wanted in her own life. Waves of love passed over her, shaded with lust and passion. She turned to Damon. "I love you." She kissed him softly before turning to face Harry. "I love you." She kissed him.

* * * *

The different ways Harry and Damon reacted amused Allie. She watched them as they sat at the dinner table with her parents. Harry seemed comfortable and chatted with her father like they'd known each other for years. He also seemed at ease with her mothers, despite Marilyn's flirting.

Damon seemed shy and reserved. Despite her father's numerous requests, Damon still called him sir. He also called the women ma'am or my lady. Damon sat at the table at attention.

Per his longstanding habit, her father didn't talk about serious matters at the table. Allie thought he preferred to watch as Marilyn ate with her fingers instead. They ate spaghetti and her mother put on a show, much to Tanya's chagrin.

"Damon, I really wish you'd relax a little." Jim sipped at his wine. "I don't bite."

Marilyn sucked a length of spaghetti between her lips slowly. "That's Allie's job."

Jim stared at Marilyn's place at the far end of the table as he shook his head. Tanya threw a piece of bread crust at Marilyn from her place to Jim's left. Marilyn laughed. "Sorry."

"N-no, you're n-not." Tanya glared. "Jim's r-r-right, though." She glanced down the table to Damon. "J-just r-relax."

Paige looked across the table at Damon. "You'll have to relax sometime."

Janelle looked passed Allie to where Paige sat. "After dinner, honey."

"Yeah, right." Paige smiled.

Harry glanced across the table at Allie, and then looked to Damon on his left. "Paige is right though. Just take a deep breath, drink more wine, and relax." He grinned. "Besides, when have you ever seen a room blessed with so many beautiful women?"

Damon laughed nervously. "That's true." He looked to his left as Marilyn did the trick with another piece of spaghetti, staring at Jim at the other end of the table.

Janelle reached to her right to pat Allie's hand. "You're right. They are sweet."

"I don't mind when you do that, really." Paige looked to Marilyn on her right, and then glanced at Tanya. "But if she throws a knife at you, she may hit me."

Allie saw Marilyn's eyes get their come-fuck-me look as she turned to her right. "Am I bothering you, Damon?" She put her hand on his.

Damon's mouth worked several times without sound. "Um, no. I mean no, Ma'am." He snatched his hand from the table and rested it in his lap.

"Mom." Allie joined Tanya in glaring at Marilyn. A wave of jealousy hit her. Maybe even anger.

The look vanished instantly from Marilyn's eyes. "Sorry. Old habits die hard!" Her eyes went back to their normal deep sapphire blue. "I really am harmless."

Harry laughed. "You're going to kill him."

"She m-m-might." Tanya looked across the table at Janelle. "Aren't you g-going to help us st-stop her?"

Janelle laughed. "Not me! She's done this for at least seven hundred years." She reached to her left to take Jim's hand. "That's how we ended up with a table for five."

Jim chuckled. "Can we steer the conversation to something less controversial?" He looked straight down the table at Marilyn. "Please?"

"Sure, baby." Marilyn smiled at Damon and Harry. "You'll get used to this in a few years."

"That's good news." In what Allie thought showed rare tact for Harry, he glanced at Jim. "How are things going for getting the system secured?"

"Not too bad, actually." He sipped his wine and flagged the steward for a refill. "Going to be a long rebuilding process, though."

"That's what I hear. Sounds like the place is a mess."

The conversation focused on Arup for the remainder of dinner. When the group moved to the sitting room, the stewards brought around drinks. Allie knew her parents developed some regimented habits over the centuries, but she watched Damon and Harry as everyone took their seats. Jim sat in an old armchair that he always used. Marilyn perched on the right arm as Janelle sat on the left. Tanya and Paige sat on the small loveseat just next to the armchair.

Harry smiled at them. "Sitting on the arms of the chair doesn't look all that comfortable to me."

Marilyn sighed. "It must be, though. We've done it for a long time."

Jim patted her knee. "Let's not go there again." He looked at Allie. "I think you're on, little one."

She took Harry's hand in her right and Damon's in her left. "Right." She sighed. "I guess there's no secret that we're together as a family now."

"So what else is new?" His lopsided grin appeared.

Harry looked around the room before he spoke. "I think we've got the cart a little before the horse."

Jim frowned. "Why's that?"

"Because Damon and I haven't even asked you for permission to marry Allie."

Allie's heart jumped. She opened her mouth to speak, but she couldn't make words come out, only a slight choking noise. Beads of sweat formed on her forehead.

The room became very quiet as Jim's grin slowly returned. "As long as Allie says yes, you won't hear me complain."

Damon turned to his right on the sofa the three shared to face her. "Allie, will you marry Harry and I?"

Harry's smile faded to the most solemn look she could recall ever seeing on his face. "Please, Allie. Marry Damon and I."

Tears ran down her face as she looked from one man to the other. "Oh my God! This is really it? No more lame proposals."

"No, at least we hope this isn't lame." Harry kissed her hand. "Was that a yes or a no?"

"Yes." Her smile felt good through the tears. "Of course I'll marry you both."

Chapter 20

Changes

"You're really getting married, then?"

Harry laughed a little. "Yeah, I really am." He watched Devon with amusement. "That puts you squarely on the hook."

"It does that." Devon looked puzzled. "I don't understand the idea of loving two people, though."

"Hell, I'm doing it and I'm not sure I understand." Harry shrugged. "I do love Allie and Damon both, though."

"I can understand that you love one of them, just not both. I'm not sure about that part."

"Maybe you'll understand one day."

"Maybe." Devon smiled. "What's this I hear that you plan to leave the Fleet?"

"I'm leaning that way. After all, what will I do to follow this act?"

"Damned if I know, but it would be a shame."

"Tanya has offered me work with her computers."

"Not the same, Harry. No more real puzzles to solve while you chase the rabbits." Devon grinned.

"That's true, but I think I may have had enough puzzles to last me."

"Besides, your wife is rich." Devon grinned.

"That too." Harry leaned back in his chair. "And my husband is working full time."

Devon shook his head. "Two people. Damn."

Harry watched his former boss. He now outranked Devon. "Does the fact that Damon and I are as involved as Allie and I bother you?"

"No, not at all." Devon stared at him for a moment. "That you would even ask that question makes me wonder if it bothers you, though."

Harry thought, remembering when he first understood his feelings for Damon. "There was a time that it did bother me. A short time, granted, but I had those thoughts. Then I realized that it made no difference at all." He sighed as he smiled. "All I know is that I care about Damon almost as much as I do Allie. I'm not willing to give up either of them."

"That's the important thing." Devon smiled. "Do you think women know that we men worry about being loved and being able to love someone?"

"I know one woman who knows that very well."

Devon laughed a little. "I actually envy you."

"Better be careful with that. Envy is one of the seven deadly sins."

"I guess I do. If I'm earning eternal damnation, it should be for something a lot more fun than envy."

Harry laughed. "I hear that!" He frowned as he thought about the seven deadly sins. "I guess this relationship I'm in makes me guilty of at least three of them."

"Which ones?"

"I'm guilty of greed, gluttony, and lust." Harry smiled. "The three deadly sins."

* * * *

As they walked to the Café, Allie walked with Harry on her right arm and Damon to her left.

"We love you, Allie." Harry kissed her cheek. ." He smiled as they entered the elevator. "We could all play elevator roulette."

Allie giggled.

Damon looked puzzled. "What's elevator roulette?"

Allie stood on her toes to kiss his nose. "You'll see one day soon."

They found a table away from the dance floor and Rebecca came to take their orders. "Hi! Your parents came by last night, Allie, and I understand that congratulations are in order for the three of you."

"Thanks." Allie smiled. "I'm happy. I won't speak for Harry and Damon, but they'd better be happy."

Rebecca laughed. "They'd better. What can I get you tonight?"

Rebecca left for the kitchen to place their orders. Harry thought for a moment. "I think that it's your turn for the first dance, Damon."

"Right." He stood and held his hand out to Harry. "Dance with me?"

"I'd be honored."

Allie laughed as the men went to the dance floor. She watched her men dancing. She knew they weren't really *her* men. She certainly didn't own them, but more important, the group formed what Marilyn, wearing her biologist hat, might call a symbiotic relationship. While Harry and Damon didn't make her complete or whole, they formed a team. Each one brought not only their own unique strengths to the team, but their inimitable weaknesses as well. The resulting team became not only stronger than any individual, but also greater than the sum of the parts. Harry and Damon weren't *her* men any more than she was *their* woman, but God help the person, man or woman, who tried to come between them.

They came back to the table just as Rebecca brought their dinners. Allie ordered lobster and decided that Marilyn might be on to something. She picked up a chunk of the meat in her fingers and slowly licked it into her mouth, making sure that Harry and Damon watched.

Harry blinked at her. "Damn it."

"You too?" Damon sighed.

She ruined the seductive effect when she giggled. "That's the same look Daddy gives Marilyn." The stares they gave her set off a cascade of shivers through her body.

"Probably for the same reasons, too." Harry frowned. "Sorry. Most people aren't comfortable thinking about their parents having sex."

"Not me." She laughed. "Daddy and my moms are like rabbits. I think I got over being embarrassed by them when I caught Mom and Paige giving Daddy a blowjob in the kitchen."

Damon's eyes went wide. "Oh my God! When did that happen?"

"The first time, I think I was about ten."

"The first time?"

"Yeah. For the most recent, I caught Mom and Marilyn doing it about two months ago. Only they were in his office."

"Jesus!" Harry laughed. "I really didn't need to know that about Jim and your moms!"

"Me either." Damon looked troubled, three frown lines appearing between his eyes. He watched as Allie ate another piece of lobster.

Allie had the giggles. The look on Damon's face made an odd mixture of desire and embarrassed panic. Harry looked amused. "I'm sorry. I'll stop now."

* * * *

On their way home, Allie reached around Damon to stop the elevator. "What are you doing?"

Harry smiled. "Elevator roulette."

Allie kissed Harry, and then pushed Damon against the wall of the car. She unbuttoned her pants, letting them fall to her ankles. "Don't worry." She grabbled with Damon's pants until she released his flaccid cock. Bending over, Allie licked the head of his dick.

Harry dropped his pants. He moved in close behind her and slipped his cock into her pussy. Damon's erection built rapidly as she sucked him.

As Harry fucked her cunt, his thrusts forced her mouth onto Damon's dick. She heard Damon's low moans as she reached to the control panel and started the elevator moving again.

Damon jerked. "What are you doing?"

Harry laughed. "Elevator roulette."

"What if someone catches us?" Damon's voice came out high pitched with the nervous question.

"That's the thrill of it all."

"But..."

Allie pulled his cock from her mouth. "Don't you find that exciting?" She licked the tip of his dick. "You—seem—excited." She grunted with Harry's thrusting.

"Just—relax—man." Harry's grunting made his voice choppy, too.

"Relax? Yeah, right!"

Allie noticed that despite his protests, Damon's cock reached its full length and girth. The filling sensation of his dick sliding down her throat made her heart pound. Harry's hands gripped her hips as he thrust into her. The scent of Damon's cock filled her nose and mingled with the almost antiseptic air of the elevator, giving a blend of sweet sterility to the act.

Allie's orgasm built quickly. She licked rapidly on the head of Damon's cock as she stroked his length with her fist. Harry's dick slipped quickly in her soaked cunt. As her climax hit her, Harry gave a mighty thrust. The force of his push caused Damon's dick to run fully down her throat. As Harry's cum flowed deep inside her pussy, Damon twitched, and his cum spurted into her throat.

Gasping for breath, the three worked to get their clothes in some semblance of order. The elevator doors opened on their deck.

Harry smiled, holding the door open. He looked at Damon where he leaned against the car wall panting. "Well?"

"That was fun."

"Want to go again?"

Allie smiled "I do!"

Harry let the doors close.

Allie and Damon knelt side by side giving Harry head when the car stopped and the doors opened. Marilyn stood waiting with the blank expression of someone waiting for an elevator.

She stared for a moment, and then blinked rapidly. "Oh shit oh dear!"

Harry's cock went limp almost instantly.

Marilyn shrugged and stepped into the elevator. She turned her back to the three and pressed the button for her floor.

When the elevator stopped, Marilyn stepped off. "Are you three coming?"

Allie pulled her lips from the head of Harry's now hard cock. Damon took her place. "Not yet, Mom. Give us a few minutes."

* * * *

"Since getting to know your moms and dad, I'm a little amazed by how..." Harry trailed off, thinking. "I guess by how real and normal they are. If I met them on the street, I'd never suspect who they are." Allie sat between him and Damon on the sofa while they listened to music.

Damon seemed to know the name and artist for every song.

Allie nodded. "I sometimes think that Daddy doesn't take the whole Emperor thing very seriously, but then he'll do or say something that leaves no doubt about the power he has."

"What about your moms?" Damon listened to the song playing. He smiled. "*Locomotive Breath* by Jethro Tull. Do they do that, too? They don't act like I would imagine an empress should act."

"They do, but less than Daddy. I think Marilyn is the worst about doing it when she deals with military people." Allie shrugged. "There's no question about her being Daddy's favorite and she's also the oldest. Sometimes, she can be very much the senior Empress."

He thought for a moment. Harry imagined that Marilyn could be a tough customer when she wanted. He thought about her flirtatiousness and wondered what she might be hiding. "I can see her doing that."

"She does." Allie eyed him and Damon.

Damon hesitated for a moment, and then he stood and stretched. "I think I'm going for a walk."

"Give us a minute, and we'll go with you." Harry moved to stand.

"No, you two stay here." He smiled. "I want you to have a little time alone. I'll be back in an hour or so."

"Well, all right." Harry smiled. "I guess I owe you one."

He shook his head. "Not at all." Damon left.

Allie paused for a moment. "I want to ask you something."

"Sure."

"Are you OK with what the three of us have?"

He paused. "I really am. More than OK, in fact."

"That's all good, then." She brushed her fingers over the smooth hair on his face. "I just wondered."

"Do I act like I'm not OK?"

"No, not at all. I just know that you weren't very keen on sharing me before."

"Like I said, with the right person, I always knew I could do that." He sighed. "Damon is the right person. I'm not sure if there is another such person out there, but if so, I could even see a forth joining us sometime."

She laughed. "That's getting a little ahead in the game, isn't it?"

"Maybe." Harry shrugged. "I just know that I can love more than person now."

"It amazes me sometimes that we managed to find one another. Out of the quadrillions of people in the galaxy, we ended up in the same place."

He smiled. "Don't you believe in serendipity?"

"I guess I do."

"What about synchronicity?"

She chuckled. "Yeah, I do."

"And fate?"

"Always."

"That's good. Everyone should believe in something."

"What do you believe, Harry?"

He smiled. "I believe I'm going to make love to you."

"Not if I beat you to it." Allie grabbed his face in her hands, and pressed her lips to his.

As his beard tickled her face, the scent of his skin mixed with the spices of his cologne to bombard her senses. Her head reeled with the sudden flood of sweetness that hit her, and she tasted his scent as much as smelled him.

His hands moved over her back to caress her shoulders. The touch of his firm, warm hands sent an electric shock through her. The heat of the sensation made her shiver, and Allie remembered the day in the room with her mother's communications gear when the icy cold of the coolants mixed with the white-hot arcs of electricity. Allie imagined the nearly unlimited power that flowed through the makeshift communications lab. It offered only a fraction of the energy that flowed between her and Harry.

As Harry's hands moved over her, the music played in the background. She heard some old song that she heard before. She wished Damon were here to tell her the title. The soloist went on about how he couldn't stop loving someone.

She knew the feeling very well.

Harry's hands slowly opened her robe, and he lifted her in his arms. Shrugging out of his robe, he eased them both to the floor of the sitting room. He sat down, crossing his legs, and lowered her onto his lap facing him.

As he lowered her, Allie wrapped her legs around his waist, and his rigid cock slipped into her pussy. They rocked together, faces only centimeters apart, and his breath blew warmly against her face. The rush of the hot air played over her skin as they stared into each other's eyes, foreheads touching. When his breath, hot and sweet, mixed with the intensity of his stare, Allie shuddered.

His arms rested around her waist as he stroked her back and sides. The skin of his hands made smooth passes over her, almost tickling her with the butterfly-wing touches.

They moved together slowly and with deliberate purpose. She saw the sweat that ran down Harry's face, sticking his long hair to his face and neck. She knew her perspiration did the same, and the sweat on their bodies made his chest rub slickly against her breasts.

She rocked easily on his cock as it slid easily in and out of her soaked pussy making soft, wet noises as they thrust together. The odor of their compounded sweat mixed with the aroma of her juices to float up between their bodies, driving her senses wild.

Her climax moved slowly toward her, but suddenly leapt out and grabbed her body in its velvet fist, squeezing her in its pleasant firmness. Harry's eyes clenched, and she saw the bands of muscle in his neck tense, standing out like cables.

They shook together as they climaxed. Allie bucked and bounced on his lap, and Harry thrust up against her as their orgasms made them quake and writhe.

When their vibrations calmed, Harry lifted her from his lap and eased her back to lie on the soft carpet. He reclined beside her, and put his arms around her.

They rested together, never speaking but sharing a soft kiss now and then. The door swished open, and Damon stepped inside.

He froze for an instant. "Um, did I not stay away long enough?"

She smiled. "I think your timing is perfect."

Harry laughed. "Come over her and join us."

Damon lie down on her other side and the men cuddled her for a long time.

The intercom buzzed, and Harry answered.

Her dad's image swam into view on the screen. "Hi. Did I wake you?" He grinned. "Or interrupt anything?"

"No, not yet."

"Good. I need to see all three of you first thing in the morning."

* * * *

They chatted until they reached the large wooden doors to Jim's office. He came around the desk to hug Allie. After a moment's hesitation, he hugged Damon, and then Harry.

"Please, sit down." When they had taken chairs, he smiled. "Glad to see everyone."

"Thanks." Harry glanced at Damon and then Allie. "You sounded a little cryptic about why you wanted to see us."

Jim smiled. "I have a problem that you two can help me with."

Allie didn't like the look on her father's face. He had something up his sleeve, and she didn't know what. "Why don't you tell us what this is about?"

"I will. Jonas Remslure won't be here for at least nine or ten months to take over Arup, so the military government will need to last that long. That means I need someone in charge I can trust." His lopsided grin came to his face.

Allie knew she didn't like where this conversation headed. "What are you trying to say?"

"Simple. I want Harry and Damon as the joint military governors of Arup until Jonas gets here."

Damon's mouth opened and closed several times. Allie didn't see Harry react at all. He at least made his voice work. "I don't know anything about running a government."

Her dad smiled. "What makes you think I know anything about it?"

"Good point."

"I thought so." Jim looked at Damon. "Can you talk yet?"

"I think so. Harry's right. We have no idea what we're doing."

"That's the good part." Her dad's grin held firm. "You don't know enough to do anything wrong. Besides, I have a long history of sending my sons-in-law to do this sort of thing."

It sank in on Allie that he said nine or ten months. She knew *Boone* wouldn't sit in the Arup system that long. "If they do this, I'm going with them."

Jim shrugged. "I expected nothing else."

"If you want me to do this, I'll do the best job I can, but I have no clue what to do." Harry frowned a little. "There is a downside to it all, though."

The look on her father's face told Allie he figured everything out long before they reached his office. "What would that be?"

"We'll have to move up the wedding."

Chapter 21

Moving On

Allie woke alone in the big bed. The slightly orange sun of Arup shown through the window and she stretched as it washed over her. On Arup for ten months, Allie still loved the sunrise.

She'd grown up on *Boone*. Until this assignment on Arup with Harry and Damon, Allie thought she had spent about a year total on various planets. Something in her bones, maybe the tug of real gravity generated by mass and not artificial gravity created by some manipulation of the strings and membranes making up the universe, told her that she belonged on a planet. Humans evolved on a planet, not in free space.

The only problem Allie could see came down to getting out of this bed alone. The Arupian beds were too soft for her. She rolled to the edge, but couldn't clamor over the rail. She sighed and used the call button. Responding quickly to Allie's call, Chin'ree, the Arupian housekeeper, came to the bedside.

"Are you stuck again?" Chin'ree's grasp of English was much better than Allie's skills with Arupian. She spoke with a slight hissing accent.

"Seems that way." Allie held Chin'ree's large paws as she sat up and swung her legs over the side of the bed. "Where are Harry and Damon?"

"They're in the dining room, already working on some problem with the election."

Chin'ree helped her to stand. "Thank you."

"You're welcome. Do you need me to help you dress?"

Allie laughed. "I can handle that part, so long as I stay away from the bed."

"Just call if you need me." Allie watched Chin'ree go back to her other duties. The Arupian woman stood half again as tall as Allie and massed three times as much, but Allie knew she was as gentle as a kitten. She winced at the analogy.

Since their arrival on Arup, Harry and Damon placed a ban on all derogatory references and names used to describe Arupians. No Fleet personnel used the old wartime nicknames of kittens, cats, kitties, or, especially, fur balls. All people, Arupian and human, now were people. Equals and partners.

Chin'ree served as the chief housekeeper and personal assistant to Allie. She found Chin'ree a caring and loving woman. Allie liked her, as she liked almost all the Arupians she met over the last ten months.

She finished dressing and went to the dining room. Harry and Damon talked with Hall'doo, the chief of Arupian police.

Harry sighed. "All right. We can't use the civic center for a polling place. What else is there in the city that will hold that many people?"

Hall'doo made a purring sound. "There is the university exercise center."

"How many people will that hold?" Even after ten months, Allie liked the way Damon's Lieutenant Colonel uniform looked on him.

"At the same time, around ten thousand. Maybe twelve."

"That should work, then." Harry nodded. She wondered if Harry's retiring from Fleet was the right thing for him to do at the end of this assignment. She managed to stifle the laugh that thinking about Paige liking sailors brought on her.

Damon looked at Harry for a moment, and Allie saw the telltale expressions that they communicated with their implants. "OK, Hall'doo. We'll leave this to you. Let us know if you need anything."

"Yes, Sir." Hall'doo left to make the things needed for the election happen.

Harry saw her. "Good morning." He came and kissed her. "How did you sleep?"

"Great." Damon stood next to her. "Hi." She kissed him.

"Morning. We decided to just let you sleep."

Last month, Allie reached the point where she couldn't get comfortable in bed. Her sleep suffered, often only sleeping an hour or two at a time. "Thanks. I probably needed that."

"We thought so." Harry rubbed her belly, caressing the bulge of her eight-month pregnancy. "Both our babies needed to rest."

Allie laughed.

Damon chuckled. "You need to teach me to do that, Harry."

"Rub her belly?"

"No! Make her laugh."

"Oh! That's easy." Harry reached for her ribs.

"If you tickle me, I'll break your fucking arm."

Harry pulled his hand back quickly. "Right."

Chin'ree brought breakfast to the table. Allie looked up at her. "Will the kids be here today?" Chin'ree's two children often visited the government house and Allie liked to watch them play. Only four years old, the children would run through the palace grounds. Despite the comparison, Allie thought they acted like all kittens. They ran, chasing invisible prey. They would hide, and then pounce at each other and even adults who strayed too close. Still only standing to Allie's breasts, the children could leap, from a standing start, to more than twice her height.

Chin'ree smiled. "Yes, they'll be here after school, about 1500."

Allie smiled. "That's good." Allie never considered herself very maternal. Like so many expectant mothers she knew, her interests in children peaked when she became pregnant. No human children lived on Arup, and she saw Chin'ree's children as her surrogate kids. At least until her baby would be born next month.

She thought that might be because she spent so much time with them. Chin'ree and her husband, along with the children, lived on the palace grounds. Her husband Krell'mar worked as a guard at the palace. Chin'ree smiled and headed back to the kitchen.

"You're spoiling her kids." Harry patted her hand. "Tells me what we have to look forward to."

Allie laughed. "My parents spoiled me, so why should we do anything different? Besides, we all know that if this is a girl, you two will be insufferable!"

"You're probably right about that." Damon sipped at his coffee. "I know Harry will."

"Now wait just a minute! You're as bad as I am!"

"Am I? Which of us fawned all over Miranda at the going away party?"

Harry sighed. "She's just a kid!"

Allie watched while the men bantered about her kid sister. "She's almost sixteen."

Harry laughed. "Besides, she's cute."

"Remember that thing about breaking your arm?" Allie smiled at him. "You'll both spoil this baby rotten. I know how you are."

"So what if we do?" Damon shrugged. "We're her Daddies. We're supposed to spoil her."

"I guess that's true." Allie kissed their hands. "So, how are things looking for the elections?"

"If we can get the polling places lined out, it will come off well." Harry laughed. "I think Jonas may have his hands full, though. The Arupians are very social, but the old government repressed them, not allowing public assemblies."

Damon smiled. "And now they're trying to make up for that in a few months."

Allie thought for a moment. "Do you think we'll still be here when the baby is born?"

"I don't know." Harry leaned far back in his chair, stretching his hands over his head. "I need to get more sleep. Anyway, it will probably be close."

Allie suddenly wanted to have her baby on a planet, not a spaceship. "I want to stay here until the baby is born."

She saw the look pass between Harry and Damon, but she saw no indication they spoke by implant. Harry squeezed her hand. "If that's what you want, we can make it happen."

She thought for a moment, gathering her thoughts before she spoke. "I want our baby born here, on a planet, instead of *Boone*." She sighed. "Claire is the only one of my sisters and brothers not born on *Boone*. Being here has made me think about things." She smiled at her husbands. "I think we belong on a planet. I know we're a spacefaring people, but at least our baby can be born on a planet."

"Like Harry said, if that's what you want, then that's the way things will be." Damon kissed her hand.

* * * *

Allie watched Chin'ree's children playing in the gardens. Niel'doo, the little boy, tried to roar at times, but he still needed to grow a bit before he could match the shuddering sound an adult male Arupian could release. Allie watched them play and saw that evolution allowed Arupians, like all creatures, to fit perfectly into their world. Their blue-gray fur blended perfectly with the vegetation and the children all but vanished as they hunted their imaginary prey.

She smiled as she thought about the changes in her life the last year. In chronological order, she met Damon, met Harry, lost Damon, almost lost Harry, got Damon back, almost lost Harry again, gotten married, and now she expected a baby. She laughed as she thought it had been a busy year.

Even with the ups and downs, the year was the happiest she could remember in her life. She never knew true happiness before now, though.

Allie believed she had the best men in the galaxy as her husbands. The family they formed went much further than that, though. Harry and Damon were her best friends, confidants, and lovers. Even that didn't tell the tale, and she knew better. They were all best friends.

A small pang of guilt crossed her mind. Because of the heavier gravity of Arup, 1.12 of Earth standard, the doctors advised that Allie not have sex. Other than blowjobs and handjobs, Allie followed the advice. Damon and Harry made love, usually with her present, but she knew they both wanted to have sex with her.

The fact that she couldn't have sex for medical reasons didn't make her feel guilty. The guilt stemmed from that she really found little interest in her for sex right now. Her mothers and Claire told her this would happen while she carried the baby. Just because it was normal, that didn't mean she liked it.

On the other hand, Harry and Damon never complained, and she knew they didn't conceal anything from her. For some reason she didn't understand, their love and understanding made her feel good.

The children darted to the bench where she sat and took up places on each side of her. Allie smiled at them. "Tired?"

Niel'doo smiled a toothy grin. "Yes. Did you hear my roar?" Their

English abilities improved everyday.

"I did, and you frightened me!"

His sister, Hans'ree, shook her head. "He did not frighten me." She held her chin high in defiance.

"You're a stupid girl."

Allie laughed. "You shouldn't say your sister is stupid."

He looked at his feet for a moment. "I'm sorry, Hans'ree."

"That's all right."

Allie pulled a bag of dried fruit from her pocket and offered the children the treat. Omnivores, the Arupians liked many of the same foods as humans. As she chewed, Allie saw Hans'ree staring at the bulge of her belly.

"Allie, can we touch your baby again?"

The children marveled at the moving baby inside her. "Sure." Allie lifted her shirt as the young Arupians put their paws on her belly and pressed their ears to her skin listening for the heartbeat. Allie wondered at times if the infatuation might be a predatory instinct. Her communicator chirped, and she tapped the switched. "Jenkins."

"Hi, love." Damon made a kissing sound. "Chin'ree wanted me to tell you that the kids have homework tonight."

She looked at the children. Their shoulders slumped. "All right. We're on our way back." She closed the link.

Niel'doo sighed. "Do we have to go back?"

"Yes, we do. You need to study so you do well in school." She gathered the sad children into her arms. "I'm going to miss you both when I have to leave."

* * * *

Harry worked in his office late. At every turn, overlooked details of the elections seemed to crop up. The pressure wore on him more than he hoped it might. The elections for the advisory council were set for a week from today.

Damon left early, saying he didn't feel well. Harry knew Damon wanted to be alone with Allie for a while. The idea certainly didn't bother him. Even with the love between him and Damon, the competitive spirit remained. He smiled remembering the fight from last year, using a bet to give it an air of respectability. The fight was over Allie. No question about that.

Allie's recent comments about wanting to stay on Arup until after she gave birth nagged at his mind. He wondered that might lead to leaving Boone and living on a planet. Like many people in the Fleet, Harry didn't like planets. They tended to exist in one extreme or the other. Either terribly crowded or terribly deserted, planets didn't have a happy medium. They also stayed in one place.

It could be, he thought, simply another phase of Allie's pregnancy. At least it was better than the fits of anger she went through several months ago. She threw things, and she had a wicked fastball.

Harry knew it didn't matter to him, though. He loved Allie with everything in him, and he would do anything for her. Despite the rivalry with Damon, Harry loved him, too.

The three, soon four, made a family.

* * * *

Damon sat with Allie on the sofa. They kissed and touched each other, and the excitement she always stirred in him blazed. The bulge of her pregnancy pressed against him as they hugged.

Damon spent the last eight months trying to understand his own feelings about Allie's pregnancy. He knew that, as a jarhead, he didn't know much about people and feelings, things Gabe always called touchy feely. Damon wondered if a man was supposed to feel the combined warmth and chills he experienced when he looked at her. Allie always gave him shivers, just with a look, but since she became pregnant, the feelings changed in some way he couldn't fully grasp.

Harry commented to him when they found out she carried the baby that something in the leftover evolution of men made them find the woman carrying their child amazingly attractive. No doubt that Harry is smart, smarter than him, but Damon thought Harry missed this particular target. He found Allie unbelievably attractive, pregnant or not. He couldn't argue that something had changed, though.

His lips slipped from hers, and he snuggled in her long hair, the scent as fresh as the first time he kissed her. The soft waves rubbed his face and caused him to quiver.

His mind falling into a military mode, Damon knew that the way he loved Allie could be dangerous. He understood full well that if the need arose for him to choose between protecting her and protecting the Empire, Allie would win the conflict in his mind. Fifteen years of training and learned reactions would fade in an instant to protect her, regardless of the price.

Her soft hands ran over his head, gently caressing him as they kissed. Damon wanted her, but he wanted her and the baby safe even more. He smiled to himself thinking that he had no trouble controlling his urges because he loved and needed her far more than he wanted her. He wanted her more than anything.

* * * *

When Harry walked into their quarters, Allie tried to stand from the sofa to meet him. She didn't make it. Far too large and soft, Arupian furniture gave humans problems getting up. Being pregnant made it worse for her.

Harry laughed. "Just stay put and I'll come to you." He sat down next to her on the sofa, and then kissed her deeply. He leaned passed her to kiss Damon. "Feeling better?"

Damon nodded. "I think so. I'm just tired."

Harry nudged her. "Yeah, you wimpy Marines can't keep up with us Fleet types."

"Yeah, right."

"I didn't need a gun while we played soldier on the moon."

"It's a weapon, not a gun." Damon smiled. "But your point is well taken."

Allie tried not to laugh. Laughing made her need to pee, and she feared wetting herself. "You do know that the two of you have turned into an old married couple, always bickering at each other, right?"

Harry shrugged. "I guess we have."

"I can see that part of it." Damon smiled. "I can think of worse things, though."

Allie risked a giggle. "Did you eat, Harry?"

He laughed. "You could say that. Chin'ree fussed over me and brought a huge meal to my office. She stayed and watched me while I ate."

"That's my girl!" Allie tried another giggle and stayed dry. "So, what should we do this evening?"

Damon sighed. "If you weren't pregnant, we could think of something."

Allie stung from his comment. "I'm sorry. Really, I am."

Harry glared at Damon. "No, Allie! He didn't mean it like that! There's nothing for you to be sorry about. You're doing exactly what you should do, for yourself, our baby, and for us as a family."

When she looked at Damon, she saw only concern on his face. "I'm the one who's sorry. That didn't come out the way I wanted it to sound." He thought for a moment, staring into her eyes. "I wanted it to come out funny, but it didn't work."

Allie wiped at the tears welling in her eyes. Her emotions still ran amok at times. She managed a small smile. "You should leave the humor to Harry."

"I should." He kissed her lips very softly, like a butterfly. "I'm sorry."

"It's all right." She found that she cuddled into Harry's arms. "I love you both."

Harry's strong arms squeezed her. "We love you, too." He kissed her hair.

Damon leaned to her and kissed her again, deeply this time. His tongue darted in her mouth as he pulled her head to his. Allie's breath puffed quickly passed her lips and her heart thundered in her ears when he pulled away.

She smiled a little. Allie moved to kneel on the floor in front of the men. Damon gently held her shoulders. "No, love." His powerful arms lifted her back to sit between him and Harry.

Allie frowned. "I don't want to ruin the moment, but don't you want a blowjob?"

Damon smiled. "Of course I do, but I don't want you to do anything you don't want to do." He exchanged a look with Harry. "We know you're not too interested right now."

Harry brushed his hand over her cheek. "We also know that's normal." He shrugged. "I'm not sure I have the words to say this in a way that makes sense, but I'm so damn excited about the baby that I'm not terribly interested in sex, either."

She looked at Damon, and then at Harry again. "Harry, don't patronize me, please."

"I'm not. Seriously, all I can think about is you and our baby." He shrugged again. "Sex with you is nothing short of fantastic because I love you so much, and I can feel how much you love me. It feels better to have my arms around you and our baby."

Allie studied Harry's face. He made a terrible liar, and she saw no hint of deception on his face. She didn't know if she believed him because of his expression or because she loved him. She turned to Damon and watched his face for a moment. He made a worse liar than Harry.

Damon smiled. "I love you, and I love our baby. I'm more than happy being as close to you both as I can get."

Tears stung her eyes, but Allie didn't think her emotions were out of control again. She touched their faces with her fingertips. She thought of many things to say, but all of them sounded like clichés to her mind. She finally selected a simple cliché. "I love you both."

* * * *

Harry stretched and ran his hands through his long hair. "Well, looks like we're just about done here."

Allie smiled. He and Damon were near exhaustion, but the time they could rest approached fast now. The elections of two weeks ago went well and the new council waited for Jonas to arrive in three days. Harry and Damon could dissolve the military government, and that would finish the work. At least that would finish the military and government work. Her due date only ten days away, Allie knew that her family would have a new job to work on then. She laughed a little.

Damon smiled at her. "What's so funny?"

"I'm thinking that none of us is going to get much rest. Just about when you unload Arup on Jonas, we'll have a new baby to take care of."

"I can think of worse things than that."

Harry nodded. "Me too." His face went slack for a moment. "I'm a daddy."

Damon's face took on the same expression. "Shit. Me too."

Allie managed to stifle her laugh. "Yes, you are."

"I guess I've been so swamped the last nine months for it to really hit me." Harry frowned deeply. "I don't know anything about being a daddy!"

"You didn't know anything about running a planet, either. You've both done a great job with that, though." She took their hands in hers. "You'll be great daddies."

"I don't know. Harry's right. What do we know about this daddy gig?"

"You'll do a great job." Allie smiled. "I asked Mom why Daddy is so good at being a daddy. She told me that any man with normal biology could be a father. It takes a special man to make a daddy. You're the most special men I've every known."

Harry seemed to shake himself a little. "It's too late to back out now, so we'll just do our best." He glanced at Damon for a moment. "Have you thought about what we should do after we're done here?"

"Yeah, I have, but this isn't my decision." She smiled. "It's our decision."

Damon chuckled. "OK, I can accept that, but what are your thoughts?"

"*Boone* is home for me. That's where I was born and where I grew up."

"That sounds like you want to go back there." Harry sipped at his coffee. "I had the impression you wanted to go to a planet."

"I think I did for a while." Allie thought for a moment. "Something about being on a planet told me that's where we belong, as a species. I'm not so sure about that anymore."

Damon frowned. "Maybe I'm confused, but why the sudden change of heart? Twice."

She laughed. "Humanity has been in space for more than four thousand years. We almost exterminated ourselves in the Doom Time. If Grandpa and Grandma, and all the others, hadn't taken action to move people from Earth, we'd be extinct now."

Harry nodded. "Yeah, space saved humanity." He waved toward the window where the black night sky of Arup waited. Stars in unfamiliar constellations twinkled, and the two moons floated through the patterns. "That, my loves, is our destiny."

"It is."

"Our parents and grandparents gave us the future." Harry smiled. "They gave us the universe as our playground. Yeah, sometimes we fall off the swing and skin our knees. Sometimes a bully shows up in the playground." Harry's face went soft and his eyes focused far out into space as he stared through the window. He sat silently for a long time, and she wondered what he thought about. He sighed softly. He turned back to the table and stared at Damon for a moment. He smiled when he looked at her, and his whole face smiled at her. His eyes twinkled as the fine smile lines spread over his face. "I want our kids to have the gifts that we have."

Damon nodded. "I want that for our children, too."

Chills ran through her body as she watched her husbands opening their souls to her. She knew she didn't need to tell them that she agreed. They knew, somehow, that she shared their thoughts. "I'll call Daddy and have him come pick us up."

Harry laughed a little as he turned back to the window. "Back to *Boone*." He faced her and Damon again. "Together again."

THE POLYAMOROUS PRINCESS

THE END

WWW.MELODEEAARON.COM

Other books by Melodee Aaron at www.sirenpublishing.com/melodeeaaron

An Ike Payne Adventure 1

Sergeant Ike Payne: Cop, aspiring author, Marine. She has power, respect, friendship, and the only career she's ever wanted. She also has a locked room murder attempt and 24,000 suspects.

Tensions mount to solve the crime, and Ike is thrown together with Devon Henson, a young lieutenant, to find the killers and protect the crew and civilians aboard His Majesty's Starship Boone.

Ike and Devon's passions rise as shadowy terrorists take over the computers controlling the ship and begin a rampage of death and destruction that pulls Ike and Devon, alone and out-gunned, into a deadly confrontation with the leader of the terrorist group.

No matter the technology, battle always comes down to a woman and a gun. Their survival, and that of everyone on Boone, depends on the Love of Payne.

An Ike Payne Adventure 2

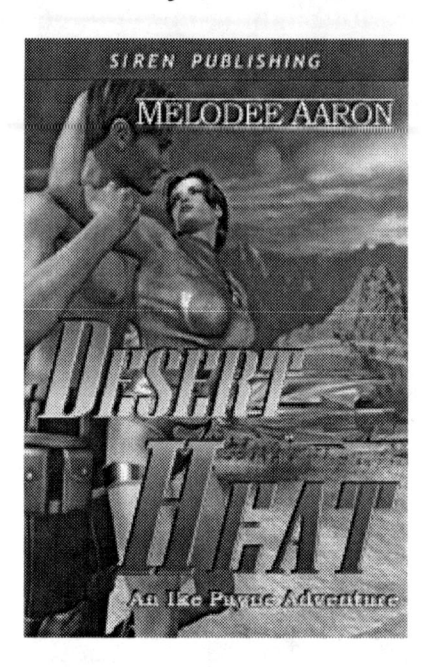

Ike's life is complicated. She's the Marine General in charge of security for His Majesty's Starship Boone. Her husband, Devon, is suffering problems with his memory since he was injured in the battle with the Palean Liberation Front a year ago. Ike has to escort the spoiled Princess Miranda to Nerumie to settle a civil war.

Just when things might take a turn for the better, their ship crashes in the deep desert. The crash strands Ike, Devon, Miranda, and Sergeant Jack Ingram with little food and less water. The temperature swings from half that of boiling water to far below freezing, and killer animals stalk them in the darkness and from the skies.

Attraction, love, and lust weave a web through the group as they deal with their growing feelings for each other. Discoveries of hidden feelings made under the orange sun of Nerumie cause tempers to flair. Passions rage between the four, testing devotion and love to the limits as they fight for survival in the desert heat.

REVIEWS

For the Love of Payne

4 Stars/Orgasmic: "There is nothing like an adventurous, action-packed story told from a woman's point of view. *An Ike Payne Adventure: For the Love of Payne* is filled with wonderful characters, but Ike is the one who had me enthralled and kept me turning the pages. Ike is perfect. She has a sense of duty, but is not hard nosed, as one might assume. There is a sensitive side to her that caused me to relate to her position as a marine sergeant and her desire to be a sensual woman. Ike is very aware of her sexuality. That made the sex in this novel outrageous and a turn on. Devon is interesting enough with his often clumsy behavior. That characteristic endeared him to me and made me wait on Ike to help him put everything back to right. When I first thought of a hero for Ike, Devon did not come to mind, but that is what makes him so special. He is different and therefore appealing. Overall, I believe *An Ike Payne Adventure: For the Love of Payne* is a good read that will leave anyone wanting more." —**Suni Farrar,** *Just Erotic Romance Reviews*

Desert Heat

4.5 Stars/Hot: "What can I say; Melodee Aaron produced another best seller. *An Ike Payne Adventure 2: Desert Heat* was even better than the first installment. The original story introduced me to Ike and Devon, while the follow up novel carried me on a journey with the couple and brought Miranda and Sergeant Jack Ingram into the fold. I am guilty of loving sequels that follow a lead character over a period. Sue me. I had the pleasure of knowing Devon as he became more comfortable with himself. He was a different man, more self-assured and assertive. In my humble opinion, it showed in his lovemaking. Between Ike and Devon it was a constant battle of who desired the other more. Their active sex life caused me a very restless night...Even the sub-characters were interesting. They added something new, and vivacious to the tale. I'm so excited. I just know there is going to be another chapter in the Ike Payne saga and I cannot wait." —**Suni Farrar,** *Just Erotic Romance Reviews*

Siren Publishing, Inc.
www.SirenPublishing.com